I0831230

THE CAMPAIGN

A POLITICAL THRILLER

HUNTER SCHAAL

ISBN 979-8-9996460-0-2 (Hardcover)

ISBN 979-8-9996460-2-6 (Paperback)

ISBN 979-8-9996460-1-9 (eBook)

Cover Design by Allison Schaal

Author Photograph by Reagan Lange

First Edition

Printed In the United States of America

1 2 3 4 5 25 24 23 22 21

To Victory,
My First Lady.

Aut inveniam viam aut faciam.

I will either find a way or make one.

-Hannibal

Prologue

November 2028 | Denver, Colorado

He stood at the edge of history, bathed in floodlights and flanked by flags, his silhouette cutting clean through the thin Colorado air. One hundred thousand people held their breath, waiting for the man they'd chosen to chart a new course for the country. And there he was, centered beneath the blinding white stage lights, poised like the story's hero.

His voice, calm but firm, threaded through the cold air with the kind of conviction that made people forget just how ugly the road to this moment had been.

"History has shaped us into the nation we are today," he said, his words slow and deliberate. "It's written in our scars from civil war and our triumphs from civil rights. We've endured collapse, clawed through depression, and emerged from the shadows of terror. Time and again, we rise; not because we are perfect, but because we are unwilling to surrender to the darkness."

The crowd stirred, not in a frenzy, but in reflection. It was a familiar sentiment, but the way he delivered it made it feel like a prophecy.

"But today," he continued, "our challenge is not foreign. It is neither ideological, religious, nor economic. It is us. We are a nation at war with itself, not by blood or by border, but by the slow corrosion of trust. Trust in one another. Trust in the system. Trust in the idea of America."

The wind cut through Civic Center Park, stiff and biting, yet no one moved.

"A house divided against itself cannot stand," the man said, invoking Lincoln, not for applause, but to mark a line in the sand. "And yet here we are, splintered into factions, our discourse poisoned by tribalism, our institutions bent beneath the weight of cynicism. The extremes have consumed the middle. We don't talk, we target. We don't compromise, we cancel. We don't debate, we destroy."

He let the silence settle, knowing the power it held.

"This campaign—this moment—it's about victory. It's about course correction. I did not run to represent a party. I ran because I believe, still, in the fiction of unity, that from many, we might again become one."

Applause broke, not all at once, but gradually, like a tide giving way to the moon. It wasn't for the rhetoric. It was for the chance to believe again.

He raised a hand, not to stop them, but to steady them.

"I offer no easy answers. I offer no fantasies. Only this: We must try. Try to speak honestly. Try to govern transparently. Try to remember that democracy, like trust, dies in darkness, and we have spent too long in the dark. If we are to rebuild what has been broken, we must open the doors. We must open the books. And we must open our ears to each other."

The wind came again. The crowd leaned in. His voice dropped, but the fire stayed lit.

"I will not hide behind bureaucracy. I will not rule from behind closed doors. You deserve to see how power is wielded in your name. And if that truth is uncomfortable, then so be it. Let discomfort lead to reform."

A beat. Then a promise.

"*E pluribus unum*," he said. "Out of many, one. That is the story we were meant to tell. That is the nation we still have a chance to become."

And for a single, fleeting moment, the kind that history rarely names until it's already gone, it almost felt like the country might begin again.

On the first Tuesday of November, 2028, the country waited, but nowhere felt the pulse of that night like Denver. The Mile High City, crisp under a 37-degree dusk, seemed to vibrate with anticipation. Traffic came to a standstill from Fort Collins to Colorado Springs. Horns, flags, flashbulbs. From the rooftop bars of LoDo to the cul-de-sacs of Aurora, the city glowed with something closer to conviction than celebration. Not even a Broncos Super Bowl victory had gripped Denver like this. Because this wasn't sports. It wasn't a spectacle. It was power, seizing shape before our eyes.

For the first time in its history, Denver had produced a president. Theodore Bright, Ted, had gone from the city council chambers to the U.S. Senate, each step choreographed, each title a rung. Now, he stood on the final one. Just hours earlier, he had unseated Republican President Norman Hayden in a 336-to-202 Electoral College landslide. The win had felt less like a surprise than an inevitability. Hayden's collapse had been in the making for months. But inevitability doesn't lessen impact. When the networks called it, the crowd didn't just cheer, they chanted. *Bright. Bright. Bright.* His campaign posters, once soft pastel calls to optimism —*The Future is Bright, Bright for a Better America* —now curl on lampposts like scripture. And the man who once cut ribbons at rec centers now stood at the edge of the West Wing.

Ted's victory in the 2028 Presidential Election marked the third consecutive one-term presidency; something this country hadn't seen in more than a century. Trump, then Biden, now Hayden; all either defeated or discarded before their time. Just fifteen months earlier, Hayden, the once-beloved Florida governor, seemed untouchable. He'd ridden high approval ratings into his re-election year. But power is a hungry thing, and it doesn't run on memory. His administration stumbled. Then unraveled. When the scandals came, they didn't come slowly. And when the voters turned, they didn't look back. The old names were fading. New ones, like Bright's, were already etched in marble before the dust had time to settle.

In Denver, the air felt thinner than usual. Not because of the altitude. Because of the weight. People poured into the streets, not just for Ted, but for what the moment seemed to mean: that change was still possible, that power could still shift with a single vote. The celebration wasn't just loud. It was desperate. A kind of joyful exhale after months of unease. This was more than a city rallying behind one of its own. It was a country learning, all over again, how quickly everything can change.

Ted's win didn't feel like a campaign victory; it felt like a correction. A recalibration of something that had been broken for too long. His rise offered more than policy or party; it provided a narrative people were longing to believe again. That America could still reward good men. That decency wasn't obsolete. That politics, for all its brutality, might still be a vessel for hope.

He didn't shout. He didn't sneer. He spoke in complete sentences and walked with humility. He looked like the future, even if his ideals belonged to the past. People weren't just voting for him; they were also supporting him. They were anchoring themselves to him. Trusting him with their disappointments. Betting, one more time, that the system might still be worth something. And Ted, steady, likable, endlessly disciplined, gave them something to hold on to.

But the dream has a price. Behind the cheering crowds and campaign posters, behind the easy smile and soaring speeches, power was doing what it always does. It was taking its toll. The public saw the symbol. Few saw the scars.

"A political campaign is a dehumanizing rite. Its only purpose is power, and it tends to bring out the worst in men. Repetition, exhaustion, anxiety, and pressure must be endured cheerfully. Instincts have to be disguised. Sleep and privacy are elusive. Each day brings some new temptation to compromise a little." Jack Newfield wrote that in 1968, but it could've been said last week. The machinery hadn't changed, only the names. In 2028, his words echoed through every pivot, betrayal, and moral compromise that brought Ted Bright to this moment. The dream might live on, but the men who chase it rarely walk away untouched.

Norman Hayden hadn't stumbled into the presidency. He'd carved a path, bridging the populist right and centrist moderates, blending dogma with polish. In 2024, that formula worked. Democrats called him beatable, but no one believed it. He governed like a man above challenge. And for a time, he was. But power has a half-life. It decays. The scandals didn't need to be explosive; they only needed to be relentless. The damage wasn't dramatic; it was cumulative. By the time his approval began to crater, the GOP's bench was empty, and Ted Bright had already begun his ascent. He didn't win by rage or revolution. He won by offering something cleaner. Calmer. A version of America that people wanted to believe in again. And that's how you displace a man who thinks he can't be beaten; not with chaos, but with clarity.

The nation's attention turned to a single square of land carved between marble columns and glass towers. Civic Center Park, nestled between Denver's City Hall and the Colorado State Capitol, brimmed with nearly

100,000 guests, packed shoulder to shoulder in anticipation of the night's central event: Ted's victory address.

I had stood on debate stages against Ted Bright once; fought him in polls, outmaneuvered him in Iowa, outlasted him in South Carolina. Now, I stood in his shadow, waiting behind the haloed stage that crowned the end of our shared journey. The Secret Service hated being here. It was too tight. Too exposed. I'd pushed for Mile High, Ball Arena, even the Colorado Convention Center. But Ted wouldn't budge. He chose Civic Center Park long before the first vote was cast. He wanted to speak from the place where his political story began: between City Hall and the Capitol, the courthouse in view, with the skyline he once governed at his back. The symbolism was clean, potent, and unmistakable.

"This is where I started," he told me once. "Let the world see where I came from—and what I'm stepping into."

Now, with the election night won and the Capitol dome a glowing spectacle behind him, Civic Center Park becomes the center of the universe, at least for tonight. The mountain air is sharp, tinged with the scent of marijuana and exhaust, distinctly Denver. Massive screens beam live coverage across the country. Every major network is here: CNN, FOX, NBC, ABC, *Meet the Press, The Political Pulse.* Foreign correspondents broadcast in French, Japanese, Portuguese. Millions tune in across time zones and continents, watching the man America just elected take the stage.

And somewhere behind the stage, the cameras, and the spotlight, I wait, watching, too.

I wasn't just watching history. I was in it. Vice President-elect Landon Wolfe. A title that still felt like a borrowed coat: heavy, unfamiliar, not quite mine. But I'd earned it. One maneuver at a time.

As the city surged with anticipation, I wasn't at Civic Center Park, not yet. I was five blocks away, sealed inside the campaign's makeshift war room on the top floor of the Wellington E. Webb Office Building, watching history unfold beside the man who'd just made it. Outside the glass walls, the celebration raged; champagne corks ricocheting off drywall, interns hugging and crying, someone blasting Sinatra loud enough to rattle the vents. Inside, Ted and I sat in a silence that felt almost sacred. President-elect. Vice President-elect. The titles were real now, though they hadn't quite settled into our bones.

I hadn't set out to be anyone's number two. Months earlier, I launched my own bid for the presidency. I had the war record, the message, the right enemies. But none of it could cut through the noise of *Bright Fever*. From Columbia to Sacramento, crowds didn't just support Ted, they anointed him. By the time we hit Chicago for the convention, the numbers were clear. He was the nominee. I was the footnote.

Ted didn't want me. His first choice had been River McCoy, the affable senator from Georgia. McCoy was built for the job, charming, unthreatening, dependable. A golden retriever in a blue suit. But picking him meant sacrificing not just his Senate seat, but likely another in the special election as well. With the Democrats clinging to a razor-thin majority, it was too steep a gamble. So, in a last-minute shift dressed up as bold strategy, they chose me. The man Ted had spent a year dismantling on debate stages. His so-called "bridge to the veteran vote," the pundits claimed. To me, it felt more like a shotgun wedding.

Lydia Barnes didn't hide her fury. She'd been with me since I entered the race; a strategist, a truth-teller, the one person I trusted to say the things I didn't want to hear. She saw the Brights for what they were: a family obsessed with image, legacy, and loyalty to their own bloodline. "They'll use you," she warned, "chew you up, hang your skin on the wall." I didn't argue.

Ted had that polished veneer. A smile meant for cameras, not people. He spoke like a man with a mirror behind his eyes, always calculating, consistently positioning. I never trusted him. Never liked him either. But in politics, liking someone isn't the point. Standing behind them on stage? That's just part of the job.

So I said yes.

Why? Partly because of the Solomon Islands. On paper, it was a civil war. In the situation room, it was something else entirely: power projection, control of key trade routes, a standoff with China masquerading as diplomacy. I had served in Iraq and Afghanistan. I understood the stakes. I knew the threat. I wanted a seat at the table when the next war was planned.

The other reason? Simpler. I wanted power. If I couldn't get the top job, I'd take the second, so long as it came with an elevator heading up.

Ted didn't make it easy. In the primaries, he and Rey Hughes, his communications chief and campaign enforcer, dragged my name through the mud. They floated stories about my drinking, resurrected old ghosts, questioned my judgment, my loyalty, my stability. But I didn't flinch. I knew what the game was. And so did he.

That's why I took the deal. Because power doesn't ask if you like the person handing it to you. It just asks if you're willing to take it.

The quiet between Ted and me didn't last. One by one, his inner circle filed into the room, family, trusted advisors, the ones who'd seen it all.

The space itself spoke of control, dressed in quiet luxury. West Elm leather couches. Flat-screens on the walls replaying the night's coverage from competing networks. Rey Hughes sank into the chair across from Ted. Philip and Edward Bright flanked me on the couch, while Gwen Bright, the family's matriarch, wrapped her arms around Evelyn Bright in a warm, celebratory hug. Laughter and chatter rose quickly, until Ted raised a hand. The room fell still.

All eyes rested on the coffee table, where Ted's private line, a sleek black iPhone reserved for the gravest calls, sat idle under the glare of the overhead lights. The screen remained dark, until it didn't. The moment the Virginia area code lit up, the room froze. President Norman Hayden's name appeared, stark against the glow. Ted didn't flinch. He answered on the second ring.

"Mr. President," he said, voice even and composed.

"Senator," Hayden answered, sounding worn out, like he'd been living with the loss long before the numbers made it official.

"Congressman Wolfe is here with me," Ted added, giving me a slight nod. "What can we do for you, Norman?"

"Ted, there's no script for a call like this. Only tradition. You ran a strong race. You and Wolfe pulled off what most people thought was impossible. I'm calling to concede, and to congratulate you. I believe you'll make a fine president."

There it was. The handoff. Clean, formal, heavy with subtext. I kept my eyes on Ted. He let the moment breathe before answering, just long enough to add weight.

"Thank you, Mr. President. That means a great deal."

The conversation then moved into procedural territory, discussing transition briefings, intelligence memos, and diplomatic coordination. Official language for a very real shift in power. Ted asked everyone to give him a moment alone to finish the call. We all stepped out. The door shut behind us with a soft but final click.

Outside, the energy roared back to life. Staffers laughed and hugged, the press angled for quotes, the buzz of victory saturating the air. I spotted Ellie Poole weaving through it all, purposeful as ever. Lavender dress, composed expression. Her eyes locked with mine, and for just a second, that familiar, knowing smile flickered across her face.

"Mr. Vice President-elect Wolfe," she said as she handed me a document. "Here's the speech I've drafted. It hits all the necessary notes: unity, continuity, and a shared vision with Ted. Restoring virtue, rebuilding strength."

I thumbed through it, not really reading. The phrasing was crisp, the structure balanced. It was precisely what the moment called for.

"Thank you, Ellie. You've done your part brilliantly."

I tucked the speech into my inner jacket pocket. I meant the compliment, not about the speech, but about her. Ellie had been with me from the start, long before the Bright family entered the picture. Where Lydia sharpened my instincts, Ellie gave them shape. Her words gave mine teeth. She wasn't just a speechwriter. She understood the stakes in a way few others did.

Past the secure zone, Secret Service agents began sweeping the halls. The motorcade was forming. We'd be headed to Civic Center Park any minute. The night had already written itself in history. The crowd was waiting. The victory was absolute. And under those bright lights, the world would see it, for Ted, and for me.

We arrived within minutes. Downtown Denver pulsed with life; crowds packed into the streets, electricity in the air. The city had become something alive, breathing in rhythm with the chants and cheers of a nation looking ahead. Tens of thousands lined the barricades, waving signs that read *Bright-Wolfe 2028* and *Colorado's Son. America's President.* Their voices rose like a tide, defying the cold November air.

The motorcade descended into the underground parking garage beneath the Capitol. Above us, the sound of the crowd dulled into a low rumble, like thunder trapped in a box. The Secret Service moved quickly, guiding us through a concrete hallway where the air was still and dry. Controlled. Contained.

Backstage, the shift was immediate. A white tent had been set up behind the stage, wide enough to hold a small army. It was a green room in name only, meant to be a place of rest, but thick with nerves. Gas heaters filled the space with warmth, though it felt forced. Hollow. I drew a breath and held it, just long enough to feel my chest tighten, then let it go.

Inside, the campaign staff moved with nervous purpose. Photographers adjusted lenses, the advance team clipped earpieces in place, and communications aides whispered final notes. Everyone played their part. But beneath the bustle was something quieter: reverence. Ted wasn't just the candidate anymore. He was the next president.

A photographer lifted his camera. Ted and I stood shoulder to shoulder, turned to the lens. Smiled. Flash.

It wasn't the first photo Ted and I had taken together. But it would be the last.

I already knew what was coming. The same way you sense a tremor before the ground shifts. This photo would be everywhere; in newspapers, campaign retrospectives, textbooks, patriotic montages with orchestral swells. But it would be a lie. It would freeze us in unity, in victory. It wouldn't show what happened next. What I did next.

Ted turned to me as the photographer stepped away.

His posture changed. The weight of the night seemed to settle across his shoulders like something too heavy to shake. His smile vanished.

"You know what you are, Landon?" he said, just low enough for me to hear. "You're the fog that rolls in after the battle, covering the dead. You wait, you hide, then you scavenge what's left."

His voice was calm. Intentional. Sharp.

"I've watched you slither through every campaign room, every donor dinner, every backroom handshake, hoping no one would see the fangs."

He let it hang there, eyes locked on mine.

"But despite everything... despite you... I want this to work. I want a real partnership. Like Eisenhower and Nixon, before it all went south. Like Clinton and Gore, when it still mattered."

He looked over at Gwen. At Evelyn. At Edward and Philip. Then back to me.

"You and I—this country—we don't get a second shot at this. So here it is, plain as I can offer it. We start fresh. Clean slate. You give me loyalty, I'll give you respect."

He held out his hand.

I took it.

His grip was firm. Not warm. Not trusting. It felt like two rivals shaking hands on stage, playing their part for the cameras; tight, rehearsed, destined to fall apart once the lights were off.

"You have my word," I said.

We both knew it meant nothing.

Ted stepped toward his family, the glow of the stage lights catching the edge of his hair, outlining him in gold like something just shy of legend. Gwen waited with her arms open, and the rest of them —his children, his grandchildren —closed in around him. One by one, he hugged them all. His legacy, standing there in flesh and blood, gathered to witness the pinnacle of his life's ambition.

I sat in a folding chair beside Lydia and Ellie. The weight of the moment pressed down on us, thick and silent. In front of us, a small TV buzzed with static light, flickering as it streamed the scene outside. The stage, just minutes ago lit in red, white, and blue, stood quiet now, flags unmoving, the podium alone under the dimming glow. The noise of the crowd gave way to a hush, stagehands guiding the atmosphere like they were calling a curtain. It was the kind of quiet that could break under its own tension.

Then the announcer's voice boomed through the speakers.

"Ladies and gentlemen, please welcome to the stage, the next President of the United States, Theodore Bright!"

The crowd erupted. It wasn't just noise, it was force. A hundred thousand voices surging at once, crashing like waves across Civic Center Park. Fleetwood Mac's *Don't Stop* kicked in, and the Bright family stepped into the brilliance of center stage.

They moved across the platform like they belonged there, waving, smiling, soaking in every second. Ted took his time walking to the podium, letting it all sink in.

"Don't stop thinking about tomorrow..."

The song rose behind him, a promise wrapped in melody. The message was loud and clean.

Hope. Unity. Renewal.

But I knew better.

Not every spotlight reveals the truth.

Some cast shadows deeper than anyone realizes.

Ted Bright's victory speech, delivered under blinding lights and the roar of a hundred thousand voices, marks the final chapter of *The Campaign.* And while it may seem strange to begin a story at its end, some stories demand it. Some truths don't unfold: they detonate. This night wasn't just the end of a presidential race; it was the result of a long, deliberate equation. A moment forged not by fate, but by those willing to twist the gears of power behind closed doors.

Yes, *The Campaign* follows the road to the 2028 election, but it's more than that. This was never Ted Bright's story, no matter how bright the spotlight burned. It's mine. The story of how a man like me, dismissed, overlooked, and buried under the weight of other people's ambitions, found his way to the center. Not to win. Not even to survive. But to leave a mark no one could ignore. What happened at Civic Center Park wasn't destiny. It was designed. And the reckoning started long before the confetti hit the ground.

PART ONE

EXILE

1

Exit Polls

November 2016

I sat there alone, the weight of the moment pressing down on me. A half-drunk glass of whiskey and gin sat in my right hand, its contents slowly losing their warmth as the November night outside grew colder. The curtains of the hotel suite were drawn back, offering a view of the Des Moines, Iowa, skyline, a city that held so much meaning for me. But on this particular night, it felt different, as if the town itself was bracing for a seismic shift.

It was November 8th, 2016, Election Night. I found myself at The Farmhouse, a luxurious four-star hotel that seemed out of place in the heart of Iowa. From the balcony of my room, I could see Wells Fargo Arena, the home of Iowa's minor league teams. Adjacent to it stood Hy-Vee Hall, the major convention center where we had planned a party for my reelection to Congress; an event that would never occur.

I had been a member of the U.S. House of Representatives since 2009, representing Iowa's 3rd Congressional District. Over the years, I had become known as a progressive legislator who tirelessly championed the interests of my constituents, especially veterans and rural communities. My journey began when I rode the coattails of President Barack Obama into office, and during my eight years in Congress, I made a mark.

I served on multiple committees, each reflecting my commitment to different causes. The House Committee on Agriculture enabled me to support farmers and rural communities through measures such as farm subsidies and sustainable agricultural practices. The Armed Services Committee was where I contributed to discussions on national defense, military readiness, and the well-being of veterans. I played a role in the passage of the Affordable Care Act, a cause close to my heart, through the House Committee on Energy and Commerce.

In my time in Congress, I believed I had done my job well. I had expected to win a fifth term representing the people of Iowa, but the 2016 election would prove to be a shock to us all. My opponent, Morgan McClain, a Republican candidate and a mom from Indianola, had managed to ride the same kind of wave I had eight years prior.

She had a limited political background, her primary qualification being her service on the Indianola Community School Board. However, McClain had taken a page from Donald Trump's playbook, who was at the top of the Republican ticket. Her campaign echoed the cry to "drain the swamp," a populist chant that struck a chord with voters.

Despite my accomplishments and dedication to healthcare, farmers, and veterans, McClain successfully painted me as an "Establishment Liberal," alleging that I would take orders from Nancy Pelosi and Hillary Clinton. It was a narrative that resonated with many, even though I considered myself more of an independent with a commitment to the people I served.

As the election results came in, I sat in my hotel suite, alone and disheartened. The rhetoric of draining the swamp had prevailed, and Morgan McClain emerged as the victor. Experience seemed to matter little in this election; what mattered was the perception of change and a commitment to the people.

I stared at the television, my glass now empty, the room darkening with the approaching morning. The impossible had happened, a Donald

Trump Presidency. Although it was distressing to watch a man I loathed win the White House, each time the results of my race appeared on the screen, I closed my eyes and took another swig, attempting to dull the pain of defeat and the uncertainty of the future. The night had become a blur, but the weight of the moment hung heavy in the air.

I was well into my fourth serving of the Jameson-Sipsmith concoction, the room reeking of stale liquor, when a firm knock echoed through the hotel suite. The door swung open, revealing my wife, Kelly, a shadow of her usual vibrant self. With her light ash brown hair cascading past her shoulders, she stood at 5'8, an air of disappointment clinging to her. Behind her, our five-year-old twin daughters, April and Kelsey, clung to her legs, their innocence a stark contrast to the turbulent atmosphere around them.

Their arrival disrupted my hazy solitude, causing me to rise unsteadily from my chair, my 6'2 frame struggling to maintain balance. As I stumbled towards them, Kelly extended a hand to steady me, her touch both reassuring and cautious. She straightened my loosely hanging tie against my wrinkled white dress shirt and planted a bittersweet kiss on my cheek.

"Landon, I'm sorry," Kelly said.

I tried to regain my composure, but the slurred words spilled out uncontrollably. "Sorry about what?"

"The loss. The election," Kelly replied, her voice laced with sympathy.

"Ah, yes, thank you for the reminder," I retorted, bitterness oozing through the haze.

"Sweetie," Kelly continued, "we truly regret this. I do, and the girls do too. Your entire team downstairs is devastated."

"My team? They feel awful?" I stood up, feeling the room spin. Closing my eyes, I shook my head, attempting to clear the fog. Frustration boiled over, my voice rising. "They should feel awful. They failed in their responsibilities. If they had done their jobs, we'd be celebrating across the street with my constituents. Their incompetence has consequences, and I'm the one bearing the brunt of it! Fuck!"

"Landon!" Kelly snapped. "Watch your language in front of the kids."

"Come on, Kelly. It's nothing they haven't heard before." I waved dismissively, the alcohol fueling my defiance. "Besides, you know I'm right. Those volunteers, those goddamn volunteers, didn't fulfill their duties. They didn't make enough phone calls; they didn't collect enough votes."

Kelly rolled her eyes, her frustration apparent as she looked me up and down. She was just trying to help, but her words were doing more harm than good. Each utterance from her seemed to tense my muscles further, like a ticking time bomb.

"On the bright side," Kelly tried to ease the situation, "now we can take that family vacation we've talked about. You'll have time to take the girls to kindergarten. You'll be around more."

Still standing, I brushed off the suggestion. "I don't want to think about that right now. I don't have time to think about the girls. I need to plan my next move, my next course of action."

"Honey, there is no next move."

"There has to be. I could call for a recount. There's still a chance I could win. I could even consider buying some votes," I rambled, my voice growing more erratic with each word.

"Landon, there won't be a recount. You lost by over fifteen points. She won. The people have spoken."

"Damn it, Kelly! You don't get it. Those volunteers," I pointed downward, "cost me my job, and now I have to fix it. I have to do their job!"

Kelly's eyes narrowed, her anger palpable. "You're seeing this all wrong."

"What do you mean?" I asked, taking another swig of the alcohol.

"It wasn't your volunteers who messed up; it was you, Landon. You mishandled your own campaign."

"What?" I repeated, alcohol-induced confusion setting in.

"You mishandled your campaign by ignoring your constituents' needs. You never listened to their suggestions, and you turned your back on your friends and family when they needed you the most. That's why they voted you out."

In a fit of drunken rage, I raised my right hand and slapped Kelly across the face. Tears welled up in her eyes, and behind her, I saw my twin girls, April and Kelsey, hiding and crying in unison. They hated it when their parents argued, just like any child would. But what could I do? On that November night in 2016, I believed my words, actions, and argument with Kelly were justified.

I pointed to my chest and said, "I know what it takes to win a campaign. I know what the people of Iowa need and want. What do they even know? They're just backwoods wannabe city folks who know nothing but corn and soybeans. They don't understand the struggle of securing funding for government projects, sitting on committees, and passing laws. They're clueless."

"They know something," Kelly said, recovering from the blow.

"What?" I shouted.

"They know you're no longer fit for office and that you don't care about them anymore. McClain was right. You've become part of the establishment." She punctuated her words by slapping me across the face.

The sting from her hand didn't faze me. It was her words. *"Part of the establishment"* pierced deeper than any slap. In that moment, I felt like

Julius Caesar—betrayed not just by allies, but by my own blood. Kelly had lost faith in me. She was my Brutus.

"Damn it!" I shouted. "You too?"

"Landon," her voice rose, "it's the truth. Look at yourself right now. You've terrified our daughters, you've assaulted me, and the hotel guests can hear everything you're saying."

"Leave," I told Kelly, slamming the half-filled drink into the television, creating a crack that distorted Anderson Cooper's image. "I have every reason to be upset. I've lost my job tonight, and now I have to witness that pussy-grabbing billionaire occupy the White House and undermine our entire goddamn democracy."

"Landon!" Kelly shouted once again, reprimanding my language.

"It's the truth, Kelly. If you don't want to hear our new reality, just leave me alone."

And she did. Kelly collected the girls' and her suitcases, and the three of them left. I returned to my chair, sitting alone in the dimly lit room with the curtains now drawn closed. As the television's fractured glow filled the room, I wept, alone in the darkness, drowning my sorrows.

I arrived in Washington two days later, the heavy weight of defeat still lingering in my mind. The previous day had been filled with a cold shower, a bottle of Advil, and the somber concession speech that marked the end of my congressional career. My wife, Kelly, and our twin daughters had returned home without me, their absence a painful reminder of the strained relationship between Kelly and me.

Our marriage had been on shaky ground even before the election, and the incident at the Farmhouse Hotel had only exacerbated our problems. Kelly had repeatedly expressed her concerns about my drinking, and she had a valid point. I had developed a habit of drinking excessively, moving beyond my usual daily indulgence of Budweiser, which I called "diesels," to consuming hard liquor every hour. Each drink had become a part of my daily routine, a coping mechanism for the stresses of my unraveling political life.

But my drinking wasn't the only issue in our marriage. As a father, I had been absent, working long hours and rarely spending time with my girls. Kelly often reminded me of a promise I had made when we found out we were expecting twins, a promise to be nothing like my own absent father, Craig Wolfe. Her reminders stung, as if she were comparing me to a man I despised.

As I returned to Capitol Hill, the pitying glances from my colleagues were inescapable. These stares came from those fortunate enough to have secured another term, while I confronted the harsh reality of defeat. No one had prepared me for this loss, and I was handling it with anything but grace.

My drinking was an open secret on the Hill. When I wasn't in session or attending committee meetings, I would slip away from my office, seeking refuge in the nearest bar or liquor store, or sometimes I would pour myself another drink right there at my desk, hidden from view. Alcohol had become my constant companion, but it was far from my only indulgence. At least once a month, when Kelly was away visiting her parents, I would dive into a world of excess, throwing lavish parties, surrounded by escorts and the seductive haze of cocaine. The line between debauchery and normalcy blurred as I lost myself in lap dances and the intoxicating allure of my reckless lifestyle. In my distorted reality, every excess seemed justified, a necessary escape from the crushing weight of my own making.

Hiding this lifestyle was manageable at first, but as the drinking, drugs, and affairs spiraled out of control, it became increasingly difficult to distinguish reality from the façade I had built. Who was Landon Wolfe, really? In the public eye, I was the charismatic congressional ally, a rising star with a promising future. Behind closed doors, however, I was a failure, no different from the deadbeat my father had been. I wasn't always this person, consumed by addiction and driven by vice at every turn. That's not who Landon Wolfe used to be. But as my power and prestige on Capitol Hill expanded, the allure of an extravagant lifestyle became irresistible. I reveled in the power and wealth, prioritizing them above everything else; my wife, my children, and the constituents back in Iowa who once believed in me. My addiction became a shadow that followed me, growing darker as I chased the hollow promises of indulgence and escapism.

As the calendar turned from November to December, I struggled to put the election loss behind me. I made half-hearted attempts to reconnect with my daughters and to be a better husband to Kelly, but every effort seemed in vain. My alcohol addiction was transforming me into a bitter and angry person, and the toll was evident at home. The constant drinking fueled my frustration and resentment, making it nearly impossible to maintain any semblance of calm or affection. The days leading up to my departure from Washington were marked by a relentless barrage of reminders of my personal and professional failures. The ridicule from colleagues, whether Republican or Democrat, was ceaseless and cruel. Each sneer and mocking comment was a dagger, amplifying the internal chaos and exacerbating the already strained atmosphere at home. Despite my attempts to rebuild what was left of my marriage, it became increasingly clear that both Kelly and I knew deep down that it was a futile endeavor. Our relationship, already battered by my vices, seemed destined to crumble under the weight of our shared disillusionment.

I sat at my desk in late December, caught between the cusp of Christmas and the crushing weight of my political defeat. The burden of failure was palpable, especially in a rare moment when I wasn't drinking in my office. My secretary, Jennifer Owens, interrupted the silence to announce a visitor. Despite my surprise, I instructed her to send them in. Moments later, Senator Ramon Vazquez of Pennsylvania, a former Congressman recently elevated to the Senate and currently serving as the Democratic Party's whip in the upper chamber on Capitol Hill, walked through the door. At 5'9", with a balding head and a strong Hispanic heritage, Ramon's face was etched with frustration, clearly indicating this was a meeting he did not want to have.

"Senator Vazquez, what do I owe this pleasure?" I greeted him with a forced smile, extending my hand as I rose from my chair.

"Cut the façade, Landon. We need to talk." Ramon's tone was sharp and direct, catching me off guard. Ramon and I had once been close friends, our relationship blossoming from my early days as a freshman congressman into one of mentorship and camaraderie over the eight years we'd known each other. However, since his ascension to the Senate, our friendship had become estranged. Yet, in my inebriated state, I still clung to the belief that we were friends.

"Is this how you treat all your friends now, Ramon?" I shot back, attempting to mask my surprise with sarcasm.

"No," he replied, his voice ice-cold. "Just you. Sit down."

Without protest, I slumped into my chair behind the desk. "Alright, Senator," I said, my tone shifting, "what can I do for you today?"

"Do you know how big of an embarrassment to the party you are?" Ramon snapped, his voice tight with frustration. "If I were the whip in the House, I would have written up articles of expulsion for you. The way you are behaving is entirely unprofessional."

Confused, I responded, "I happen to think the way I am presenting myself is adequate to the moment. I'm disappointed by the election result, but I am trying to move past it. I don't think my absence from Washington will be long. I'll be back. Better than before."

Ramon's eyes narrowed as he delivered another harsh reality. "I don't believe you'll ever be back in Washington, not in your current state. You are a shell of the man I met back in 2009."

"And what is that supposed to mean?" I shot back, irritation creeping into my voice.

"It means you've lost yourself, Landon," Ramon replied sharply. "The man I knew was driven, passionate, and had a sense of purpose. Now, all I see is someone drowning in his own sorrows, unable to face reality."

"Well, pardon me, not everyone can be a hot shot senator now, can we?" I retorted, sarcasm dripping from my words.

"You're a fool, Landon," Ramon shot back. "I got to this point in my career through hard work, dedication, and a sound mind."

Ramon paused, the frustration in his eyes giving way to a flicker of something more vulnerable. "I was once in your shoes, you know. Lost and addicted. I had the power and recognition, but I felt unfulfilled with my life. Then my first wife died."

He let the words hang in the air for a moment, the weight of his past pain evident.

"I nearly killed myself with the lifestyle I was choosing. Now, I know our friendship has not been the same as in years past, but I am coming to you as a friend, a friend telling you that I am worried about you."

"If this is your way of saying you'll miss seeing me in these hallowed halls, Senator, don't worry about me. I'll be fine. Like I said, I'll be back," I replied, trying to brush off the concern.

"Landon, will you open your fucking eyes and listen to the words I'm saying?" Ramon insisted, his voice rising with frustration. "I'm trying to give you advice, so you don't kill yourself!"

I sat up in my chair, my eyes locking onto Ramon's. "Excuse me? Who gives you the right to dictate someone's life?"

Ramon took a deep breath, shifting to a calmer tone. "I'm not dictating your life, Landon. I'm genuinely concerned about you. You're fortunate you haven't faced removal from office due to disorderly conduct. This election loss may sting, but I fear your issues run deeper. Much deeper."

I gave a slight chuckle. "Well, I guess this conversation is over."

"I'm not done with you," Ramon said firmly.

"Oh really? What would you like to add? Since you were appointed to party whip, you haven't spoken to me for four years. Now, just as I'm out the door, you show up telling me I'm living a sinful life. Come on, Senator, did you forget this is politics?"

"You know I'm right, Landon," Ramon responded, his tone unyielding. "I care about you, Congressman. I'm here today because I believe you're squandering your life, and you're too drunk to see it."

I stared at him in silence, absorbing his words. It was a rarity for someone other than my wife to label me a drunk. I felt a surge of anger and a desire to throw punches, but I managed to restrain myself. Instead of reaching for physical violence, I went for my desk drawer and retrieved a bottle of scotch, pouring myself a drink.

"Are you serious?" Ramon said.

As I brought the glass to my lips, Ramon abruptly stood from his chair and slapped the glass from my hand, causing it to crash onto the carpet, spilling its contents.

"Nice move, dumbass," I responded with annoyance. "You better hope that doesn't leave a stain."

Ramon's voice took on a more serious tone, though it felt rehearsed, as if he'd given this same speech a dozen times before. "Wolfe, you need to listen. The drinking, this reckless lifestyle; it's going to destroy you, if it hasn't already. You're not just an embarrassment to the party and your family; you're an embarrassment to yourself. What kind of example are you setting for April and Kelsey?" His voice rose, but the passion felt hollow.

"Stop," I interrupted, raising a hand.

"Landon, I'm not here as a colleague. I'm here as a friend," Ramon said, though the words felt more like a checkbox than an expression of genuine care.

I stared at him, unsure whether to laugh or be offended. "A friend?" I thought. But still, something in his tone finally cut through my usual stubbornness.

"You have a bright political future, whether you realize it or not," he continued, his words lacking the warmth they once had. "I saw that potential in you the day we met. But none of that will come to pass if you keep going down this path. Drinking, partying, it's all going to waste."

I leaned back, crossing my arms. "If I'm such a rising star, why did Iowa turn its back on me?"

Ramon shook his head. "I don't have the answer to that, but if I had to guess, I'd say it's your demeanor. Anyone can see you're intoxicated half the time. Hasn't anyone brought that up before?"

"Just Kelly," I replied. "If my staff mentioned it, I must've missed it... or fired them."

Ramon leaned forward, his voice steady but lacking warmth. "It's okay to seek help, Wolfe. Nobody makes it through life alone."

I attempted a grin, hoping to deflect his seriousness. "Well, I've always thought of myself as a lone wolf. Guess it's in my DNA."

My attempt at humor fell flat. Ramon wasn't amused. He launched into a familiar story: his struggles with drugs and alcohol, the way his second wife, Camila, helped him find faith, and how that faith pulled him out of addiction. Now, he said, he made time, when he could, to lead sobriety groups, to sit with men who were where he once was. It was a polished narrative, almost too perfect in its delivery, like a speech he'd given one too many times. Still, I couldn't ignore the conviction behind it, or the fact that he'd chosen to share it with me now.

I glanced at the bottle of scotch on my desk and, with a heavy sigh, slid it back into the drawer. A cocktail of emotions swirled within me. Part of me felt a flicker of hope; maybe the untapped potential Ramon had mentioned was real. But beneath that, the bitterness still simmered. Iowa had turned its back on me, dismissed my years of service. That betrayal still stung, and I wasn't ready to let go of that anger just yet.

"Do you really think I've still got a future in politics?" I asked, the doubt creeping into my voice as I sought some semblance of validation.

Ramon paused, his expression unreadable. "Like I said earlier, I can't gauge the full extent of the damage. But if you can turn your life around, really commit to it, there's no reason you couldn't make a comeback."

I leaned forward, my curiosity piqued despite myself. "A comeback, huh? Maybe even a run for senator? The presidency?"

Ramon hesitated, clearly not eager to feed into my delusions of grandeur. "Let's not get ahead of ourselves, Wolfe. The first step is cutting out the alcohol and cleaning up your act. If you manage that, maybe you could take on McClain in two years and reclaim your seat. But one thing at a time."

I couldn't help but roll my eyes at this suggestion. In the wake of my unexpected defeat, I had convinced myself that my time as a United States Congressman had reached its unceremonious end. The thought of running against Morgan McClain in 2018, or any subsequent year, held no allure. She could represent Iowa's Third District for as long as she pleased, or until Iowa grew tired of her as they did me.

If I were to reenter the political arena, my aspirations would soar far higher. In the days since that lonely evening atop the Farmhouse Hotel, I had harbored the idea of a revenge tour, akin to the legendary exploits of Nixon. The concept had been brewing within me long before Senator Vazquez visited my office. His visit, however, had provided me with a starting point, a spark of inspiration. It had solidified my resolve that the world would one day remember the name Landon Wolfe, transcending the mere title of U.S. Congressman. The desire to make Iowa rue their choice to vote me out fueled my determination like never before.

"Landon, would you just grow the hell up already?" Kelly's voice sliced through the air, filled with frustration and exhaustion.

It was the third blow-up we'd had that day, but honestly, it felt like the hundredth in the past year. My exit from politics was supposed to be a fresh start, a chance to rebuild our marriage, maybe even save it. Kelly had tried—God, she'd tried. After I lost the election, she didn't let my mood swings, drunken rants, or erratic behavior get to her. She gave me space, let me cope however I needed to.

We even went to Jamaica a week after moving back to Iowa in mid-January, thinking a getaway might help. Warm weather, tropical drinks, a break from reality; it was supposed to help. But that vacation turned into another disaster. For someone trying to quit drinking, being in an all-inclusive resort was a nightmare. I couldn't escape it. Whether it was in the room, at the bar, or sitting by the pool, a drink was always in reach.

Kelly knew I was struggling, and she let it slide. Hell, she even drank with me. We had an unspoken agreement that, for the time being, we were supposed to relax and take it easy. I promised her I'd cut back when we got home. But let's be real, it was all bullshit. Even when we weren't fighting on that trip, something between us was broken. The closeness we used to have? Gone. The sex was there, sure, but it was mechanical, nothing like it used to be. Some nights, Kelly stayed in with the kids while I hit the bars, flirting with strangers, pretending I wasn't the trainwreck I'd become.

When we got back to Iowa, the cracks were wide open. The cold slapped us in the face, and so did reality. One morning, after another freezing night, Kelly asked me about my plans and whether I'd looked into finding a job. I shot back with some half-assed joke about "not until November 2018." That pissed her off, of course.

"When the hell are you going to stop sulking about losing?" Kelly snapped. "You're acting like such a goddamn child!"

"I wasn't being serious," I mumbled, not wanting to deal with the conversation.

"I don't care if you were serious or not," she fired back, her voice sharp. "The election's over. It's done. The people voted you out, Landon! They don't want you! So what are you going to do now? Our savings aren't going to last forever while you mope around, pretending this isn't happening."

Her patience was gone, and I knew it wasn't just a result of hormones or a bad day. It had been three months since that humiliating loss to the stay-at-home mom from Indianola, and I still hadn't come to terms with it. Shit, I didn't want to. I wasn't ready to just "move on" like Kelly wanted.

"We're fine, financially," I said dismissively. "I don't need to jump into some bullshit job just to save face."

"Bullshit job?" Kelly's voice rose to a near yell. "What's more embarrassing than you right now? Your behavior? The way you drink yourself stupid? Jesus, I've been covering for you with my friends, my family, pretending everything's okay! But it's not. I'm sick of it, Landon. I'm sick of you!"

I glared at her, bitterness creeping into my words. "You knew what you were signing up for. You married a politician."

"No, I didn't!" she shouted, her face flushed with rage. "I married a man who loved me. A man who gave a damn about this family. Not the pathetic asshole who'd rather drink himself numb than even look at me anymore!"

The words hit hard, and she was right. I wasn't that guy anymore. And part of me hated her for pointing it out. But I couldn't admit that to her. Not now.

"Are we seriously doing this again?" I sighed, shaking my head. I wasn't in the mood for another round of guilt-tripping. Grabbing my bag, I headed for the door, snatching my car keys off the counter.

"Where the hell are you going now?" Kelly's voice echoed as I reached the garage.

"I'm going to find a fucking job," I spat back, slamming the door behind me without another word.

Our fourth argument of the day erupted late in the afternoon, just before dinner. I'd come back from another pointless job hunt, the whole day spent at the local library wondering how in the world I was supposed to live up to Vazquez's words: "You have the potential to do great things." What potential? What great things? Stuck in this backwater town in Iowa, applying for meaningless 9-to-5 jobs, I couldn't see it. I hated it here. And the decision to move back was gnawing at me more and more every day.

The fight with Kelly kicked off over dinner. I stepped through the garage door, and the stench hit me before I even saw the kitchen; fried fish, thick and oily, clinging to the air like a punishment. Cod sandwiches. My stomach turned. I hated fish. Always had. And Kelly knew that. The golden filets on the counter looked like they'd been pulled straight from a Gorton's commercial; the grinning fisherman in his yellow raincoat mocking me from memory. She wasn't trying to feed me. She was trying to make a point. And it worked.

Still fuming from another wasted day chasing dead-end job leads, I'd stopped at O'Malley's to drown my frustration. Three diesel drafts in, I stumbled out reeking of cheap beer and desperation, hoping, maybe foolishly, for something decent waiting at home. Instead, I walked into a scene ripped from a Hallmark card: Kelly humming in the kitchen, as if nothing was wrong, the kids scrubbed clean and zipped into their pajamas.

Kelsey ran to me with a squeal and threw her arms around my legs. I bent down, kissed the top of her head, tried to summon something close to a smile. But the rot in my gut wouldn't let go. The mood had set in hours ago, and now it was poisoning everything.

"Fish sandwiches? Really?" I asked, trying to keep the irritation out of my voice. "Couldn't we just have something simple, like pizza?"

Kelly shot me that look; the one she'd been giving me more and more lately. The one that screamed: *I've had enough of your shit*. "This is simple."

"Well, I don't like fish sandwiches," I snapped. "They remind me of being poor."

"I like them, Daddy," April chimed in, oblivious to the growing tension.

I ignored her. "I don't think I'm eating this," I said flatly.

Kelly's frustration spilled over. "Landon, would you just grow the hell up?"

"No. The smell makes me want to puke. I'm lying down." I moved toward the fridge, reaching for the Jameson stashed above it.

That's when Kelly stood up from the table. "If you're lying down, you won't need this," she said, snatching the bottle out of my hand before I could even react.

"Give it back," I demanded, my voice low and threatening.

"No," she shot back, cold and unflinching. "You're drunk. Again. And I'm sick of it. You've hit your limit for the day."

She twisted the cap off and started pouring it down the sink, her defiance palpable.

"Are you out of your fucking mind?" I barked, storming toward her.

"I'm doing what I should've done months ago," she said, her tone sharp, unwavering. "You said you'd stop drinking, but clearly you're never going to unless someone forces you to."

What happened next will haunt me until the day I die. The fury, the liquor, the crushing weight of failure; they all collided in one explosive second. I snapped. I lunged at her, hands trembling with rage, and grabbed her harder than I ever meant to. I slammed her against the fridge with a violence that echoed through the house. The sound, her body hitting metal, the dull thud of impact, ripped through me. The bottle we'd been fighting over slipped from my grip and shattered on the floor, spraying glass across the tile like splinters of light.

And then—silence.

Just the jagged edges of what I'd done, staring back at me.

"Kelly... Jesus... let me help," I stammered, panic rising in my chest.

She was crying. My daughters stood frozen in the doorway, their faces pale with fear. The house was thick with the heavy, awful silence of what had just happened.

"Don't touch me. Don't do anything," Kelly hissed, wiping her tears away as she pulled herself up off the floor, wincing as she avoided the glass. She marched out of the kitchen, and I could see the resolve in her eyes. This was it. She was done.

She told the girls to put their shoes on. They were leaving, and I knew they weren't coming back. I stood there, like a ghost, unable to speak, unable to move. Silent. Broken.

A week later, divorce papers arrived in the mail. Kelly was done. She didn't press charges, even though I knew she could have. She had bruises, but she spared me that humiliation. I signed the papers without a fight, knowing I didn't deserve a second chance. I'd pushed her too far, crossed a line I could never uncross.

And as I put pen to paper, a grim, sobering truth sank in: if I didn't grow up, if I didn't change, there'd be nothing left of me worth saving.

2

Rising From the Ashes

Spring 2018

"My name is Landon Wolfe, and today, I celebrate one year of sobriety," I proudly announced to a gathering of twenty diverse individuals from Capitol Hill.

The basement meeting space filled with applause and cheers from both current and former congresspeople, senators, and staffers, all united in their support of my remarkable milestone. An entire year had passed since I made the life-altering decision to leave behind my tumultuous, alcohol-fueled existence. It hadn't been an easy journey, but the personal transformation was more than worth it.

My path to sobriety had begun when I checked myself into Serenity Haven Recovery Retreat in the serene heart of Everwood, Oregon, on the 16th of April 2017. Nestled amidst the tranquil Oregon Forest, this secluded haven offered me not only the chance to conquer my addiction but also to contemplate my next political move. I harbored a deep-seated determination to silence the skeptics and prove them wrong.

I'd committed to a 90-day treatment program with the compassionate healthcare professionals at Serenity Haven. My initial apprehension felt akin to the nerves I felt stepping into Army boot camp for the very first time. But those fears quickly waned as I was enveloped in a warm and understanding community. Here, nobody knew me as a former United States Congressman. To the dedicated staff and fellow patients, I was simply a person seeking a second chance at life, striving to overcome the shackles of addiction.

The first week tested my resolve, but as I settled into the clinic's daily routine, I started to feel a sense of empowerment. Water became my constant companion, a quiet symbol of renewal and cleansing. And Lemonhead, of all things, found their way into my pocket. The tart sting on my tongue offered a strange comfort, a small weapon against the cravings that never seemed to sleep.

As the days marched on, I realized I could conquer the world. Addiction no longer controlled my narrative. When I completed my treatment, I had successfully endured ninety alcohol-free days, marking the longest span of sobriety I'd experienced in nearly two decades.

Rehab provided more than just sobriety; it offered me clarity. It was in those quiet moments that I came to the stark realization that returning to Iowa held no promise or purpose for me. Kelly and my daughters had moved on, forging new lives in South Carolina. Returning to Iowa would only serve as a painful reminder of my past mistakes.

With my life in transition, I decided to return to Washington. While it might not have been the perfect alternative to Iowa, it held the promise of support from compassionate individuals ready to help me rebuild my life. Senator Vazquez's support group became my lifeline, providing the crucial sense that I was not alone in my fight for sobriety.

In my career, I secured a position at the Ekeler Project, a healthcare nonprofit in the D.C. area, where we shared a common belief in the universal right to quality healthcare. The Ekeler family, Chris and Renee, founders of the foundation, had suffered their own tragic loss when their son James succumbed to cancer. My sister's early passing when I was just fourteen provided a shared bond based on the foundation's mission – advocating for legislation that eased the burden of medical hardships on families.

With my experience from working on the Affordable Care Act and my well-established connections in Congress, I was hired as one of the three dedicated lobbyists for the Ekeler Project. The Ekelers, unaware of my congressional fall from grace, welcomed me into their ranks.

Spring of 2018 marked a turning point in my life. A whole year of sobriety, a job that fueled a passion, and the feeling of genuine happiness had settled in. Little did I know that this newfound contentment would soon be tested as I left my one-year sobriety celebration.

It was a crisp Monday afternoon as I left the gathering, walking along the crowded streets of D.C. toward the Capitol South Metro Station. The cherry blossoms were in full bloom, casting pink and white petals into the breeze. Under the clear 71-degree sky, everything felt oddly serene for a city always on the move.

Arriving at the station, I swiped my MetroCard, and the turnstile clicked me through as I headed down the escalator toward the platform. The rhythmic hum of the trains echoed around me as I found a seat on the Silver Line. Settling in, I pulled out my phone, ready to zone out like every other commuter on their daily ride.

I started scrolling through social media, though the underground service was spotty as usual. My feed was a repetitive cycle of posts about President Trump, both for and against, interspersed with the occasional attempt at humor from friends. Nothing caught my interest. I was about to close the app and just embrace the silence when something stopped me—a post from Kelly.

My ex-wife had always kept her distance from social media, claiming it was depressing and a complete waste of time. So, seeing a post from her was rare, almost unheard of. Since our divorce a year ago, Kelly and I had only spoken when necessary, mostly about our daughters. I'd only seen the girls three times over the past year due to conflicting schedules and the distance between us. Although our marriage failed, Kelly didn't harbor resentment toward me, and I couldn't entirely blame her for what happened. We both had our roles in its collapse, and while neither of us ever tried to reconcile, we remained cordial for the sake of our daughters.

So, when her post popped up on my feed, curiosity got the better of me. It was a collage of photos from her weekend, and I instinctively clicked on the first one, though it took its time loading. There were twenty-eight pictures in total, but I didn't even get past the first.

In the opening image, Kelly beamed brightly, standing next to a man I didn't recognize. The scene felt jarring, yet familiar. I figured he must be her new boyfriend, though I hadn't heard anything about him before. But it quickly became apparent that he wasn't just a boyfriend, he was her fiancé. There, on her hand, was a massive diamond ring, sparkling enough to announce it even before I fully processed the caption.

Her new fiancé was tagged: Daniel Mathis. Something about the name pulled me in, so I clicked on his profile. It was flooded with political ads and campaign slogans: "Mathis for Governor," "Vote Mathis," "South Carolina's Future: Mathis Making the Difference."

I couldn't help but let out a bitter laugh. Politics? Kelly wanted nothing to do with that world during our marriage. How had she gone from loathing it to marrying into it again?

Confusion, then anger, swirled in my gut. By the next metro stop, still three stations away from where I was headed, I got off the train and made my way to the street above. I needed air. People rushed by me, but my mind was stuck on Kelly. With a decent signal again, I dialed her number.

She answered on the second ring.

"Hey, Landon. How's it going?" Kelly's voice was warm and familiar, just like always.

I took a moment to steady myself, breathing deeply. "Things are going well. Did I mention I landed a job with a non-profit here in D.C.? We're working on some incredible projects, really making a difference."

Her enthusiasm was genuine. "That's amazing! I'm really happy you found something you love."

I couldn't help but throw in a little jab. "Yeah, I could say the same to you."

There was a brief silence before she spoke again. "So, I guess you saw the post?"

"Yeah, I did," I said, trying to sound upbeat. "What's his name?"

"Daniel. Daniel Mathis."

"Kelly Mathis," I mused aloud. "Has a nice ring to it."

She laughed softly, the sound easing a bit of the tension. "Thanks, Landon."

I took the chance to ask more. "So, what does Daniel do?"

"He's a teacher," she answered, casually.

The word stuck with me, not matching what I'd seen earlier. I had done a little digging, okay, maybe more than a little, and his Facebook page was all campaign material. Was she lying? Or just trying to soften the blow?

"Teacher?" I repeated, faking innocence. "Funny, I thought I saw he was running for governor."

Kelly hesitated but finally confessed. "That's true. Daniel has been teaching for fifteen years, but he's also deeply involved in the community. He has worked on educational programs and job initiatives; he has really made a difference. People love him."

I pushed a little further. "So, what made him want to run for governor of South Carolina?"

Kelly's voice shifted, becoming more animated. "He was encouraged by a lot of people, but he was hesitant at first. Honestly, I'm the one who convinced him to go for it."

I blinked in surprise. "Wait, it was your idea?"

"Yes!" she said with excitement. "I believe in him. And we both think he has a real chance."

As she continued talking about her fiancé, I crossed the street, feeling a bit unsteady. Kelly had always been indifferent, if not outright dismissive, about politics when we were together. And now, she was deeply involved, even excited. It hit me hard. As if things weren't painful enough, Daniel looked eerily similar to me. He had brown hair, a similar height, and was now running for office. It was as if I were being replaced, both in her life and in my daughters' lives.

I found a ledge near a flowerpot and sat down. "Well, Kelly," I began, forcing a smile into my voice, "I just want to say congratulations. I'm glad you've found someone who makes you happy. What do the girls think of him?"

"Oh, they adore him," she said brightly. "He reads them bedtime stories and tucks them in every night. It's the sweetest thing."

Each word felt like a jab. Kelly might as well have said, "Look what you're missing, you pathetic drunk!" I blinked back the tears stinging my eyes, rage simmering beneath my skin. No matter how absent I'd been, I was still their father. I couldn't just be replaced. Could I?

"Congrats, Kel," I said, my voice tight. "I just wanted to call and say congratulations. I've got to run, there's a meeting I need to get to," I lied. "But seriously, I'm happy for you and Daniel. Tell the girls Daddy says hi."

After we said our goodbyes and ended the call, I walked another block before the weight of my emotions became too much to bear. I found a bench and sank down, staring blankly at the road ahead. Tears began to fall, and a storm of feelings churned inside me: hurt, anger, and a deep sense of loss. It hit me like a punch to the gut; I was replaced. Drowning in self-pity, I didn't notice the young woman who approached until she spoke. She looked to be in her late twenties, her strawberry blonde hair catching the light as she asked gently if I was okay. I forced a smile and lied, telling her I was fine.

"The senator will see you now, congressman," Aspen, the front desk secretary, announced, inviting me inside.

Every third Thursday of the month, I found myself stepping into Senator Ramon Vazquez's office, a standing appointment that had become a lifeline. Despite his demanding role in the Senate, he never missed our one-on-one counseling sessions, constantly carving out time for those of us in the support group. The turbulent months after I left Congress, signed divorce papers, and began the uphill battle of sobriety, Ramon had been my anchor. His door was always open, his support unwavering, and in those quiet, unfiltered conversations, I found the strength to keep going, a flicker of peace in the chaos of my unraveling life.

Over a year had passed since I'd last touched alcohol or drugs, but my inner demons persisted. Feelings of betrayal, persecution, and purposelessness gnawed at me. I felt unwanted and adrift, and the news of Kelly's engagement to Daniel Mathis had once again opened a fresh wound in my soul. As I sat down in Vazquez's office for our meeting, I had an agenda and a bone to pick.

"Landon!" Senator Vazquez greeted me with his usual warmth. "So good to see you. How are you doing today?"

I forced a grin, but it didn't reach my eyes. "I'm breathing," I said, my voice clipped. "Got a lot swirling in my head, but I'm here. What about you?"

He chuckled. "Just sat through a two-hour filibuster. Honestly, I'm just glad to be out of chambers."

We both gave a half-hearted laugh as we settled into our usual spots, him in the chair by the window, me on the couch that somehow always felt too soft when I was this tense.

"I'd be lying if I said I didn't miss those days," I admitted, my tone sharp with longing. "It's only been a year, but it feels like ten. Every time I watch C-SPAN, I feel like I'm watching someone else live the life I was supposed to have."

Vazquez nodded thoughtfully, then gently shifted gears. "Well, let me start with the usual: How's the sobriety? I know we talked Monday, but tradition's tradition. It's how we open every third Thursday."

I didn't answer right away. I looked down at the coffee table, tracing the edge with my thumb. "You want the truth?" I finally said. "Monday night—same damn day I celebrated a full year sober—I blew it. Just one drink. But it was one too many."

His expression didn't change, but I saw the concern in his eyes.

I continued, the words tumbling out now. "Kelly's getting married. I found out that afternoon. And all I could think about was being replaced, not just by her, but by the world. I had my shot, and I fumbled it; now everyone else gets to move on while I stay stuck. I needed to feel something, anything, and that bottle was still too good at pretending it could help."

"The guy's a carbon copy of me," I spat, eyes narrowed. "Well, except for being a drunken asshole."

Vazquez didn't flinch. "Landon, Kelly didn't replace you."

I shook my head, jaw clenched. "Come on. Look at him. He's polished, he's charming, he's running for governor. You seriously expect me to believe she just happened to fall for that guy? No. She chose him to humiliate me. She's making a statement: 'Look who I have now. Look who's actually got his life together.' She's doing this on purpose."

Vazquez raised a hand, steady and calm, like he was trying to rein in a wild horse. "I don't believe that's true. You're spiraling, Landon. Kelly moving on isn't about you; it's about her finding peace. Maybe even healing."

But I wasn't interested in peace. Not now. I leaned forward, fists digging into my knees. "You know what really tears me up inside?"

He didn't say a word, just nodded, letting the silence make space for me.

"I called the girls last night. Wanted to hear their voices, maybe feel like their dad again. I asked them what they thought about Daniel." I paused, voice cracking as I remembered the sting. "And in those tiny, innocent voices, they lit up. Said they couldn't wait for him to be governor. That they loved him."

I looked away, swallowing the lump rising in my throat. "He's using my daughters to boost his image. Their bedtime hugs are now campaign optics.

Vazquez didn't hesitate. "Landon... what did you expect them to say? They're seven. They haven't seen you in months. From where they're standing, you disappeared. And Daniel? He's there. He picks them up from school. He tucks them in. Kids that age don't understand your pain or your progress. They only understand presence."

I sat in that truth, staring at the floor like it might offer an escape. "I know," I muttered. "I do. But what am I supposed to do? Uproot my life? Move to South Carolina just to chase after them? What kind of father does that make me, one who abandons his purpose for guilt?"

Vazquez didn't flinch. "It makes you a father who fights for his children."

"Yeah, well, Kelly would see it as sabotage. A political stunt to tank her fiancé's campaign. She'd find a way to spin it."

"She might surprise you," he said, not unkindly.

I took a sip of the water he'd handed me earlier. It felt like swallowing dust.

"Do you at least see where I'm coming from?" I asked. "Tell me I'm not crazy for being angry about this."

He let out a slow breath. "I see it. More than you know." His voice softened. "When my first wife died, I spiraled. The bottle was my only company for two years. I missed birthdays, school plays... moments I'll never get back. And it ate me alive. But one day I realized that my kids were still there, waiting. Not asking for perfection, just presence. That's all they wanted. That's all April and Kelsey want too."

I didn't say anything for a long time. Just stared out the window behind him, where the Capitol dome stood tall and untouchable. Vazquez's words settled over me like a heavy coat I wasn't ready to shrug off.

I knew he was right.

But deep down, another voice whispered; *You're not done yet. You belong back in the fight.* And I wasn't sure which pull was stronger: the need to be a father, or the hunger to reclaim the life I'd lost.

Maybe both.

"Can we talk about something else?" I asked, my voice lower now, tired of sitting in the wreckage of my personal life.

Vazquez nodded. "Sure. What's on your mind?"

I didn't dance around it. "My political future."

That got his attention. He sat up a little straighter. "Alright. Shoot."

"I want to run for president in 2020."

He blinked. And then—he laughed. Not cruel, but not kind either. It stung like hell.

"What's so funny?" I asked, my jaw tightening.

"You," he said, shaking his head. "You can't run for president."

"Why the hell not?"

"Donald Trump, for starters," he said flatly. "You'd be a chew toy in his campaign. He'd light you up before the primaries even started."

"I can take him," I snapped. "He's a loudmouth with a Twitter account. I've debated governors, senators; I know how to land a punch."

He smirked like I'd just proved his point. "Landon, you think clever debate lines are going to stop him? Trump doesn't play by the rules. He drags people into the mud and makes them thank him for it. Cruz, Rubio, Bush; remember what he did to them? You think you'd fare better? You've been out of the game. You've got a history. Rehab. Divorce. Public flameout. He'd call you 'Wounded Wolfe' and make it trend."

I felt heat rising in my neck. "I'm not some washed-up has-been, Ramon. I'm thirty-nine. I'm sharp, I'm driven, and I actually give a damn. I'm not a Clinton; I'm not a Biden; I'm not dragging baggage from the Cold War. I'm the future of this party, and I know it."

"No," he said, all the warmth gone from his voice. "You're not running in 2020. It's not happening."

I leaned forward, glaring. "You don't get to make that decision."

"I do when no one else will say what you need to hear," he shot back. "You run, and your past becomes national news. Rehab, missed custody visits, that clip from the CNN panel where you lost it, any of it could tank you. You'd be sacrificing what's left of your name just to chase a ghost."

I opened my mouth to argue, but he cut me off.

"Name *one* politician who's come back from what you've been through and won a presidential primary. Just one."

I said nothing. Because there weren't any.

"Exactly," he said. "Look, if you're serious about rebuilding your life, start smaller. Take a House seat. Run for Senate. Hell, go after the governor's mansion in Iowa. Just don't walk back into the ring thinking it's still your time when the crowd's not even watching."

I stood up abruptly. My pulse was thundering. "This isn't about the governorship. It's not about Trump or proving I'm not done. I lost everything: my wife, my kids, my seat, and now she's marrying some clown who's about to be governor. I'm not gonna let that be the last word."

"Sit down," Vazquez said, sharp now, almost fatherly. "This isn't about Daniel. This isn't about Kelly. You're making this about ego because that's easier than admitting you screwed up. She left because you vanished, Landon. You buried yourself in ambition until there was nothing left to come home to."

I stared at him, breathing heavy. "You don't get to talk to me like that."

"And you don't get to rewrite history just because it hurts," he replied, his tone finally softening. "I know what it's like to lose everything. I know how tempting it is to chase something big just so you don't have to sit still and feel the smallness of your life. But if you ever want your daughters to know who you are, not the politician, the *man,* you need to stop chasing headlines. You need to show up. Start there."

His words settled over the room like dust. I couldn't breathe under it.

I grabbed my jacket without a word.

"Landon," he called after me, quieter now, "you want to come back? Then build something real. Something that lasts. The Oval Office will still be there in four or eight years. But your girls won't be seven forever."

I paused at the door, hand on the handle. I didn't look back.

"Thanks for the honesty," I muttered, before closing the door behind me.

I walked the length of the National Mall, each monument a silent witness to the weight of history, and now, my own unraveling. The Washington Monument stood like a needle against the sky, the World War II Memorial rippled with still water, and the names etched into the Vietnam Wall seemed to whisper caution. By the time I reached the steps of the Lincoln Memorial, my thoughts were no longer my own; they belonged to Vazquez's voice, still echoing in my ears. He was right. As much as I hated to admit it, I wasn't ready. Not yet.

The fire in me hadn't dimmed; if anything, it burned hotter. I wanted to prove them all wrong. Ramon. Kelly. Daniel. Iowa. Everyone who'd written me off. But for now, revenge would have to wait. Timing is everything in politics—and in redemption. When I struck next, it would be with precision, not desperation.

So I made a quiet vow beneath Lincoln's gaze: I would leave Washington behind. The Ekeler Project. The mess. The noise. I'd go to South Carolina, where my daughters lived, and where Daniel Mathis had taken my place. I'd do the hard thing, be present. Be steady. Let them see a father, not a politician. As spring thawed the chill from the air, I disappeared from D.C., not defeated, but preparing. Let them forget the name Landon Wolfe. One day soon, they'd remember, and they'd never see me coming.

3

Political Wilderness

2019-2026

By May 2018, I had resettled in the quiet, salt-tinged air of Sunhaven Cove, a sleepy coastal town just south of Charleston. It wasn't the power centers of Washington or the pulse of a campaign trail, but that was the point. Sunhaven Cove offered a kind of stillness I hadn't known in years, the kind that forces you to slow down and listen to the silence. Kelly and the girls lived a few hours north in Belleview Springs, closer to Columbia. We'd negotiated a rhythm; every other weekend with April and Kelsey. It meant keeping a polite distance from Daniel, playing civil for the sake of the girls. I could live with that. For now.

Of course, I hadn't come to South Carolina just to play dad every other weekend. Sunhaven Cove was a refuge, yes—but also a launchpad. I needed time to think, to rebuild, to reshape who I was becoming. The beachfront house gave me quiet, and Marion College Law School gave me purpose. I didn't know what my next move would be in politics, but I knew it started here, far from the cameras, in a place where no one was watching.

Education had never come easily. My sister's illness derailed what little routine we had growing up, and school often took a backseat to long nights in hospital waiting rooms and stretches of missed classes. Still, my mother, resilient, God-fearing, and impossibly patient, instilled in me the value of learning like a mantra. She never got the chance to finish her own education, but she was determined I wouldn't waste mine. It took longer than most, but I kept that promise. I earned my GED at twenty-two, just before shipping off to basic training.

The Army gave me discipline, but it also gave me direction. Between deployments to Iraq and Afghanistan, I studied in barracks and tents, fueled by ambition and the G.I. Bill. I pursued a dual degree in environmental and political science through an online program, keeping one eye always on the future. Those degrees, and a bit of charm, opened political doors. But I knew degrees alone weren't enough to climb higher. One mentor's words stuck with me: "If you want to lead, keep learning."

So in the fall of 2019, I enrolled at Marion College School of Law to pursue a J.D. in Public Policy. The coursework, which included regulatory systems, constitutional law, and policy analysis, felt more like familiar ground than foreign territory. With savings, side work, and a stubborn sense of purpose, I worked my way through the program. It wasn't just about education anymore; it was about legitimacy. In a world where perception is power, a law degree gave me both. I wasn't just the veteran or the ex-Congressman with a past; I was rebuilding myself into something stronger, brick by brick.

March 2024

"What do you mean Dan won't endorse me?" I snapped, my voice sharper than I intended as I paced the hardwood floors of my beach house, phone pressed tight against my ear.

There was a pause. Then Kelly's voice came through, cautious, measured. "I'm sorry, Landon. He said he just... can't."

"Can't?" I echoed, stopping in my tracks. "Kelly, we're family, or close enough. I've been civil. I've been present. The least he could do is return a favor."

"He's the governor," she said, her voice tightening. "It's not that simple."

"You think I don't know that?" I bit back. "You think I don't understand how politics works? That's exactly why I need him. One word from Daniel and I'm back in the fight."

There was a long sigh on the other end, the kind I remembered from when things between us were starting to unravel. "Landon... I can't change his mind."

The line went quiet for a beat. Then—"Goodbye, Landon."

The call ended.

I stood there, phone still in my hand, staring at nothing. March 2024. Nearly two years since I walked across the stage at Marion College, J.D. in hand. I'd done everything right, on paper. Working full-time at Enigma Trust in Charleston, heading up the war games division, shaping battlefield scenarios for the Pentagon's elite. It was prestigious work. Strategic. Respected.

And completely hollow.

The pull of D.C. hadn't let go. It gnawed at me in quiet moments, on the drive to work, during late nights on the porch, watching the tide roll in. With a congressional race approaching, I decided to take a chance in South Carolina's District 1. The incumbent, a Democrat, was vulnerable, but I wasn't naive. I knew I needed an edge. In a bold move, I switched my party affiliation to Independent.

Switching to independent was risky, sure. But I believed the district was ready for a candidate who wasn't tethered to party lines. And with my record, my story, I thought I could be that candidate. Still, I knew I needed to be realistic. Independence in name meant very little without credibility. Without backing.

Daniel Mathis was supposed to be that credibility.

He owed me, at least, that's what I told myself. I'd watched him rise, supported Kelly and the girls through his campaign, bit my tongue more times than I could count. He knew I was serious about this race. And when I asked him directly, while picking up April and Kelsey, he gave me a politician's smile and said, "I'll think about it."

That was weeks ago.

The call to Kelly was my final attempt to persuade him to move off the fence.

Now, it was clear, he wasn't budging.

But why? That's what I couldn't shake. Why would he refuse to support me? What was he afraid of? What was he hiding?

I didn't have the answer.

But I would find it.

Using Daniel's personal number, I dialed his phone, my tone reflecting my urgency and frustration. The phone rang once and then went to voicemail. I made a second attempt, but it went straight to voicemail again. My persistence led me to make three more calls before I finally left a message, my frustration evident.

"I am not going to be ignored, Dan," I declared sternly. "I expect you to return my call and discuss this like a man, rather than sending Kelly to handle your business."

Despite my insistence, Daniel never returned my calls, leaving me to fend for myself. My campaign for District 1 was abruptly cut short, polling at a dismal five percent, and I had no choice but to withdraw due to my financial constraints.

With no better path forward, I pivoted, reluctantly, toward another run for Congress. It wasn't the grand comeback I had envisioned. Still, I hoped it might serve as a springboard, something to pull me back into the national conversation. If a presidential campaign was ever to be more than a distant dream, I needed to rebuild from somewhere, and the House seemed like my best shot.

But reality came crashing down. The campaign unraveled faster than I could have imagined. I was polling in the single digits, my war chest was nearly empty, and the people I once considered allies had grown silent. The defeat was more than political; it was personal. I felt abandoned. If I was serious about reaching the highest office in the land, I had to rethink everything. Influence required leverage, and leverage meant relationships. I would have to start playing the long game, investing in others, earning trust, and slowly reclaiming relevance.

With a heavy heart, I returned to Enigma Trust, the uncertainty of my political future weighing heavily on my mind. In solitude, I contemplated my next steps and diligently worked to reshape my public image, one day at a time.

February 2026

The jazz was soft, almost an afterthought, just loud enough to smooth over awkward pauses. The lighting was low, the kind of amber glow that made everyone look a little better than they really were. It was a place built for quiet power lunches and discreet affairs. Our table was tucked near the window, a fresh loaf of bread between us, still warm but untouched. The smell of grilled steak and garlic vegetables hung in the air, sharp enough to cut through the small talk.

I swirled the straw in my lemonade, eyes steady on Senator Ramon Vazquez. It had been a while since we'd seen each other face to face, too long, really, and tonight was about more than catching up.

"You're up for reelection this fall, right?" I asked casually, leaning back.

Ramon nodded. "Yeah. And it already looks like a war zone. The field's crowding early."

"I figured as much," I said. "Word travels. You've got a real fight ahead."

He shrugged, a knowing half-smile playing at the edge of his mouth. "Welcome to the Senate."

I leaned forward slightly, voice lowering just enough to signal a shift in tone. "Look, Ramon, I think I can help. You remember my role at Enigma Trust?"

"Director of War Games, something like that?"

"Exactly. My team conducts advanced simulations and cybersecurity audits, testing vulnerabilities and analyzing threats. We're good at what we do. What if I conducted a comprehensive security audit of your campaign operations? Communications, donor files, internal strategies, the works. Quiet, thorough, and airtight."

Ramon paused, brow furrowing as he tore a piece of bread in his hands. "That's a generous offer," he said slowly. "But we've already got a few folks in D.C. watching our systems, and honestly, I don't think we have the budget for another layer."

"I'm not talking about billing you," I said, waving it off. "It'd be pro bono. My way of helping a friend. And it's not about replacing your team, it's about adding an extra line of defense. Independent eyes. If something slips through the cracks, you'll want to know before your opponent does."

He studied me for a beat, then nodded. "You really think it could make a difference?"

"In this climate? Absolutely. Data breaches are campaign killers. This allows you to go public with a message that you're not just running a campaign, but securing one. That kind of foresight builds trust."

Vazquez sat back, thoughtful. "Well... I can't argue with that. And I appreciate it, Landon. It means a lot."

I gave a slight smile, meeting his gaze. "Just planting seeds, Ramon. I help you now, maybe someday you help me."

He smiled in return, not saying a word, but he didn't have to. In politics, nothing stays free for long. Tonight, I wasn't doing a favor. I was making a down payment.

July 2026

The war room at Enigma Trust was quiet, but never still. A low, steady hum from the overhead lights mingled with the soft buzz of electronic equipment. Fluorescent fixtures cast a pale, sterile glow across the gray carpet and the oval table that anchored the room. Along the walls, digital monitors pulsed with movement: maps, data feeds, news tickers. One of them showed the Solomon Islands in deep crimson, a hotspot of unrest, a symbol of failure.

Three of us sat at the table, I and two longtime colleagues, men who had seen war from the inside and knew the difference between rhetoric and resolve. Our tablets lit the space before us with intelligence updates, intercepted transmissions, and reports of mounting atrocities: villages shelled, leaders executed, families torn apart by tribal and political lines.

This wasn't just a conflict. It was a powder keg.

We'd been watching it for years, Enigma Trust and a few scattered allies in the intelligence community. The Solomon Islands had long been a geopolitical pressure point. A former British colony still licking its wounds from decades of uneven development, tribalism, and foreign interference. Now, in the summer of 2026, the country was splintering. The Solomon Liberation Front, a Chinese-backed insurgency, had turned its rhetoric into a war machine. The United States, ever desperate to maintain its influence in the Pacific, clung to the fractured government in Honiara like a man gripping a fraying rope.

We all knew it: this wasn't just a regional civil war. It was the first real proxy war of a new era.

And our president was about to speak.

Collins, seated to my right, pointed a remote at the largest screen and turned up the volume. The channel shifted to GlobalLink News Network, cutting in with a red banner:

PRESIDENT HAYDEN TO ADDRESS SOLOMON ISLANDS CRISIS LIVE.

A few seconds passed, then the image sharpened. Republican President Norman Hayden, midway through his second year in office, stepped into view on the South Lawn of the White House. Young, impeccably dressed, with that air of rehearsed concern that came off more like a press secretary's performance than a commander-in-chief's resolve.

He began speaking. The crowd fell still.

"We strongly condemn all foreign interference in the South Pacific," Hayden said, his voice firm but lacking edge. "We are engaged in active diplomatic dialogue with the government of the Solomon Islands and our allies across the region..."

I barely heard the rest. The tone was measured. Predictable. Weak.

"Secretary of State Prescott has opened lines of communication with both parties, including members of the Liberation Front," Hayden continued, as if acknowledging terrorists as equal partners was some kind of diplomatic masterstroke. "We believe peace is possible, and we urge global cooperation in condemning further violence. The United States remains committed to stability, to diplomacy, and to a peaceful future in the Pacific."

When he finished, the camera lingered for a moment; Hayden standing before the press, his eyes trying to sell conviction, his lips curled into a faint, practiced smile.

Then came the explosion.

"You've got to be fucking kidding me," Torres muttered, tossing his pen onto the table. "That's it? Talks? While China's building runways on Guadalcanal and dropping crates of weapons into jungle camps?"

I didn't answer right away. I just stared at the screen, the image of Hayden now fading into a commercial break.

"This is how we lose the region," I said, finally.

Collins looked at me. "Say that again."

"We've seen this playbook before. Regional instability, insurgent groups backed by a global adversary, the U.S. floundering with statements and summits. It doesn't work. It never works. We should support the Solomon government with training, advisors, and boots on the ground, if necessary. Hayden's trying to run the world like a college debate team."

"He doesn't have a spine," Torres said. "You do."

I turned toward him. He wasn't smiling. He wasn't being kind. He was being honest.

"You should be calling the shots, Landon," he said. "Not him."

The words hit harder than I expected. Not because they were new; I'd heard versions of them before, but because this time, in this moment, they didn't sound like flattery.

They sounded like a call to arms.

For a long moment, I didn't speak. I just stared at the quieted screen, my own reflection faint in the black glass. The office around me faded. The hum of electronics dulled to nothing. In its place came something else, something older. A pulse, steady and rising. The feeling I used to have during late nights on the Hill, during classified briefings, during campaign stops, and backroom negotiations. A sense of gravity. Of destiny.

I had buried it for years. After my failed congressional run in 2024. After I walked away from Washington, vowing I was finished chasing ghosts. I had told myself that power was a temptation, not a calling.

But I may have been wrong.

Maybe it wasn't about revenge anymore. Perhaps it was about my responsibility.

The men in that room had looked to me. Not just for ideas, but for answers. For leadership. And deep down, I knew they weren't alone.

I stood, my chair scraping quietly behind me. "Maybe it's time," I said softly.

Torres glanced up. "Time for what?"

"For someone to remind this country what leadership looks like."

I walked out of the room without another word, my mind already racing ahead. Not to the next briefing or meeting. But to something larger.

Something more dangerous.

Not war in the South Pacific.

But a battle on home soil.

A fight for the future of American power.

And this time, I wasn't going to be a spectator.

The Capitol office was as polished as ever, marble floors gleaming beneath the midday sun, portraits of long-dead legislators watching over the modern political theater. I strode up to the front desk with practiced ease, my voice calm and assured.

"Good afternoon," I said, offering the receptionist a smile. "I'm here to see Senator Vazquez."

The young woman behind the desk glanced up, her expression skeptical. Her fingers hovered over the keyboard. "Do you have an appointment?"

I kept my tone light, almost amused. "No. But that shouldn't be an issue."

She blinked, clearly unconvinced. Just as she opened her mouth to object, a new voice cut across the lobby like a whipcrack.

"No one sees the senator without an appointment."

I turned.

She approached like a lawyer walking into court, measured, confident, unwilling to entertain nonsense. Mid-thirties. Her tailored cream pantsuit looked expensive but functional, and the heels clicking beneath her gave her an extra inch of authority she didn't really need. Straight strawberry-blonde hair, sharp jawline, and eyes that looked like they'd read too many briefing memos and trusted none of them.

She didn't offer a name. She didn't have to. Power speaks without introduction.

I smiled, not backing down. "Just tell Ramon I'm here," I said to the secretary, deliberately using the senator's first name. "I'm an old friend."

The strawberry-blonde woman stepped between us. "I said no one sees the senator without an appointment."

Her posture was defensive. Irritated. Like she'd seen a hundred men like me walk in unannounced, thinking charm could bypass protocol.

"If you don't leave," she added crisply, "I'll call Capitol Police."

I kept my expression calm, but added just the right amount of smugness. "I don't see the harm in giving Senator Vazquez a quick call and telling him Congressman Landon Wolfe is here. He'll want to see me."

Her reaction was immediate; an eye roll that was more tactical than emotional. "I see several problems," she muttered, deadpan.

I tried another angle. "Is this how you treat other members of the Hill?"

Technically, I hadn't held office in over a decade. But once you've walked those halls with a vote in your hand, the scent of power doesn't fade so easily.

She stared me down for a beat, jaw set. Then, with a sigh, she turned to the secretary and gave a tired nod.

"Page the senator. Ask if he'll see... the congressman."

The receptionist hesitated, then obeyed. I stood there, trying to appear relaxed, even as the seconds dragged. The woman in the cream suit folded her arms, never once breaking eye contact. I could tell she didn't like me. Or maybe she just didn't like surprises. I respected that.

Finally, the secretary looked up. "He'll see you."

Of course he would.

I stepped past the checkpoint and down the corridor, led by an intern toward the senator's office. When the door opened, I was met by a man who looked exactly how I remembered him: graying at the temples, expensive tie knotted too tight, eyes that had learned long ago how to smile without meaning it.

"Congressman Wolfe," Ramon Vazquez said, offering his hand. His tone was stiff, the greeting formal. When our hands met, he pulled me into one of those half-embrace, half-political photo-op hugs.

"It's been a while," he added.

"Likewise," I replied, forcing a smile.

But he wasn't looking at me anymore. His eyes had already flicked to the clock on the wall.

The door to Senator Ramon Vazquez's office creaked open like a groan of protest, as though the very walls resented my arrival. Stepping inside, I was again struck by the heavy scent of leather and wood polish, as well as the museum-like stillness of a room untouched by time. A flag drooped in the corner, like forgotten promises, and the sepia-toned photographs lining the walls —snapshots from campaigns long won —reminded me that this was a man rooted in tradition, even if the world around him had moved on.

The senator stood by a mini fridge, pulling out a water, his expression tight, like he'd just bitten into something sour. He gestured toward the cream-suited woman walking into the office. "Landon," he said, barely masking his irritation, "this is Ms. Lydia Barnes. She's managing my reelection campaign. One of the sharpest political minds I've worked with." His tone shifted to something polite and clipped. "Hope you don't mind her sitting in. We've got a strategy session right after this."

"Of course," I said quickly, extending a hand. "Pleasure to meet you."

Lydia stood with practiced grace and took my hand. Her grip was firm, her gaze assessing. "You look familiar," she murmured, brow slightly furrowed. "Have we met before?"

I offered a half-smile. "Yes, just out there, in the lobby."

But she shook her head slowly, thoughtful. "No. It's something else. I'll remember eventually. I always do."

There was a quiet confidence in her tone, the kind that didn't need permission to command a room. I could see why Vazquez respected her; she was no token aide; she was a chess player in a room full of checkers.

We took our seats, me on the worn leather couch, Ramon across from me in his armchair, Lydia settling beside him with her tablet perched on one knee. The senator and I exchanged the usual pleasantries, catching up briefly. I asked about the Enigma Trust audit I offered earlier that year, and it was Lydia who responded.

"It was thorough," she said, eyes flickering to her notes. "Found a vulnerability in the email system—weak passwords across several accounts."

I nodded. "Glad the guys caught it. Hopefully it's resolved."

"It's been addressed," she replied evenly, already moving on.

A short silence followed, filled only by the hum of the air vent and the ticking of a wall clock. Vazquez's eyes finally lifted to meet mine; calm, expectant, and faintly irritated.

Then Ramon leaned forward, clasping his hands together. "So, Landon, what brings you back to D.C.? Why have you demanded to see me?"

I hesitated, just long enough to feel how small the room suddenly seemed, then straightened, trying to match the weight of the moment.

"Eight years ago, I came to you with a half-baked idea about running for president. You were right, I wasn't ready. But since then, I've stayed sober, gone back to school, rebuilt what I could of my life. And I believe it's time."

I let the words land, then added, with full conviction, "I'm going to run for president in 2028."

For a moment, Vazquez just stared. Then he blinked, once. Slowly. The faintest curve of disbelief tugged at the corner of his mouth.

"The presidency?" he said softly, almost to himself.

Lydia stopped typing mid-note. The hum of the vent felt louder.

"Well," she said after a beat, "I'm not sure I'm in any position to weigh in. We just met, though I swear I still know you from somewhere."

I tried to steady myself. His silence was worse than laughter. I filled it the only way I knew how; with words.

"I want to make real change," I continued, my voice steady. "Universal healthcare. A total overhaul of our education system. I want to restore America's global leadership. We've let China overstep for too long. I want to push them back, starting with the Solomon Islands. We need to return to a purpose-driven policy."

I exhaled. Then I looked between the two. "Thoughts?"

Lydia chimed in, "Bold. Vague, but bold."

I dismissed Ms. Barnes' comment, shifting my focus to Ramon.

Vazquez leaned back, exhaling slowly. "Landon, you've come a long way. I respect that. I do. But I can't support this."

My face didn't move, but something inside me recoiled. "Why not?"

He hesitated, choosing his words. "President Hayden is polling well, mid-fifties. He's done... a decent job. He'll be hard to beat."

I studied him, searching for even a hint of pride, some sign that he was impressed. There was none. Only calculation.

"That's exactly why I should run," I said. "He's soft on China, his 'America First' plan is hollow, and he's taken this country in the wrong direction. His foreign policy is cowardly."

"I disagree," Vazquez said cooly. "For the first time in a long time, I support the sitting president, Republican or not."

"He's isolating us."

"And where in the Constitution does it say we're the world's police?"

I laughed bitterly. "How about history? Or common sense?"

"Agree to disagree," Vazquez muttered, clearly done with the debate.

"Is that your only objection? Hayden's popularity?"

Ramon shook his head. "There's more. The presidency demands everything. You'll be torn apart in the press. Do you have donors lined up?"

"Not yet. I've got savings. Small donors. I'll mortgage my house if I have to."

That was the last straw for him. Vazquez laughed, full-bodied and incredulous. But there was no humor in it, only pity.

"You think that's enough? Landon, this isn't city council. It's a billion-dollar race. You're not ready."

The laughter hung between us like smoke. I stared at him, half expecting him to take it back. He didn't.

My jaw clenched. "I've been preparing for years."

He stared at me, the warmth draining from his face. "You think being sober and writing op-eds qualifies you to run a country?"

Something in me faltered; a half-second of doubt, then hardened.

"I am going to do this, Ramon," I said, heat rising in my chest. "With or without your blessing."

Lydia, who had remained silent through the storm, finally spoke, voice like a scalpel. "You're passionate, Mr. Wolfe. But you're treating this like a passion project, not a war. Passion alone doesn't win primaries. It gets devoured by infrastructure and money. You need power to seize power."

The room went still again. Even Vazquez seemed to consider her words.

I turned to her, stung but unwilling to show it. "I have a platform—ideas. That's power."

"That's idealism," she corrected. "Not power."

Her tone wasn't cruel. Just true. And that made it cut deeper.

Ramon stood now, his voice firm. "You want a shot at the presidency? Run for Congress again. Senate. Build a base. Come back in 2032. 2036. *That's* a plan."

I stayed seated a moment longer, breathing hard, staring at the carpet until my vision blurred. Then I rose.

"I'm not waiting another goddamn decade! I already lost ten years rebuilding from rock bottom. I lost my wife. I barely speak to my kids. This is my moment."

"Then take it," Ramon snapped. "But don't come crying to me when you fall flat on your ass."

That broke something loose. I didn't feel anger at first, just exhaustion. Then it came all at once. "You've always doubted me," I said, voice shaking with rage. "I supported you. Every bill. Every speech. I believed in you. And you write me off like I'm some lunatic with a slogan."

My voice dropped, cold and deliberate. "You're an empty suit with a flag pin: hollow, polished, and too scared to stand for anything that might cost you something."

"Watch your tone," he warned, voice like steel. "You may not hold office anymore, but you *will* respect mine."

I met his glare with one of my own. "Fine. I'll watch my damn mouth."

I stormed toward the door. My hand hit the knob. "I should've known better," I muttered, just loud enough for both of them to hear.

The door slammed behind me like a closing casket, sealing away the last shred of goodwill between us. All that remained was the sound of my footsteps in the marble corridor, and the bitter taste of another bridge gone up in smoke.

As I stormed down the corridor, the polished marble beneath my shoes echoed like gunshots in an empty cathedral. I was trying, failing, to settle my breath, but the rage inside me refused to dissipate. My pulse throbbed in my ears. The exchange with Vazquez had unraveled me more than I wanted to admit.

Seventeen years. At times, I had been his anchor, his fixer, his goddamn lifeline. I helped prop up his campaign when he was struggling in the House. I connected him to the right people in the Pentagon to give his Veterans Bill the credibility it needed. I was there when the cameras weren't, when the donors dried up, when he thought about quitting. I gave him everything but my liver. And in return? He bought me a couple of coffees during rehab and checked in once every other Christmas.

Our friendship hadn't just frayed, it had rotted. I used to think it was a partnership, but I see now it was more like a parasitic vine: Vazquez climbed, I withered. I was the scaffolding for his ascent, forgotten the moment he touched marble.

I was a few strides from the exit when I heard rapid footsteps behind me; heels clicking like a metronome out of sync with my fury.

"Senator Wolfe!" Lydia Barnes called, breathless but composed. Her voice was sharp enough to cut glass.

I stopped, barely masking the exasperation curling my lip. "It's *Congressman,"* I muttered without turning.

"I know," she said, catching up. "Force of habit."

"What do you want, Ms. Barnes?" I asked, each word dipped in acid.

"You want the honest answer?" She gave a slight tilt of her head, calculating. "I want to help you."

I barked out a hollow laugh. "Help me? You work for *him.* You're the messenger girl for the man who just tried to slit my political throat."

She stepped closer, too close. "I don't carry anyone's water, Congressman. Not even Vazquez's. I saw what happened in there. And whether you like it or not, that was your campaign's funeral, unless you let someone like me resurrect it."

I stared at her, the weight of cynicism dragging at my shoulders. "I'm not interested."

"You should be," she said, tone coiled and calm. "You walk out of here thinking you're David with a slingshot, but all I see is a man bleeding out with no staff, no money, and no plan."

"I said no." I gripped the door handle.

She stepped between me and the door, eyes blazing. "Look, I want to know what your vision *really* is. What kind of country you want to build. Because I heard a flicker of something real in there, buried under all that wounded pride. You've got anger, Wolfe, but do you have a map? A mission?"

I shook my head. "Save the pitch for someone else."

"You want to beat Vazquez? Get the last laugh? Win the nomination? Then let me help you shape the story. Let me *run* your campaign."

I glared at her. "You think this is a game?"

She smirked slightly. "Of course it's a game. The difference is, I know how to win it."

"Go to hell."

"You're gonna need someone," she said, unfazed. "I've got more experience in presidential politics than you do. That's not ego. That's math."

I opened the door. "Here's some math for you," I muttered, and without looking back, I flipped her the bird over my shoulder.

The door slammed behind me, and with it, whatever Lydia Barnes thought she had to offer. I didn't know what the hell I was walking into next, but I knew one thing.

I was done being someone else's stepping stone.

PART TWO

ASCENSION

4

Grassroots

2026

I hadn't been able to sleep.

The McLean residency, with its cold modernity and Amazon Echo-Alexa silence, felt more like a safe house than a home. Enigma Trust furnished it well enough, with vaulted ceilings, a state-of-the-art kitchen, and some attempt at art on the walls, but the place still felt borrowed and sterile. Temporary. Like everything else in my life.

I spent the better part of the night circling a pool table in the den, a bottle of sparkling water within reach, the cue stick serving as my substitute for a more dangerous habit. The only sound in the house came from the clack of billiard balls. Rhythmic. Predictable. Unlike the rest of my week.

I lined up the thirteen ball, an orange-striped one, my least favorite, and sank it in one sharp shot.

Then came the doorbell. Sharp. Invasive. Wrong.

I set the cue down slowly, frowning as I crossed the tiled floor toward the front of the house. No one should be here. Not now. Not unless they were trying to sell me something, or bury a knife in my back.

When I opened the door, she was standing there like she owned the place.

Lydia Barnes.

Strawberry-blonde hair swept back in a severe bun, a tailored white blouse tight enough to draw the eye, but it wasn't an accident. Her black slacks hugged her waist like they'd been measured twice. And beneath that crisp white top, the telltale lift of a push-up bra wasn't subtle. Neither was the intent behind it.

I caught myself glancing, once, then looked her square in the face.

"Ms. Barnes," I muttered. "What the hell are you doing here? How'd you even find this place?"

She smiled like she'd just beaten me at chess. "Enigma Trust isn't as private as they think. Now, is that any way to greet the woman who's here to launch your political future?"

My brow tightened. "Didn't I tell you to go to hell?"

"You did," she said brightly. "I just don't take no for an answer."

Before I could shut the door or respond, she stepped past me, heels clicking against the floor like a declaration of war, and entered the foyer as if she'd paid the mortgage herself. Her perfume followed her in, faint but engineered, the kind of scent that said: *I'm not here by accident.*

I turned, watching her scan the room with sharp, appraising eyes.

"Nice place," she said, her voice laced with amusement. "But it's missing something... oh right—power."

"What do you want, Lydia?"

She turned to face me, folding her arms just under her chest, knowing exactly where my eyes had drifted a second too long. "I'm here to talk about your campaign. I'm assuming you've had time to prepare your proposal for me?"

I gave a bitter laugh. "Proposal? You mean the one where I told you to buzz off? Yeah, it's still active."

She chuckled, unbothered. "You're angry, fine. I'd be too. But let's not pretend you don't want this. I saw it in your eyes, even if Vazquez didn't."

I narrowed my gaze. "You're wasting your time."

"No," she said, stepping toward me now, slow and deliberate. "I'm investing it."

I didn't move. Just stood there while Lydia looked at me like a general sizing up a new battlefield.

"You need someone who knows how to play this game," she continued. "And you do want to play, Landon. Don't insult both of us by pretending you don't."

I shook my head. "You don't know a damn thing about me."

Her smile tightened, sharp now. "I know you've got rage to burn, a grudge against half the party, and a chip on your shoulder the size of the Beltway. That's not nothing. That's fuel."

I stared at her, unimpressed. "You can leave now."

Lydia didn't flinch. She stepped deeper into the room like she hadn't heard me, or more likely, didn't care.

"You've got fire," she said, her eyes scanning the space, then landing on the pool cue in the corner. "But you don't have a plan. Not yet."

"I told you back at the Hill, I'm not interested."

"No, you told me to go to hell. Which, for a guy with three sober birthdays, wasn't your most emotionally regulated moment."

I blinked. The jab was surgical, and she knew it. She didn't raise her voice, didn't gloat. She just let it hang there.

She walked past the pool table and sat on the edge of the couch, crossing her legs. "I've seen candidates more unstable than you go the distance. The difference is, they had someone ruthless enough to make them believe it was possible."

I didn't move. I didn't speak. I wanted to throw her out, to keep my walls up, to hold onto what little pride I had left after the day I'd just had. But her words cut deeper than I'd admit, because maybe she was right. Perhaps I didn't have a plan.

She tilted her head. "What do you want, Congressman? To make history? Or just prove to your ex-wife and Vazquez you're still breathing?"

I exhaled through my nose and motioned toward the armchair across from her.

"Fine. Let's talk."

Lydia smiled, not smugly, but like a chess player who'd just traded pawns and knew she had the board exactly where she wanted it.

We sat across from each other in the quiet of the McLean house, the soft hum of the refrigerator in the next room the only sound. Lydia sat on the couch, her legs crossed with precision, eyes fixed on me like a hawk circling its prey.

I leaned forward, elbows on my knees, hands clasped together to keep them from fidgeting. "Why do I want to be president? That's what you want to know?"

She tilted her head, smirking like she already knew the answer. "Don't give me the vague pitch you gave Vazquez in his office," she said. "I want to know what's beneath the surface. The truth. No bullshit."

I sat back, exhaling slowly.

"At Enigma Trust, our job is to monitor threats before they metastasize. To make sure the Pentagon and the White House don't fall asleep at the wheel. For the last few years, we've been watching the Solomon Islands crisis fester; what started as a whisper on the edge of the Pacific has turned into a scream. China is now involved, building ports, bribing ministers, and militarizing trade routes. It's a damn powder keg. And what's Hayden doing? Hosting summits and grinning through banquets. He thinks handshakes and photo ops are going to solve a geopolitical crisis."

I shook my head, jaw tight.

"A few weeks ago, he gave one of those scripted, teleprompter-heavy addresses, empty words about peace and partnership. It was during that speech that I realized something. My calling... it isn't about proving my ex-wife wrong. Or making my daughters proud. Or even getting the last laugh on Vazquez. Those are echoes. Not reasons."

I leaned in now, voice steady. "My calling is to bring fear back to the United States' name. Not chaos. Not warmongering. But fear. Respect. Deterrence. We've let the world walk all over us for too long: China, Russia, the whole damn G20. Trade deals that gut our workers. Military restraint that invites aggression. Meanwhile, the Solomon Government is pleading for help, and our president's too busy working on his handicap to care."

Lydia raised an eyebrow, but didn't interrupt. She didn't need to. I could feel her attention sharpening.

"No," I said, preempting the question I saw forming in her expression. "I don't want war. I want peace—through strength. Reagan understood that. He knew the only way to prevent conflict was to make damn sure your enemies feared starting one."

I stood and began pacing, the energy in my chest too much to contain.

"The second the world stops respecting America is the second our republic begins to die. Our democracy and our values don't exist in a vacuum. They only exist as long as the world believes in our ability to defend them. Aiding the Solomon Islands isn't about charity. It's about responsibility. It's about reshaping our foreign policy, ending this damn isolationist slide that started with Trump, dragged on with Biden, and now festers under Hayden."

I turned back to her.

"We need the world. And like it or not, the world needs us. The Founding Fathers understood that tyranny isn't always foreign; it can come from within. Hell, the Declaration lays it out: *when a long train of abuses and usurpations... evinces a design to reduce them under absolute despotism, it is their right, it is their duty, to throw off such government.* That's not just a line from 1776. It's a doctrine. One our country has forgotten."

Lydia took it all in, her expression unreadable: calculating, thoughtful, then finally shifting to something close to satisfaction. She leaned forward, resting her arms on her knees.

"Well, that's more like it," she said softly. "There it is. The real Landon Wolfe."

She let the silence linger a moment, then added, "You're right about the Solomons. But maybe for a different reason than you think."

I narrowed my eyes.

"My family, specifically Barnes Industries, has interests across Southeast Asia. Logistics, defense support, energy infrastructure. If the U.S. moves into the Solomon Islands, there's an opportunity. Security contracts. Reconstruction. All the predictable spillover. My father used to say: War may be unpredictable, but the balance sheet rarely is."

"So that's what this is?" I said, not bothering to hide the edge in my voice. "You want to help me become president so your family can cash in?"

She smiled, unbothered. "I want to help you become president because you have the fire and the vision to reshape this country. My family? They're just the jet fuel. You've got the engine. And right now, you're sitting on a runway."

She stood and crossed to the wet bar, not to pour a drink, but to inspect the crystal decanter. She tapped the glass, then turned back to me.

"I can jumpstart your campaign, Landon. Staff. Funding. Infrastructure. Everything you'll need to get off the ground. You just have to say yes."

I didn't answer right away. The fire in my gut was burning, sure, but so was the nausea. I'd seen too many men in Washington trade their convictions for convenience, vision for favors. Lydia wasn't offering me a hand. She was offering me a deal. And deals always come with strings.

I leaned back slightly, studying her.

"Outside of writing checks... what exactly do you offer me?" I asked. "Vazquez said you're one of the sharpest minds in Washington. What can you actually do to help me reach my goal?"

She raised an eyebrow, but didn't interrupt.

"And don't you work for him?" I added. "He made it pretty damn clear what he thinks of my campaign. I doubt he'd let you walk away from his reelection to help run what he'd call 'a fairytale.'"

Lydia's expression shifted, becoming less polished and more raw. "Vazquez is a prick," she said flatly. "An empty suit who likes the sound of his own voice more than actual strategy. I'll sit in a meeting, give him a solid plan, and he'll dismiss it. Then Fisher, my subordinate, might I add, repackages it with a slightly different spin, and suddenly Vazquez is all ears."

She folded her arms, jaw tightening. "Vazquez turns off his brain the second he sees a uterus in the room. Doesn't matter how right I am. Doesn't matter that half of what's gotten him this far was my work behind the scenes. He wants a mirror, not a mind."

"And you're done playing the mirror," I said quietly.

She nodded. "I can leave him. Hell, I can crush him. I know every donor, every leverage point, every crack in the machine. All I need is a reason. You give me that reason."

I ran my tongue along the inside of my cheek, weighing it all. "And if we fall short of our goal? What then?" I asked. "Do I become some indebted servant to Barnes Industries? A mouthpiece for your family's interests?"

Lydia laughed, sharp, rich, and unbothered.

"Congressman," she said with a grin, "we're not going to lose. Trust me on that."

I looked at her, really looked. She wasn't bluffing. She was all in, cards already on the table.

Truth was, no one else had treated me like this. Not since the Army. Not since the divorce. Not since I first arrived in Washington and realized just how small one man's voice could be. But Lydia, she saw me. She heard the anger behind the ideals, the vision beneath the ambition.

And if she and her family stood to profit, so what? If I got what I wanted, revenge, relevance, a shot at reshaping this country, wasn't that worth the trade?

I nodded slowly.

"Alright," I said. "Let's do it."

She rose, smoothing the front of her blazer and rolling her shoulders back, composed, ready for battle.

She walked towards the door. As she reached for the handle, I called out, "It wasn't the clothes."

She glanced back, waiting.

"You won because you didn't flinch."

Her smile sharpened, amused but merciless.

"You don't have a shot with me, Wolfe," she said coolly. "But you're smart enough to know that's not why I'm here."

I watched her walk away, her stride measured, deliberate, every step a message that she was in control.

When I closed the door, I stood in the entryway for a long while, listening to the silence. And for the first time in years, I didn't feel alone in the war I was about to start.

I had just made a deal with the devil.

But at least this devil believed in me.

The scent of fresh hay and diesel clung to the cold Iowa air as I stepped out of the rental and into the frost-kissed fields of Jasper County. Lydia had spent the past several weeks crafting my rollout, tightening my image, testing language, and building a groundswell online, but we both knew the real work started in places like this. Barns before boardrooms. Feed lots before fundraisers.

This wasn't my first trip to Iowa. But it was the first time I returned not as a congressman searching for headlines, but as a man courting a movement.

George Rowlands greeted me with a handshake that could crack a fence post. Weathered. Firm. Authentic in a way that you can't fake, no matter how many consultants you pay.

"Landon Wolfe," I said with a nod, smiling like I meant it. "Appreciate you having me out here."

George eyed me with the skepticism of a man who'd seen a few too many empty promises pass through his fields. "Heard you might be runnin' for president," he said. "So, what's the pitch? What makes you different from Hayden? Or the half-dozen others sniffin' around my front porch this week?"

I glanced out over the rows of tilled soil behind him. I could see the John Deere in the distance, caked in rust and memory. "The pitch?" I repeated softly. "I guess that's the part I'm trying to unlearn."

He waited.

"I'm not here to sell you something, George. I'm here because I remember what it's like to look around and wonder if Washington even remembers you exist." I paused. "And yeah... I'm seriously exploring a run. Haven't said it out loud yet, but I'm not hiding either."

George folded his arms. "You've got the boots and the charm. But so did Hayden when he came through here four years ago."

I nodded slowly. "And look where that got us."

We stood in silence for a beat, the wind carrying the faint sound of cattle lowing in the distance. Then, as if on cue, the conversation turned outward, toward the world. George asked about the Solomon Islands. China. Global entanglements. Whether I thought we had the stomach anymore to hold the line out there.

I dug my hands into my coat pockets.

"When I was in Congress," I began, "I said a lot of things that sounded good in a press release. But here's the truth: the Solomon Islands aren't just some speck on a map. They're a test—one of many. A test of whether the United States still has the resolve to be more than a spectator in the defining power struggle of our time."

George didn't blink. I kept going.

"We can't police the world. I get that. But we also can't afford to pretend that what happens overseas won't end up on our doorstep. China is expanding in all areas: economically, militarily, and digitally. And places like the Solomons? They're where the new Cold War is being fought. Quietly. Strategically."

I looked him square in the eyes.

"We have to show up. With diplomacy, yes, but also with consistency. With strength. If we abandon our allies, we leave a vacuum. And history shows us who fills those."

He let that hang for a moment, then grunted in approval. "You sound like you've thought about this."

"I have," I said. "More than I should've. And not because I'm trying to check a box on some foreign policy debate stage, but because I'm tired of leaders who think strength is all bark or all bullets. It's both. It's knowing when to talk... and when to walk."

A hint of a smile touched George's face. "Well, you're better than the last guy who stopped by here promising the world and not knowing where the Solomons were on a globe."

We shook hands again before I climbed into the SUV. As we pulled away from the farm, I glanced back at the silhouette of George Rowlands, an honest man with soil under his nails and politics in his heart, whether he admitted it or not.

That conversation hadn't gone viral. No cameras. No applause lines. Just two Americans, talking about what mattered.

The ripple effect of Lydia Barnes's decision came fast and without warning. Days after she walked away from the Vazquez campaign, Lydia began assembling a team, not of loyalists, but of professionals who believed in building something different. Within a week, two new names appeared around the kitchen table of our makeshift headquarters: Dr. Ellie Poole and Terry Park.

Dr. Poole was a communications savant, the kind of woman cable news bookers prayed would say yes. A former media consultant to senators and CEOs, she held a PhD in political rhetoric. She had a reputation for transforming candidates who didn't look the part and turning them into contenders. Lydia brought her in not to stage-manage me, but to make me legible to voters again; after the headlines, the divorce, the exile.

Ellie didn't waste time. My schedule filled with media training sessions: how to hold a room, how to modulate tone, when to lean in, when to say less. She reworked my speeches with surgical precision, cutting the fluff, sharpening the message. I traded rolled-up sleeves for tailored jackets, updated my haircut, and, yes, on her advice, tidied up my eyebrows. Nothing drastic. Just cleaner. Calmer. Presidential.

But Ellie did more than coach. She reminded me how to listen, how to speak with sincerity without sounding like I was trying. She was the one who pushed me back into community meetings and church basements, not for cameras, but for the rhythm. For the people. "Relatability isn't a strategy," she said once, flipping through polling numbers. "It's muscle memory."

Then there was Terry Park.

Terry didn't smile much, but that was fine; his job wasn't charm. Lydia brought him on as Campaign Operations Director, a title that undersold his value. Terry was logistics, infrastructure, and contingency plans rolled into one. He built out the backend of the campaign like a military operation, streamlining data systems, internal communications, travel routes, donor pipelines, and crisis drills. If Ellie was the voice, Terry was the spine.

They didn't always agree. Terry found Ellie too idealistic; Ellie found Terry too mechanical, but together, they made the machine run. Lydia stood at the center of it all, not micromanaging but orchestrating. I watched her become what she'd always claimed to hate: a political operator. But she was good. Too good to deny.

With their help, the whispers turned into headlines. The "maybe" candidacy morphed into speculation. And even though I hadn't officially declared, we all knew what this was becoming. I started traveling again, taking quiet visits to early primary states, visiting small towns in Iowa, and exploring backroads in South Carolina. Places that knew my name from years ago.

For the first time in years, I felt like I had something to say, and people were starting to listen.

I hadn't declared myself a candidate yet. But the checks were being written. The calls were being returned. And somewhere between the first media hit and a town hall in Des Moines, the man I used to be started to fade behind the man I was becoming.

The grandeur of the Rockies stood silent and snow-draped outside the tall windows of the Brights' mountain cabin. Inside, the crackle of a wood-burning fireplace warmed the room, mingling with the scent of pine, cinnamon, and Gwen Bright's famous sugar cookies. The Evergreen tree glittered with decades of ornaments, school projects, souvenirs, and heirlooms; each one telling a chapter of the family's story. Ten stockings hung neatly over the stone hearth, just as they had every year since the children were small.

Senator Ted Bright stood at the edge of the hearth, dressed in a thick red sweater and jeans, a mug of coffee warming his hands. He was a commanding figure even in stillness, tall and broad-shouldered, with a mop of salt-and-pepper hair combed back from his brows and a neatly trimmed beard that gave him a statesman's air. His piercing blue eyes, bright with intelligence and years of public service, held both warmth and a quiet weight. He looked every bit the seasoned leader and patriarch, a man shaped by the rugged Colorado terrain he'd served for decades.

Beside him, Gwen sat curled into a plush armchair, her hand resting gently on his knee with the quiet strength of a lifelong partner. Her blonde hair, still gracefully swept back despite a few silver strands, framed a face marked by years of devotion, poise, and resilience. Around them, their three adult children were nestled on the long couch: Evelyn, polished and poised, her mother's mirror in both looks and demeanor; Philip, the eldest, with Gwen's blond hair and his father's confidence; and Edward, the youngest, who, unlike his siblings, bore his father's dark hair and striking features, though he sat slightly apart, quiet, his gaze fixed on the flames. On the rug by the pine-scented tree, the Bright grandchildren squirmed with impatience, casting wide-eyed glances at the stack of wrapped gifts, waiting for permission to plunge into Christmas delight.

Ted cleared his throat gently, and the room quieted.

"I want to start by saying Merry Christmas," he said, his voice deep and steady. "It means more than you know to have everyone here. Gwen and I have cherished these moments for decades now; family first, always. But before we open presents... I've got something I need to say."

He paused, gathering his thoughts as the firelight flickered across his face.

"I've been giving serious thought to 2028. And I want you all to hear it from me first: I'm thinking about running for President.

For a moment, the room was silent. Then Philip, the oldest, leaned forward, eyes wide with excitement.

"Dad, that's huge. Honestly, you've been preparing for this your whole life. You've got the record, the name, the reputation—this is your moment."

Evelyn nodded, offering her father a warm smile. "I agree. You've always served with integrity. The country needs someone who doesn't flinch at hard truths. And you're one of the few who can lead with both strength and compassion."

Ted's eyes moved to Edward, whose gaze was fixed on the fire. The youngest of the Bright children and Ted's namesake, Edward had long carried the unspoken title of the family's black sheep. His struggles with addiction, failed ventures, and a history of public missteps had cast a long shadow over his once-promising potential. Where Ted shared an easy, almost instinctive bond with Philip and Evelyn, his relationship with Edward was knotted by disappointment and unspoken grievances. Even now, on Christmas morning, the space between them felt more like a quiet truce than a true reconciliation.

"I'm not saying don't do it," Edward began, "but running for President... It's not just you who runs. We all do. Campaigns chew families up, Dad.

They expose everything. And I'm not sure we've all got the stomach for another round of that."

Ted nodded, appreciating his youngest son's honesty. "Fair. That's a good point, Ed."

He turned toward a nearby whiteboard propped beside the mantle. "Let's make this simple. How about we go around the room and discuss the reasons for and against? I'll play scribe. Evy, want to kick us off?"

Evelyn leaned forward. "Pro: You're a consensus builder. The country's fractured, Dad. You've built coalitions in the statehouse and the Senate. People need someone who can talk to both sides without compromising their principles."

Ted wrote it down: **Unifier – track record of bipartisanship.**

Gwen chimed in next. "Pro: Legacy. You've spent your life in service, Ted. But this... this would be your highest call. Not for power, but to leave behind a country better than you found it."

Ted's marker hovered as he wrote: **Legacy — finish the work.**

Alyssa, Philip's wife, raised her hand playfully. "Con: Baldness."

Ted raised a brow. "Excuse me?"

She laughed. "Stress. You'll lose your hair. Or Philip will. Someone's going bald."

Ted grinned and scribbled **Baldness — campaign stress** into the 'against' column.

Edward, still leaning back, added, "I'll offer a serious one: family fatigue. Your life has always been about public service, but that has meant missing many birthdays and canceled holidays. This is a whole new level of sacrifice, not just for you, but for us too."

Ted nodded again, quietly writing, **Cost to family — personal toll.**

There was a moment of reflection before Evelyn spoke again. "But also, think about what's happening globally. We're in a leadership vacuum. You have foreign policy experience and moral clarity. That's rare. You won't pander to strongmen. You believe in the alliances that have kept peace for decades."

Ted's gaze lingered on her. He gave her a grateful look and wrote, **Strong, principled foreign policy.**

Edward shifted, finally meeting his father's eyes. "I may have my doubts, but... You don't back down from the hard stuff. That's one thing I respect. And if you do this, do it for the right reasons. Not because you *can,* but because you *should."*

The room fell quiet as Ted stepped back and surveyed the board. The pros outweighed the cons, but more than that, they reflected something deeper: shared values, faith in his leadership, and belief in his character.

Ted smiled, placed the cap back on the marker, and set the board aside.

"Alright," he said with a grin. "That's enough presidential talk for one morning. It's time for stockings and cookies."

The grandchildren squealed with delight as the adults laughed, the weight of the ambition giving way to the joy of family and the peace of Christmas morning.

Returning from my morning jog through the misty trails of the North Carolina woods, I carried with me the crisp air of the wilderness and the dull ache of exertion in my legs. I was speaking later that day, but any anticipation I felt quickly shifted when I stepped into the modest campaign lodge.

My team was crowded around the television, their attention fixed. Even the interns, usually half-scrolling on their phones, were glued to the screen. I wiped sweat from my brow and turned toward the broadcast.

On the screen, in a packed hall in Newport, Rhode Island, Senator Kennedy Hickman stood at a grand podium draped in red, white, and blue bunting. The crowd, diverse and energized, was mostly comprised of women and young people, holding signs that read "HICKMAN 2028" and "The Future Is Female." Cheers rippled like waves as Hickman stepped forward, her tailored white suit a symbolic nod to the suffragettes.

"This moment is bigger than a campaign," Hickman began, her voice firm and full of conviction. "This is a movement. For every woman who's been told to wait her turn. For every daughter who's been underestimated. For every mother who's worked twice as hard for half the pay, this is our time."

The crowd erupted. Women in the front row were already crying. Young girls on their mothers' shoulders waved miniature flags. Lydia, seated on the couch, let out a low whistle. "She knows exactly who she's talking to."

"I'm running for President of the United States," Hickman declared, "because equality should not be a question, but a given. "It's time for women to earn the same paycheck for the same work. To have autonomy over our own bodies without apology. To lead not only in our households, but in the highest offices of this nation."

Every pause she took was met with thunderous applause.

"No more asking politely for equity. No more waiting patiently for progress. If you're tired of being told to smile, sit down, or stand aside, this campaign is for you."

The camera cut to signs that read: "My Body. My Rights." and "Daughters Deserve More."

I folded my arms, catching my breath, still sweating from the jog, but I hardly noticed. The energy on screen was undeniable. Even from a thousand miles away, I could feel it.

She then moved on to young voters. "To our students drowning in debt, to the twenty-somethings priced out of the housing market, to the new graduates asking if the American Dream still exists, I see you. I *am* you. And I will fight for you."

Her voice rose again, soaring like a chorus over the crowd. "We will pass equal pay legislation. We will codify Roe. We will expand education access. We will reclaim the promise of America for every woman and every young person whose voice has been dismissed. This is not a revolution, it's a course correction."

A standing ovation followed her closing line: "I'm Kennedy Hickman, and I believe that when women rise, America rises."

The crowd chanted her name as she stepped down from the podium, embraced by her teenage daughter and husband. The room had the electricity of a history-making moment. For a split second, I wasn't thinking about my campaign. I was just watching the future unfold.

The screen shifted to *The Political Pulse* studio in D.C., where the analysts dove in.

"Well, there it is," said a silver-haired commentator with a tight smile. "Senator Hickman has officially launched what promises to be one of the most ideologically progressive campaigns we've seen in years."

"She made a strong appeal to women and Gen Z voters," another chimed in. "But let's not forget, she's barely halfway through her first term in the Senate. That inexperience could be a real liability."

A female analyst jumped in, rolling her eyes. "We've heard this before. Barack Obama had just as much experience in 2008, and look what happened. This isn't about time served, it's about qualifications. Hickman's a Harvard grad. A Wall Street executive. A senator. And she just commanded that stage like a front-runner."

The conversation turned to strategy and early-state polling, but I barely heard it. I stood quietly, towel in hand, thoughts churning. Hickman had seized the moment. And now, the race was officially on.

My own announcement was days away. Would my message land with the same force? Could I connect across demographics the way she had?

I didn't have an answer, only the growing awareness that the bar had just been set.

Beneath the dusky sky along the Charleston waterfront, I stood before a crowd of 450. Their faces glowed beneath the lights strung across the pavilion, eyes lifted with expectation, hope, and curiosity. It wasn't the biggest crowd South Carolina had ever seen, but it was ours. And it was enough to spark a fire.

"My name is Landon Wolfe," I began, my voice steady, carried by the wind off the Atlantic. "And I'm running for president of the United States."

The applause was immediate, quick, and forceful, but I raised a hand to still it. I hadn't come to deliver platitudes.

"I'm running because this country is starving, for leadership, for conviction, for a future that isn't shaped by fear, but by ambition. From the shop floors of Milwaukee to the shipping docks in Savannah, Americans aren't asking for handouts; they're asking for a chance. And it's time we gave it to them."

I spoke about the need for bold investment in American innovation, the promise of clean energy that doesn't bankrupt working families, and the necessity of rebuilding an education system that doesn't leave our next generation behind. The crowd nodded, some cheering, others recording, but I saw them listening, leaning in.

Then I pivoted.

"But I didn't come here tonight just to talk about domestic policy," I said. "The world is watching us, and right now, they see drift. They see weakness."

The wind picked up as if on cue.

"In the Solomon Islands, in Eastern Europe, in the Taiwan Strait, the forces of instability are gaining ground while America dithers. Let me be clear: we can't lead at home if we retreat abroad. We need a foreign policy that is strong, smart, and moral. One that defends our allies, deters our adversaries, and upholds the promise of American leadership; not just as a power, but as a partner."

That drew genuine applause, more than I expected. Maybe America was hungry for it, too.

"I'm not running to manage decline," I said, locking eyes with as many faces as I could. "I'm running to build again. To believe again. To lead again."

The cheers swelled. For a moment, it felt like Charleston itself was roaring back.

I stepped back from the podium, heart pounding, not with nerves, but with purpose. This was the start. The night the campaign became real.

And the fight for America's future officially began.

5

Campaign Trail

Spring to Summer 2027

Senator Ted Bright's announcement came on a crisp Friday morning, March 12, 2027, and with it arrived a tidal wave of media attention. Standing before a cheering crowd in his home state of Colorado, Bright unveiled his campaign with a confident smile and a slogan tailor-made for the digital age: *"The Future Is Bright."* It was a phrase that echoed across newsrooms, late-night talk shows, and voter inboxes by sundown. The media wasted no time dubbing Bright the first *serious* contender for the Democratic nomination; an experienced lawmaker with a clean image, deep donor ties, and most critically, a campaign warhorse behind the curtain: Rey Hughes.

Rey Hughes was a name that stirred both respect and fear in the political underworld. A fast-talking Cajun from the Louisiana bayou, Hughes had earned his reputation as a ruthless campaign strategist during the last presidential cycle, helping propel Norman Hayden to the presidency with a mix of populist flair, below-the-belt tactics, and a dogged instinct for the jugular. Four years later, Hughes had ditched Hayden like a worn-out saddle and was now firmly attached to Ted Bright's rising star.

Political insiders scrambled to interpret the shift. Was it ideological? Strategic? Or just another case of Hughes backing the best bet on the board?

In one of his first post-announcement appearances on *The Political Pulse,* Hughes leaned back in his chair, grinning like a gambler with pocket aces. He wore a wrinkled seersucker suit and a bolo tie, sipping sweet tea from a mason jar like he was holding court on a front porch instead of a national news studio.

"Now look here," Hughes said, his Southern drawl stretching like molasses over gravel. "I was raised around racetracks. My daddy taught me early—you don't fall in love with the horse, you fall in love with the odds. Four years ago, Hayden was the stallion to beat. But that boy's lost a few strides. Ain't no shame in it. Happens to all champions. But this year? This year the thoroughbred's name is Teddy Bright."

He pointed straight at the camera, as if he were preaching to the American people.

"See, Teddy's got what the others don't. He's clean. He's sharp. He doesn't spook easily. And he has that government résumé that folks can actually respect. The man knows how Washington works without bein' soaked in the swamp. That's a delicate balance, friend."

On another network appearance, he doubled down:

"Let me tell you somethin' real clear," he said, wagging a finger. "Experience ain't just a résumé line. It's a weapon. And Teddy's got it holstered and ready. Me? I'm just the ol' gunslinger keepin' the other cowboys nervous."

When asked why he abandoned the sitting president for a challenger, Hughes didn't flinch.

"I ain't married to no politician," he said, grinning. "I marry momentum. And Teddy Bright? He's the one wearin' the white hat this time. You either back the horse that's runnin' or you end up sittin' in the mud watchin' history pass you by."

Hughes' over-the-top style and unpredictable metaphors made him a magnet for soundbites and a headache for fact-checkers, but his influence was undeniable. With Hughes steering the ship and Bright steady at the helm, the campaign quickly dominated early coverage, eclipsing the noise of earlier announcements, including mine.

My January campaign launch in Charleston had ignited solid buzz, skillfully crafted by Lydia, Ellie, and Terry. It reminded voters that I hadn't disappeared, and that I wasn't done yet. However, as the campaign gained momentum, Ted Bright's entry shifted the narrative. In the eyes of the press, Ted was not just another candidate—he was *the* candidate to beat.

Between January and March, six candidates had jumped into the race, but none landed the kind of punch Bright did. Then, barely a week later, another trio-including the powerful Senator Ivan Chang of California, joined the fray, tightening the noose on every campaign's margin for error.

From that moment forward, every handshake mattered. Every stump speech carried weight. My team and I pressed ahead through Iowa, New Hampshire, South Carolina, and Nevada with measured grit. I couldn't afford to posture or play politics; I had to *earn* it.

Ted had the money, the momentum, and Rey Hughes lighting fires wherever he went.

But I had something else. I had the fight.

And in this crowded race, no one, not even the early favorite, could afford to underestimate the long trail ahead.

"Good morning, Mr. President. Guy Whitehead is here," announced Chief of Staff Chuck Albert as he stepped into the Oval Office. "We'd like to go over your reelection."

"Send him in," President Norman Hayden said, setting down a folder and adjusting the cuffs of his navy blue suit. Though not tall, Hayden carried himself with quiet authority; his black hair dusted with grey, his eyes steady and penetrating, his posture upright like a man who knew exactly where he stood.

Guy Whitehead entered briskly, clutching a slim tablet and a folder thick with data. A seasoned campaign strategist with a talent for turning numbers into narratives, Guy didn't bother with small talk.

"Approval's holding strong at fifty-six percent nationally," he began without preamble, tapping on his tablet. "That puts you in a better position than most incumbents at this stage. Especially with the economy trending in your favor and no major Democrat primary threat."

Hayden leaned back in his chair, steepling his fingers. "That's all good. But which one of them should I be watching?"

Whitehead didn't hesitate. "Ivan Chang."

Hayden raised an eyebrow. "Chang?"

"He's the DNC's chosen one," Guy replied. "Young, polished, first-generation American. He has charisma and Silicon Valley money backing him. The party's consolidating early. Behind closed doors, he's the one they're preparing for the general."

Chuck Albert added, "They're lining him up like it's his coronation. Media loves the narrative: immigrant son, outsider energy, data-driven reformer."

"Don't let the clean image fool you," Guy continued. "He's a serious contender. If history tells us anything, it's that the DNC doesn't leave its golden boy behind. They'll rig the machine to make sure he gets to November."

Hayden's jaw tightened slightly. "And Bright?"

Guy gave a slight shrug. "Bright's a wildcard. Strong launch. His numbers are solid out of the gate. But Rey Hughes is the story there."

At the name, Hayden's expression cooled.

"He's a snake," the president said. "I'm glad I cut my ties when I did."

"You're not wrong," Chuck said. "But he's slippery, and he knows how to throw elbows in the primary. Might bruise up the field before Chang even gets through."

Whitehead nodded. "Which could work in our favor; if the Democrats tear each other apart, you stay above the noise."

Hayden exhaled through his nose, calm but alert. "Let them fight, then. I'll keep governing."

They spent the next half hour reviewing battleground polling, demographic trends, and early messaging ideas. There was no sense of panic. Hayden was a sitting president with a strong hand. But even kings had to keep an eye on the board.

As the meeting came to a close, Hayden stood and buttoned his coat.

"Let's keep an eye on Chang," he said. "And if Bright's team starts making noise, I want a profile on every staffer he's hired since January."

"Yes, sir," Guy said with a smirk. "We'll be ready. It's going to be one hell of a race."

The clock struck six in the morning as I stepped into one of the many libraries scattered across the University of Wisconsin campus. It marked the third day of my Memorial Day Weekend campaign tour, the second day in Wisconsin. My arrival at the library was early, ensuring ample time for the makeup artist's skillful touch and last-minute preparations for my interview with NBC correspondent Chuck Todd on his renowned Sunday talk show, *Meet the Press.*

Ellie Poole's words echoed in my mind as she reviewed my talking points. "This interview is your first major conversation with the American people since your days in Congress. Chuck's going to press you. He'll ask who you are, what you stand for."

I looked up from the notes in my lap. "Should I try to be myself? Or should I go in polished?"

Ellie didn't hesitate. "Be yourself. Be different. You've given speeches. You've shaken hands and posed for photos. But this? This is your chance to speak to millions. Separate yourself. Tell them why you're running."

"Gotcha," I nodded, just as a makeup artist gently dusted my forehead, preparing me for the spotlight.

The makeshift set was nestled among the library stacks, transformed by soft lights and mounted cameras. A pair of production assistants hovered, one adjusting my mic and earpiece, the other smoothing my collar. I took my seat, back straight, eyes on the camera.

In my earpiece, Chuck Todd's voice cut through: "Good morning, Congressman Landon Wolfe. I appreciate you taking time out of your campaign to sit down and talk with me."

"The pleasure is mine. Thank you for having me," I responded, steady and calm.

"I want to begin with a poll from *The Washington Post.* It says forty-eight percent of Americans still aren't sure who you are. That's nearly half the country. How do you respond, Congressman?"

I smiled, knowing this one would come. "Chuck, I don't see that number as a problem; I see it as potential. That's forty-eight percent of Americans who are curious. They're tuning in right now to learn more. And I welcome that. I'm not a household name because I haven't spent the last decade climbing the rungs in Washington. I've been outside the machine, living in the real world, where decisions in D.C. actually land."

Todd followed up quickly. "So then, why are you running for president?"

"Because I believe America is ready for a leader who doesn't come from the club of career politicians. I'm not running to protect a legacy or appease donors. I'm running because the soul of this country is being starved of honest leadership.

"Our politics have become performative. Partisan. Broken. I've seen what Washington does to good people, and I've seen what happens when those good people stay silent. I've been out of Congress for ten years, and during that time, I've worked with rural hospitals, community colleges, small business owners, and veterans' families. I've seen the gap between what politicians say and what people need. And that gap is growing.

"My vision for this country starts with rebuilding the foundation: education, healthcare, economic fairness. We need an America where your zip code doesn't determine your opportunity."

Todd leaned forward. "You brought up education. That hasn't always been a central part of your legislative career. What's changed?"

"Everything," I said. "I became a father. I volunteered in public schools. I met teachers buying their own supplies while juggling two jobs. My plan begins with increasing teacher pay and investing in early childhood education, particularly in underserved communities. But it goes beyond that. We need to treat education as a lifelong commitment. Community college should be tuition-free. Apprenticeships should be normalized. I want to see high school seniors choosing between college, trade school, or launching a startup, with real support behind each path."

Todd nodded. "Let's talk healthcare."

"Let's," I said. "Because we've talked around it for too long. Healthcare isn't just a policy debate—it's a kitchen table issue. My plan is to expand Medicaid and make the public option a reality. Prescription drug costs? We're going to bring down the costs by finally allowing Medicare to negotiate directly with pharmaceutical companies. Mental health can't be a footnote. It should be integrated into every level of care, because no one should have to wait six months to see a therapist."

Todd glanced at his notes, then back up. "You mentioned your outsider status. That might appeal to some. But it's also true you haven't served in public office in over a decade. Doesn't that lack of recent experience put you at a disadvantage?"

"Not at all," I said, meeting his gaze. "In fact, I think it's one of my greatest assets. Washington has become so insulated that it's forgotten how to listen. I've spent the last eleven years *listening*. To farmers in Iowa who can't afford flood insurance. To young parents crushed by childcare costs. To veterans navigating a VA system that treats them like numbers. That's the experience that matters.

"Norman Hayden talks about putting America first. But his version of that means walls, tariffs, and shutting the door on the world. My vision of 'America first' means strengthening our schools, healing our healthcare system, investing in clean energy, and building an economy that works for *everyone,* not just those with lobbyists. You can't lead America forward by looking backward."

Chuck Todd leaned back, visibly thoughtful.

"Experience matters, yes. But if experience means being a cog in a broken machine, then I'll proudly be the outsider holding a wrench." I commanded.

A brief pause passed between us.

"Well, Congressman Wolfe, we're out of time. I appreciate your candid answers."

"Thank you, Chuck," I said. "I appreciate the conversation."

The red light on the camera blinked off. I exhaled slowly, peeling the mic off. Backstage, Ellie was grinning ear to ear.

"You did it," she said. "You introduced America to Landon Wolfe."

I nodded, not in celebration, but in determination.

This was just the beginning.

Senator Ivan Chang's morning began with an obligatory appearance at First Presbyterian Church on Sycamore Street in McDonough, Georgia.

Clad in a tailored navy suit and polished Oxfords that looked more at home in a San Francisco boardroom than a Southern pew, Chang sat motionless through the service, his expression unreadable beneath his designer frames. As hymns echoed through the sanctuary and the pastor spoke of grace and humility, Chang's gaze flicked briefly toward the stained-glass windows, then back to his smartwatch. He nodded at the right moments, barely, but made no effort to blend in. To the congregation, he looked more like a tech executive trapped in a Sunday ritual than a man of public faith.

For those watching closely, it was clear: this wasn't devotion. It was optics.

Aides flanked the senator as he left the church the moment the benediction ended, not bothering with small talk or handshakes. This was a box checked, another line on the campaign itinerary. Outside, his motorcade waited with the engine running.

Next stop: Antwone's Steak House.

The crowd had been gathering for over an hour. Local volunteers in Chang-branded polos handed out flyers and QR codes that linked to sleek campaign videos and policy pages. Inside, the familiar aroma of grilled sirloin and fried okra mingled with the buzz of campaign excitement. The owner, a lifelong Democrat and the restaurant's matriarch, had closed the place to the public for the day, eager to host what felt like a brush with history.

When Chang entered, the room erupted in applause. He raised a hand, offered a brief, practiced smile. The stage had been dressed to resemble a town hall, but everything about his entrance had the rhythm of a product launch.

"Good afternoon, Georgia," he said, gripping the mic with the casual confidence of a TED Talk speaker. "Look, I know what you're thinking: another politician making another stop in another town. But I'm not here to make promises the old way. I'm here to talk about intervention, intelligent, targeted intervention that drives outcomes."

He paced slowly, letting his words hang.

"We are at the front end of a new economic reality, one driven by automation, digital currencies, and scalable AI solutions. And the question is: Will we lead it, or will we let the rest of the world eat our lunch?"

He let the question simmer before pressing on, voice now rising with controlled urgency.

"I've spent the last fifteen years building partnerships with entrepreneurs, innovators, and investors who are shaping the next generation of American jobs. These aren't hypotheticals. These are prototypes. And we can bring that momentum to every forgotten zip code in America, including rural Georgia. That's the promise of *inclusive disruption."*

The crowd blinked, some nodding, others unsure what "inclusive disruption" meant, but it sounded fresh. It sounded big.

"Now, on climate: it's not just a moral issue. It's a market opportunity. We're talking about smart grids, modular solar, advanced battery storage, and we're going to build it here. Not in Beijing. Not in Berlin. Right here in the U.S."

Applause broke out again. Chang smiled, this time more naturally.

"My administration will incentivize innovation; public-private partnerships that bring tech to the people, not just to the coasts. That's how we make clean energy profitable, how we upskill workers, how we rebuild a future that's actually worth inheriting."

He closed with a line that had been workshopped to perfection: "The next era of American leadership won't come from nostalgia. It'll come from new energy: digital, environmental, and political. Let's build it together."

The applause was loud. Not raucous, measured, enthusiastic. Ivan Chang had done what he came to do. He'd made his appearance, delivered his data-driven sermon, and reminded everyone in the room that the

Democratic Party already had their nominee. Now they just had to catch up to his vision.

The auditorium was stifling, the late July humidity of central Ohio pressing down like a wool blanket. Ceiling fans did little more than stir the warm air as Senator Ted Bright took the stage at Harley High School, dressed plainly: faded blue jeans, a white button-down shirt with the sleeves rolled to his elbows, and a gold rectangular leather-banded watch on his left wrist, scuffed at the edges, but still ticking. It was the kind of detail that stuck with people. A reminder that Bright wasn't just *campaigning* in places like this; he came from them.

"The story they keep telling us," Ted began, voice steady and clear despite the heat, "is that we're too far gone. That America's too angry, too tribal, too broken to come back together."

He let the words sit for a moment, then stepped forward, meeting the eyes of the crowd: veterans, teachers, young couples, union workers.

"But I don't believe that. I *can't* believe that. Because I remember a different America. I remember cookouts where my grandfather, a Republican who never missed a Sunday at church, laughed shoulder to shoulder with my uncle, who voted blue and lived with his boyfriend. I remember my mom writing postcards for Democratic causes while my dad taught economics and quoted Reagan. We didn't agree on everything. But we still sat at the same table. We still believed in something bigger than ourselves."

The crowd stirred, with a few nods and murmurs of agreement. Bright's tone grew stronger, more urgent, not angry, but animated by a sense of moral clarity.

"We've let cable news and clickbait convince us that compromise is weakness. That your neighbor is your enemy. But I'm telling you, as an American, as a Christian, as someone who's raised kids in this world—that's a lie. And it's time we stopped living in it."

He paused, wiping his forehead with a handkerchief, his shirt clinging slightly to his back. The room was hot, but he wasn't slowing down.

"This campaign, it's not just about me. It's about *us.* About building a coalition that puts country before party, facts before fear, and solutions before slogans. I'm not running to be a Democratic president. I'm running to be *America's* president. And that means listening, not just to those who agree with me, but also to those who don't. Especially those who don't."

A soft applause began to ripple, then grew, not thunderous, but honest. The kind that came from people who had stopped clapping for politicians years ago.

"Some people say bipartisanship is dead," Ted finished, his voice calm again, almost reflective. "But I think it's just waiting. Waiting for someone, for all of us, to pick it up again and carry it forward. Like our parents did. Like our grandparents did. We can do it again. We *have* to."

The room stood still. Not frozen, but listening.

For decades, Washington had been defined by trench warfare politics, with red versus blue, a win-at-all-costs mentality. But in that moment, as the cicadas hummed outside and sweat beaded on foreheads inside, something felt different. Ted Bright wasn't just asking for votes.

He was inviting a movement.

The midday sun beat down on the campaign bus as it rumbled through a two-lane stretch of wheat fields and silo towns. I leaned against the window, watching the blur of middle America roll by: amber fields, rusted tractors, hand-painted signs that said everything and nothing at once. I'd shaken a thousand hands in the past week, smiled at twice as many, and yet the numbers hadn't budged. Seven months in, and I was still stuck in fifth.

Inside the bus, the rhythm was restless. The faint bustle of the A/C battled the summer heat. Terry sat toward the back, buried in data like a surgeon in an operating room, laser-focused, always precise. Ellie had commandeered the center table, coffee in hand, scrolling furiously through a feed of attack ads from Chang's camp. Lydia, always poised, always dangerous, perched at the front, her laptop open, her eyes hard. Even in this light, her presence cut through the noise.

"I think it's time we hit back," Ellie said, her voice cutting through the low hum of the bus. She didn't look up from her screen. "Hard. Chang's painting Landon as inexperienced. Hickman's implying he's Lydia's puppet. And Bright—Bright's selling unity like it's a magic trick, but no one's calling him out on the sleight of hand. They've all taken shots, while we've stayed clean."

My eyes flicked toward her, but before I could say anything, Terry spoke up from the back without missing a keystroke.

"No," he said flatly. "It's not the move."

Ellie turned toward him, eyebrows raised. "Why not?"

Terry sat back, folded his arms, cool and composed as always. "Because they don't work. Not the way you think. Attack ads are white noise now.

People see 'em, tune out, or worse, they think you're just another desperate politician flinging mud to climb out of a hole. We lose credibility."

Ellie leaned forward, voice sharpening. "We're in *fifth,* Terry. Fifth. And we've got less than six months to make a move. The nice-guy approach isn't breaking through."

"We're not just playing nice," Terry said. "We're playing smart. Substance over spectacle. Voters want someone who looks like they're above it all."

"No, they don't," Lydia said, her tone razor-sharp. She shut her laptop with a firm click and stood. "They *say* they do, but when someone throws the first punch, and lands it, that's who they remember."

Terry didn't flinch. "Lydia—"

"No," she snapped. "You're wrong. You're thinking like a pollster. I'm thinking like someone who's trying to win. If we play this right, we don't come across as petty; we come across as *fearless.* Calculated. Honest, even."

She stepped closer, fire in her eyes now. "Bright's speeches are empty calories. Chang's cozied up with the DNC establishment, and Hickman hasn't worked for anything in her life. We don't need to go nuclear. We go surgical. We strike with purpose. And when we do, people will stop and say: *Who is this Landon Wolfe, and why the hell does he have the guts to say what we're all thinking?"*

Terry glanced at me, then back at his screen. "You're gambling."

Lydia didn't blink. "I'm investing."

I felt the shift in the air. Something about Lydia's words... they snapped the campaign into focus. For months, we'd been grinding; kissing babies, shaking hands, holding town halls with barely-there local coverage. And still, fifth.

But now?

Now I could feel it. The electricity. The fire in my chest. I looked at each of them: Ellie ready to torch the field, Terry already working out damage control, Lydia with the look of someone who smelled blood in the water.

"Do it," I said. "I trust your instinct."

Ellie grinned, already typing. "We'll lead with contrast spots. Controlled aggression. One-minute clips hammering Bright's voting record. Chang's donors. Hickman's hypocrisy."

"Social media will light up," Lydia added. "We time our drops, prime the narrative, then follow with ads in targeted markets. Focus groups will eat it up."

"I'll prep the counters," Terry muttered, resigned but locked in. "And get us lawyered up."

The ideas started flowing, fast and furious; ad spots, taglines, viral moments, influencer blitzes. Outside the bus, the Midwest rolled on quietly, green, unbothered.

But inside?

We were done waiting.

It was time to fight back.

6

Tipping the First Domino

Late Summer 2027

In the weeks that followed, we dropped the gloves.

No more pleasantries. No more restraint. If we were going to climb out of fifth place, we had to play the game the way it was being played: hard and loud. Our team blitzed the field, zeroing in on every major opponent standing between us and the nomination: Ted Bright, Kennedy Hickman, Ivan Chang, and yes, even the sitting president.

At a packed rally in Carson City, I lit into Senator Bright's legacy, calling him the epitome of political inertia. Our ads leaned into his decades in government with a cold stare at the record: missed opportunities, safe votes, speeches without substance. The closing line said it all: *"Bright talks about the past. I'm fighting for your future."* His campaign fired back, crying foul. But we'd already moved on.

Next came Kennedy Hickman. Her manufactured image, her polished speeches, easy targets. We portrayed her as out of touch, born into a life that most Americans couldn't dream of. The line we pushed: *"Hickman's silver spoon won't feed the nation."* Her team called us petty. We called it precision.

Ivan Chang got no pass either. We painted him as the DNC's darling: reliable, obedient, forgettable. Our tagline? *"Not another DNC puppet."* His rebuttal was to call me irrelevant. But irrelevance doesn't trend. We did.

Then we went for the big one: President Norman Hayden. No one expected it. But we hit him on foreign policy, hammering his isolationist response to the Solomon Island Crisis. *"Putting America first should never mean leaving the world behind."* It was bold. It was risky. And it made headlines.

The counterattacks came quickly, and the media frenzy was even faster. Critics called us desperate. Voters called us gutsy. And the polls? They ticked up.

We weren't the darlings of the party. But for the first time, people were paying attention.

The building was eerily quiet, having been emptied by the night crew long ago. Just Lydia and I remained; two flickering lights in a darkened campaign headquarters, staring down a crisis we never saw coming.

I stood over my desk, jaw clenched, phone in hand. On the screen: a headline that could gut our campaign in one stroke.

Barnes Industries Secretly Brokered Defense Tech Deals with Foreign Powers, Sources Say.

The words blurred for a second as I reread them, certain I'd misread. But no, it was real. It wasn't a rumor or a spin. It was a leak. The kind of things that ended careers.

The article didn't name Lydia directly, but it didn't have to. Anyone paying attention would know. Her fingerprints were all over it. According to the piece, Barnes Industries had quietly funneled proprietary American tech to a so-called "allied nation", a rival in everything but name, during her father's twilight years. Lydia, barely out of college at the time, was in the thick of it, running interference with regulators and manipulating congressional contracts to keep it buried. Back then, she wasn't just a rising star. She was a fixer. A cleaner. A Barnes.

I stared at the screen until my reflection blurred into the headline. Every instinct in me screamed this couldn't be happening, not now. Not after we were finally showing progress.

"I trusted you," I muttered, the fury barely contained. My voice shook: rage, betrayal, disbelief, some lethal cocktail I couldn't swallow fast enough. "You thought this would just stay buried? That I'd never find out? Jesus, Lydia—how long were you planning to keep this from me?"

Lydia didn't move. She stood against the filing cabinet, arms folded like armor, her mouth tight. A faint twitch in her jaw gave her away, just for a second.

"I didn't bury anything," she said coolly. "I neutralized a threat. Years ago."

Her calm made my pulse jump. For a heartbeat, I almost laughed—she sounded proud. Like this was strategy and not scandal.

"Bullshit." I slammed the phone down so hard it bounced. "This isn't some rogue tweet or a bad oppo dump. Your family sold out national fucking security, Lydia. You pushed it through. You *lied* to me."

She met my stare without blinking. "I protected you."

"No, you protected *yourself,* and dragged me into the blast radius without saying a goddamn word."

Her eyes flashed. "You think you'd even *have* a campaign without me? Without my connections, my money, my father's black book?" She stepped forward, voice rising. "You'd be back at Enigma Trust running war games in some classified basement, screaming into the void while no one gave a shit."

"Maybe I would," I growled. "But at least I wouldn't be dancing through a fucking minefield with a bomb strapped to my campaign manager's chest."

"I told you," she snapped, stepping into me, "it was handled. It was ancient fucking history. If this is coming out now, someone *resurrected* it, and they did it to get to *you."*

"Because you didn't kill it," I hissed. "You just made it bleed quietly."

She smirked, bitter and fast. "Welcome to politics, Landon."

The words hit harder than any shout could have. I felt my throat tighten. I wanted to lash out, to make her feel even a fraction of the panic ripping through me, but I couldn't decide if I was angrier at her or at myself for letting it happen.

I wanted to scream. To fire her. To bury this whole mess six feet under and walk out the door.

My mind was already drafting the statement: "Effective immediately, Lydia Barnes has stepped down." I could see the headlines, the speculation, the blood in the water. But my hands wouldn't move. I couldn't. Not yet.

Instead, I just said, "I should fire you."

Her reply came without hesitation, razor-sharp.

"Then do it."

The silence between us tightened like a noose.

She stared at me, daring me. Calling my bluff. Because we knew—I couldn't. I wouldn't. Firing Lydia Barnes would be like cutting the brakes on a speeding car and hoping for the best.

I hated her in that moment. And I needed her more than I ever had.

"I made you," she said, stepping even closer. "No donors. No headlines. No party support. You were a fucking ghost until I walked you into that fundraiser in Georgetown and made them listen."

"Don't flatter yourself," I muttered, jaw clenched.

"Don't lie to yourself," she shot back. "You needed a monster, and I showed up. You don't get to play innocent now."

I looked away because she was right. Somewhere deep down, I'd known it all along. I hadn't wanted a partner. I'd wanted a weapon.

I turned away, hands on my hips, trying to breathe. The world was spinning faster than I could hold it.

"If this blows up," I said, "it's over. You get that right?"

She nodded, all business now. "I'll handle it. No press. No fingerprints."

"This has Rey Hughes written all over it," I muttered.

"Or someone working for him." She said. "Bright's team is full of old-school beltway snakes. I'll cut the head off."

I looked at her again, really taking in her features. She wasn't shaken. She was *focused.* Her eyes had that Barnes glint I'd come to fear and rely on in equal measure.

"You're dangerous," I said. "Too dangerous to keep. Too dangerous to lose."

Her expression softened, barely. "That's why I'm still here."

I nodded slowly. The room was quiet again.

"From now on," I said, voice low, "there are no more secrets. You don't make another move unless I know about it."

She arched a brow. "Is this the part where you leash the devil?"

"No. This is the part where I stop pretending I'm not one, too."

She gave the faintest smile, dark, knowing. And without another word, she turned and walked out, heels like a politician's smile, practiced, polished, and utterly lethal.

The door shut, and the silence that followed was deafening. For a moment, I almost reached for the phone, to call someone, anyone, but there was no one left to call.

I sat down behind the desk, still buzzing from the fight.

God help me.

The line between us and the abyss had vanished, and I was done pretending I wanted to come back.

The carrier loomed like a floating fortress, steel bones glinting under the relentless Virginia sun. The Elizabeth River shimmered nearby, its calm surface a cruel contrast to the chaos these decks had seen. Above, the sky was blinding blue, too serene for a world spinning toward a darker chapter.

Inside the narrow corridors of the ship, the scent of oil, sweat, and sea clung to everything, sharp and constant. I moved past sailors and officers with steady purpose, nodding here, clapping a shoulder there. I wasn't in the Navy, but I'd worn a uniform too. I knew the cadence of a base, the weight of deployment in a man's eyes. I wasn't just here to shake hands. I was here to listen.

Two Navy men leaned against a bulkhead, still in their deployment khakis, faces sun-leathered and hollowed out from months in the field. I caught the end of a muttered joke about chow in the mess hall.

"Bet the Air Force would call it a war crime," I said with a smirk.

That got a laugh.

"Those flyboys wouldn't last two days underway," one of them, Petty Officer Westbrook, said.

"Two days?" the other, Ramirez, scoffed. "They cry if the hotel coffee's lukewarm."

We all chuckled; soldiers and sailors, speaking the same language. Different branch, same mission.

Petty Officer First Class Ramirez's eyes shifted, darkening. "You just off the campaign trail, sir?"

"Always," I said, reading the change in his tone. "You two just get back?"

"Solomon Islands," Westbrook said. The words hit like a shot of cold water. "About six days ago."

I stepped in closer. "I've heard the reports."

"They don't tell you shit," Ramirez muttered. "Fox News runs pieces about humanitarian efforts, schools being rebuilt. That's a goddamn mirage."

Westbrook nodded grimly. "Sir, we saw kids starving in alleys, gunfights breaking out in marketplaces. The Separatists are no longer just a rogue group. They've got Chinese arms. Chinese money. Hell, we even intercepted encrypted comms we couldn't crack; Mandarin dialects we hadn't even heard before."

I frowned. "Hayden says diplomacy is holding."

"Diplomacy?" Ramirez spat at the word like it tasted rotten. "We were airlifting bodies, sir. Civilians. Ours. Locals. Anyone who got caught in the crossfire. The government over there is barely functioning, and China's building influence while we talk about *strategic patience."*

I leaned against the wall, the noise of the ship seeming to dull around me. "You're telling me we're losing."

Westbrook looked dead in the eye. "We already lost. We're just pretending we haven't."

Silence fell between us for a beat, heavy as ballast.

Ramirez's voice lowered, but it stuck like a hammer. "The Solomons aren't just a regional issue, sir. It's a proving ground. China's watching how we respond. So is the rest of the world."

"Hayden's asleep at the wheel," I muttered.

"He's not asleep," Westbrook said. "He's afraid. And people are dying for it."

I thanked them, not because I didn't have more to ask, but because I couldn't trust what I'd say next. Rage was building in me, not the cheap kind that fades with headlines, but the real thing. The type that boils slow and turns into action.

Walking back through the ship's passageways, their words echoed louder than the boots on metal. This was no longer just a crisis. It was the fault line of a new global order.

The Iowa State Fair had long served as a benchmark of political theater; part performance, part pilgrimage. That summer, it marked an uneasy truce. Seven of the twelve Democratic presidential contenders, wearied by a season of barbed debates and brutal polling, converged to project an image of unity. It was staged, of course. But it mattered.

For me, the fairgrounds held more than political opportunity; they stirred something deeper. A murmur of childhood, a memory of family, of simpler days before the weight of legacy. Though I rarely invoked my Iowan roots on the trail, they lived in me still, quiet, stubborn, unshakeable. Even after the bitter loss more than a decade ago, when the state turned cold and distant, something in the soil still called me back.

The moment I stepped onto the sun-drenched grounds, I was hit by a familiar, heady mix of smoke, sugar, and sweat. Grills crackled, oil bubbled, and the smell of fried food clung to the air like tradition itself. Stalls boasted everything from skewered pork chops to deep-fried Twinkies. The indulgence was unapologetic, almost sacred. But the fair was more than gluttony. It was Iowa's grand stage, a pageant of democracy, where the mundane and the monumental collided in the shadow of the presidential sweepstakes.

Despite the national party's attempt to reorder the primary calendar, Iowans hadn't relinquished their pride of place. They clung to their first-in-the-nation identity like an heirloom, and they wore their civic duty with a farmer's steadiness; weathered, skeptical, enduring.

We scattered across the grounds. Terry, Ellie, and Lydia, each led their respective teams into the throng, distributing handbills and striking up conversations, anchoring our message in faces and names. Meanwhile, I moved deliberately. I shook hands. I listened. I asked about irrigation systems and yield projections, as well as quarterback transfers and rivalries that spanned generations. In Des Moines, especially in District 3, where memories of past divisions lingered, I knew I had ground to make up. But even there, conversations unfolded with a surprising warmth.

"Good to see you again, Congressman."

"You've still got my vote."

Simple words. But in this heartland crucible, they carried weight. Not everyone had turned away.

The fair's unofficial centerpiece, the presidential corn kernel poll, offered a moment of levity that somehow felt gravely symbolic. Each attendee was handed a single corn kernel, a tactile vote of confidence to be dropped into a tin bucket labeled with their chosen candidate. The rituals had the charm of a county fair and the intensity of a straw poll. Children laughed as they cast kernels beside their parents. Volunteers cheered each clink. The buckets grew heavy with hope, one kernel at a time.

It was, objectively, a gimmick. But it felt like something more. A small ceremony in a long campaign. A reminder that participation, no matter how symbolic, still mattered.

As the afternoon sun turned a lazy gold and the smell of grilled corn mingled with cotton candy and diesel generators, the fairgrounds swelled with anticipation. Buckets would soon be lifted. Kernels counted. Then came the soapbox speeches, the real reason we were there.

Behind the stage, tucked inside a cavernous white tent cooled by industrial fans and guarded by volunteers with clipboards, the candidates gathered. The heat outside was punishing, but inside the tent, there was a strange camaraderie —a temporary fraternity of adversaries. Senator Patrick Callahan of Massachusetts leaned back in his chair, brows furrowed over a bottle of Gatorade. Senator Ivan Chang scrolled through notes on his phone. Kennedy Hickman was already pacing, practicing her lines under her breath.

I nodded to Callahan, exchanged brief words with Governor Casey Fox, and offered a half-smile to businesswoman Jade Knox, who returned it with a knowing glance. We had all come to play the part. And we all knew the stakes.

I settled into my seat and sipped from a bottle of water, the condensation dampening the edge of my sleeve. Lydia appeared beside me, tablet in hand, her brow set with quiet focus. She looked up, and for a moment, the din faded.

"It's been a good day," she said, her voice low, private.

"It has," I replied, matching her tone. "Better than I expected."

She didn't quite smile. But the corners of her mouth shifted, barely. "They're remembering who you are."

I glanced toward the tent flap where the light spilled through in a honeyed glow, and I thought of the kernels, the buckets, the murmurs of old support returning like cautious waves.

"I hope so," I said.

As we shared amused glances, the energy in the tent shifted. Ted Bright entered like a stage cue, flanked by his photogenic children, campaign star Rey Hughes, and an entourage of polished aides. The whole scene had the theatrical flair of a royal entrance; part political muscle, part pageant.

Lydia's posture went rigid the moment she saw them. Her gaze locked onto Evelyn Bright, and something behind her eyes flickered, contempt, yes, but something deeper too. Evelyn moved with poised elegance, her sunlit curls nearly mirroring those of her older brother, Philip. They looked like they'd stepped off the cover of a J. Crew catalog. Behind them trailed Edward, the youngest: dark-haired, silent, and visibly uncomfortable, like he hadn't been born for the spotlight but had no choice but to follow it.

I turned to Lydia, catching the tension in her jaw. "Problem?" I asked quietly.

She didn't look at me. "Brights," she muttered, venom coating the word. "Like a modern-day Kennedy cosplay, only faker. All image. No depth. Evelyn especially... she's a cobra with a blowout."

Terry gave a low whistle, clearly entertained. "That's dramatic, even for you."

Lydia finally glanced at him, her tone flat. "It's not drama when it's accurate." Her voice was low but cutting. "She doesn't just win, she makes sure you lose everything along the way. Philip? He's just her echo. Whatever she whispers, he shouts. And Ted's so obsessed with legacy he doesn't even notice—or care."

Ellie, ever the inquisitive one, tilted her head. "Okay, but seriously, what did Evelyn do to you? This sounds personal."

Lydia didn't answer right away. Her lips pressed together, and her expression grew distant, like she was staring through Evelyn instead of at her. "We've crossed paths," she said at last. "Let's just say I've seen the Bright machine up close. And it doesn't matter how hard you work or how right you are; if you're in their way, they'll grind you down until there's nothing left."

There was a finality to her voice that silenced the rest of us. Something had happened, something big. And whatever it was, it had left scars. Lydia had learned to hide behind sharp words and steel-eyed glances.

I looked back toward the Brights. They were laughing now, Evelyn charming some local reporter. Philip shaking hands, Edward lingering on the edge like he wanted to disappear. Picture-perfect, polished, untouchable.

Lydia stood abruptly. "I need a break," she said, already walking.

She veered toward the far end of the tent where a catered snack bar stood beneath a string of soft white lights. Her heels clicked against the floor as she moved with purpose, controlled and sharp, as if each step were a release valve.

I watched her go, lingering just long enough to see her grab a bottle of sparkling water and lean against the high-top table near the back, eyes fixed on the ice bucket like it had personally offended her.

She hadn't left the tent. She wasn't trying to escape the Brights; she was bracing herself for them.

Lydia made her way to the snack bar, her stride sharp and deliberate. She didn't glance toward the Brights, but I could tell she felt their presence like a stone in her shoe. Her fingers wrapped around her water just as someone stepped up beside her.

"Didn't peg you as the sparkling water type," came a low voice. "Thought you'd go with something stronger.

Lydia turned her head slightly. Edward Bright.

He stood with his usual unbothered air; shirt crisp, posture relaxed, but eyes far more observant than his siblings'. He didn't radiate the same smug entitlement as Evelyn or Philip. No, Edward was quieter. Slippery in a different way.

"Didn't peg you as the mingling type," Lydia replied, tone neutral, not cold, but far from warm.

Edward gave a slight smirk. "I'm not. But every now and then, the crowd gets interesting."

She opened the bottle, took a slow sip. "And here I was thinking the snack bar would be Bright-free. Guess I was wrong."

He leaned against the counter, elbows propped like he had all the time in the world. "I could take the hint and leave."

"You could," she said, offering a polite smile that didn't reach her eyes, "but we both know you won't."

Edward chuckled, folding his arms. "Touché. You've got a reputation, you know. Brilliant. Sharp. Even dangerous."

Lydia's brow lifted slightly. "Funny, I didn't think the Brights talked about anyone but themselves—unless they were planning to ruin something."

"Evelyn talks," he said simply. Philip nods. I listen."

"Must get exhausting," she said. "Being the brooding outlier in a family of golden children."

"Depends on the day," Edward replied, his gaze flicking briefly to where his siblings were still charming the crowd with rehearsed ease. "Today's... tolerable."

She tilted her head. "Why are you really talking to me, Edward?"

He didn't answer immediately, but something softened in his stance, not slackness, but intent; a shift. "Maybe I'm just curious," he said. "Or maybe I respect someone who doesn't pretend to like us. Not even a little."

His gaze held hers for half a second too long. Not leering. Just honest. That was worse. Lydia caught a flicker of something else —interest, perhaps admiration. A weakness, if she ever saw one.

Lydia snorted softly. "Well, I'm glad we can skip the pretending part."

A moment passed, and Edward's smirk faded into something quieter. "You know, you and Evelyn... It's a shame what happened between you two."

Lydia didn't flinch, but her grip on the bottle tightened ever so slightly. Her voice, when it came, was cool and unyielding. "If you're trying to score points by bringing that up, don't bother."

Edward held her gaze, his expression unreadable. "Not trying to score anything. Just saying, it didn't have to end the way it did."

Lydia let out a dry laugh, sharp as glass. "You're right. It didn't. But your sister made her choice"

There was a flicker; regret, maybe, or something close to it, in Edward's eyes, but it vanished just as quickly as it came.

"And I made mine," Lydia added. "So unless you're here to defend her, don't waste your breath."

He paused, then shrugged. "I may carry the name, Lydia, but I'm not their shadow. Not always."

She studied him, searching for the angle. There was always an angle with the Brights. But Edward? He was harder to pin down.

Perhaps he truly saw her, not just the mask, but the machinery beneath. Lydia filed the moment away like a loaded round. Sooner or later, every weakness had its use.

"Well," she said, voice cool again as she grabbed a small plate of pretzels. "Enjoy the snacks, Edward."

"I always do," he said, but there was something more behind the words, like he was testing her reaction, waiting for something to crack.

But Lydia didn't crack.

She turned and walked back toward our table, her expression unreadable. Still, there was something just beneath the surface. A flicker. Not quiet anger. Not quite interest.

I watched her sit down beside me, her face calm but eyes a shade darker than before.

"What was that about?" I asked quietly.

She unscrewed the cap of her water, staring ahead. "Edward Bright. Trying to be clever. Maybe even... human."

I gave her a look. "Did it work?"

She didn't answer right away. Then, with a breath of disbelief, she said, "The worst part is, I think he meant it. And I still don't trust him."

She looked back toward the snack bar where Edward lingered, speaking now to an aide, but his eyes briefly met hers across the room. A flicker of something passed between them, recognition, perhaps. Or maybe a warning.

Whatever it was, I could tell the game had just shifted.

I leaned in. "Think Edward's a threat?"

Lydia's smirk returned. "I think he's a Bright. That's enough."

Then she met my gaze, her tone steeled with resolve. "But if he wants to play, I'm not backing down."

"Good," I said, returning the smirk.

Senator Ivan Chang adjusted the cuffs of his dress shirt, annoyed by the damp cling of cotton against his back.

"My shirt's ruined," he muttered, voice low and clipped. "I'm not stepping up there looking like I just crawled out of a sauna."

His campaign manager hovered nearby, dabbing his own forehead with a tissue. "There's a clean one on the bus, Senator. I'll send someone."

Chang waved him off. "Make it quick. I want white, crisp, not one of those dreadful gingham things." He leaned back in the folding chair, eyes scanning the tent like a CEO inspecting a factory floor. "Can someone turn down the sun?"

That's when Rey Hughes appeared, smiling like he knew something everyone else didn't.

He moved through the green room tent with a casual swagger, the kind that said he'd already won whatever game was being played. A half-eaten corndog dangled from one hand, his sleeves rolled to the elbow, boots leaving little clouds of dust in their wake. He walked like a man who'd grown up on red clay and never forgot it.

"Senator," Hughes said, dragging the syllables like honey over gravel. "Mighty fine weather for a reckoning, ain't it?"

Chang looked up, squinting. "Mr. Hughes." His smile was thin. "I was wondering when the sideshow would find its way over here."

"Oh now, don't get snippy." Hughes pulled up a chair without asking and sat, his legs spread wide as if he owned the table. "Just thought I'd mosey over and congratulate you. You're doin' well out there." He took a bite of the corndog. "Real... *efficient* showing."

Chang gave a single blink. "Is that meant to mean something?"

Hughes leaned in, resting his elbows on the table. "Saw your boy just now. Looked mighty busy with them corn kernels."

Chang's brow furrowed, but his voice stayed cool. "Excuse me?"

"Oh, I ain't accusin' nobody," Hughes said, raising a hand mockingly. "Just sayin' it's curious, real curious, how a teenager ends up transferin' a handful of Bright's votes into your bucket. Like he mistook the damn thing for a popcorn bin at the movies."

Chang sat up straighter, ice threading his voice. "My son would never do that. Are you seriously suggesting—"

"I ain't suggestin', Senator." Hughes's tone hardened. "I'm *tellin'* you what I saw. Your golden boy got sticky fingers. Maybe he thought it was part of the tradition, like bobbing for apples or deep-fryin' anything that moves."

The young man in question, standing nervously nearby, paled. "Dad—I didn't—he's twisting this—"

Chang cut him off with a glare. "Enough." Then to Hughes: "You're overstepping."

"Overstepping?" Hughes grinned, cocking his head. "That's what we're callin' it now when someone tells the truth? I figured a man of your stature would own up, or at least pretend better."

"You're not here for the truth," Chang snapped. "You're here to stir chaos. That's all Ted Bright's campaign knows how to do: create noise, lob accusations, and pray something sticks."

"You sure got a lot of sound in that fancy mouth for someone who supposedly ain't guilty," Hughes said, letting the silence stretch a beat too long. "Hell, Senator. You act like this little vote doesn't matter, and yet you're sweatin' bullets over it."

Chang's chair screeched as he stood. His voice dropped into something cold and sharp. "You think this matters to me? Some hokey vote with corn kernels in buckets? This isn't a campaign; it's a circus. And Iowa's just the first tent."

Hughes stood too, slowly, the grin never leaving his face.

Chang didn't stop.

"These people? Please. They grow corn and change oil. And they think that gives them the right to shape foreign policy? Iowa doesn't decide presidents—money does. Power does. These yokels will follow whoever we tell them to when the time comes."

Silence. The whole tent had gone still.

Chang looked around, chest heaving slightly, then noticed the staffer across the room, holding a phone, eyes wide. The blinking red light on the camera app said it all.

Rey Hughes smiled like a man who'd just reeled in the biggest catfish of his life.

"Well," he drawled, stepping back, "don't let me keep you from meltin' down in peace."

He tipped his head and walked away, leaving Chang standing alone in the heat, realizing too late that his mouth had just become the story.

One by one, the scales creaked beneath the weight of expectation. Buckets of corn kernels, each dropped by fairgoers casting their votes, were hoisted and measured in front of a restless crowd still buzzing from the spectacle they'd just witnessed. The Iowa State Fair's corn kernel poll wasn't scientific, but it was symbolic, and this year, it felt seismic.

Governor Casey Fox came in last, his polished optimism failing to connect. Jade Knox followed, her outsider pitch drowned in the noise of the moment. Senator Kennedy Hickman landed in fifth, then came Patrick Callahan in fourth, his usual bluster tempered by the crowd's unsettled mood. Ted Bright's name brought a scattered round of applause; third place, solid but unspectacular.

Only two buckets remained: mine and Ivan Chang's.

But Chang wasn't there.

He and his entourage had left the fairgrounds the moment the soapbox speeches began, slipping away as the candidates lined up to speak directly to the voters he had just dismissed as "corn-growing yokels." What followed was less a series of campaign pitches and more a public trail of Chang's elitism. One by one, we condemned the arrogance that had just been unmasked, each speech sharpened not with ambition, but with outrage. The crowd leaned in, not for policy, but for principle.

Now, as the final two buckets sat heavy on the scales, the emcee called the result.

"Senator Ivan Chang—first place."

A roar erupted, but it was jagged, uneven. Cheers were loud, but so were the boos, cutting through the celebration like static through a broadcast. News of Chang's meltdown was spreading, first by whispers, then by phone screens.

His bucket was heavier. His support, at least for now, was real. But he was nowhere to be seen.

I turned to spot Ted Bright standing with Rey Hughes near the edge of the crowd. They weren't smiling. Not exactly. Their expressions were taut, split between concern and satisfaction. Hughes whispered something, and Ted gave a tight smirk, like two men watching a plan go off with just enough of a bang.

Chang had the trophy.

But not the crowd.

As the door closed behind me, the familiarity of the Farmhouse Hotel wrapped around me like a ghost, unwelcome but necessary.

The wallpaper hadn't changed. Neither had the heavy drapes nor the creaky wood floors. It was here, years ago, that I watched my political career unravel. The night I lost my congressional seat. The night everything broke between Kelly and me, even if I didn't see it yet. The night I swore, quietly, bitterly, I'd make them all regret ever doubting me.

Ellie had tried to book a different hotel when she found out about it. She was worried it would trigger something. But I told her no.

"This is a ghost I need to confront," I said. "I want closure."

And it was true. The Farmhouse wasn't just a monument to failure; it was a checkpoint. A reminder of where I started, and how far I'd come. Back then, I was broken. Now, I was rebuilding.

Not to restore what was lost.

But to claim something bigger.

I peeled off my sweat-soaked shirt and tossed it aside. In the mirror, I no longer saw the defeated congressman. I saw a warrior, sharpened by loss and steadied by time. My campaign had moved to fourth in the polls. But this was Iowa. Not the finish line, just the first shot in a long war. We weren't playing for tomorrow's headline. We were playing for the nomination.

The knock came just as I sank into the couch.

I knew who it was before I opened the door.

Lydia swept in like a woman on fire.

"You watching CNN?"

"No," I said. "Didn't feel like punishment tonight."

"You should," she grinned, remote already in hand. "The Chang meltdown's going national."

She flicked on the TV. The screen lit up with headlines:

Chang Can't Handle the Iowa Heat

They Grow Corn and Change Oil

Is This the End of the Golden Boy?

A clip played on loop: Chang, red-faced and snarling, his voice cracking as he lashed out at Rey Hughes in full view of a dozen phones.

Two CNN commentators argued on a split screen.

"This is going to hurt Chang," one said, voice tight with certainty. "Iowa might not be the first primary state for Democrats anymore, but you can bet South Carolina heard Chang loud and clear. Makes you wonder what he thinks of them."

"It's tasteless, sure. But let's be real, this is modern politics. Outrage today, forgotten tomorrow. I condemn the comments, but... this is part of the game."

"Even so," the first commentator continued, "Rey Hughes clearly struck a nerve. You have to wonder if it was intentional."

Lydia muted the TV.

We sat in silence. The room thrummed with tension. Lydia's smile was electric.

I leaned back, arms crossed. "I don't know if this'll end Chang's campaign," I said slowly, "but the golden boy's gonna have his chain a lot tighter by the DNC."

Lydia nodded. "He'll never speak off-script again."

"Which makes him predictable," I added.

"Which makes him beatable," she finished.

We locked eyes.

There it was, the unspoken truth.

This hadn't been luck. It hadn't been Hughes.

It had been *us*.

"Rey thought he was baiting Chang into a trap," Lydia said, pacing now. "He never saw that he was the bait."

"You played him."

"We played him," she corrected.

She stopped in front of me, eyes gleaming.

"I gave Hughes just enough rope," she said. "Flattered him, fed his ego. Suggested that if he went after Chang publicly, it'd make Bright look strong, alpha. He loved it. Couldn't wait to corner Chang with the kernel vote and light the match."

"And Chang did what Chang does," I said.

"Exactly," she smirked. "Ego met ego. One exploded. The other walked away with clean hands."

I didn't smile. I didn't need to. The fire in my chest told me everything I needed to know: it worked. Every word, every whisper we planted, every ego we stroked, it had all paid off.

"This was never about fixing a summer straw poll," she said. "It wasn't about Iowa or Rey Hughes thinking he had some killer soundbite. This was our warning shot."

I nodded. "To everyone."

Hughes thought he was being clever. He thought *he* was the one sticking it to Chang. But Lydia and I gave him the nudge. Fed him the line. Let him think it was his. And Ted? God, Ted, still doesn't get it. He's out there making statements like he's moderating a debate in a church basement, like this was just some misstep on the trail. He doesn't realize the real target was him.

"We made them react," Lydia said. "We made them flinch."

"Good," I said. "Let them flinch. Let them run."

We weren't here to play defense. Not anymore. This was a message.

Lydia smiled with the quiet satisfaction of someone watching the first domino fall.

Ted thought tonight was about Chang.

He doesn't realize we just opened the trap under his feet.

7

Senator Vazquez's Veto

October 2027

The days after the Iowa State Fair were everything we hoped for, and nothing we expected.

The media crowned Rey Hughes the unlikely hero of the moment, painting him as the scrappy Southern truth-teller who had taken Ivan Chang to the political woodshed over a corndog and a mic. Within forty-eight hours, Hughes was on every network that would have him, sliding between condemnation and folksy charm like he'd rehearsed the whole act in front of a mirror. When pressed, softly, of course, on whether the ambush had been planned, he chuckled with that syrupy drawl of his and dismissed it as a misunderstanding. A poor choice of words from a tired candidate. A heat-of-the-moment reaction. Nothing more.

I watched him sell it with almost a strange admiration. After all, he believed it too.

No one suspected Lydia and me. Why would they? Hughes did all the talking. He led the charge. He "controlled" the narrative. And Ted Bright, bless his clueless heart, thought he was the one who benefited most from it. He had no idea we'd baited the trap for both of them.

But whatever we stirred up in Iowa didn't last.

Florida was a different beast altogether.

We touched down in the Panhandle three days later, running a string of town halls and closed-door events near military bases, where we hoped my foreign policy pitch would land better than in Des Moines. It didn't. The Solomon Islands? The education overhaul? The national service plan? None of it resonated. The room didn't turn on me, they just never leaned in. That's worse, in a way. Disinterest is a quieter death.

Floridians weren't biting. And if they were leaning toward any Democrat, it wasn't me; it was Bright. I tried not to read too much into it at first. It was early in the race. But by the time we crossed the state line out of Tallahassee, the polling confirmed what I already felt: we were tied for fourth. Deadlocked with Hickman, barely ahead of Callahan. Bright was in the lead.

And of course, this was Hayden's backyard. Florida had gone red last time, and if history was any indicator, it would again next November. Neither I nor Ted stood much of a chance here in the general. But this wasn't about November, not yet. That was still fourteen months ahead. The primaries hadn't even started, and already Bright was running laps around the rest of us in the polls. That's what stung.

For now, I was willing to let Florida go. Not forever, but for now. Bright had the momentum, the media buzz, and the donors lining up to crown him the heir apparent. Let him have the panhandle crowds and the polite applause from military families. I'd regroup.

The truth was, my campaign felt like a seesaw, high one day, crashing the next. We left Iowa with fire in our lungs and whispers in the press. But Florida brought us back to earth. And just as we were packing up to leave, another poll dropped, a national one. And it didn't care about the games we'd played in Iowa. It reminded me we still had a mountain to climb.

I tossed the paper down onto the seat beside me like it had burned my hand.

"That's a downright lie," I said flatly, staring out the small oval window of the jet. Clouds drifted past us like nothing happened, like the rest of the country wasn't buzzing about whether or not I was fit to be president because I didn't wear a wedding ring.

Ellie reached for the printout, skimming the top lines. "It's the follow-up poll. The one about your daughters."

"They're implying I'm an absent father," I muttered. "That I haven't seen them in years. Like I abandoned them."

Terry looked up from his laptop, frowning. "It's not even subtle. It reads like a hit piece wrapped in data."

I turned to face them, hands on my hips. "The divorce? Fine. People can judge. But being *single*? Since when did that disqualify someone from leading the free world?"

Lydia didn't flinch. "Since forever, Landon. Not officially. But let's be honest. Every president for the last two hundred years has either had a picture-perfect family or faked one well enough to pass inspection."

"It's not the divorce," Ellie added gently. "It's that you're alone now. No partner. No emotional anchor. People think that means unstable. Or worse, unaccountable."

I let out a dry laugh. "So I'm a security threat because I don't have a plus-one?"

"No," Lydia said. "They're afraid you'll start acting like one."

I turned toward her, eyebrow raised.

"They're imagining headlines," she continued. "Landon Wolfe, seen leaving a D.C. hotel with a staffer. Or caught in a scandal with some donor's daughter. It's not fair, but the image writes itself."

"I've kept my name clean."

"And they're still suspicious," Terry said, shaking his head. "They think being single means you'll be distracted; womanizing, reckless. You're not just fighting Bright or Chang. You're fighting the ghost of every politician who's ever screwed around."

I sat down, the leather seat creaking beneath me. "I'm not getting married. Not anytime soon, at least."

Terry looked me in the eye. "So how do we kill the narrative?"

The aircraft hummed with nothing but the sound of its engines.

Then Lydia, ever the strategist, spoke with the calm of someone who'd already run the scenario three times in her head.

"We get ahead of it," she said. "We make it clear you're single by *choice,* not by dysfunction. That you're focused, grounded. Not chasing skirts. Not broken. Just... committed. To this campaign and to the country."

Ellie leaned in. "We could do a profile. A sit-down interview. Something personal. Talk about your daughters. Your routines. The sacrifices you've made. Make people *see* the version of you we see."

"And the version we *need* them to see," Lydia added. "A man who doesn't need a spouse to be stable. Who's honest, self-aware, and not hiding from anything."

I nodded slowly, the anger still simmering under my ribs, but beginning to give way to strategy.

"Alright," I said. "If America wants to make this personal, then let's make it personal. But on our terms."

The jet cut through the dark, carrying us to the next stop, and the next fight.

The stage was dressed in quiet Americana, modern, but familiar. A well-lit living room set featured clean-lined furniture, warm earth tones, framed photos on the mantle, and a soft glow from a floor lamp in the corner. It evoked comfort, not kitsch; a contemporary home where trust could be built one honest word at a time. The message was intentional: stability, family, and sincerity, all carefully crafted to appear genuine. The inspiration was no secret; Richard Nixon's famous Checkers Speech loomed large over the moment, and that was the point.

But this wasn't about a dog or campaign funds. This was about a man without a First Lady. And a country wondering if that was okay.

I sat on a sleek, low-profile armchair, my legs crossed, my suit crisp yet relaxed. No teleprompter. No press. Just one camera, one country, and one truth. Lydia had called it "Wolfe Unfiltered." But I knew what it really was: my chance to level with the American people.

I leaned in, hands steepled.

"Marriages fail," I said plainly. "I'm sure some of you watching know what I'm talking about. Kelly and I didn't just grow apart... I drew us apart."

The silence that followed was intentional.

I told them about the alcoholism—how it nearly ended me. I told them about Senator Ramon Vazquez, who found me at my lowest and refused to let me stay there.

"My new lease on life... It's something I take seriously," I said. "Marriage is sacred. Not something I'll enter into for the sake of optics. I won't get married just because a poll says I'd be more electable. Either the American people like me for the man I am, or they don't."

Then came the testimonies that no political strategist could script.

Veterans, men I'd bled and wept with in Iraq and Afghanistan, joined me on set. One by one, they spoke. Not of politics, but of brotherhood. Of quiet leadership in chaos. Of sacrifice and steel resolve.

"Wolfe was the glue," one of them said, his voice cracking. "When it got dark, he made sure the lights came back on."

Then came the pivot. Two figures walked onto the stage: my daughters, April and Kelsey. The moment they sat beside me, the air changed. No more campaign. No more polish. Just a dad with his girls. For a fleeting moment, I almost believed it myself; that this was real, that I wasn't just putting my daughters in front of a camera to make America forget what I'd already missed. But that's exactly what I was doing. And it was working.

Kelsey teased me for my terrible cooking. April laughed about how I cried during *Finding Nemo.* They weren't rehearsed. They weren't guarded. They were real. And for the first time, I could feel the nation lean forward.

"Being divorced doesn't make me less of a father," I said, looking at them, not the camera. "If anything, it made me more present. More aware of how fleeting time is. These girls, " I pulled them close. "They're my legacy."

The moment was soft. But it was strong.

The special ended with the three of us curled up on a deep sectional, a soft throw draped over our legs, watching home videos on the sleek flatscreen mounted in the corner. Me in scrubs, holding baby April. Kelsey's third-grade science fair. Laughter. Real life.

It worked.

By the next morning, the headlines were electric:

Wolfe's Checkers Moment: Honesty Over Optics.

Can a Single Man Be President? America Says Yes.

Wolfe Surges After Intimate Address.

Polls showed a six-point bump. We overtook Senator Hickman for third nationally.

But success always stirs the hornet's nest.

A few days later, my ex-wife, Kelly, and her husband, now, former South Carolina Governor Daniel Mathis, appeared on a morning news show, visibly frustrated. Kelly accused me of "using April and Kelsey as political props," her voice bitter with anger.

Later that evening, after a town hall in Greenville, South Carolina, a local reporter asked me about it. I didn't blink.

"I'd like to remind Governor Mathis," I said evenly, "that it was *my* daughters who took *him* to Columbia."

A sharp pause followed, but I didn't elaborate. I didn't need to. Everyone remembered the glossy campaign posters, the Fourth of July parade, the staged hugs and kisses. My daughters were no strangers to political theater. This time, though, they weren't props. They were participants.

Some critics howled. But the damage was done, to them, not me. The American people had seen something that couldn't be spun: authenticity.

And in a political era thick with artifice, that was gold.

The campaign was riding high. My televised address had done precisely what it needed to, maybe more. Poll numbers surged. Donations poured in. And for the first time, the endorsement list wasn't just hopeful mayors or ambitious state senators; it now included heavyweights like Virginia Governor Greg Winters. We had momentum. But I wasn't satisfied.

There was one name still missing.

Senator Ramon Vazquez.

Our relationship had always been unbalanced; I was chasing the approval, while he kept the distance. I used to think it was mutual respect. Maybe even friendship. But looking back, it was mostly projection. I admired him. He tolerated me. That became painfully clear a year earlier, when I walked into his Senate office to tell him I was running for president. We'd gone toe-to-toe when he refused to back me. Then I took Lydia Barnes, his chief campaign architect, with me when I left.

We hadn't spoken since.

Lydia's departure rattled his reelection campaign. She had been his campaign manager in title, but Ramon often ignored her strategies in favor of advice from her male assistant. Ideas she had developed were regularly dismissed, only to be accepted when repeated by someone with a deeper voice. Still, Lydia was the one holding the operation together. After she left, the campaign floundered. Ramon managed to win reelection, but just barely. Lydia always maintained that if he had trusted her and kept her, he would've won in a landslide.

Still, I couldn't shake the feeling that we weren't finished. As strained as it was, the history between us ran deep. Vazquez had seen me at my worst; drunk, directionless, angry, and still believed enough in me back then to help me get clean and show me the outlines of a future I didn't think I deserved. For better or worse, he helped set me on this path. And now, as I prepared to hold a rally in Reading, Pennsylvania, his hometown, it felt wrong to do so without his blessing.

So I invited him down to Sunhaven Cove.

A weekend of ocean fishing. Just the two of us. An olive branch disguised as a getaway. I told myself it was about repairing a friendship. But deep down, I knew what I really needed: his endorsement. Not just because it would play well in the press, or boost my numbers in Pennsylvania, but because some part of me still wanted his approval. Maybe even his respect.

The SUV's low growl cut through the ocean breeze as it crunched to a stop on the gravel drive. Senator Ramon Vazquez stepped out, all polish and control: navy suit, silver tie, that same smug air he'd always carried like a uniform. He didn't belong here, not on my turf, not in Sunhaven Cove.

I stood barefoot on the porch, dressed down in a fisherman's sweater and cargo shorts, sweet tea already in hand. The salty air clung to us as we shook hands.

"Ramon," I said coolly. "Glad you made it."

"Landon," he nodded. "You've been busy. Making waves."

Small talk followed us as we strolled toward the dock; two old friends, or maybe just two men who used to lie to each other better. He dismissed his driver and waved off the security detail, confident that the sleepy coastal setting posed no threat. Trusting his instincts, they drove into town. We climbed aboard the boat, and I cast us off into the open water, my hands moving automatically as I guided the sail with ease.

"Hell of a view," he muttered as we glided away from shore.

"Best part of the state," I said, eyes scanning the horizon. "Let's see what the ocean gives us today."

For a while, the silence between us felt natural, even pleasant. Two men escaping the circus. But I hadn't brought him out here to fish. I brought him here to talk.

A small, controlled part of me liked the pretense; the calm, the ordinary motion of ropes and water. It made the ask land softer, or so I told myself.

Once we were anchored and lines were cast, I broke the stillness.

"Next month I'll be in Reading for their Veterans' Day parade," I said, keeping my tone casual as I watched the water lap against the boat. "I've got a speaking engagement afterward. Given you're from the area, I was wondering if you'd like to join me."

Vazquez didn't respond right away. He adjusted his rod, eyes fixed on the horizon. When he finally spoke, there was an edge to his voice. "What exactly are you proposing?" he asked, not bothering to hide his exasperation. "I haven't shown my face at that parade in years. It'd look awkward, like I suddenly care."

I nodded slightly, acknowledging the weight of his past without backing down. "Maybe. But I believe the people of Reading will welcome you back. It could be a good homecoming."

He let out a short laugh, dry and tinged with irritation. "So you think you know my people better than I do?" he said with a glance. "Wolfe, why do you want me crashing your rally?" His laughter echoed across the water, leaving behind a ripple of silence.

I met his gaze. "I need your endorsement."

Saying it felt like stepping off a ledge. The word "need" tasted like admission, like the very weakness he'd always accused me of.

He didn't even look at me. "Jesus Christ, Landon," he sighed. "This again?"

"It's not a hard ask," I said. "You're from the district. A personal endorsement, just a few fucking words from you, and my campaign flips the entire northeastern bloc."

Vazquez finally turned to me, eyes hard. "What did I tell you in D.C.? I'm not endorsing you. That's not changing."

I kept my voice low, but firm. "Why the hell not?"

His face twisted into that same fucking smirk I remembered from the Capitol cloakrooms. "Because you're dangerous, Wolfe. Because you're not running for the country—you're running to prove a goddamn point. You want to win just to say *fuck you* to everyone who didn't believe in you. You think that's leadership?"

"You don't know what the hell you're talking about," I snapped.

"Oh, I do," he said, voice rising. "You're still that bitter little prick who got cut off in committee meetings and ran off to drink himself sick in the parking lot. You haven't changed, you just got sober enough to wrap your vengeance in policy talking points."

I stood up, chest tight. "I'm fighting for healthcare. For education. Real shit. Shit, you used to give a damn about before you sold your spine to the establishment."

He sneered. "This isn't about policy, and you know it. Hell, you'd burn the damn system down just to watch the ashes blow back in someone's face."

I stepped toward him. "You preach about second chances. You told me I had promise. You *used* to believe in me."

"No," he said coldly. "I pitied you. There's a difference."

That stopped me cold. My hands curled into fists at my side.

"You want the truth, Landon? You were useful. You were broken, easy to manage, desperate for validation. But I've seen what's really under the surface now. You're poison. And I won't go down with you."

"I don't need you," I muttered. "I'll win without your fucking help."

"You're not going to win," he said, matter-of-fact. "You're going to implode. Everyone sees it but you. And when you do, it'll be spectacular. You'll be remembered as the man who thought anger was enough to run a country."

I turned away, jaw clenched. "You're a coward."

"And you're delusional," he spat. "You talk about Lydia like she's some savior. She'll cut your throat the second it suits her. Just like she left me."

He stood now, pacing the edge of the boat, voice rising with each step. "She walked out on my campaign in the middle of a war zone; left me for dead when the polls were tanking, donors were panicking, and the media was circling like vultures. You think she's loyal? She almost cost me my livelihood. My damn legacy."

I didn't say anything. The surf lapped against the boat hull. A gull screamed above. He turned back to me.

"I was hesitant to leak that story about her family. The one about them trading defense tech to foreign clients. I really was." He paused. "But I'm glad I did."

My mouth went dry. For a moment the boat seemed to tilt as if the world had shifted on its axis.

My chest tightened.

"I fed it to the *Post*. I had the receipts, years of shady transfers buried under shell corporations with her father's signature on half of them. I thought it would bury her. And you." He jabbed a finger at me. "But you survived. You both did. That witch walked out of the fire cleaner than she went in."

I stared at him, my blood boiling. "You sick son of a bitch," I hissed, stepping closer. "You could've destroyed everything I've worked for. My campaign could've collapsed. My team, my reputation—gone!"

"Your campaign?" he sneered. "You think that campaign belongs to you? You think any of this is yours?" He shook his head, laughing bitterly. "You're a puppet, Landon. You always have been. Lydia Barnes is the one pulling the strings."

"That's not true."

"Isn't it?" he shot back. "Lydia feeds you the lines. She makes the calls. The Barnes family bankrolls you, shapes you, uses you." He stepped in, nose almost touching mine. "You don't even own yourself."

I clenched my jaw.

"Won't be long until she kicks you to the curb," he continued, a grin spreading across his face. "Just like Kelly did."

The name landed like a slap.

Everything narrowed. Rather more than the words, it was the look in his eyes, the certainty that he had already written the ending for me if he wanted to.

I looked him dead in the eye. "Careful, Ramon."

"Why?" he said, his voice now laced with poison. "Because I said what you're afraid to admit? That none of this, none of what you've built, is real without her? You're not a leader. You're a placeholder. A seat warmer for the Barnes dynasty."

Enraged beyond words, I lunged. My palms struck his chest with full force, and Vazquez staggered back, slipping on the slick deck before tumbling over the edge of the boat. His body plunged into the black, churning

Atlantic with a hollow splash that was quickly swallowed by the vast silence around us.

No shore. Not witnesses. Just open water stretching endlessly in every direction.

My chest heaved, adrenaline surging. Being around Ramon had always felt like dancing with a live wire, dangerous, volatile, and bound to leave a scar. But this wasn't a dance anymore.

This was war.

And I wasn't his pawn. I was the executioner.

Vazquez surfaced, coughing and sputtering, saltwater streaking his face, his suit soaked and sagging like dead weight. But even now, even adrift in the sea, his mouth still moved.

"Now you've done it," he spat. "Just wait till the press hears about this. 'Landon Wolfe, quick-tempered as ever, assaults sitting senator.' You'll be lucky to survive the week."

He lifted a hand toward the boat, a smug half-smile clinging to his face, as if he believed I'd reach down and haul him back to safety.

I didn't move.

There was no room left for reason. No space for second chances.

Everything slowed, my heartbeat loud as a drum, the world narrowing to his face, until it felt like the moment existed outside time. In that slow ring, his face wasn't an enemy's, but a man I'd once sought to impress. That flip of recognition came and went faster than I could name it.

I knelt at the edge, seized his soaked collar, and yanked him closer—close enough to see the flicker of fear ignite behind his eyes.

"You don't get to threaten me," I said, my voice low and calm, the fury now cold and focused. "Not anymore."

And then, without hesitation, I shoved him under.

His limbs flailed in panic, his fingers clawing at my arms, tearing skin and drawing blood, but I held. Held until the fight drained from his body, until the sea claimed him completely.

I stood, breathing hard, salt and blood dripping from my hands.

Out here, the water took whatever it wanted.

Tonight, it took Ramon Vazquez.

And it left me with only silence, and fire.

8

Recovery

October 2027

Releasing his body, I collapsed back onto the deck, chest heaving. Vazquez floated away in silence, arms splayed wide like some martyr to the cause. But there was no sainthood in that man, only rot, buried under a thousand layers of ego and paranoia.

Death wasn't new to me. It had trailed me like a shadow since I was seventeen. First came my sister, cancer, slow and merciless. I used to sit at her bedside, pretending her hair was just "thinning," not falling out. Then my mother, weeks after I was sworn into Congress, a drunk driver on Highway 30 slammed into her Buick on a rainy afternoon. And then, the army. Afghanistan. Iraq. Death had visited often enough to wear out its welcome, and now it barely registered at all. You learn not to look at the faces. You just move on to the next task. That's what death became: a job to finish.

The Atlantic took Vazquez without protest, a silent transaction between the living and the lost. I watched until he was just a blot against the water's shimmer, then reached for my phone. My fingers were still wet with seawater and blood.

One bar of signal. Just enough.

"Lydia," I said when she picked up. "We have a situation."

A pause. "Define situation."

"I need the fixer," I said flatly. "I need the old you. The Barnes who tied up loose ends, not just ordered ad buys and staged town halls. You still her?"

Another pause. This one, shorter.

"Where are you?" she asked.

"About two miles off Sunhaven Cove. You'll meet me at the north jetty. Bring a set of clothes and a trash bag."

She hung up without another word.. That was the Lydia I needed.

I found the old Igloo cooler buried beneath a pile of boat rags, mostly empty except for a few dusty glass bottles of Budweiser. I cracked one open, chugged down half, and poured the rest across the floor of the deck. I broke another bottle near the helm, flung shards across the console, then kicked the cooler until it cracked and spilled.

Beer. Broken glass. One drunk senator. It could sell—especially with the right press whispering in the right ears.

I took the salt-stiff rag and wiped down the rail, the seatbacks, the helm. Blood leaves a trail if you're careless, and I couldn't afford carelessness anymore. My own fishing pole lay splintered where it had fallen, the line still trailing limp into the water. I snapped the remaining section across my knee and fed it to the sea, watching the pieces drift away while Vazquez's rod stayed untouched in its holder; one ghost of the day left behind. When I was satisfied, I lifted the anchor and let the boat drift, the breeze pushing it further toward open water, toward where Vazquez still floated.

Then I stripped to my undershirt, tucked my phone into a waterproof pouch, and dove into the sea.

The cold punched me in the lungs, but I kept moving. Stroke. Breathe. Stroke. Breathe. Every moment erased evidence, cleansing the last hour from my skin. The shoreline was just a blur for most of the swim, the pale outline of the dunes barely visible beyond the haze.

By the time I reached the edge of my property, the sun was low, bleeding orange across the horizon. Lydia waited just where she said she'd be, leaning against her black sedan, a duffel in hand.

"Strip," she ordered. No hello, no lecture. Just tactical clarity. "Clothes in the bag. Towel off, then get in."

I obeyed. Lydia tossed me the towel. I toweled off and dressed quickly, in dark jeans and a campaign fleece. My hands were steady, too steady, not from discipline, but from detachment. Death didn't rattle me anymore. This wasn't a breaking point. It was a problem to solve.

I zipped up the campaign fleece, the soft fabric concealing the bruises blooming along my forearms. My hair was still damp, the salt crusting at my temples, but at least the cold Atlantic had washed most of the blood away. Lydia drove fast, eyes fixed on the road, the gears of her mind spinning just as fast as the wheels beneath us.

"You need to be seen," she said, sharp and sure. "Now. Somewhere public. With witnesses."

"Where?" I asked, my voice low.

"I called you," she continued, laying out the script like a seasoned press secretary. "Told you Bennett Yarrow was looking for you. You told Ramon you hated to cut things short, but Yarrow—he's a whale. A finance titan. You've been chasing him for weeks. He hinted at a six-figure donation, maybe more."

She glanced at me, then back to the road.

"You told Vazquez you had to head into Charleston. Said, 'I hate to cancel, but this is the kind of guy who only picks up once.' Then you offered him the boat. Said, 'You came all the way down here from D.C., take it out, fish for a while. I'm sure you could use the solitude."

I leaned into the side mirror and combed my fingers through my hair, trying to undo the ocean. My scalp still burned with salt. My hands were steady, but my pulse hadn't slowed. Not yet.

"I'll get Yarrow on the line when we get to HQ," Lydia said. "You'll talk to him. Make small talk. Say you're glad he picked up. Maybe even close the deal. Whatever you do, keep your voice calm."

She looked over at me again, her jaw tight.

"Leave Vazquez and the press to me and Ellie."

I nodded once, silent. The lie was clean. Precise. Just enough truth to pass a background check. Still, something about it sat wrong in my gut, not guilt, just the awareness that I was now balancing on a wire strung between two disasters.

The searchlights sliced across the Atlantic like pale, anxious hands, combing the sea for a man everyone already suspected was gone. Coast Guard vessels roamed the darkening waters, their engines humming low like a prayer. The sky had bruised into twilight, and every wave they cut through felt like a countdown.

Inside the house, the warmth of the overhead lights did nothing to cut the chill. Capitol Police. Local officers. Two members of Vazquez's personal security team. All of them packed into the living room like they were waiting for me to crack. But I didn't.

I sat at the edge of the couch, elbows on my knees, voice just unsteady enough to be convincing.

"I had to head into Charleston," I began. "I got a call from Lydia Barnes, my campaign director. She said Bennett Yarrow had finally reached out."

"Yarrow?" asked one of the detectives, flipping a page into his notepad.

"Finance guy," I said. "Big player. We'd been trying to get in front of him for weeks. Suddenly he's ready to talk—today of all days. I couldn't say no. I told Ramon I hated to cancel, especially since he'd come all the way from D.C., but I figured he'd enjoy a little time to himself. He said he would. Took the boat out alone."

"And you left when, exactly?"

"Maybe twenty minutes after Vazquez's detail left. Got changed, grabbed the truck, headed straight into the city."

"Where did you meet Mr. Yarrow?"

"At his office. Top floor of the Ellington Building. I'm sure their receptionist can confirm it. We talked for a while. I think he's coming around."

Their pens scratched paper, and I could see Lydia standing near the window, arms crossed, her eyes flicking between me and the officers. She'd already made the calls before we ever stepped foot back in Sunhaven. Yarrow had his script. He didn't need to lie; he just needed to take the meeting, answer questions, and make it seem like today was exactly what I said it would be.

They kept circling the same questions. Times. Details. Why I didn't call Ramon when I got back. Had he mentioned any plans to swim, drink, take medication?

Each answer rolled out the way Ellie rehearsed it with me in the car. Calm. Concerned. Like a man who couldn't imagine his friend might end up dead.

The senator's driver, a barrel-chested former Marine named Wilkins, looked pale when I'd called him. "He didn't come back?" he asked, voice tight.

"No," I said. "I thought he was still on the water."

Wilkins arrived fast, bringing two other detail members with him. One paced. One stared at me like he wanted to break my jaw. I let him. It helped the story.

Then came the crackle.

"This is CG-2587. We've located the vessel. No one aboard."

Silence dropped like an anchor. Everyone froze. The officers glanced at one another. Someone whispered, "Jesus."

I leaned forward, elbows still planted, face slack with worry. "They found the boat?"

"Yes, sir," came the voice through the radio. "Drifting northeast, anchor lifted but still secured."

The room fell heavy with tension. My pulse slowed, not from relief, but from anticipation. The story had held. So far.

Thirty more minutes passed in static and footsteps and quiet conversations. Then the final call came.

"Recovered a body. Male. Mid 60s. No ID on him, but... matches the senator's description."

No one looked at me. Not right away. They stared at the floor, at the furniture, at their own reflections in the window.

"Apparent drowning," the voice finished.

I let my eyes close, just briefly. The performance wasn't over, but the climax had hit.

The week after Ramon's death felt like a year. Every hour was a new headline, a new theory, a new question I had to pretend not to hear. I spent my days in interviews with local authorities, federal agents, campaign advisors, all asking variations of the same thing: What happened that morning on the water?

I gave them what they wanted—what we *needed* them to hear. The same story, word for word, no embellishments, no contradictions. I stuck to it with the discipline of a man who had rehearsed it a hundred times in the mirror. Because I had.

Meanwhile, Lydia moved like a phantom in the background; silent, swift, and surgical. She never asked for permission. She never needed to. A phone call here, a favor there. A quiet donation to a coroner's reelection campaign. A discreet lunch with a state health official. I didn't ask for the details, I didn't have to. I just knew by the end of the week, the autopsy report had been... adjusted.

Drowning. That much was true. But the toxicology screen now told a different story. Blood alcohol content at 0.8. Just enough to raise eyebrows. Just enough to make people whisper.

It was brilliant in its cruelty. Senator Ramon Vazquez, the face of sobriety on Capitol Hill. Founder of "Clean & Clear," that self-run support group for staffers and aides trying to get clean. He had gone public about his own past with addiction, wore it like a badge of honor. And now, just like that, the whispers were growing: maybe he'd fallen off the wagon. Perhaps the pressure had gotten to him. Maybe he wasn't who we all thought he was.

Lydia painted the canvas with precision. A staffer found an empty mini bottle in his car. A hotel clerk in Charleston claimed Ramon had been acting "erratic" the night before. None of it could be fully proven. None of it had to be. All it needed to do was cast doubt.

And it worked.

The media storm raged on. They circled like sharks, hungry for contradiction, for blood in the water. I didn't give them any. Instead, I gave them sadness. Sincerity. The signs of a man grieving.

I stood in front of the press again, outside our campaign headquarters in Charleston, the old brick building casting long shadows in the afternoon light. Same stone-faced journalists. Same cameras clicking like distant gunfire. I let my voice crack. I let my hand tremble just slightly as I pulled out the note Ramon had once written me in rehab. *"You get one shot at life, Landon. Don't waste it lying to yourself."* I read that line aloud. I let it hang in the air.

"My friend is dead," I said. "And instead of mourning him, *honoring* him, you're all turning this into some political spectacle. If I weren't running for president, would you be asking these questions? Or would this just be what it is—a tragedy?"

A silence fell over the crowd, the kind that doesn't come often in a world addicted to noise.

I left the podium not as a suspect, but as a man grieving his friend.

That was the story we sold. And for now, they were buying it.

The air inside the headquarters was thick with sweat, stress, and the faint scent of burnt coffee. Outside, the press had finally backed off; there shouted questions dissolving into the Charleston humidity like gunpowder smoke after a volley. I stepped through the heavy door of the old brick building and into the war room that had become our second home, where victories were tallied, lies were refined, and strategy lived and died by the hour.

Lydia was already seated at the conference table, her tablet in hand, scrolling with agitation. Terry stood nearby, arms crossed, suit wrinkled from the sleepless week he'd dragged himself through. Ellie lingered by the door, silent, alert, always watching the room like a hawk.

Lydia didn't wait. "We've lost the ground we spent months bleeding for."

She turned the tablet around and shoved it in my direction. Polling data glared back at me: numbers, percentages, color-coded graphs that told a story of collapse.

"We're sixth," she said flatly. "Sixth. Behind Fox."

Governor Casey Fox. That grinning, toothpick-chewing phony who'd coasted on charm and a well-timed flood relief photo op. It would've been funny if it weren't so pathetic.

Lydia kept going. "The narrative's gotten away from us. What you said on air bought us time, but it wasn't enough. Vazquez's death is sticking. They're painting you as callous. As suspicious."

Ellie remained stone-faced. She knew the truth, same as Lydia.

Terry didn't.

I sat, slowly, letting my fingers tap once against the wood grain of the table. "This is all reactionary. It'll blow over."

Lydia's glare hardened, but I went on.

"That's the beauty of the era we live in, isn't it? Our attention spans are weak. This—" I waved vaguely toward the door, toward the headlines still spinning in the ether, "—this is just the shiny new toy. Sooner than later, a new story will spark, and we'll rebound."

Terry wasn't nodding. He was staring.

"There's nothing shiny about a man dying, Landon," he said quietly.

Silence. Lydia broke it with a bitter scoff.

"This is politics," she snapped. "People die. The story dies with them, or it doesn't. We don't control the tragedy, but we do control the narrative."

Terry's jaw clenched. "Control the narrative? Is that what we're doing now?"

He wasn't angry, yet. Just tired. But it was the kind of tired that cracks something deeper.

"I've spent the last week putting out fires I didn't light," he said, voice rising just a hair. "I've defended you in donor calls, soothed volunteers, redirected media inquiries. But this thing with Yarrow? The boat? The sealed reports? I wasn't informed about any of it. Why?"

Lydia's reply was sharp and rehearsed. "It was a tight window. Sensitive intel. No time for a roundtable."

Terry looked between us, the lines in his face deepening with unease. "That's not how we've done things. Not until now."

I didn't blink. "This was a tragic accident. Nothing more."

But something shifted in his eyes.

He wasn't buying it. Not fully.

"You expect me to believe," Terry said slowly, "that after over a year of no contact, you and Vazquez suddenly meet alone at your house? No aides, no press, no security detail, just the two of you. And now he's dead? I know you were trying to get his endorsement, but I didn't know it would be off the record."

He didn't accuse. He didn't need to.

"I expect you to trust me," I said calmly. "That's what you've always done."

Terry didn't answer right away. Instead, he glanced at Lydia, then Ellie, then back at me. Whatever faith he'd held was fracturing. I saw it. Felt it. And yet, he said nothing more. Just nodded once, a reluctant signal of continued loyalty; if only for now.

Lydia, tense and tired, turned her fire elsewhere. A poor aide walked in with coffee and the wrong folder, catching the full blast of her wrath. "If you can't label things correctly, don't label them at all," she snapped, snatching the folder from their hands. The kid blinked, turned, and disappeared before I could offer even a half-hearted gesture of sympathy.

The room quieted again, but not in peace. We were tired. Splintered.

Terry stayed a moment longer, then muttered something about making a few calls and slipped out, the door clicking shut behind him.

I waited until I heard his footsteps fade down the hall.

"He's going to be a problem," Lydia said.

I stood and walked to the window. Outside, the city moved on like it always had, blind to what its favorite son had done.

"No," I murmured. "He's going to be a choice."

I didn't have to turn to know Lydia was smiling.

We were past the point of no return. The truth, whatever version of it still remained, had become just another variable in the equation of power. The campaign wasn't about ideas anymore. It wasn't even about the presidency.

It was about survival.

And survival demanded sacrifice.

9

Blood on the Stage

January 2028

The East Room of the White House was filled with a heavy stillness, despite the presence of reporters, aides, and cameras. Rows of gold-trimmed chairs faced the podium, and the towering windows allowed the late afternoon light to cast long shadows across the polished floor. President Norman Hayden stood alone before the nation, flanked by the American flag and the presidential seal. He gripped the edges of the lectern, not out of nerves, but resolve.

"My fellow Americans," he began, his voice even, though his tone carried the wear of sleepless nights. "I come before you today with an update on the deteriorating situation in the Solomon Islands; a crisis that, for months, we hoped could be de-escalated through diplomacy and partnership."

He paused, glancing briefly to his right where his national security team sat off-camera. Then back to the teleprompter, but his delivery stayed personal, off-script, even as it wasn't.

"The United States has a long-standing commitment to peace and stability in the Indo-Pacific. But over the last several weeks, the Solomon Liberation Front, a violent separatist faction, has advanced rapidly, destabilizing the region and threatening the sovereignty of the Solomon Islands' elected government. These developments have been fueled, in no small part, by external support, particularly from the People's Republic of China, which has continued to provide strategic and material backing to separatist forces."

A murmur rippled through the press pool.

"For months, my administration pursued every available diplomatic channel. We engaged Beijing directly. We worked with regional allies through the Pacific Islands Forum. We offered support to the Solomon Islands government under the framework of economic cooperation, governance reform, and security partnership. But the time for diplomacy alone has passed."

Hayden leaned forward slightly, voice firm.

"This morning, after consultation with congressional leadership from both parties, I have signed into law a targeted emergency assistance package to support the government of Prime Minister Talifa and the Solomon Islands. This includes humanitarian aid, civil defense equipment, and non-lethal intelligence support. In addition, I have authorized the deployment of a limited U.S. military contingent—2,500 troops—to be stationed on Guadalcanal and surrounding areas to assist in stabilization efforts, secure critical infrastructure, and advise local forces in containing the threat posed by the SLF."

Camera shutters clicked. Some aides in the back exchanged glances. But Hayden didn't waver.

"This is not an occupation. This is not an open-ended conflict. Our mission is to stabilize, support, and step back as soon as conditions allow. We are coordinating closely with our allies in Australia, New Zealand, and Japan, and this deployment is part of a broader regional strategy to prevent further escalation and ensure the Pacific remains free and open, not controlled by coercion or chaos."

He gave a slight nod, signaling the end of his prepared remarks.

"I know the cost of sending American troops overseas. I do not make this decision lightly. But when democracies are undermined and violent actors are emboldened by foreign powers, we must respond with clarity and conviction. The Solomon Islands are not just a faraway place on a map. They are a test, a test of our values, our leadership, and our commitment to a free and stable world."

The room remained quiet for a moment as Hayden stepped away from the podium, leaving the gravity of his words to settle. The president's gait was slow but unyielding as he exited through the side corridor, the eyes of the nation trailing him, not just for what he had said, but for what might now come next.

The anticipation of tonight's debate hung in the air like humidity before a storm. South Carolina was just days away from casting the first votes of the 2028 Democratic Primary, and the stakes couldn't have been higher. I'd just wrapped my final walkthrough of the stage: podium lighting, sound check, the obligatory nods to producers pretending not to care who wins, and now I stood alone in my dressing room, jacket off, shirt collar loosened, watching the replay of President Hayden's address.

There he was, in the East Room, sleeves crisp, jaw tight, posture heavy. And for once, God help me, for once, the man looked like the commander-in-chief.

I sat there, motionless, watching as Hayden laid it out: an aid package approved by Congress, 2,500 troops deploying to the Solomon Islands, and a blunt acknowledgment that diplomacy had failed. That part hit me harder than I expected. For months, he had danced around this crisis, pretending like the Chinese weren't pouring fuel on the fire, pretending like the Solomon Liberation Front wasn't marching toward total control of the archipelago. And now? Now he'd finally faced it. Took a stand. Called it what it was.

I didn't clap. But I wanted to.

He made the right call.

Two and a half months ago, I couldn't string together a headline that didn't have *Vazquez* in it. Every damn question was about the senator's death. Every whisper in Washington was about guilt, optics, motive. We'd gone into full containment mode, redirecting press cycles, reshaping our ads, practically rewriting the entire South Carolina field plan. And somehow, through sheer will and a merciless schedule, we'd clawed back to fourth in the national polls. Not quite where we were before it all came crashing down, but close to it. Close enough to matter. Close enough to make tonight count.

But now, watching Hayden, watching history shift in real time, I knew something had changed.

This wasn't going to be just another foreign policy blip. This wasn't a one-day headline. This was the beginning of something bigger.

I thought back to the sailors I'd spoken with up in Norfolk. Navy men stationed in the Pacific, their stories peppered with frustration; stories of encroaching influence, of watching Chinese warships edge closer to territories we once thought untouchable. They'd told me, plain as day, that the Solomons weren't just a strategic foothold, they were a test. A test of presence. A test of will. And we were failing it.

Until now.

Now, the question wasn't whether we'd respond, but whether we were ready for what came next. Because the Solomon Islands wouldn't stay an isolated headline. They'd shape the campaign. Shape the conversation. Force every candidate to answer whether they believed in American leadership or American retreat.

I could already hear the debate questions forming in my mind. *Should we send troops? Should we pull back? Do the Solomon Islands even matter to the American people?*

And I knew what I would say.

They matter because weakness invites war. They matter because silence has a cost. And they matter because for all the ways I've criticized this president—and I still will—I can't fault him for doing the right thing today.

I shut off the TV. Rolled my sleeves up. Looked at my reflection.

Tonight wouldn't just be about bouncing back.

It'd be about who was ready to lead when the world caught fire.

And I was damn ready.

With less than an hour to go, the noise of the outside world dimmed behind the thick dressing room door. I adjusted my tie, the fabric stiff against my collarbone, more from nerves than starch. The mirror stared back at me, composed, polished, ready. Every move, every breath I took now mattered. Then Lydia's voice cut through the calm.

"Ted Bright wants to see you. Just came through," she said, arms crossed, face unreadable.

I exhaled sharply through my nose. Of course, Ted wanted to see me. The oldest trick in the book: disrupt the rhythm, wedge into the pre-show silence, get inside your opponent's head before the lights even flick on.

"He's playing games," I said.

Lydia smirked. "Always is."

Still, I stood. Curiosity was a powerful itch, and despite every logical nerve in my body telling me to stay put, my feet were already moving. Lydia fell in step beside me. As we turned down the hallway, past campaign aides buzzing like bees in panic, she leaned in close and whispered low enough that only I heard.

"Careful," she murmured. "The Brights have that same glow you see on cult brochures. All smiles, no soul."

I bit back a grin. Classic Lydia. No love lost between her and that family. Especially not Evelyn. Lydia never trusted politicians who'd never tasted failure. The Brights, with their magazine covers and curated charm, had glided for too long.

We entered the dressing room and were greeted with a tableau of perfectly staged chaos. Ted stood at the center like the conductor of a family choir; Evelyn perched nearby, flipping through cue cards, and Rey Hughes leaned against the wall, the very picture of Southern eccentricity. A campaign staffer buzzed in the background, adjusting the lights as if this were a TV set instead of a backstage war room.

"Landon!" Ted called, spreading his arms as if I were a long-lost brother. "Ms. Barnes, welcome."

He didn't wait. "I just want to say, how good was Iowa, huh? Chang melting down in that humidity? 'They grow corn and change oil,'" he laughed, nudging Rey. "Still kills me. You and me, Landon, we cracked him open like a peanut."

I flicked my eyes to Lydia. Her face was frozen in the tight-lipped smile she reserved for people she'd love to destroy. She knew, as I did, that Iowa had never been a partnership. Ted had been the unwitting decoy; the bull charging into a trap we'd baited. He thought he'd been leading when really, he'd been our biggest target.

"I remember," I said, offering nothing else.

Ted, oblivious, pressed on. "That's why I called you here. Tonight's debate—it's a pivotal one. We have Hickman on one side and Chang on the other. If we want to advance to the next round, we need to give the voters something decisive. Unified. Like Iowa. We push them. Make 'em sweat."

Rey Hughes chimed in, slow drawl slathered over his words like molasses. "We got a real chance here to shake some branches, let the weak ones fall. Just need a nudge and a grin."

I nodded faintly, more to keep him talking than because I agreed. Ted stepped closer now, eyes trying to lock onto mine with a false sense of camaraderie.

"You in, Landon?" he asked. "Let's give the people a show."

I let the question hang.

In a room like this, every silence has weight. I could see Lydia watching me, one eyebrow cocked. She knew the game. Knew I did too.

I stepped forward just enough to meet Ted's gaze.

"Look, Ted, I think we both know what Iowa really was. You may have seen it as a joint venture. We saw it differently. And frankly, I'm not here tonight to play tag-team politics."

His smile didn't fade, but the eyes twitched, just a flicker, just enough. "Landon, don't make the mistake of thinking you're above strategy. It's how you win."

"I'm not above anything," I said. "I just prefer strategy that doesn't involve doing someone else's dirty work. Especially not on live television."

Ted opened his mouth to respond, but I cut him off with a simple, "Thank you for the offer," and turned to leave.

As we exited the room, I could feel their eyes on our backs. Lydia didn't speak until we were halfway down the hall.

"He still thinks he's the one holding the strings," she said, almost to herself.

I smiled. "Let him. Makes it easier to cut them later."

The hum of the debate stage drew closer. Bright lights. Hot air. The storm was coming. And I was ready to step into it alone.

The stage lights pulsed like a heartbeat in the distance, casting long, artificial rays across the curtain's edge. The moderator's voice echoed faintly from the auditorium, reciting the rules like a funeral liturgy—orderly, precise, utterly detached from the bloodsport we were about to enter.

I stood just beyond the velvet curtain, center of gravity low, breath even, mind surgical. I'd rehearsed every line, every pivot, every escalation. I was ready.

Then came the drawl.

"Well butter my backside and call me a biscuit, if it ain't Landon Wolfe," Rey Hughes purred behind me. "All dressed up with nowhere to go but down."

I didn't flinch. Just closed my eyes for a beat. I should have seen this coming.

"You should've taken the offer back there," Rey went on, voice as slick as snake oil. "But you're the stubborn kind. I get it. Daddy probably taught you that, or maybe he just left too early to teach you anything at all."

I turned, slow and deliberate. Rey was close, closer than I liked, grinning like a man who enjoyed the sound of his own threats. His bolo tie glinted under the side-stage lights like a cheap dagger. He pulled a flask from his coat, unscrewed it, and took a dramatic swig. The scent hit me before the sound of the cap falling shut: bourbon. Oaky. Expensive.

He did it for show. For me. Ted's idea, no doubt.

"That the stuff you used to drink?" Rey asked, mock-curious. "You always struck me as a whiskey man. The kind that drinks to forget just how average he is."

I smiled faintly, cool, practiced. "That supposed to rattle me?"

"No," he said, wiping his mouth with the back of his hand. "Rattlin's for copperheads. I'm more of a constrictor. Slow and tight, 'til you forget what breathin' even feels like."

He leaned in. I could smell the booze on his breath now. "Chang and Hickman? We'll do what needs doin'. But you? You made it personal. So I'll tell you plain, there's more than one way to skin a candidate, and you're about to find out just how deep we'll cut."

I let the silence sit, then looked him square in the eyes. My voice came out calm. Not loud, not sharp, just... still.

"Rey," I said, "I don't think you know exactly what I'm capable of."

For a moment, his grin froze. His pupils twitched, like a man not sure if the dog he just kicked might have teeth. I saw it, the flicker. Then it was gone, replaced by that greasy drawl.

"Well now," he said, chuckling low, "ain't you just full of mystery."

I turned away.

"Y'know," he called after me, "you might wanna keep an eye on the crowd tonight."

I paused.

"She's out there," he said, voice barely above a whisper. "Kelly. I'm fairly certain I saw her in the second row. Thought you'd want to know."

That one stuck; not like a dagger, more like a splinter. Not because I believed him. But because I wasn't sure, I didn't.

I didn't turn back. I walked forward, the spotlight bleeding into the corners of my vision, the roar of the crowd rising in my chest like a second heartbeat.

Behind me, Rey Hughes faded into the shadows.

They packed us into the Performing Arts Center in Charleston like it was a title fight—and it was. Seven candidates. One nominee. Millions watching from their living rooms, popcorn in one hand, remote in the other, waiting to see who would land the first blow. The air inside was dense with heat, studio lights, and ambition. Even the moderator looked like he might bolt for the door.

It started, as always, with Senator Ivan Chang.

Hair slicked, tie razor-sharp, he leaned into his podium like it was a pulpit. The cameras loved him; their golden boy from California, all ego and eloquence.

"We are living in a time of grotesque inequality," he boomed, his voice controlled by heavy messianic urgency. "A system built for billionaires has failed the rest of us. So no more band-aids. We need a bold restructuring of our economy. That's why I'm proposing a universal basic income, funded by a wealth tax on the one percent."

He paced the stage with the assurance of someone who had memorized every applause line. "We will embrace automation and clean energy, but we won't leave anyone behind. Healthcare. Housing. Education. These aren't luxuries. They are rights. And I will fight for them all."

The crowd erupted, half in applause, half in disbelief. That was Ivan's gift. He could split a room like Moses at the Red Sea.

Then came Ted Bright. Always smiling. Always circling.

He cocked his head toward Ivan like a man indulging a child's fantasy. "That's quite the utopian gospel, Senator Chang," he said, each word laced with polite contempt. "But let's stop pretending you're a revolutionary when you're being bankrolled by the Democratic National Committee and their Silicon Valley checkbooks."

A few gasps, a few chuckles. Ted thrived on this, cutting deep with a grin on his face.

"My friends," he turned to the audience now, voice silky smooth, "we don't need a federal allowance. We need freedom—economic freedom. I'll cut taxes for small businesses and unleash the American economy without punishing success. Chang's plan is fantasy. A velvet-wrapped socialism that will bankrupt us all."

Applause, boos, more murmurs. The moderators glared at each other like EMTs at a car crash.

Governor Fox jumped in next, clearing his throat with forced gravity. "We don't need a revolution," he said plainly. "Under President Hayden, the economy is stable. Unemployment is down. Wages are up. We stay the course."

Wrong answer.

It was like tossing chum into shark-infested waters.

"Stable?" Callahan practically barked, his thick Boston accent slicing through the noise. "Gas prices are up. Utility bills are gutting families. You think that's stable?"

Senator Patrick Callahan wasn't a slick talker, but damn if he didn't sound like he meant every word. "We've delayed our move away from fossil fuels for decades. That ends with me. We'll lead in wind, solar, and nuclear, and create jobs doing it."

He thumped the side of his podium like it was a bar table in Southie. "This isn't just about going green. It's about securing our future, and getting China's boot off our necks."

I didn't agree with everything Callahan said, but the man knew how to throw a punch.

Then it was my turn.

I stepped forward and gripped the edge of the podium, not to steady myself, but to anchor my voice in the chaos.

"Let's not pretend this economy is shaped by one man in the White House," I began. "The rot runs deeper. It's been built, brick by brick, by decades of failed leadership; many of them standing on this very stage."

The audience tensed. No applause. Just silence. Perfect.

"We can't keep pretending we're an island. Isolationist politics have set us back. President Hayden's America First campaign? It's a slogan, not a solution. The only thing worse than bad trade deals is no trade deals at all."

Hickman's eyes lit up, eager for blood.

"Mr. Wolfe," she said, smiling sweetly with a knife behind her teeth, "isn't that just a polished way of saying you'll ship American jobs overseas?"

There it was. The accusation every globalist expected.

"No, Senator," I said calmly. "It's saying I won't lie to the American people. We're in a global economy. If we want to lead, we have to engage. Not run from it like scared children."

She opened her mouth, but I kept going.

"Every farmer hurt by trade wars, every factory shuttered because we slammed the door on foreign markets; that's not protectionism. That's surrender. I say we fight. We compete. We lead. We don't hide."

Some in the crowd cheered. Others folded their arms. But I could feel it; I was changing the weather in the room.

The moderator cleared his throat, trying to regain control. "We're going to pivot now to foreign—"

"Hold on," Hickman said, raising her hand like the queen of the classroom. "I haven't had my say yet."

She turned to the camera and delivered her pitch like a pre-recorded finance commercial. "I've spent my career balancing budgets, on Wall Street and in Congress. My plan will raise wages, protect women's healthcare, and build a future young Americans can believe in."

She sounded practiced. Plastic-like.

So I did what I do best.

"No offense, Senator," I said, "but I don't think the working class is looking to Wall Street for salvation."

The audience stirred.

"You talk about understanding real people, but the truth is, you've never lived like one. I have. I've worked minimum wage. I've skipped meals. I've lived what you treat as case studies."

Hickman's smile cracked, then vanished.

"Careful, Congressman," she hissed. "Struggle doesn't give you a monopoly on truth."

"No," I replied, "but it gives me perspective."

The moderator tried again, but it was too late. Voices overlapped. Bright was mocking Chang again. Callahan was shouting about drilling permits. Fox tried to defend President Hayden, only to be drowned out by a thunder of jeers. Hickman looked ready to leap over her podium and claw at my throat.

It wasn't a debate anymore.

It was a free-for-all.

And it stayed that way until the moderators finally threw us to commercial.

"You're on the wrong side of history, Congressman."

Callahan's voice boomed like a damn cannon, cutting through the noise as the moderators welcomed us back from commercial. We were neck-deep in foreign policy now, and the Solomon Islands crisis had taken center stage.

I had laid out my position earlier: clear, firm, and unapologetic. Stabilize the Solomon government. Show strength. Deploy more than just a token force. I wasn't asking for war, but I wasn't going to let Beijing carve up the Pacific while we sent strongly worded letters.

But nobody wanted to hear it.

Now they were circling, every last one of them. A pack of polished jackals.

"You're proposing escalation with China," Callahan continued, eyes locked on mine. "That's not strategy, that's suicide. You want to start a war no one asked for."

"I'm proposing deterrence," I snapped. "I've run enough scenarios at Enigma Trust to know what happens when we hesitate. We let the Solomon government fall, and we open the door to chaos in the Pacific. You call that peace, I call it surrender."

A smattering of applause, scattered and nervous. Mostly silence. I scanned the stage. Not a single ally.

Kennedy Hickman narrowed her eyes. "You sound like you want boots on the ground before the ink is dry on the intelligence."

"Better than waiting until there's blood in the water," I shot back.

But the attacks kept coming; reckless, dangerous, warmonger. I took the hits, held the line. Until Ivan Chang raised his hand.

"Let's shift to something equally important," he said, calm as ever. "Mental health."

I didn't like the way he said it.

Chang cleared his throat, all concern and gravity. "We don't talk enough about the emotional toll leadership takes. The pressure we face. The weight of decisions that change lives. But leadership also means transparency. Accountability."

He turned to me.

"And Congressman Wolfe, you've spoken openly about your struggles—with mental health, substance abuse. You've shown courage in that. But many Americans are asking a hard question: Are you well enough now to lead?"

My spine stiffened. There it was.

"I've said it before, and I'll say it again, I've walked through dark times. But I've also come out the other side. I've sought help. I've stayed sober. That journey doesn't make me weak, it makes me more prepared to serve."

Chang gave a slow nod, the kind that says *'noted,'* and *ignored it.*

That's when Bright pounced.

"Let's be honest," he said, eyes gleaming. "You've admitted your drinking spiraled into depression. You disappeared for nearly a decade. Do the

American people really want someone who has danced that close to the edge making decisions with the nuclear codes?"

The audience murmured. The moderators did nothing.

I breathed deep. "I didn't 'disappear,' I got help. I faced my demons while others bury theirs behind a PR team and a pharmaceutical sponsor."

It didn't matter.

Chang came in again, this time with a faint smile. "Wasn't it your boat where Senator Ramon Vazquez was found dead? Intoxicated? With alcohol you provided?"

A hush fell over the room. The cameras shifted, hungry, zooming in.

I stared at him. "Senator Vazquez was my closest friend in recovery. He relapsed, and he died. It was a tragedy, not a scandal. To drag his name through the mud is grotesque."

But they weren't finished.

The camera cut to the audience, and found her.

Kelly.

My ex-wife. Her expression unreadable as the lens framed her in perfect high-definition heartbreak.

"Tell us," Kennedy Hickman said, voice smooth as poison, "how does your ex-wife feel about your newfound clarity? Or should we ask Governor Mathis, since she left you for him?"

The air turned to ash. I didn't move.

"She stood by you until the drinking got worse," Bright added, twisting the dagger. "Politics pushed you over the edge once. What's to stop it from happening again?"

No one was talking about foreign policy anymore.

No one cared about the Solomon Islands.

This wasn't a debate. This was an execution.

Hughes had warned me. I should've known. They hadn't just come for my ideas; they came to bury me. To drag out every scar, every misstep, and parade it like a headline on a teleprompter.

I opened my mouth to respond, but the moderator finally cut in, voice brittle. "We're moving on to the next question."

Too late.

The damage was done.

I sat there, hands clenched behind my podium, the weight of their words sinking in. My past, my grief, my shame, my failures, laid bare under the lights. And all of it weaponized.

As the next candidate answered some hollow question about education reform, I kept my eyes on Bright. On Hickman. On Chang.

And I made a silent promise.

You'll regret this.

Every single one of you.

This wasn't over.

Not even close.

10

Primary Colors

South Carolina, February 2028

The air was molten when I stormed into the dressing room, rage crackling around me like wildfire under glass.

"Fuck!" I roared, launching my phone across the room. It hit the wall with a brutal *crack,* the screen erupting into splinters. Good. Let something bleed tonight.

My fists clenched as I paced like a madman, trying to process the ambush I'd just walked off stage from. The lights, the crowd, the cameras, it all felt like a setup. And I'd been the fool in the center ring, dancing for the slaughter.

No one said a word. Lydia stood near the mirror, arms crossed, watching me like a surgeon watches a patient bleed out. Terry leaned against the counter, lips pressed tight. Ellie looked like she was holding her breath.

"They *humiliated* me," I spat, ripping off my tie and slamming it onto the chair. "I got played like a goddamn rookie up there."

"You didn't," Lydia said, calm but firm. "They went low. You didn't. That matters."

"Oh, does it?" I snapped. "Because from where I stood, it looked like I got ambushed by three fucking jackals, and all I could do was stand there and smile while they tore me apart."

Terry tried to chime in. "The post-debate buzz is swinging your way, Landon. You came off controlled. Presidential."

"I came off weak," I barked. "And Bright—" I stopped, breathing hard, the fury bubbling back up. "That smug, plastic son of a bitch. He *knew* exactly what he was doing."

I turned to Lydia, stabbing a finger in her direction. "And Hughes warned me. He told me before I went on stage. Said I should've played ball with Ted. Said if I didn't, I'd regret it. I told him no. Told him *we* were smarter than them." My voice cracked with rage. "Guess what? Ted outplayed us. All of us. He offered every damn candidate a deal. Told them to tear each other to shreds and let him stand above the carnage, clean, charming, and bipartisan."

I jabbed at the air. "And we *let* him. We *helped* him." My voice dropped to a growl. "We should've seen it coming. And I blame you," I hissed, turning back to Lydia. "I blame myself. We got played like amateurs."

Lydia didn't flinch. "And now we know the game," she said coldly. "And we're going to make them regret ever thinking they could outmaneuver us."

Ellie stepped forward, trying to offer some relief. "Landon, people saw through it. The backlash on social media is real. Pundits are hammering the moderators, calling it a disgrace. And you—" she looked me in the eye—"you came off as composed. Dignified. Human. A leader."

I didn't feel like any of those things. I felt exposed. Cornered. But even I could hear the sliver of opportunity in their voices.

Terry nodded. "The narrative's shifting in real-time. The media's saying you showed grace under pressure. The others looked petty. Angry. *Desperate."*

I sank into the chair, rubbing my eyes, trying to hold onto the ember of hope in the storm of humiliation. "They're really saying that?"

"They are," Ellie said. "Landon, this isn't over. Far from it."

But I wasn't interested in recovery. I was interested in revenge.

I looked back at Lydia. Her face was calm, but her eyes were dark and calculating. The wheels were already turning. "How fast can we hit back?" I asked.

She smiled, cold and thin. "I've already made calls. We're pulling threads on Chang, Callahan, even that little shit from Rhode Island. But Bright?" Her smile grew. "We'll gut him slowly."

Terry raised a hand. "We need to be smart. No emotional retaliation. Let the dust settle, then hit them when they least expect it."

I gave a bitter laugh. "Fine. But don't think I'm letting this go. The Brights want a war? They've got one. And next time we're on a stage together... I won't be the one bleeding."

Playing by the rules in politics only gets you so far. I knew that better than anyone. Sitting alone in my office, the light from the floor lamp casting long shadows across the desk, I could still feel the sting from that godforsaken debate. Hickman's smug grin, Chang's fake integrity, and Bright's sanctimony, like a coordinated hit, one after the other, calculated and cruel.

My fingers tapped against the arm of the chair, twitching with the urge to strike back. A younger version of me would've done it already: called a press conference, lit the match, and watched it all burn. But Terry, ever the pragmatist, had advised restraint.

"Let the public see you as the man under fire," he'd said. "People love an underdog. Sympathy wins hearts. Save the bloodletting for when it counts."

I hated it, but he was right.

That didn't mean we weren't sharpening our knives.

Lydia had turned into a ghost, haunting data servers, donor registries, and opposition research files with a surgical precision I'd come to admire, even fear. Every few hours, she'd surface with something new. And this time, it wasn't scraps. It was dynamite.

She started with Kennedy Hickman, the media darling from Rhode Island, hailed as the future of progressive politics. Hickman had built her candidacy on fiery speeches about women's rights and economic justice. But to Lydia, the louder someone shouted, the more they were usually hiding.

"She's new to the Senate, but not to power," Lydia said, scrolling through an old financial ethics report. "Before politics, she spent fifteen years climbing the ranks at Creswell & Locke."

Wall Street had minted her fortune. However, Lydia discovered that Hickman's time at the firm told a different story than the one presented on her campaign website.

"She supervised a division that deliberately underpaid female analysts," Lydia explained. "One of the women even filed an internal complaint about gender-based promotion disparities. Hickman signed the dismissal order herself."

But it didn't end there. Lydia had uncovered a testimony from a whistleblower lawsuit, sealed but leaked, showing Hickman helped cover up a scandal involving a male executive accused of coercing junior employees into relationships. Hickman, the supposed champion of women's empowerment, authorized a seven-figure hush payment to cover it up.

"She's built this righteous brand as a feminist trailblazer," Lydia said, eyes locked on the screen. "But the truth? She made her millions by protecting predators and keeping ambitious women silent."

Then came Chang.

He'd been the toughest. Clean image. Meticulous records. Carefully curated public persona.

But Lydia had cracked the firewall, literally.

"Ivan Chang's campaign accepted over $2.3 million in bundled donations from a PAC registered in the Virgin Islands," she said, eyes locked on the digital paper trail. "But the real money's coming from offshore Chinese firms tied to the United Front Work Department."

That hit me like a brick.

"Wait—you're saying he's—"

"In bed with Beijing. Or at least lying on the sheets." She smirked. "There's encrypted communication logs between his senior strategist and a Chinese tech executive under surveillance. Talks about 'policy cooperation' and 'trade openness' in exchange for further contributions."

I stood up, the blood hot in my chest.

"Chang's not just corrupt, he's compromised," I said.

"And we paint him as a Manchurian candidate," Lydia replied. "It'll be the end of him."

The Brights would come later. That war was personal, and I wanted it to be slow and precise.

But something else was stirring. Something I hadn't expected.

I picked up the phone and called Kelly.

I don't know what I was hoping for. Maybe clarity. Maybe closure. Perhaps just the sound of a familiar voice that didn't want something from me. She picked up on the third ring.

"Oh my God," she said before I could even speak. "Jesus, Landon... they gutted you."

I laughed, bitter and low. "Yeah, well, politics isn't for the faint of heart."

"Tell me about it." Her voice softened. "The vultures, the cameras... the way they talk about me, like I was just some trophy Daniel picked up along the way."

There was a pause.

"I didn't leave you for him," she said. "And I sure as hell didn't sign up for being a political pawn."

I didn't say anything. I didn't have to.

Then, the twist I never saw coming.

"I've been talking to Daniel," she said. "He wants to help."

I almost dropped the phone.

"You're kidding."

"No. Daniel was at the debate too. He thinks what they did to you was disgusting. He's willing to endorse you, publicly. Says it's time you get a fair shake."

Daniel Mathis, the man who'd married my ex-wife, helped raise my daughters, and kept his distance from every campaign I'd ever tried to run in South Carolina, was now offering his support?

"Why?" I asked, my voice skeptical, tight.

"Because he knows you," Kelly replied. "Better than they do. And fran kly... so do I."

By the end of the week, the story had flipped.

Kelly made a televised appearance; poised, articulate, unflinching. She didn't rewrite history, but she dismantled the fiction Bright and Chang were selling.

"Our marriage ended, but that doesn't mean Landon Wolfe is who they say he is," she told a packed press pool in Columbia. "He's not perfect, but he's real. He fights for what he believes in, and he doesn't deserve to be dragged through the mud to sell someone else's lies."

Then Daniel took the podium.

"For years, I've watched this man get torn apart. And for what? Because he doesn't fit into the polished mold? Because he speaks his mind? No. Landon Wolfe loves this country. He always has. And he has my endorsement."

You could hear the shockwaves across the state.

South Carolina had just tilted.

And I knew—we weren't just surviving anymore. We were winning.

Excitement surged through the Clemson University gymnasium as students packed shoulder-to-shoulder in the bleachers, their voices echoing against the walls like thunder. It was the final morning before the South Carolina primary, and Senator Kennedy Hickman had come for one last rally, one last push to prove that her momentum wasn't just coastal buzz; it was real, and it was moving.

When she walked on stage, the room erupted in cheers. She smiled, confident but composed, her sharp navy blazer and crisp posture reminding everyone she wasn't here to charm. She was here to lead.

"Let's hear it for the Tigers!" she called into the mic, drawing a wave of whistles and applause. Her voice carried with practiced ease, smooth but never soft. "I don't think I've ever seen this much energy before noon."

Laughter rippled across the crowd. She gave them a moment, then settled into the message.

"I came here today not just to ask for your vote, but to talk about where we're going, and how we get there. Because this election, believe it or not, isn't just about beating Chang or Bright. It's about whether this country decides to rebuild or retreat."

The crowd grew quieter. Focused.

"For too long, we've had leaders who react to problems instead of solving them. Who wait for the next crisis instead of preventing the last one from happening again. That ends with me." Hickman stepped forward, voice steady. "I've spent my career in systems—economic, political, social—and I can tell you: when the game is rigged, you don't just play it better. You rewrite the rules."

A burst of applause met her declaration. She continued.

"We're going to bring integrity back to government, not by promising miracles, but by doing the hard, often thankless work of reform. Ending no-bid contracts. Cutting waste. Holding every federal agency accountable, top to bottom. You shouldn't need a lobbyist to get heard in Washington."

Students in the back raised their fists, nodding along. Hickman let the energy build.

"We're going to tackle the climate crisis not with slogans, but with strategy. Investments in clean tech, public transit, and carbon capture, driven by science, not superstition. And yes, we're going to take on the corporate polluters who've been profiting from destruction for decades."

Her voice didn't waiver. She wasn't speaking in abstractions; this was a blueprint.

"I believe in a country where working hard actually means something again. Where small businesses aren't drowned out by monopolies. Where, if you clock in, you can afford a place to live and health care that won't bankrupt you. Where your zip code doesn't determine your lifespan."

Applause swelled again, students rising to their feet.

"And to every young person here who feels like they've inherited a broken country—guess what? You have. But you also have the chance to fix it. You're not the leaders of tomorrow. You're the leaders of right now."

The gym was alive with noise. Chants of Hickman's name broke out from a corner near the stage, spreading slowly, unsurely, then with complete conviction: "Hick-man! Hick-man!"

She smiled, eyes shining. "I'm not perfect. I'm not the loudest. But I am the one who will work like hell for you every single day. Not for headlines. Not for donors. But for results."

And in that moment, she wasn't a senator from Rhode Island, or a woman trying to crack the ceiling others had only scratched; she was a force. A candidate who had found her footing not in flash, but in firepower and facts. As the crowd roared around her, Kennedy Hickman raised her hand, waved once, and stepped away from the podium.

As the sun rose over South Carolina, the polls had me in third place, narrowly. Pundits still buzzed about Ted Bright, calling him the steady hand of the race, the man to beat. Chang was falling off. Mathis's endorsement had injected new life into our ground game, and our internal numbers showed what the media hadn't yet caught up to: this was a three-way race, and I was gaining ground.

Still, there were other things on my mind.

I arrived at Enigma Trust that morning, just outside Charleston, not as a candidate, but as something else; someone who remembered what it meant to be behind the curtain. The old brick compound sat quiet; the buzz of analysts and operatives had been replaced by the hum of server rooms and half-lit hallways. Weekend protocol, maybe. Or it was just that kind of day.

Mitch Ferguson met me at the door to what used to be my office. Now his. He had a face like a Cold War technocrat: slicked back hair, horn-rimmed glasses, a habit of squinting like he was always trying to see the next problem before it arrived.

"Congressman Wolfe," he said with a nod. No handshake. No press cameras. Just the two of us and the weight of whatever he had called me here for.

I stepped inside. The room looked the same, only colder. Same blinds, same outdated map of the Indo-Pacific on the back wall. But my books were gone. My picture of April and Kelsey, too.

"You didn't redecorate," I said, half a smirk.

Mitch sat behind the desk, hands folded. "Didn't want to erase the ghosts. Some of them still come in handy."

I sat across from him, the air in the room turning heavier by the second.

"This is about the Solomons," I said.

He nodded slowly. "It's unraveling. Faster than anyone predicted. The aid package was a PR move, and the troop deployment? Glorified security guards. They're barely allowed to engage. The Liberation Front is expanding. China's embedding advisors, funding infrastructure, buying off local officials. The Prime Minister has no control."

"Taneoka?" I asked.

Mitch shook his head. "Talifa. Jonas Taneoka is who the SLF wants in power. Talifa is still the PM, but just barely. According to Emile Rollins, the assassination plot is real. And close."

I felt my back straighten at the name. Emile Rollins didn't raise alarms unless the floor was about to collapse. A CIA analyst who has worked closely with Enigma Trust for years, Rollins was the kind of man who only surfaced when the world was about to shift.

"What's he saying?"

"Two nights ago, Rollins met with a trusted intermediary out of Honiara. The SLF is no longer just agitating. They've made a decision. Talifa is in their way. He's trying to push back against Chinese influence, making small moves that are enough to make him a threat. They want him dead. Soon."

I stared past Mitch, my eyes catching the glint of the Pacific map. "And if they kill him?"

"They claim it won't be a coup. Just a 'spontaneous' change in leadership. A national movement, they'll call it. But we both know the playbook. Taneoka's the one they want. Educated in Beijing. Speaks fluent Mandarin. He's packaged like a populist, but he's nothing more than a proxy."

"And the White House?"

"Hayden's response has been... diplomatic. He thinks our troops are 'stabilizing the situation.' However, the truth is that they're outnumbered and outmaneuvered. They're policing intersections while Chinese advisors hold cabinet meetings. Hayden doesn't want to escalate. He thinks it's a local matter, a post-colonial mess we shouldn't own."

I exhaled sharply. "The President doesn't understand the stakes."

"No," Mitch said. "He doesn't care about them."

A silence passed between us.

"You didn't bring me in here to be briefed," I said.

Mitch studied me for a moment. Then he nodded. "No. I brought you here because you're the only one left who might still object to this. You've been sounding alarms for months now, and no one's listening. Not State. Not the Pentagon. Not Hayden."

"I don't hold any real power," I reminded him.

"But you hold a spotlight," he said. "And Rollins thinks that's enough. You raise the issue, highlight what's happening, speak plainly, and force the media to dig deeper; maybe Hayden will be forced to respond. Public pressure, international scrutiny, anything to slow the SLF before the bullets start flying."

I stood and crossed to the map, tapping my finger on Guadalcanal. "They want to kill a sitting head of state while we stand around with rifles and blindfolds. We don't even call it an occupation, because that would mean we'd have to admit responsibility."

Mitch turned toward me. "That's exactly right."

I let the silence hang. I wasn't naïve. I knew what Mitch wanted: not a statesman, not a diplomat. A fuse. Something volatile enough to force movement.

I turned back to face him.

"You want me to call attention to this?" I said. "Drag it onto the debate stage, more than I have. Raise hell at a press conference. Leak a memo. Make it loud."

"I want you to make it real," Mitch said. "Before it's too late."

I nodded slowly. I knew what that meant.

If I spoke, I'd be accused of saber-rattling. Of warmongering. Of politicizing foreign instability for personal gain. But if I stayed silent, if we all did, we'd wake up one day and find a Chinese-backed puppet regime in the Solomons, and no one would remember how it got that far.

"I'll think about how to move," I said, reaching for the door.

Mitch didn't stop me. "Just don't think too long."

I stepped into the hall, Lydia already calling me about the first returns from Columbia. But my head was somewhere else, on a small island in the Pacific, where a man named Talifa was living on borrowed time.

Lydia stepped into my office at 5:45 PM, just as the first wave of polls started to close across the state. She didn't say anything at first, just offered a calm, knowing nod that made me feel like we'd already won. I hated that about her. That quiet confidence. That maddening certainty. She never flinched, not in public, not in private. She believed in this thing from day one, believed in *me,* even when I wasn't so sure.

It was my first election night since 2016, my first time stepping into a war room with something real on the line again. And I felt good. Confident. The energy in the final 72 hours had been electric, and the numbers were finally bending our way. But I'd felt this before. I remembered that same swell of hope, that same rising certainty... right before the floor gave out beneath me. In politics, nothing is promised. Not even the feeling that you're about to win.

The campaign floor was alive. Phones rang. Screens blinked. Volunteers shouted updates over the din of clattering keyboards and polling site feeds. I straightened my jacket, forced a deep breath, and stepped into the command center, our so-called bunker, where optimism and anxiety collided over stale coffee and glowing precinct maps.

Terry, Lydia, and Ellie were already there. The television wall glowed like a stained-glass window of twenty-first-century idolatry; news anchors, exit poll analysts, and live shots from Charleston precincts. Beneath it, a massive interactive map of South Carolina sprawled across the wall, lit up with precinct data that hadn't fully processed yet. Red, blue, green. Lines and numbers. My name. Bright's. Chang's. And Hickman's.

"Three-way battle emerging in the Palmetto State," a voice buzzed from one of the news feeds. "But all eyes are on Senator Ted Bright tonight. His ground game, his energy, his message; there's something electric about this campaign. Voters are calling it Bright Fever."

"He's giving people Obama vibes. A modern-day Jack Kennedy with Gen Z polish," a younger anchor grinned, practically glowing.

I nearly laughed; Bright was pushing sixty and barely knew how to unlock his iPad. Gen Z Polish? Please. The man still printed his emails before reading them.

I closed my eyes, just for a second. Let it pass through me like nausea. This wasn't an analysis, it was a coronation. They were no longer covering a campaign. They were anointing a savior.

The room buzzed as more returns trickled in. I circled the table, my fingertips dragging along the edge, pretending I was calm and steady, but the truth was I felt like I was walking a high wire without a net.

Then it hit.

BREAKING NEWS flashed across the top of one of the monitors. A live crawl unfurled beneath it: a screenshot of Senator Ivan Chang's *X* account.

"My best wishes go out to Senator Patrick Callahan, who sadly left the campaign earlier today. May God continue to bless you and your family."

The room froze.

I stepped closer to the screen, my stomach twisting. "What the hell is this?" I asked, eyes scanning the words again as if I'd misread them.

The implications hit fast, sharp, and hard. If Callahan had actually dropped out, if even the *idea* took root in the minds of enough undecided voters, his modest but loyal base could be scattered in a heartbeat. And in a race this tight, even a few thousand disoriented supporters could shift the balance. Toward Chang. Or toward me. Or maybe toward chaos.

Terry was already on the phone. Ellie was pulling up social feeds. Lydia didn't move, eyes locked on the screen like she was trying to burn a hole through it.

"If it's true," I said slowly, "we need to be in front of this. We need to reach Callahan voters *now.*"

But even as I said it, I felt the dread clawing up my spine. Not because I feared what Chang had done, but because I knew how easily it could work. In politics, perception mattered more than truth. If voters *thought* Callahan had pulled out, many of them would just move on, cast their ballots for someone else, and never look back.

"Someone confirm it," I snapped, my voice cutting through the tension. "Did Callahan actually suspend his campaign?"

A few seconds later, one of the interns, a nervous kid with an oversized headset and a laptop in his lap, spoke up. " I-I'm seeing something now. Callahan didn't drop out. He flew home to Boston this afternoon. His daughter's sick, just the flu, apparently. His team put out a statement an hour ago saying he's still in the race, just not on the trail tonight."

"Then why post that?" Ellie asked, referring to Chang's post.

"Because it doesn't have to be true," I muttered. "It just has to *look* true. Just long enough to spook the right voters."

Lydia finally turned to me. "It won't matter."

I raised an eyebrow. "You don't think?"

She shook her head. Calm and certain. "We've got the momentum. That kind of stunt only works when you're losing ground. Chang's flailing."

Maybe she was right. Or perhaps she was just saying what I needed to hear. Either way, the damage, if any, had already been done.

I looked back at the screen; the crawl was still running, like a slow leak beneath the blaring headline. I didn't know if Chang's stunt would cost me votes or win me some. I only knew one thing:

We were in the middle of a dogfight. And the night had only just begun.

By 7:05, we were getting results from the Lowcountry.

We were still in third.

No one said anything, but the tension in the room thickened like smoke. I could feel it in the silence; staffers leaning forward in their chairs, phones clenched tight in their hands, watching the map like it might change if they stared hard enough.

Ellie hovered near the data desk, refreshing exit poll projections every few seconds. Lydia didn't speak. She didn't have to. Her eyes were locked on the map, her fingers drumming slow, deliberate taps against the armrest of her chair.

And then, the map shifted.

Ten counties reporting. I was winning six of them.

Charleston.

Dorchester.

Sumter.

The margins weren't enormous, but they were enough to shift the tone. By 8:30 PM, the narrative was bending. No longer *Bright versus Chang.* Suddenly it was Wolfe, the former congressman, the man who supposedly flamed out in 2016, surging into contention.

"People are responding to your messaging, Landon," Ellie said, smiling. "It's real."

I forced a laugh. "Early results are like first impressions, Ellie. They can be deceiving."

But deep down, I felt it. The tremor under the surface. The invisible current snapping loose. Every few minutes, another volunteer shouted precinct numbers, and more cheers rippled through the room. The giant county map on the main screen started bleeding my name.

By 9:10, CNN interrupted its regular election night broadcast. A split-screen: Ted Bright in Columbia, waving at a half-full ballroom... and me, standing dead center in a war room that now felt alive.

"This is not what the Bright campaign expected," one of the talking heads admitted. "We are witnessing a legitimate upset in the making tonight."

By 10:15, Lydia finally looked up from her phone.

"Greenville just came in," she said, almost like an afterthought. "You're up three points there."

My heart kicked once, hard.

We hadn't invested much in Greenville; it was too expensive, too crowded with competing messages. We were supposed to *hold the line* there. Instead, we were taking ground.

Ellie pressed a hand to her mouth. Terry let out a low, disbelieving laugh. The room buzzed with cautious hope.

Then Columbia flipped.

Ten minutes later, Richland County added another layer of proof: the base wasn't just showing up; they were *turning out.* More than expected. More than *Bright* expected.

Someone turned the volume up on MSNBC. I watched the chyron update in real time, like someone had typed it with shaking hands:

"*Wolfe Leads in South Carolina: Another Surprise in a Volatile Primary Season.*"

The room shifted again.

Now there was shouting. Movement. Laughter. One of the interns, Julian, literally started crying. I hadn't even realized he was old enough to vote.

By 11:30 it was official.

"Landon Wolfe Projected Winner—South Carolina Democratic Primary."

The room exploded.

Cheers, applause, hugs, backslaps. A bottle of champagne I didn't even know we had got popped near the back. Ellie jumped into Terry's arms. People screamed and people sobbed. Phones rang and buzzed and pinged with texts from people we never expected to hear from again: rivals, reporters, consultants from rival campaigns.

I just stood there, motionless, watching the screen like I didn't quite believe it.

Because for all the effort, for all the planning and precinct math and get-out-the-vote speeches, I hadn't really *expected* this.

Not *tonight.*

Then I felt Lydia's hand on my arm.

"Told you," she said quietly, without even looking at me.

And for once, I didn't have anything to say back.

I just looked out at my team, at the chaos, the celebration, the sparks of hope lighting the room like fireworks, and tried to breathe it all in.

Because everything had changed.

And somehow, we were still standing.

11

Ballots and Battlegrounds

Super Tuesday | Spring 2028

"I have fought tooth and nail, strategized endlessly, and poured my heart and soul into this campaign. But today, with a heavy heart, I must step back from the race for President of the United States. This decision wasn't easy, nor was it made in haste. After intense discussions with my family and advisors, we have reached a consensus that my true leadership lies in the Senate. Though our aspirations fell short, we achieved a great deal over this tumultuous year. The lessons learned will not be forgotten as I continue my journey. To my unwavering supporters, I extend my deepest gratitude. Thank you for standing by my side."

Senator Kennedy Hickman stood beneath the glare of TV cameras, her trademark composure cracking just enough to feel real. Her voice was strong, but her posture betrayed the weight of defeat; her shoulders were tight, and her chin was lifted too deliberately. Beside her, her husband and daughter stood like well-rehearsed pillars of unity, eyes glassy but dry. They knew this wasn't the ending she wanted, but it was the one she'd been steered toward, one misstep at a time.

What finished her wasn't just the anemic fourth-place finishes in South Carolina and New Hampshire, or the fifth-place finishes in Michigan and Georgia. It wasn't just the polling freefall or the money drying up like rain on pavement. It was the story.

It began as a whisper on the political blogs, just a thread on Reddit that was initially dismissed as unimportant. But within a week, it had exploded across every outlet from *Politico* to *CNN.* The reporting was meticulous, damning, and timed with surgical precision. Years ago, during her tenure as a managing director at Creswell & Locke, Hickman had overseen a division where women in identical roles consistently received 23% less pay than their male counterparts. Worse still, the firm had quietly settled a seven-figure sexual misconduct lawsuit, one Hickman had personally signed off on as part of the internal review committee. No admission of guilt, no paper trail, until there was.

The press pounced. The "pro-woman candidate" narrative, the proud advocate for single-payer maternity leave legislation, and the viral moment with the girl in the pink blazer on TikTok; it all collapsed under the weight of her Wall Street past. The betrayal was almost too perfect. Morning talk shows dissected the hypocrisy like vultures around a carcass. "You can't preach feminism on the trail and bury women in the boardroom," one anchor said. The phrase stuck. Protesters began showing up at campaign events with signs that read *Equal Pay, Not Hush Pay.*

Hickman's campaign tried to weather the storm, attempting to turn the tide back to her legislative record and claim that she'd inherited those systems and worked to change them. But the damage was done. Trust was broken. The women who once saw themselves in her stopped attending her rallies. The money disappeared next. Donors didn't like the scent of blood. Neither did voters.

No one knew where the leak came from. The story had too much sourcing, too much detail for it to be random, but there was no digital fingerprint, no disgruntled staffer stepping into the light. Just silence. A vacuum.

I watched it unfold as if I were watching someone drown through glass.

We never celebrated her fall. Lydia and I both knew it wasn't about Hickman personally. It was about narrowing the field, turning the chaos into a binary choice. Clearing the brush. Creating contrast.

Now, standing behind that podium, Hickman bowed out with dignity. However, her exit wasn't a clean resignation; it was a carefully orchestrated exit.

And we were pulling the strings.

Following South Carolina, the battlefield thinned. Casey Fox gave a gracious, if defeated, farewell. Senator Hickman cited a need to return to "legislative priorities." Pierre Guire, the self-made billionaire who spoke more about NFTs than foreign policy, quietly bowed out after Nevada. All that remained was a dying Knox campaign, Patrick Callahan wheezing toward Super Tuesday like a man out of breath, Ivan Chang disappointing his backers, and the two storms colliding: Ted Bright's messianic rise and my own bruised, bloody march through the primaries.

I had done well enough, finishing second in Georgia and close in Michigan, but nothing replicated the firestorm that South Carolina gave us. And Ted? Ted was catching wildfire in a bottle. His crowds surged. His message sharpened. His name was becoming the kind of word people whispered with hope, or fear. "Bright fever," they called it.

And the fever was spreading.

So, we went west. Into the lion's den. Colorado. We should've gone to the Springs for the military crowd, but Lydia insisted on Broomfield. "More suburban families. Lower risk. We're not trying to win, just show face." It was a dogshit rally. Thin crowd. Cold wind. A damn middle school gymnasium. Little to no press. Just the echo of my own words bouncing off aluminum bleachers and checked-out volunteers.

The moment we were wheels up, the silence on the plane was palpable. I stared out the window, watching the flat dark sprawl of Denver bleed into the night, before I snapped.

"Jesus Christ, Lydia. What the fuck was that?"

She didn't even flinch. Just crossed one leg over the other and looked at her tablet like I wasn't even there.

"I'm serious," I said, louder now. "We just spent sixty grand and three days of momentum to wave at thirty-eight people and two local news interns. We look pathetic."

Lydia didn't look up. "You needed to be seen in Bright's territory. It wasn't about crowd size."

"Oh, spare me the bullshit." I unbuckled and stood. Terry glanced up from the galley. Ellie didn't even blink. This wasn't new. "We're not running some metaphorical poetry campaign. I need wins. Not symbolic losses that pad out your little strategic vision board."

She finally looked up, and her eyes were ice. "You done?"

"No. Not even close." I stepped forward, voice tightening. "You sold me on this plan. You told me we'd win this thing. You said *we weren't going to lose."*

"And we won't," she said, like it was a script.

"We *are,* Lydia. We are *losing.* We've been stuck in neutral since South Carolina. I thought you were this master strategist, the cold-blooded genius. But we're getting steamrolled. And you're telling me to keep calm while we bleed out on a gym floor in fucking Broomfield?"

That did it. Lydia stood.

"You want to talk about bleeding out? You're the one choking the campaign to death every goddamn day, Landon. You want to blame me? Fine. But don't forget who's holding the checkbook, the contacts, the damn playbook. You think your little firebrand speeches and scowls win elections? No. I do."

"You think this is all about money?" I shouted. "You think you can buy your way to the presidency?"

"No," she snapped. "But I can *build* my way there. Brick by brick. Which is more than I can say for you, running around like a toddler with a stick of dynamite strapped to his back."

My face flushed. I could feel it. The blood rushing to my ears, pounding in time with my fists.

"You really want to do this now?" I said, stepping in close. "You want to drag this out in front of Ellie and Terry?"

"They're used to it," she said without looking.

"You think you're in charge, don't you?"

I *am* in charge," she said, calm and savage. "Because you clearly can't be. You're impulsive. You're volatile. You're a walking liability wrapped in a decent haircut."

I turned away, jaw clenched. "You always knew who I was."

"Yeah," she said coldly. "I just didn't realize you'd unravel this fast."

That's when she hit me where it hurt.

"Look at what happened with Vazquez," she said, stepping forward. "Look me in the eye and tell me that was rational. That was presidential. That wasn't some *unhinged* reaction to a bad headline."

My stomach flipped. "Don't you fucking bring him up—"

"Why not?" Her voice lowered to a whisper. "I cleaned it up. I buried the story. I saved your goddamn life—and this campaign. And now you dare to question my judgement?"

I was silent. The whole cabin was. Even the engines seemed quieter.

She stepped closer.

"You want to win? Then start acting like a fucking president. Not a drunk uncle at a goddamn family reunion. I've played the game, Landon. I've seen men like you fall apart because they couldn't distinguish between power and control. Power isn't yelling. It's waiting. Planning. Cutting once, *clean.* You want to win? Then shut the hell up and *listen to me."*

I sat down hard in my seat, the rage boiling but directionless now. Lydia stood over me like a prosecutor. I didn't look at her. I couldn't.

She leaned in, her voice low.

"If you keep blowing up every time we hit turbulence, you won't make it to the convention. Ted Bright will wipe the floor with you, and I'll be on a beach in Santorini while you're screaming at a mirror in some cable news greenroom. You hear me?"

I nodded once. Barely.

She straightened, exhaled, and turned toward the back of the plane.

Terry poured another cup of coffee. Ellie looked out the window.

And I sat there, burning.

Not because she was wrong.

But because she was right.

And that scared the hell out of me.

The air in Chinatown was thick with incense and steam from sidewalk vendors, the rhythmic cadence of Mandarin mixing with the low thrum of traffic and distant applause from supporters gathered for his next stop. For a moment, Senator Ivan Chang allowed himself to breathe it in; his people, his city, his state. California was his to lose, and he knew it. Michigan had been the breakthrough. Bright was bruised. Wolfe was boxed in. Super Tuesday was next.

He walked through the crowd like a king, his usual smirk tucked just beneath a crisp navy overcoat. The staff called it "Chang Mode", that rare sweet spot where ego, confidence, and momentum aligned perfectly. He'd made it through the mud of January and February. The polls were climbing. DNC donors were crawling back. The press called him the comeback kid.

Then his phone buzzed.

He ignored the first two vibrations. A staffer tried to hand him a tea from a nearby shop. He declined politely.

The third buzz came with an urgent message: CALL ME NOW —Oliver.

He stepped away from the crowd, weaving past a dragon dance troupe and into the quiet shade of a restaurant overhang. The sun suddenly felt too hot. He answered.

Oliver didn't say hello. "It's out."

Chang froze. "What's out?"

There was a pause, followed by the unmistakable sound of a laptop slamming shut.

"The report. Axios. It's... bad. They have the donation chain. Shell companies. Private dinners. The Xinjiang Development Group meeting. The pipeline bid out of Sacramento."

Ivan's mouth opened, but nothing came out.

"They're calling it compromised influence. Backchanneling. A 'pattern of collaboration.' It's all in the story. Front page. Syndicated within the hour."

Chang staggered backward like he'd been struck. His back hit the brick wall of the restaurant behind him. The color drained from his face.

"They're saying I sold access?"

"They're saying you traded it. For intel."

A hollow beat passed between them.

Oliver added, quietly, "They've got names, Ivan. Not just yours."

"Jesus," Chang whispered, hand trembling as he pressed it to his forehead. His thoughts fired in a dozen directions. *How? When? Who?*

He looked out into the street where a local news camera was beginning to set up. His campaign advance team waved him forward, smiling, unaware of the incoming meteor.

He couldn't move.

"Get the car," he barked, voice cracking. "Tell them I'm not doing the rally."

He hung up.

The SUV arrived within minutes. Chang climbed in, yanked the door shut, and stared through the tinted glass as San Francisco faded behind him. His mind screamed. The pressure behind his eyes built until he felt nauseous. He had always prided himself on being the smartest man in the room. That arrogance, once his armor, now weighed him down like an anchor.

They think I'm a foreign agent.

I'm done.

I'm fucking done.

"How did they get this?" he muttered aloud, though no one answered. "That file... it was locked. Who leaked it?"

He thought of Bright. Maybe his people had found something. But this wasn't their style. Rey Hughes was ruthless, yes, but not precise, not like this. This was coordinated. Timed to the minute. It didn't feel like campaign dirt. It felt like a bullet between the ribs.

No leaks had ever come from Wolfe's team either. Not directly. Landon played dirty, sure, but he didn't play this quietly.

So who did?

His hands shook. For the first time since his first Senate race, Ivan Chang couldn't speak. Couldn't spin. Couldn't think of a line, a pivot, or a defense.

His voice finally broke through in a whisper: "They've killed me."

Not politically wounded. Not bruised.

Killed.

The hum of conversation drifted around the table like background music, low and steady, punctuated by the clatter of silverware and the occasional pop of laughter from nearby booths. They were tucked in a corner of a popular meat-and-three just outside downtown Birmingham, the kind of place where the iced tea was syrupy and the biscuits could stop a heart.

Ted Bright sat at the head of the table, still dressed in his rolled-up shirt sleeves and campaign slacks, his tie slightly loosened. Across from him, Rey

Hughes wore the satisfied grin of a man who'd just watched his enemy go up in smoke.

"We might just have the nomination in the bag by tomorrow," Hughes said, picking at a plate of fried catfish with the nonchalance of a man calling a ballgame in the fourth inning.

Philip Bright looked up from his phone. "You really think so?"

"Absolutely," Rey drawled. "Latest numbers got us leadin' in eleven states, tied in three, and within the margin in the last one. Hell, even them folks in Oklahoma are comin' around."

Ted gave a slight, cautious shake of his head. "Phil, don't count your chickens before they hatch. The primaries are only half the battle."

"I know, Dad," Philip replied, but the glint in his eyes said otherwise.

The campaign had been burning hot through the South. Three days, seven cities, tens of thousands of hands shaken and promises made. From Beaumont to Birmingham, Bright was drawing crowds that wrapped around courthouses and high school gyms, chanting "The Future is Bright" and waving signs like they'd seen the future and it wore cufflinks.

Even Ted couldn't deny it. *Bright fever* was catching.

Rey leaned back, stretching out like a man who'd just finished splitting wood. "I'm tellin' y'all, this race is fallin' into our lap like a pecan pie off the back porch."

Philip grinned. "Dad, it's over. Chang's done, Callahan's breathing through a straw, and the press is already calling it a two-man race."

"Damn near a one-man race," Rey added, tapping his fork on the table for emphasis. "Chang was like a coon dog chasing his tail; looked busy, made noise, but wasn't gettin' nowhere. That story that hit yesterday?" He let out a low whistle. "Put a stake clean through his campaign's heart."

Evelyn, poised and polished in her campaign blazer and pearls, tilted her head slightly. "That piece on Chang was brilliant," she said. "I don't know who you bribed or blackmailed to get that intel, Rey, but it landed like a bomb. Encrypted comms, Chinese donors, the Virgin Islands? That was surgical."

Rey's grin widened. "Well, sugar, you know me. Got friends in low places and favors banked like gold bars. Sometimes all it takes is knowin' which tree to shake."

She narrowed her eyes, skeptical. "So you're saying that wasn't you?"

He paused, just for effect, then leaned in, lowering his voice as if sharing a state secret. "Swear on my mama's pecan pie, I didn't drop that leak. But I *will* say this, whoever has been payin' attention. That play was straight outta the Hughes playbook."

Evelyn sipped her tea, her lips twitching at the corners. "Well, whoever it was, they handed us Chang's scalp on a silver platter. What's next?"

Ted, who'd been mostly quiet while the others buzzed around him, finally spoke. His voice was steady, eyes locked on Rey's. "Landon Wolfe."

The name landed with a weight that stilled the table.

Rey nodded slowly, as if turning the idea over in his head like a horseshoe before throwing it. "Wolfe," he repeated. "He's a different breed. Got that war hero sheen, talks like a preacher, fights like a boxer. But don't worry, none. He's walkin' into a trap and don't even know it."

Ted's brow furrowed. "I'm not interested in dirty tricks."

Rey chuckled. "No tricks, Senator. Just strategy. Politics ain't a Sunday picnic, it's a back-alley brawl. Wolfe's got skeletons. Perhaps not as intense as Chang's, but enough to rattle the bones. We start pressurein his platform: foreign policy, defense contracts, that Veterans' Alliance PAC of his, it'll shake loose some splinters."

Philip leaned forward. "We going public before tomorrow?"

"Maybe," Rey said. "Or maybe we hold it. Let him overperform and think he's on the rise. Then cut his legs out from under him next week. Right now, the narrative is ours. We own the airwaves, we own the message. Wolfe's just the next headline."

Evelyn's gaze drifted toward her father. "Dad?"

Ted's voice was quiet, but firm. "Just make sure we're right. If we go after Wolfe, I don't want rumors. I want facts."

Rey gave a slow, solemn nod. "Facts, Senator. And when we drop 'em, the whole country'll hear it. Like thunder before the storm."

Outside, the Alabama sun was beginning to fade, casting a golden haze through the restaurant windows. Inside, the campaign's inner circle leaned back into their meals, laughter and optimism returning. But beneath the surface, the wheels of war were turning. The next battlefield was already in their sights, and the last man standing between them and the nomination was about to learn what it meant to face the Bright machine in full force.

The war room buzzed like a hornet's nest under floodlights. Phones ringing. Fingers tapping. Screens blinking red and blue, counties coloring in like blood seeping through gauze. I'd been in my fair share of campaign nights, but nothing like this. Not with this much weight. Not with the future dangling by a thread so thin it might snap with the next refresh.

"Massachusetts goes to Callahan," someone muttered from the back.

"Maine too," another voice chimed in.

Callahan. Jesus. The man was still kicking. Like a ghost refusing to vanish. I learned forward in my chair, arms braced on my knees, the weight of a thousand county lines pressing down on my shoulders.

Then came Vermont.

"Chang."

I didn't even react. Of course, it was Chang. The bastard had more scandals than a tabloid rag, but he knew how to survive. He could be halfway to prison and still charm voters into thinking he was the victim.

"Three down, twelve to go," I murmured, not to anyone in particular. Just loud enough to hear the clock ticking louder in my head.

Lydia stood behind me, arms crossed, watching the numbers like she could bend them with will alone. "We expected the Northeast to be a wash. Our game picks up out west. Don't start writing the eulogy yet."

I nodded, but the knot in my chest wasn't loosening. Then Virginia hit.

"Bright takes Virginia."

My head jerked up. "What?"

Ellie was already moving the Virginia magnet under Bright's name. "He edged us by half a point."

"After everything with Governor Winters?" My voice came out sharper than I intended.

"He campaigned hard the last forty-eight hours," Lydia muttered. "Pulled out every trick in the book."

Of course he did. That's what Ted Bright *did.* Just when you thought he was fading, he came roaring back like a damn freight train. My jaw clenched as I stared at the map. Every state he stole felt like another brick laid in the wall between me and the nomination.

Ellie tried to soothe the blow. "We're still strong in the South. North Carolina's up next.

I didn't speak. Couldn't. All I could hear was the slow suffocation of momentum.

Then, finally, relief.

"North Carolina goes to Wolfe."

The room exhaled. A few cheers went up. Terry slapped the table. "Now *that's* more like it!"

I nodded, the corners of my mouth twitching toward something that might've been a smile if it didn't feel so damn earned. We'd bled for that win. Out-organized Ted by a mile. At least we had one to show for it.

But Ellie wasn't done.

"Texas goes to Bright."

It was like getting kicked in the gut right after standing up.

"You've got to be kidding me," Terry growled. "Texas? That was our firewall."

"It's not our firewall if voters don't care about walls," I muttered bitterly.

Bright was sweeping; state after state falling under his name like dominoes. Tennessee. Oklahoma. Alabama. Even Missouri was leaning his way. He wasn't just winning—he was *taking* them, stealing them out from under us with that damn smile and those Sunday-school speeches that made people forget he was just another polished suit with perfect hair and no spine.

Ellie stood near the board, her arms folded, staring hard at the magnet tiles as if she could will them to move differently.

"Callahan's frozen. Two states. Chang's just got Vermont. You've taken North Carolina. But Bright, he's got five, maybe six."

Lydia moved behind me, her voice low. "We still have Minnesota. We've worked that ground hard."

"We better," I snapped, then exhaled through my nose. "What about Iowa?"

Silence.

Then she said it. "Bright's leading."

I almost laughed. Typical. Of *course,* Iowa was screwing me once again. That state had been a thorn in my side since day one. Cold hands, cold people, and now cold numbers. "Iowa never liked me," I said. "Hell, I don't blame 'em. I never kissed the ring."

"Forget Iowa," Terry cut in. "Eyes on California."

California. The behemoth. The decider. Forty million people, half of them allergic to common sense and the rest too enamored with Bright's promises to see through the glitter. I already knew how this one was gonna go, but I held out hope.

Colorado came in first. "Bright in a landslide."

My shoulders slumped. "That's Ted's backyard."

"You edged Chang for second," Ellie offered.

Great. Silver medals and sorrow.

Then Utah fell. Bright again.

By midnight, I was numb. The pins kept dropping.

"Final tally," Lydia said, reading from her tablet. "Bright takes nine. You've got three—North Carolina, Arkansas, and Minnesota. Callahan's got two. Chang's stuck on one."

"And California?"

I already knew.

"Bright."

The room was quiet. Not defeated, yet, but stunned into silence.

I leaned back in my chair, running a hand down my face. Second place. Always the bridesmaid. Always a day late to the party.

And yet... we weren't done.

Three states loomed on the calendar: Florida, New York, and Illinois.

I straightened my posture, staring at the map like it owed me something. Like I could reach through the screen and drag the next state into my column.

Bright hadn't won the nomination yet. Not officially. And if he thought I was going quietly into the night, he didn't know Landon Wolfe.

PART THREE

SURVIVAL

12

A Calculated Concession

May 2028

By late May, the map was painted red, white, and bitter.

The primaries were limping to the finish line; bloated, bloody, and damn near unbearable. Every other candidate had folded. Endorsed. Vanished. Ted was already calling donors as if he had the nomination locked. As if it was all over but for the balloon drop. But I was still standing. Still running. Still pissing on his parade.

And he hated it.

He and Rey Hughes weren't looking for a win anymore. They wanted a blowout. A coronation. A clean, televised sweep into the convention with no bruises and no dissent. I refused to play along. That made me dangerous.

So they started throwing punches. Not political ones. Personal.

It began with whispers, disseminated to the right reporters at the right cocktail hours. That I'd gotten *too close* to Lydia. That I was sleeping with Ellie. That I was making late-night visits to female staffers when the trail went quiet. Then Rey dug even deeper into the gutter. He paid off some D.C. escort, called herself Crystal Cascade, if you can believe it, to claim that back in my early days on the Hill, I used to throw drug-fueled parties while my wife was back home in Iowa. According to Crystal, I was some kind of walking scandal, mixing pills with politics and women with whiskey.

It was all garbage. All lies.

But lies make great headlines.

Outside one of our rallies in Pittsburgh, the reporters were foaming at the mouth, pushing past security like they were chasing a murder confession.

"Congressman Wolfe, do you deny the allegations of romantic involvement with your campaign staff?"

I didn't flinch. I'd been expecting this ambush since the rumors first surfaced. The only thing that surprised me was how loud the cameras clicked when Lydia stepped in front of me.

"This is pathetic," she said, eyes like steel. "Desperate men throw desperate punches. Congressman Wolfe has more integrity in his little finger than Ted Bright's entire campaign operation."

Ellie followed. "They want to talk about character? Maybe they should take a look at their own mirror before smearing everyone else's."

We walked into that venue with our heads high, but inside I was boiling.

Bright wanted to break me. Turn me radioactive. Make staying in the race too toxic, too costly, and too humiliating. But that wasn't working. Next, they portrayed me as unstable. A warmonger. Dangerous.

That's what they latched onto, my speech urging American engagement in the Pacific. I said what I meant: democracy doesn't defend itself, and our allies need to know we're not turning a blind eye.

Bright twisted it into a doomsday ad that made LBJ's *Daisy Girl* look like a bedtime story. Black-and-white footage. Mushroom clouds. Children playing over air raid sirens. The narrator asked: "Would you trust Landon Wolfe with your child's future?"

Then came the dagger: Ted telling the press I'd started drinking again.

"He's not well," he said. "It's clear. His rhetoric is unhinged. America needs a steady hand, not a ticking time bomb."

That was it. I had had enough.

We were in a union hall outside Columbus when I finally deviated from the script. The crowd wasn't huge, but they were loyal. Tired, but faithful.

I walked up to the mic and didn't waste a second.

"They want to talk about addiction? Fine. Let's talk. I've been sober for ten years. That's public record. What about Ted's son, Edward? Four DUIs in the last decade. Four. And not one charge that stuck. Why? Because Daddy pulled the strings. Because when you're the frontrunner, the rules don't apply."

There were gasps. Not applause, yet. Just silence. Sharp and stunned.

"But I'm not here to drag someone else's personal demons in the mud," I said, catching myself before I crossed a line I couldn't come back from. "Because I've been there. I know what it's like to fight your own darkness."

I looked up, steady.

"But while we're talking about family values, let's talk about Evelyn Bright and her little mountain empire in Colorado. Quiet land deals. Shady shell companies. Profit margins that don't make sense unless you're playing fast and loose with the law. Sound familiar?"

Now the crowd was with me. Murmurs turned to anger. Heads nodded.

"And then there's the healthcare lie," I said, my voice rising. "Ted Bright says he wants affordable medicine. Wants to fight Big Pharma. However, he holds major stock in RXSure, a company that has increased prices on insulin *six times* in the last year. That's not healthcare reform. That's profiteering. That's corruption. And if you don't believe me, check the filings. They're public."

The room exploded. Applause. Shouting. Cameras flashing again, but this time, they were *aimed at me,* not just to capture a scandal, but a moment.

I'd drawn blood.

Ted wanted to bury me beneath a pile of gossip and fiction. But now he was covered in dirt too. He thought he could play god and kingmaker at the same time. But I was still in this race, and now, he had to deal with me in the mud he made.

Outside, the White House lawn was bathed in spring sunlight. Inside, the air was heavy with dread. President Norman Hayden sat stiffly behind the Resolute Desk, eyes pinned to a satellite image of the Solomon Islands. Red markers dotted the screen: SLF units, Chinese naval vessels, newly fortified positions.

General Preston Rhodes, Chairman of the Joint Chiefs, stepped forward. A Cold Warrior through and through, his steel-blue eyes had seen too many coups in too many places to mistake this for a coincidence.

"Mr. President," Rhodes began, voice low and firm. "Prime Minister Talifa was assassinated at 0200 local time. The SLF took credit an hour later. Jonas Taneoka has declared himself acting head of state."

President Hayden's jaw clenched. "Taneoka? I thought he was in exile."

"He was," General Glenn Bowers cut in, folding his arms. "Until Chinese intel and weapons brought him back."

General Robert McIntyre, the cerebral, shadowy head of Military Intelligence, stepped forward. "We've intercepted chatter suggesting that

Taneoka's return wasn't just backed by Beijing, it was orchestrated. This wasn't a grassroots rebellion. It was a test."

"A test?" Hayden asked, his voice tightening.

McIntyre nodded. "Of how far we're willing to let China push. And I'd say we just failed it."

Rhodes paced slowly in front of the Resolute Desk. "Taneoka's consolidation is already underway. We believe three senior pro-US officials were executed this morning. Others have fled to Malaita, but their chances are slim. The Liberation Front has control of Honiara, the ports, and—thanks to Chinese logistics—air superiority."

The room fell into an uneasy silence.

Hayden looked to his Secretary of Defense, Claudia Meyers, a pragmatic voice in the room. "Is there any viable opposition left?"

"Scattered, disorganized," she said. "And afraid. Taneoka's brutality makes Fuentes look like a transitional figure. He's not an idealist, he's an operator. Cold. Calculating. He spent five years building a network inside the SLF while in exile in Guangzhou. The minute Talifa opened his doors to Western diplomats, Taneoka marked him for death."

"Jesus," Hayden muttered.

"Sir," Bowers said, stepping forward again, "we're watching the beginning of China's Pacific Monroe Doctrine. They refer to it as the Pacific Prosperity Sphere. They want to dominate the region politically, militarily, and economically, without ever firing a shot. The Solomons are their launchpad."

Hayden rubbed the bridge of his nose. "So we've lost the islands."

Rhodes snapped his head toward the President. "No, sir. Not yet."

McIntyre followed. "But if we don't move quickly, we'll lose more than just the Solomons. Papua New Guinea is already wobbling. Fiji's leadership is under pressure. This could be the start of a chain reaction."

"And if Taneoka allows Chinese bases on Guadalcanal?" Hayden asked.

Bowers didn't hesitate. "Then they'll have eyes and missiles in striking distance of Australia, Hawaii, and every major Pacific trade route. It'll be like watching the Iron Curtain fall, except this time, over water."

The President leaned back in his chair. "I didn't sign up to be a wartime president."

"No one ever does," Rhodes said. "But leadership means facing war that comes to you."

Hayden tapped his knuckles against the desk. "What are our options?"

"Military options are limited unless we want direct confrontation," McIntyre said. "But we can begin asymmetrical responses; fund the remaining loyalists, sabotage SLF infrastructure, work through regional allies."

"Operation Hedgewall," Bowers added. "A regional containment plan. Strengthen military ties with Australia, New Zealand, Singapore, and the Philippines. And maybe, just maybe, we prepare a long-game strategy to undermine Taneoka from within."

"Regime change," Meyers said bluntly.

Rhodes looked to Hayden. "Sir, this is not just about the Solomon Islands. It's about the Pacific. If we let this go, Beijing will redraw the map."

President Hayden sat still for a long moment, staring at the flickering map. Taneoka's face, pulled from a Chinese state news feed, glared back at him from the corner screen, smug, composed, already cloaked in revolutionary rhetoric.

"I want full briefings from Pacific Command and Langley by morning," Hayden said. "And I want you all to understand something: we're not going to war. But we're not going to roll over, either. Taneoka wants to be a symbol. Let's remind him what it costs to be one."

He looked around the room, eyes landing on each general, then his Secretary of Defense.

"I won't let the next Cold War start with us asleep at the wheel. Begin contingency planning. Quietly. And get our allies on the phone."

Rhodes straightened his posture. "Understood, Mr. President."

As the room emptied, Hayden remained seated, the map still glowing on the table. He reached over and shut off the screen.

For a long time, he said nothing. But in his mind, a single truth repeated:

They had just lost the first island.

And it wouldn't be the last.

The music thumped softly through the walls. Champagne popped somewhere down the hall. I could hear the cheers, the laughter, the shallow sounds of people pretending a loss was something worth celebrating.

Out on the deck, my campaign staff was toasting a well-fought fight. Speeches had been made. Glasses raised. Some even cried. But I couldn't bring myself to join them. Not tonight. Not yet.

I stood in the study of my beach house in Sunhaven, a glass of ginger ale resting in my hand, not whiskey, though Ted's little whisper campaign would say otherwise. I wanted that story out. Let him think I was slipping. Let him think I'd already lost. That's how you get them to look away just long enough to strike.

Behind me, the door creaked open.

"You really are a buzzkill, you know that?"

Lydia.

I turned. She was framed in the doorway, silhouetted against the golden remnants of sunset. Black dress. Hair up. The flicker of candlelight caught the sharpness in her eyes. She closed the door behind her.

"You should be out there," she said, stepping inside. "Everyone's looking for you."

"I know," I replied, turning back to the window. "But I needed quiet."

"You always need quiet when you're plotting something."

I smiled faintly. Lydia knew me too well.

"They think this is over," I said. "They think we're finished."

"We are," Lydia replied, matter-of-fact. "Bright won. The math is done. He'll seal the nomination by July, and you'll be a political footnote by August."

"I've conceded," I said, swirling the transparent liquid in my glass. "Called Ted myself. Told him I'd support the party."

"But you don't mean it."

I looked over my shoulder at her. "Of course not."

Lydia strolled toward me, stopping just short of the desk. Her voice softened. "Landon... we gave it everything. You fought like hell. But 'Bright Fever'? The movement? You couldn't beat that."

I stepped toward her. "So what if I joined it?"

That stopped her.

"You want to... join Bright?" she asked, suspicion creeping in her tone.

"Think about it," I said. "Ted's the nominee. He's going to be president if the movement holds. But what if I'm the one standing beside him when he is?"

Her eyes narrowed. "You're serious."

"I want to be his running mate."

She laughed. Sharp and bitter. "You think Ted Bright, the man who used *Crystal Cascade* to bury you alive on national television, is going to turn around and ask you to be his vice president?"

"No," I said. "He's not going to ask."

I stepped closer. Our eyes locked. Her breath caught.

"I'm not going to give him a choice."

Lydia tilted her head, the wheels already turning. "Go on."

"Bright wants legacy," I said. "That's what he's addicted to. Not power—*legacy*. He wants to be remembered as a revolutionary president. The man who reshaped the American experiment. A transformational figure."

She folded her arms. "So you tell Bright what? That you'll help him get there?"

"I tell him that with me on the ticket, he doesn't just get eight years, he gets sixteen. Two administrations. His and mine. He ushers in the new era, and I lock it into history."

I walked behind the desk, lowering my voice. "I'll play the loyal heir. The apostle of the Bright Doctrine. And when the time comes..."

Lydia raised an eyebrow. "You bury him."

"Only if I have to," I said, smiling thinly. "But let's not pretend Ted doesn't have skeletons. One leak, one scandal... the media goes berserk. Congress gets its knives out. If the storm gets bad enough, if the outrage reaches a boil..."

She completed the thought. "...he resigns."

"And who's standing there, untarnished?" I asked.

"Landon Wolfe," she said, almost admiringly. "The loyal vice president. The steady hand."

I nodded. "The natural successor. America's relief valve."

She was silent for a moment, chewing on the weight of it.

"But you're missing something," Lydia said finally. "Ted has options. Hundreds of names more palatable than you. People he trusts. You really think he picks the guy who refused to bend the knee?"

"No," I said, setting my glass down. "I think Ted picks me because Edward makes him."

"Edward?" She questioned.

Her eyes didn't widen in surprise, just sharpened in interest. She moved closer, her gaze narrowing like a surgeon tracing where to cut.

"You think Edward is the key?"

"I know he is." I met her eyes. "You saw it at the Iowa State Fair. The way he looked at you. That hesitation. That want. He's insecure. Lost in that family. Ted doesn't see him, not really. Just shields him like glass. Covers up his DUIs, his failed enterprises. That kid's a ghost in his own house."

She smiled, slow and deliberate. "And you want me to say hello to a ghost."

"I want you to *see* him. The way no one else does. Just enough to make him feel something. Like he matters. Like someone finally sees the son, not the shadow."

She crossed her arms, thoughtful now. "You think Edward will start whispering in Ted's ear? Advocating for you?"

"I think he'll start feeling brave. And when that happens, he'll make mistakes. The kind we can work with."

She raised an eyebrow. "You want me to make him *messy.*"

"I want you to help him be who he already is," I said quietly.

Lydia turned from the desk and walked to the window. The lights from the party flickered against the glass. She stood there for a long moment, silhouetted by power and calculation. Then turned back to me with that look, half fox, half blade.

"You've been sitting on this, haven't you?"

"Since the moment I realized I was going to lose."

She approached slowly, her heels now silent. Dangerous things rarely made noise.

"And if it works? If Edward cracks?"

"Then Ted will do what he's always done," I said. "Protect the family. Cover it up. Pretend it never happened. And if I'm standing there with the solution in hand..." I let it hang.

She reached for my untouched drink, lifted it to her lips, then set it back down without sipping. "You're asking me to play a long, quiet game with a broken boy and a desperate father."

"I'm asking you to remind them what fear feels like."

Her eyes glittered. "Then I'll need a new dress."

Outside, the celebration went on. Music pulsed. Laughter rolled across the courtyard. But inside the study, something colder took root. Not a plan. A pressure point. The kind that would leave bruises in the morning.

We didn't toast. We didn't shake hands.

We just understood.

And that was enough.

13

Voices in the Arena

The Democratic National Convention

The view from the penthouse suite of the Hilton Chicago stretched wide and glittering, as if the city itself was offering up its skyline for judgment. Below, banners waved in Grant Park, media tents sprawled like temporary embassies, and camera lenses followed every handshake, every smile, every carefully choreographed moment of unity.

But inside the suite, the air was heavy. The kind of air that carried the scent of stress, old coffee, and too many decisions.

Senator Bright stood at the far end of the room, his tie loosened, collar unbuttoned. The hum of Lake Shore Drive traffic below was barely audible beneath the low voices and rustling of memos. The Democratic National Convention was in full swing. History had returned to Chicago, sixty years after the '68 bloodbath, and the ghosts of that week still lingered. Cops clashing with protesters. The party fractured on national television. Riots in the streets while the nominee smiled under spotlights.

Ted wasn't smiling.

A list of names sat on the table before him, crisp on paper, limp in promise. The names had been vetted, tested, polled. But none of them stuck.

"No governor wants the damn job," Ted muttered, not looking at anyone in particular. "That's the truth no one will say out loud. They smile, they nod, but it's not a promotion. Not anymore."

Rey Hughes shifted in his seat, slow and deliberate, his Louisiana drawl as smooth as bourbon. "Second-highest office in the land, boss. Some still see the value in that."

Ted gave a dry laugh and picked up a glass of water. "Tell that to Kamala Harris. Or Mike Pence, waiting for Trump to implode. Or Cheney—hell, the guy practically ran the White House and still walked away hated by half the country."

He downed the glass.

"The job's a graveyard of ambition. Half of 'em end up writing memoirs no one reads."

Rey leaned in, undeterred.

"But it's still power. The right VP steadies the ship, brings in voters you can't reach alone. Look at Obama and Biden. Different worlds, but it worked."

Ted leaned forward, planting his elbows on the table, staring hard at the list. "It worked because Barack knew how to run a campaign like a movement. I don't need a movement. I need insurance. A damn firewall."

Hughes eyed him carefully. "You talkin' policy or politics?"

"Both," Ted said. "We need someone who can absorb the heat when it comes. And it will come. Every one of those names..." He ran a pen down the list. "Too loud, too green, too compromised, or just not ready."

Governor Casey Fox; crossed out. Governor Luis Ramirez; sidelined by whispers of corruption. Senator Olivia Dowd; rising star, but too coastal. Ted had promised a ticket that could unify the party's bruised wings: progressives, moderates, and working-class voters in Rust Belt states. But his options felt thin. Manufactured.

Across the table, a communications aide spoke up, nervously: "What about a military pick? A general, maybe? That always polls well."

"No," Ted said flatly. "That's a stunt. We're not doing stunts."

Rey glanced toward the window, where the city lights blinked like signal fires. "History's starin' back at us through that glass, boss. You know it. Chicago, don't forget. Neither does the press. We get this wrong, and it's all folks'll talk about. We need a pick who doesn't just balance the ticket. We need someone who changes the narrative."

Ted stared down at his hands. His campaign had steamrolled the primaries; out-fundraised, outmaneuvered, out-messaged every rival. But that was just the rehearsal. This? This was the real stage. A general election under floodlights, with opposition research and October surprises waiting like landmines.

He looked back at the list. "None of these people fit."

Hughes leaned forward, slow and patient. "Then maybe it's not someone on the list."

Ted didn't answer. The room fell into silence, broken only by the buzz of a phone vibrating on the table. Bright didn't move. He was somewhere else, in the future, maybe. In the arena. In the thick of the fight.

He finally spoke, almost to himself. "The real campaign starts now. Not in the debates. Not in the ads. It starts with who I trust to sit one heartbeat away."

He didn't need a partner. He needed leverage. An insurance policy. A bargaining chip. Someone he could control, or someone the country couldn't ignore.

Outside, the wind shifted over the lake, and the city of Chicago exhaled. The shadows of 1968 still lingered; batons, smoke, fury, but so did the lessons. Every convention had its fracture point.

Ted Bright was about to choose his.

The hotel restaurant was all brass and linen, the kind of place where time slowed to a polite crawl and power played itself out between courses. Sunlight slanted through tall windows, casting a soft gleam across the silverware and untouched water glasses. It was quiet, refined, perfect for the sort of conversations that reshaped careers.

Senator Weeb Charles sat across from me, his blazer buttoned, his tie knotted to perfection. He looked like the ghost of the old party: silver hair, liver spots, and that unshakable air of Southern tact that made everything sound like a compliment, even when it wasn't.

"How many conventions does this make for you, Landon?" he asked, smoothing the napkin across his lap. He asked it like a man who already knew the answer.

"First," I said, offering a practiced smile. "Just soaking it all in."

He chuckled, low and gravelly, like bourbon over rocks. "Well, hell. You picked a good one. Or a cursed one. Depends on how it all shakes out."

The waiter came, took our orders —something light, something easy —and vanished again. Then the real conversation began.

He didn't say it, but I could hear the real message: *You're here. You're somebody now.* And he wasn't wrong. The Bright campaign began as a curiosity, then evolved into a movement. People were watching. People were listening. And people like Weeb didn't extend lunch invitations for nostalgia.

"You know Neal Teller, of course," Weeb said, adjusting his cufflinks like they were hiding secrets.

"South Carolina's lion," I replied. "Sure."

"He's stepping down after this term. Quietly, of course. No press yet. Health ain't what it used to be, and frankly, the man's tired."

I didn't answer. I let the silence do its job.

"We're going to need someone strong to replace him," he went on. "Someone who can win. Someone the party can trust."

That's when it dropped. The moment. The pitch.

"We want you to run, Landon. The seat's yours if you want it. Full support. Big donors. DNC infrastructure. You wouldn't have to lift a finger till 2029."

He said it as if he were offering me a Rolex, not a Senate campaign.

It should have flattered me. And it did, briefly. Neal Teller's seat wasn't just power. It was permanence. Influence. A chair at the grown-ups' table. People worked a lifetime for that kind of invitation.

But for me?

It felt like a consolation prize.

I kept my expression polite. Curious. Thoughtful. Inside, I could already feel the gears shifting. Lydia and I had mapped out the whole thing. We weren't in Chicago for a steak dinner and applause lines. We were here to pull strings, make moves. Get Ted elected, and then position ourselves for what came after.

Senator was nice. But it was *settled*. Safe. It wasn't enough.

"That's a generous offer, Senator," I said slowly. "And I'm honored you'd consider me for it."

Weeb nodded, already reading between the lines.

"But I'm afraid my timeline might not match yours," I added.

He tilted his head, his eyes narrowing just slightly. "How do you mean?"

I didn't blink. "There's been talk."

"Talk," he repeated, with a small smile. "What kind of talk?"

I held his gaze. "That I'm on the shortlist. For the Vice Presidency."

It landed like a dropped fork. Not dramatic, but noticeable. Weeb's brows rose a hair, just enough to tell me he hadn't heard that before. That I'd managed to surprise a man who rarely was.

"Well now," he said after the moment. "That's news."

He leaned back in his chair, fingers steepled in front of him. His tone was calm, but I could see the math flashing behind his eyes. Who told who. Who stood to gain. What it meant.

"You sure you want that job?" he asked finally. "It's a hell of a gamble. A Senate seat's yours for the taking. Name on the door. Six years locked in. Real power."

I gave a slight smile. "Depends on how you define real."

He laughed at that, but it didn't reach his eyes. "You're ambitious, Landon. Nothing wrong with that. But there's a difference between climbing and flying too close to the sun."

He sipped his water. I didn't respond.

Because the truth was, I didn't need to.

Let him guess. Let him wonder. That was the point.

He saw a young man turning down the Senate for a shot at the vice presidency. What he didn't see, what he couldn't, was that I wasn't playing for second place.

The rafters trembled with applause as I stepped into the blue-lit spotlight of the United Center. A sea of delegates stretched before me, cheering, clapping, swaying with their ridiculous signs and plastic flags. "Unity,"

"Hope," "Bright for America." Their excitement was tangible. Their faith is genuine. That was the part that made it so easy.

I took my place behind the podium, the warmth of the stage lights cutting through the cool draft of the arena's upper tiers. Behind me, the party's banner hung like a curtain at a high school play: stars, stripes, and slogans stitched into a dream no one dared to question. I adjusted my tie, took a deep breath, and smiled.

Fake it until you make it. Then fake it some more.

"Good evening," I said, my voice steady, my smile presidential. "Fellow Democrats, friends, believers in the promise of this nation..."

A rolling cheer swelled and broke across the floor. I let it carry for a beat, then gently raised my hand for silence. The crowd obeyed.

"Tonight, we gather in a city that has been both a crucible and a proving ground for our party. A city of firsts and failures. A city that remembers. Some of you might recall what happened here sixty years ago..."

A murmur passed through the crowd; those old enough to know, young enough to have been taught.

"In 1968, we were a party at war with itself. The streets outside were filled with protestors. Inside, the establishment clung to control. And the world watched; confused, angry, disillusioned."

I paused for a moment, letting the ghosts of Chicago whisper through the cables and scaffolding.

"But tonight," I said, my voice lifting with just the right blend of hope and resolve, "we are not that party. We are not a party divided. We are a party united. Because we have learned. We have grown. We have overcome."

The applause came right on cue, enthusiastic, approving. Perfect. I let the crowd cheer. It bought me time to refocus.

I lowered my voice slightly, drawing them in. "We are Democrats. But more than that, we are Americans. And this moment, this crisis of conscience we find our country in, demands not just partisanship, but partnership."

That line wasn't mine. Ellie had written it. She said it would test well in the Midwest and among undecided voters watching from their living rooms. She was probably right.

"I came close in this race," I said, offering a gracious shrug, the kind that told people I wasn't bitter, just humbled. "But this was never about me. It was never about ego or ambition..."

It was absolutely about ego. About ambition sharpened into a weapon. About knowing when to bow so you could rise higher.

"This was always about one thing: the future of America."

Another wave of cheers. I nodded along with them, a benevolent shepherd guiding his flock.

"And so tonight, I am here not just as a former candidate, not just as a Democrat, but as someone who loves this country enough to know when to step aside for the greater good."

A long pause. You could hear the silence settle like mist.

"I am proud to endorse Ted Bright as the next President of the United States."

The roar that followed was deafening. People stood. People wept. Delegates embraced. I could see the camera lights blinking across the arena like fireflies, catching my smile as my hands were raised in salute. History, they thought, was happening. And it was. Just not the history they believed.

"Ted is a good man," I said, carefully. "A man who understands that our democracy only works when both sides, yes, both sides, are willing to reach across the aisle. To compromise. To govern with humility."

It tasted like ash in my mouth. Ted didn't believe that anymore than I did. But he had to pretend. And I had to pretend better.

"Tonight," I went on, "we begin not just a campaign, but a covenant. Between ourselves and the American people. We promise them competence, compassion, and character."

More clapping. More standing. More fools clinging to slogans and chants. I stood in the eye of their storm and smiled, still speaking.

"This is our time. Our moment. Let's go win it. Together."

The applause hit again, thunderous and long. I turned from the podium, waving, smiling, soaking in the spotlight. But inside, I was ice. I was calculating. Every beat of this speech had been designed not to support Ted, but to make me indispensable to him. A partner. A sidekick. A stepping stone.

They thought I had conceded. That I had moved on.

But I hadn't.

I stepped off the stage into a blur of lights and roaring approval. Somewhere above, in one of the luxury suites, Ted was clapping, nodding, grateful.

I adjusted my cuffs and offered a measured smile as I passed aides and delegates lining the wings.

Let them cheer for unity tonight.

I had other plans for tomorrow.

Across town from the roaring lights and flag-waving theatrics of the United Center, a quieter kind of strategy was unfolding.

The restaurant was the kind of place that didn't need a name on the awning. Tucked into a historic building on the Gold Coast, it was soft with candlelight and low music, its air scented faintly with truffle oil and restraint. Politicians, financiers, and power brokers came here not to be seen, but to be remembered—by the right people.

Lydia sat alone at a corner table, her presence as carefully measured as the vintage wine on the sommelier's cart. Her crimson dress held to classic lines; elegant, grounded, undeniable. A slim watch circled her wrist, ticking toward midnight. Her hair, with soft waves of strawberry blonde, framed a face that did not flinch from scrutiny.

She wasn't hiding tonight. She was waiting.

Five minutes past their scheduled time, her guest arrived.

Thomas Roan, CEO of Fenhurst Capital, was a man who moved through the world like he owned it. In his early sixties, his sharp features were weathered by the Pacific sun and the winters of Davos. His salt-brown hair was clipped short, his suit a dark gray European cut that didn't wrinkle even after a fifteen-hour flight.

He approached without apology, smiling slightly as he extended a hand.

"Miss Barnes," he said, his voice smooth, low.

"Mr. Roan," Lydia replied, rising just enough to offer her hand, not enough to provide deference. "I appreciate you making time. I know you just landed."

He slid into the seat across from her. "Jet lag's nothing a good dinner and better company can't cure."

They ordered without fanfare. Two courses, one bottle. No appetizers, no dessert. Lydia didn't need small talk, and Roan didn't expect it.

Fenhurst had been circling Washington's orbit for years, its investment threaded through defense logistics, rare earth minerals, and strategic ports.

With Chinese influence escalating in the South Pacific and whispers of American reengagement, the Solomon Islands were once again becoming a hinge point. Roan's interests were growing. So were Lydia's.

Still, this wasn't her mission tonight. It was simply a window.

Roan sipped his drink, his fingers tapping once against the base of the glass. "You've done well for yourself, Lydia. There was a time when no one in our world thought you'd last beyond your father's funeral."

She smiled politely, folding her napkin. "Those people underestimated the value of a second life."

"And now you're halfway to a third. Campaign manager, industrial executive, and still finding time for... dinners like this."

"Fenhurst is in a position to move quickly. Barnes Industries knows the terrain, supply chains, and infrastructure, as well as clean energy. We've worked in Micronesia and Fiji. Our logistics arm just finished a dual-port operation in Samoa." She leaned back slightly. "If the State Department's posture shifts, I'd rather we be there together when the dust settles."

Roan studied her for a moment. "So would I."

It wasn't a commitment, but it was enough to get by.

They clinked glasses; no grand pronouncements, no signatures. Just the thud of quiet agreement between two people who knew the value of timing.

Lydia stood first.

She adjusted her dress with a slight motion, brushing a wrinkle from the hip. As Roan reached for his phone to settle the bill, her attention shifted.

Across the restaurant, at a semi-circular booth beneath a hanging brass light, Edward Bright sat surrounded by three aides and a man Lydia recognized as Russell Langston; a telecom executive with deep pockets and a long memory. Langston rarely gave political money unless he sensed a storm about to break.

Edward looked the part, wearing a crisp navy jacket and a tie still perfectly knotted, despite the long day. His dark hair was combed with precision, his expression alert but guarded. He nodded occasionally, listening more than speaking. The convention badge was gone, but the conversation still carried the residue of it. Lydia could see it in the way the aides leaned forward, how Langston kept one hand on the table like he was weighing something.

Edward wanted something. Needed it, actually.

His father's Senate seat was edging toward vacancy, and the vultures in Denver and D.C. were already circling. Edward wasn't the heir anyone expected; not his father, not the party brass, and certainly not the donors. He had the charm, the voice, the camera-ready smile, but not the discipline. His arrests, the DUIs, the string of quiet settlements and whispered scandals, those didn't disappear, even with a name like Bright. Everyone had assumed his older brother, Philip, would take up the mantle when the time came. But Philip has stayed out of the spotlight, and Edward, against all odds, refused to step aside.

Support was tentative. Polite. Cautiously interested. But the Bright name was the hottest thing in American politics, and Edward knew how to wield it just enough to get the meeting. Langston wouldn't endorse him, not yet, but he was here, listening. That was more than most could manage. Lydia could see it: Edward still believed there was a place for him in the dynasty his father built. Even if he had to carve it out himself.

She didn't need to study him any further.

She already knew what came next.

Lydia offered Roan a warm smile.

"Thank you for your time," she said. "I'll have my office follow up with a memo."

Roan nodded, rising to shake her hand again. "You'll be hearing from us."

Lydia moved through the restaurant with purpose disguised as elegance. Every step was calibrated, every glance intentional. The crimson dress, tight at the waist, loose at the hem, did most of the talking.

Edward spotted her before she reached him. His eyebrows lifted, surprise at first, then something more extraordinary, more composed: interest. He was still seated at the table, surrounded by three of his father's junior staffers and Russell Langston. The group had been there for a while. Edward did a double-take. Lydia saw it land, her presence disrupting something. The conversation thinned. Langston glanced her way, then checked his watch and rose.

"Edward," Langston said, placing a hand on the young Bright's shoulder, "we'll be in touch."

Edward nodded, saying nothing. The aides followed suit, offering polite smiles and quick glances as they moved past Lydia. She didn't acknowledge them. Her eyes were locked on Edward, and his on hers. He hadn't stood. He hadn't looked away.

"Well," he said, smiling up to her. "If it isn't Lydia Barnes. Didn't expect to see you here."

She tilted her head, gave him a smile that invited him to wonder why she was smiling. "It's a free country. Or so I've been told. Is this seat taken?"

Edward gestured to the empty seat across from him. "Please—sit. Honestly, I'm glad you stopped by. Been smiling through my teeth all day."

She sat, crossing one leg over the other with just enough show. "You're looking well, Edward. Handsome and only slightly tired. Campaigning suits you."

He gave a breathy laugh. "It's been a long week and it's only Monday."

The waiter returned, and Lydia seized the moment.

"Another whiskey for the gentleman," she said, without asking, "and I'll have a Sazerac. Heavy on the rye."

Edward raised an impressed brow. "Didn't take you for a New Orleans girl."

"I'm not. I'm a Barnes girl. We like our liquor strong and our men soft around the edges."

Edward laughed; she saw the color rise in his cheeks.

He glanced toward the window that looked out toward downtown. "Big night, huh? Wolfe's speech is all anyone's talking about."

Lydia gave a slight shrug. "He did fine."

"Is that your version of praise?" Edward replied playfully.

"I've just heard better," she said, letting the tease hang.

She leaned in slightly.

"So," she said, "Are you here for your father, or for yourself?"

"Can't it be both?" He swirled the last of his drink before the new one arrived. "Officially, I'm here to network. Unofficially..." He looked down into his glass. "I'm tired of being the Bright sibling no one bets on."

She tilted her head, her expression softening. "Philip's boring. Evelyn's unbearable."

Edward exhaled, almost a sigh of relief. "Finally. Someone said it."

"I say it often," Lydia replied. "But you know that."

Their drinks arrived. Edward tossed his back fast. Too fast. She sipped hers slowly.

"You were always the interesting one, Edward," she said, eyes flicking to his hands, then his mouth. "The one with edge. Charm. Hunger."

"Yeah, well, I've got a handful of DUIs and a rehab stint that say otherwise."

"And still, you're sitting here with me. Wearing a thousand-dollar suit and talking about running for Congress." She clinked her glass gently against his. "Tell me you don't think you deserve it more than they do."

"I do," he said, sharper now. "They don't know what it means to fight for it. Not like I do."

Another round. This time, a smoky mezcal for Lydia, bourbon for Edward. His posture slouched slightly now, but he leaned in, close enough for his cologne to blend with the citrus and sweat of the city.

Lydia watched him over the rim of her glass. The shift was subtle but there; the polished son of a political dynasty giving way to the restless boy underneath. His tie had loosened. His words came back easier. She could almost see the Teflon start to peel.

She didn't speak right away. Silence worked better than charm. Let him fill it. Let him reach for her, for approval, for a lifeline. He always had that need—the Brights all did. Only Edward was honest enough to show it.

"What if I told you," she said, brushing a stray strand of hair behind her ear, "that you didn't have to do it alone?"

His grin wobbled, boyish and just a little drunk. "You're offering to run my campaign?"

"I'm offering to *win* it for you," she said. "We get ahead of the narrative, start framing you as the bold outsider, not the black sheep. You'll look like a rebel, not a relic. Voters love that."

Edward leaned back, his glass half-raised, considering her. The bourbon trembled slightly as he laughed.

She swirled her drink, then added with a knowing smile, "I need another campaign. Wolfe didn't win the nomination, but now they talk about him as if he were a statesman. That didn't happen by accident."

Edward blinked, slowly. "God, you're good."

"I'm expensive too," she whispered, "but you're worth the price."

Their legs brushed under the table. He didn't pull away. His voice, lower now, dragged slightly on the vowels.

"You remember Iowa?" he slurred, grinning. "That Fair. You wore—God, what did you wear? Something red?"

"I love wearing red," she replied, letting the corner of her lip curl. "It keeps the powerful men distracted."

"Worked then," he mumbled, "works now."

Lydia let the silence settle again. She could almost hear the hum of the bar over his breathing; the soft clink of glasses, the low jazz somewhere in the distance. Edward Bright, heir to a dynasty, was sitting three feet away, and every minute he talked, he handed her another piece of himself.

She laughed softly, then traced her finger along the rim of her glass. "I'm staying at the Conrad Hilton, off Michigan Avenue. Room 745."

Edward looked up, surprise registering lazily.

"That's—" he started, then chuckled. "No shit. I'm staying there too."

She tilted her head, the faintest ghost of a smile touching her lips. Of course he was. Same hotel, same orbit, that same hunger. Men like Edward always thought fate was flirting when really it was just opportunity, dressed in red.

"Well," she said, rising slowly, "then that saves me the trouble of calling a car."

Edward stood, one hand bracing the table. He adjusted his collar, blinked twice like he was recalibrating his balance, then followed.

For a brief second, Lydia watched him from the corner of her eye; the unsteady gait, the unguarded grin. She almost pitied him. Almost. Then the thought passed.

Outside, the air was cool and electric with the sounds of Chicago nightlife. Lydia stepped closer, not touching, but close enough to pull his center of gravity with her.

The city lights flickered against the river, a mirror of movement and color. Lydia caught their reflection in a storefront window, his frame leaning unconsciously toward hers, her smile sharp as glass.

As they walked up Michigan Avenue, Edward discussed legacy and frustration, his father's looming shadow, Evelyn's insufferable righteousness, and the ache of being the family's afterthought. Lydia let him talk, nodding at the right moments, her smile easy, her presence disarming.

She wasn't seducing him.

She wasn't recruiting him.

She was using him.

And he'd never realize it, until it was too late.

They stepped into Room 745 of the Conrad Hilton, their laughter echoing softly as the door clicked shut behind them. The suite exhaled quiet luxury: polished oak furniture, crisp white linens stretched across a king-sized bed, and dim ambient lighting that made everything, and everyone, look warmer, softer, and more forgiving. Through the tall windows,

Michigan Avenue shimmered like a river of gold, but Lydia barely spared it a glance.

She moved first, setting her clutch down on the desk, slipping out of her heels. When she turned, Edward was already close, too close. The alcohol had dulled his sense of timing and space. He kissed her with a clumsy urgency, the kind that mistook affection for possession. Lydia responded in kind, her lips meeting his, her hands gliding over his shoulders, her performance smooth and convincing.

They made their way toward the bed, still locked in that carefully choreographed embrace. Edward's hands wandered; her cheek, her neck, her breasts. He ran them down her sides and finally cupped her ass, squeezing it with a soft, almost boyish enthusiasm. Of course, he was an ass man.

Lydia played the part. Her moan was just breathy enough. Her fingers trailed the outline of his erection, coaxing a guttural groan from him. He was so easy to read, so easy to lead. She let herself be laid back on the mattress, her red dress shifting above her thighs.

But just as he reached for his belt buckle, she placed a hand on his chest, gently halting him.

"Wait," she said, rising with a laugh that was warm but sharp. "We need a drink first. Something to toast to."

Edward, flushed and panting, gave a tipsy grin and slumped back into the pillows. "You read my mind."

Lydia crossed the room to the minibar, her movements relaxed and confident. From within the folds of her bra, she withdrew a small, clear vial, unlabeled, discreet. She selected a bottle of cabernet and uncorked it with practiced ease, then poured two generous glasses. With her back to him, she tilted the vial over one of the glasses, watching as the liquid disappeared without a trace.

She turned, both glasses in hand, her smile painted on like lipstick. "Cheers," she said, handing him the glass.

He clinked it against hers. "To strategy," he slurred, and took a long, unguarded sip.

Lydia tilted her head, amused. "I've been looking forward to this," she said playfully.

Edward stood again, emboldened, embers reigniting. She turned her back to him, lifting her hair. "Unzip me?"

He obliged, fumbling slightly at the zipper. The dress peeled away like wrapping paper, revealing black lace and silk that clung to her hips and breasts with precise, deliberate flattery. His breath caught; she could feel it behind her. A lesser woman might've been flattered.

"Why don't you get comfortable on the bed?" Lydia said sweetly, turning just enough to give another look. "I'll go freshen up."

He nodded, dazed and eager, making his way back to the mattress.

Lydia walked toward the bathroom, her expression shifting as soon as her back was to him; warmth drained, mask dropped. This was not seduction. This was strategy. Cold, calculated, and necessary.

As the door to the bathroom clicked shut behind her, Edward took another sip, sank into the bed, and smiled like a man who thought he had won.

I stepped into Room 744, the carpet muffling my footsteps, the air thick with anticipation. Just ahead, the adjoining door to 745 stood slightly ajar, a silent invitation. Through the gap, I caught a glimpse of Lydia, perched casually in the armchair like a queen surveying a conquered court.

Edward's white Oxford shirt hung loose on her frame, revealing black lace beneath. Her red dress was flung across the floor like the flag of a vanquished enemy.

Our eyes met. A small smile played at her lips, sly, dangerous, victorious. I closed the door behind me.

"Is he out?" I asked, keeping my voice level quiet.

Lydia didn't move. She glanced at the bed. Edward Bright, son to a king in the making, lay sprawled across the sheets, naked and unconscious. His arm hung off the mattress like discarded luggage.

"Out cold," she said. "Between the bourbon and the dose I slipped him; he won't stir for hours."

I allowed myself a slow, controlled smile. "Just as we planned."

"Clueless," she added, standing. "Like the rest of the Bright family. They think the world owes them something. Power by birthright. Legacy by default."

She walked toward me, the shirt falling open slightly. There was a quiet fury in her step, not passion, but purpose. "They thought we were pawns. Background noise. A forgettable congressman and a campaign staffer with good heels and better instincts."

"They won't forget us after tonight," I said.

She stopped a foot in front of me. "No. They won't."

The plan was simple in theory, brutal in execution. Edward's history with the bottle, his reckless nights, his inability to control himself, had long been a quiet liability. The press had always looked the other way, protected by the family name. Tonight, we'd give them something they couldn't ignore. By morning, Ted Bright's campaign would be teetering on the brink. But we weren't here to destroy the Brights outright. No—we were giving them an out. A deal. One, they couldn't refuse.

Name me as his running mate. Or lose everything.

"Are you ready?" she asked, eyes gleaming with something like madness, and something like devotion.

I nodded.

We turned and stepped back into Room 744, closing the adjoining door behind us with a soft finality. What was about to happen couldn't be undone.

Lydia walked toward the bed. In a slow, practiced movement, she let Edward's shirt slip from her shoulders. The soft hotel light bathed her in a honeyed haze. Her lingerie clung to her like purpose. Beautiful. Dangerous. Willing.

I stood at the foot of the bed, gripping Edward's belt in my hand. It was heavier than I expected. I looked at Lydia. She gave me a small nod. No fear. Only fire.

And then I began.

I won't describe what came next; not because I regret it, but because I don't need to. Pain speaks its own language. It bruises. It bleeds. It whispers and screams. And Lydia, God help us both, never missed a beat. Every cry, every fall, every shudder was calculated.

I don't know what was real and what was theater. I don't think she knew either.

By the time I finished, the room was in ruins; linens were soaked, glass was shattered, and the echoes of violence still lingered in the corners. Lydia lay across the bed, a constellation of bruises forming on her skin. Blood trailed from her mouth. Her left eye was beginning to swell.

She looked beautiful.

Broken, but not weak. Never weak. This was strength. A kind of devotion no man could demand, and few could stomach.

I sat on the edge of the bed, breath heavy, heart steady. Lydia turned her head toward me, her voice barely audible.

"They'll believe every word."

I looked down at her. "They have no choice."

And they would. By the end of the week, Ted would be on his knees. And I'd be standing beside him. Smiling.

Morning came fast, cruel, and loud. Philip Bright kicked the door in like he was breaching a war zone. "Where the fuck is he!"

Room 744 wasn't big enough for his rage. Evelyn was right behind him, a flurry of blonde hair and stilettos. "You fat piece of shit!" she snapped, her voice slicing like glass as she spotted Edward slumped in bed. "Do you have any idea what you've done? You've destroyed the entire campaign!"

Edward groaned and shifted under the sheets, naked and half-conscious. "What... what's going on?" he mumbled.

Philip didn't answer; he lunged. Fists first. He grabbed Edward by the neck, ripped him up from the mattress like dead weight. The sheet fell away. "You raped Lydia Barnes," he spat, and then he hit him.

Hard.

Edward stumbled back, dazed and bleeding. "What the hell are you talking about?" he choked. "I didn't—"

"You shut your fucking mouth!" Philip came at him again.

"You've wrecked it all. The campaign. Dad's legacy. Our family." Philip's voice cracked on that last word.

Evelyn stood there, arms folded like a judge at sentencing. "You just couldn't keep it in your pants, could you? All that power and still thinking with your dick."

Edward found his black boxer briefs on the floor, pulled them on with shaking hands. "I don't remember anything past the restaurant," he said. "I swear, I didn't touch her. I didn't rape her."

"Liar," Evelyn hissed.

But the hits stopped. Philip stood over his younger brother, heaving a sigh. Doubt had crept in, just a crack, but enough. "What happened last night, Ed?"

"I don't know!" Edward's voice broke, raw with panic. "I drank too much. I blacked out. But I swear to God, I would never hurt Lydia."

Then came a voice from the door.

"Are you sure about that?"

Ellie Poole entered like she owned the goddamn hotel. Calm, clean, untouched by the chaos, with a look in her eyes that could freeze fire. She walked between the siblings like they weren't even there and took the center of the room.

"You want answers?" she said, already pulling out her phone. "Here's a voicemail Lydia left me at 2:37 this morning.

She pressed play.

Lydia's voice came through the speaker, raw and broken, yet rehearsed to perfection. "Ellie... please. Edward... he wouldn't stop. I begged him. I begged, but he hit me. He kept hitting me. I tried to scream, but he... oh God, he wouldn't stop.

Her sobs bled into the silence.

The room went still. The only sound was the hum of the hotel's A/C unit and the slow, rhythmic collapse of Edward's breathing.

"I didn't do this," he whispered, as if saying it out loud would change the facts. "I don't even remember being with her last night."

I stepped forward, voice flat. "There's blood on the sheets. On your shirt. Your hands are cut up. There's a claw mark across your back. You want to explain how that got here?"

Edward looked down at himself like he was seeing his own body for the first time. "I... I don't know."

Evelyn didn't speak. She just stared at him. Then slowly, she walked across the room, close enough to really look at her brother, really study him. His trembling hands. His eyes darting like a trapped animal. The pitiful, shamed posture of a man who didn't know what he'd done... but was starting to believe it was something awful.

She had seen him lie a hundred times growing up.

This wasn't one of them.

Philip's fists were still clenched, but his breathing had slowed. He, too, was watching Edward now, not with rage, but with a gut-deep fear he couldn't quite name. The kind you get when you realize the bomb already went off and you're just waiting for the shrapnel to hit you.

I opened my phone and held it out.

I didn't flinch. This was the moment the trap fully closed.

"Look."

The screen lit up with photos. Lydia's face, bloodied, bruised, and swollen. A deep red mark streaking her cheekbone. Another on her collarbone. Finger-shaped bruises on her upper arm. A hospital ID band was still around her wrist. One photo showed the imprint of a ring on her neck. Edward's class ring.

Philip leaned in, then recoiled as if he had tasted blood. "Jesus Christ..."

Evelyn covered her mouth. "No..."

"She's lying," Edward whispered, but even he didn't sound convinced.

Evelyn's voice was hollow. "She's not."

For a long moment, no one spoke.

Evelyn's gaze drifted past her brother, past the evidence, as if she could already see the headlines forming.

Then she closed her eyes, and when she opened them again, the rage was gone. Replaced with calculation. The gears had shifted. She was now seeing the bigger picture. The setup. The timing. The impossibility of proving innocence without blowing everything up.

"This was a hit job," she said finally. "A fucking political hit."

I didn't deny it.

That's when Ellie stepped forward.

Cold as the grave.

"You're right. And unless you play this exactly the way we tell you..." Her eyes found Evelyn's. "Your campaign is finished."

Evelyn turned on her like a viper. "This is extortion."

"No," Ellie said, smiling. "This is the game. Welcome to it."

"You're bluffing," Evelyn snapped. "You wouldn't dare take this public."

Ellie cocked her head. "You want to risk it? Let the press run wild with 'Ted Bright's son accused of rape'? Let your dad stand on that stage tonight while his youngest is in handcuffs?"

Philip looked at her, fury cooling into something worse: understanding. "So what's the deal?"

Ellie turned to me. "Landon Wolfe. Vice President."

Evelyn laughed. "Never. My father would never agree to that."

Ellie leaned in close. "Then I suggest you start packing. Because in about two hours, the police will be on their way to pick up Edward. And by tonight, your family's name will be radioactive."

Philip sat down; the fight drained out of him. Evelyn was still standing, still pretending to hold the high ground.

"You're disgusting," she spat at Ellie. "You staged this entire thing. You think you're some mastermind? You're just a sociopathic whore on a leash."

Ellie smiled. "And yet here you are. Begging for a leash of your own."

Evelyn lunged toward her, but I caught her arm.

"Don't," I warned. "You're already bleeding out politically. No need to go down with your pride too."

Evelyn jerked her arm away and stormed for the door. "This isn't over."

"It is if you want your father in the White House," I said.

She paused at the threshold, turned her head just enough to hiss, "Bastards."

The door slammed shut. I let out a long breath, turned to Edward, who looked like shell-shocked and small.

Silence settled, heavy as smoke. The kind that follows an explosion, when all that's left is ruin and victory.

"You'll be fine," I said to him. "Eventually. Probably."

He didn't reply.

I looked at Ellie. She looked back at me.

We didn't smile. We didn't need to.

The campaign was now ours.

"I like him," Ted said, his voice calm but carrying that familiar edge of resolve. He leaned forward, resting both palms on the table. "McCoy's a homegrown Georgia boy. Knows the ground, speaks the language. If he flips Atlanta and holds the suburbs. That's the race."

Rey Hughes let out a low whistle and grinned. "Been tellin' you, boss. Southern fight needs a Southern soldier. Hell, if we put River McCoy on the ticket, we build a wall from Atlanta to Denver. The South, The Rust Belt, they'll come home."

Ted nodded. "He's clean, tested, got pull with the unions. His rebuttal following the State of the Union earlier this year? Lit the whole rotunda on fire."

He turned to his aide. "Get him on the line. I want ten minutes with him."

The aide nodded, lifting his phone, but before he could dial, the doors to the suite exploded open. Evelyn entered like a bullet; face flushed, eyes blazing, heels clacking with purpose. Her presence sucked the oxygen from the room.

Ted straightened, surprised. "Evelyn. We were just—"

"Don't bother," she snapped. "Whatever plans you just made, you'll want to rip them up. We have a problem. A big one."

Ted blinked. "What are you talking about?"

Evelyn walked straight to the table and slapped her tablet down. "It's Edward."

Ted's confusion deepened. "What? What about Edward? What happened?"

Evelyn took a deep breath, then let it loose like a dagger. "Lydia Barnes. He attacked her. Or at least, that's what Wolfe and that bitch are saying."

The room froze.

Ted's mouth parted slightly, his voice dropping. "Attacked her?"

"They've set him up," Evelyn hissed. "Manipulated him. They've got photos, witnesses. Footage of them together. The bruises on her face? Practically made for the press. They're threatening to go to the police unless we do what they want."

"Jesus Christ," Rey muttered, standing. "This some kinda joke?"

"No joke," Evelyn said. "They've cornered us. And Wolfe, he's not bluffing. Lydia's in the hospital, making sure her face looks good on camera. We're being played, and it's working."

Rey's Southern drawl cracked through the room. "This campaign was a coronation, dammit. Now it's a hostage situation. That snake Wolfe just cut off our air."

Ted stumbled back into his seat like he'd been punched. He stared down, trying to absorb it. His hands trembled at the edge of the table for a second before he found a steadying grip. "Wolfe... did this? I am so confused."

Evelyn unlocked her tablet and slid it toward him. "This is what he's using to corner you. Lydia's face. The bruises. The narrative against Edward."

Rey's jaw tightened as he yanked out his phone. "I'm callin' Wolfe right now. Gonna put the fear of God in him, make sure he doesn't run to the goddamn cops."

Evelyn stepped in, arms crossed, her voice ice-cold. "Don't bother. I already know what he wants. He's given us an ultimatum."

Ted looked up, hollow. "What kind of ultimatum?"

"He wants to be your running mate," Evelyn said. "Vice president. No negotiations. You don't give it to him, they go to the cops, Edward gets arrested, and this campaign explodes on live television."

Silence roared in the room for a second, the kind of silence that marks the moment a life fractures along a single line.

Rey raised his voice. "You can't let that son of a bitch in, Ted. You do that, he owns your presidency. You hand him power now, you never get it back."

Ted stood up, rage rising from his chest. "Do you think I don't know that?! My son's looking at prison time. My campaign, our entire strategy, dead in the water. You think I want this? I'm out of fucking options!"

He turned, slamming his palm against the table. "Landon Wolfe. That bastard's been waiting in the shadows like a parasite, feeding off this campaign." His voice rose with every word. "He's not a politician, he's a predator. A vulture. Sitting there with that self-serving face, waiting for something to rot so he can pick at the bones."

He took a step back, hands on his hips, breathing hard. "And now he wants the vice presidency? Fine. But let's not pretend this is about public service. This is about him staging his coronation. Grandstanding at its fucking finest."

Rey stepped forward. "Ted, listen to me. You let Wolfe in; you'll never sit at the head of your own table again. He'll gut this administration from the inside. That man's unstable. I still think he killed Vazquez."

Ted's head dropped into his hands. He let out a growl that was half-sob, half-scream. "God damn it, Edward. I've spent half my life cleaning up that boy's messes. DUI in Boston. The staffer in D.C. Now this."

Evelyn didn't miss a beat. "You should've cut him loose before the campaign even started. I told you he'd be a liability."

Ted looked up. "That is your brother. My son. You're not helping."

He pivoted, pointing a trembling finger at Rey. "And you! I pay you a fortune to keep this shit from happening."

Rey didn't flinch. "I underestimated Wolfe and Ms. Barnes. Thought we had the board locked. I didn't see this move coming, and I should've."

A long, tense silence. Then, a knock at the door.

A staffer leaned in. "Sir," he said quietly, "I just got off the phone with the Senate leadership team. If you pick McCoy, we lose his seat. It's not guaranteed to stay blue, not with a special election on the horizon."

Ted didn't move.

The aide continued. "With you out of the Senate, and McCoy gone too... we lose the majority. We'd be handing Congress to the Republicans before we even swear you in."

Ted let out a slow, humorless laugh; the sound of a man realizing the chessboard's pieces were not his to move.

Ted closed his eyes. "Christ. So we don't even get to govern if we win."

"And Wolfe?" the aide added. "He doesn't cost us a seat."

Evelyn glared toward the door. "He's probably sitting somewhere right now, smug as hell, waiting for us to make the call."

Rey scoffed. "Hell of a game he's playin'. Blackmailing his way into the White House."

Ted turned to the entire room. His voice was ice. "Nobody leaks a fucking word. If even a whisper of this gets out, Wolfe's ready to go scorched earth. That man's dangerous. And right now, he's got us by the balls."

He looked at Rey.

"Set up the meeting," Ted said, voice barely above a whisper. "Bring Wolfe to me."

14

Cancer on the Presidency

September 2028

The relentless humidity that had gripped Washington through August had finally broken. A torrential downpour swept across the capital, hammering Pennsylvania Avenue and churning the lawn of the White House into thick, black mud. Thunder cracked across the skyline like a warning bell. Inside the West Wing, the storm barely registered; something worse had arrived.

Nancy Johnson, the White House Press Secretary, moved fast through the marble halls. She was normally composed, one of the few unflappable voices in an administration addicted to optics. But tonight, her blazer clung to her from sweat and rain, her heels clicked with more purpose than polish, and the lines beneath her eyes seemed to deepen with every step.

She didn't bother knocking when she reached the Chief of Staff's office, just pushed through the door and locked eyes with Chuck Albert. He was alone, standing near the far wall, looking out the window, watching the storm.

"Nancy?" he asked, surprised by the urgency on her face. "What's going on?"

She stopped just short of him, catching her breath. "We've got a problem."

He raised a brow, already calculating. "What type of problem?"

Nancy pulled her phone from her pocket, tapped the screen, and held it up. "Ruben Leon just sent me the courtesy preview."

Chuck squinted. A *Washington Post* article, still in draft mode, stared back at him. The headline was a missile.

White House Linked To Florida Money Laundering Scheme.

He didn't speak, just took the phone and read.

The article, scheduled to publish at midnight, alleged that during President Hayden's final term as Florida governor, a covert network of political appointees and contractors siphoned millions from public infrastructure projects into off-the-books accounts. The funds were laundered through a shell nonprofit, *The Florida Growth Initiative,* and distributed across a web of LLCs tied to allies of Hayden's administration. Several sources, including internal emails, claimed portions of the stolen funds were funneled into a super PAC that kickstarted Hayden's 2024 presidential campaign.

Chuck's name was mentioned several times. Not just as a participant, but as the architect.

Nancy crossed her arms tightly. "It drops in less than three hours."

Chuck finally looked up. His voice was hoarse. "How much do they have?"

"Enough to kill the reelection. Maybe the presidency."

He ran a hand down his face. "They stop short of a criminal accusation?"

"They don't have to say it outright," she said. "But they've got paper trails, bank records, an ex-state official on the record. The implication is clear, Hayden knew. And you? You ran the whole thing."

Chuck nodded once, slowly. "They're not wrong."

Nancy flinched. "You're admitting it?"

"It was 2020," Chuck said quietly. "We were locked down. The economy was shot, and tourism had all but vanished. The legislature had just approved a massive recovery bill. It was chaos; there was no oversight and no press. I diverted surplus funding from infrastructure delays into side accounts. Quietly. Legally ambiguous at worst."

"And you funneled that into the campaign?"

"Not directly. I used nonprofits, LLCs. Half the country does it. The FEC won't touch it."

"But you *did* do it."

Chuck exhaled slowly. "Hayden needed a runway. We were hemorrhaging support after the pandemic response. If we didn't start building his national profile by '21, he never would've survived the primaries."

Nancy's voice was rising now. "You stole public money."

"I repurposed it."

"That's not a defense, Chuck, that's a felony."

He turned away from her, gripping the back of a chair. The thunder rolled again.

Nancy stepped closer. "How much did he know?"

There was a long pause. Chuck's jaw flexed. "He knew the nonprofit existed. He knew it was helping the campaign. But I never told him where the money came from. He didn't ask."

"So he can claim ignorance."

"No," Chuck said. "He can claim distance. But not innocence."

Nancy's face hardened. "The headline will do damage whether he's guilty or not. You understand that, right?"

Chuck nodded. "It's my mess. I'll take the fall."

"You don't get to be a martyr," Nancy snapped. "This isn't about you anymore. The president will be dragged in front of cameras, accused of robbing the state he governed. You really think the voters will care that he only skimmed a little off the top?"

Chuck said nothing. Outside, lightning lit the window like a strobe.

"What do we do?" She said sternly.

Chuck turned finally, his face drawn but resolved. "We protect the president."

"That's not a plan," she shot back. "That's a mission statement."

He didn't flinch. "It's all we've got."

"What do I say to the press?" she asked, her voice tight. "What do we tell Hayden?"

Chuck Albert didn't hesitate. "You say nothing."

He didn't raise his voice, but the words carried weight. He began pacing across the room, composed, though the storm outside paled in comparison to the one inside his chest.

"The president is my responsibility," he continued. "He's wheels-down in Indianapolis. As soon as I can get through to him, I'll tell him."

Nancy's expression darkened. "The Democrats will come for him."

Chuck dismissed it with a wave. "They control the Senate, not the House. And the House is ours. The GOP won't impeach their sitting president in an election year; not unless we give them a reason they can't ignore."

Nancy wasn't convinced. "Public pressure's going to mount. And fast. People don't forget when their former governor stole from them. Florida is going to burn."

Chuck narrowed his eyes. "That's the real crisis. If we lose Florida, we lose the map. Without those electoral votes, our path to reelection gets thin. *Real thin.*"

"So we get ahead of it. We control what we can." Nancy said, her voice cooling.

Chuck nodded slowly. "Containment. Clarity. No one talks to the press. No off-the-record comments. We drown this thing in message discipline."

She glanced at the clock on the wall. 9:07 PM.

"Ruben's story hits at midnight. But we weren't the only ones who got the preview. Donors are going to panic. Bright will hammer us for answers, and every reporter in the Beltway will be circling this place like vultures by dawn."

"We keep moving. We work the problem. Shape the narrative," Chuck said, like a general preparing for battle.

She hesitated, then nodded. "This story isn't a flare-up, Chuck. It is going to consume everything."

"A cancer on the presidency," he said quietly.

She walked toward the door. "We're running out of time."

Chuck Albert, Chief of Staff to the President of the United States, didn't flinch. He turned his back to the room and squared his shoulders, already bracing for the storm ahead.

"We always are."

The Jefferson Hotel smelled like antique power; leather chairs, old books, and the ghosts of every deal ever struck behind closed doors. The private suite wasn't large, but it was secluded, sealed from the press and the public. That's what mattered now. Privacy. Plausible deniability.

Lydia stood near the corner, not to hide, but to survey. Detached. Composed. Like a commander studying the battlefield after the first volley.

A clock on the mantle clicked once; in that small sound everything seemed to tilt.

"He took the deal. Ten years."

I didn't flinch.

For a moment my hands looked foreign in my lap; I studied the veins as if they belonged to someone else.

I expected him to. We'd built a wall of evidence around him so airtight, a jury wasn't even necessary. The man didn't stand a chance. Worked at the Conrad Hilton. No alibi. Right complexion. Right background. Wrong place, wrong time. That's all it took. The machine needed a sacrifice, and we fed it.

Terry straightened from the wall like a spring snapping loose.

"You mean he confessed?" His voice was tight and controlled, but the fury was already there, bubbling under the surface.

Lydia didn't look at him. "His public defender pushed for a plea deal. Said a trial would make things worse. With time served, he might be out in seven."

"He's not guilty," Terry said, louder now. "And you know that."

"That's not the point," I muttered. "The campaign needed resolution. The press needed someone to crucify. Now they have their man."

The words hung between us, thin and bright, like a glass shard.

Terry laughed, short, sharp, and bitter. "So an innocent Black man goes to prison and you call that *resolution?"*

"Politics," I said. Like it was self-explanatory. Because it was.

Terry's voice cracked. "You always say that like it absolves you," he snapped. "Like 'politics' is the magic word that makes it okay to ruin lives. You used him. Just like you used Vazquez. Just like you use all of us."

I didn't flinch. "Careful, Terry. You're walking close to a line you can't uncross."

"I've already crossed it," he shot back. "You speak about justice like it's a talking point. I *live* it. Every time I walk into a room, every time I talk to voters who look like me and believe we can still make this country better; I *live* it."

He pointed toward the door, toward the world outside.

"And now I have to live with the fact that I sent one of my own to rot in a cell so you two," he gestured to me and Lydia, "could keep your hands clean. But they're not clean, Landon. No one's is."

He looked down at his palms, like he could still feel the weight of the guilt settling into his skin. "They're covered in something I can't wash off."

Lydia stepped forward. "Terry—"

"No. Don't. Don't tell me he'll be pardoned. Don't promise me he won't serve the full ten. You can't know that. You *don't* know that. And even if he does get out, it doesn't change what we did to him."

Ellie shifted in her seat but said nothing. Lydia's eyes flicked toward me for reassurance, but I gave her none. Terry's words weren't a surprise. This had been building for weeks.

"We did what had to be done," I said, low and hard. "If that's too much for you, then maybe this game isn't for you."

My voice sounded smaller than the sentence. Terry heard that.

He turned to me, eyes burning. "This isn't a game. This is a man's life. And you're not a leader, you're a fucking executioner."

I stepped toward him now, closing the space. "You want to walk away? Fine. But don't pretend like you didn't know what this was. You made your choice the day you stayed silent about Vazquez."

"I was wrong," he said, voice trembling with fury. "But I won't stay wrong."

"You leak this," Lydia said, stepping forward, her voice steeled, "and it's not just your career that ends. You understand that, right?"

The threat sat in the air like a physical thing; you could feel its weight.

"Go ahead," he said. "Try it. Ruin me. Kill me if you have to. But I'm not going to be part of this machine anymore. I won't be another piece in your corrupt little puzzle."

He turned toward Ellie. "You're really staying with them?"

She didn't move. Didn't blink. That was her answer.

Terry let out a breath, like something inside him had finally broken.

I watched him step to the door, but not before he looked at me one last time.

"I believed in you. God help me, I really did."

And then he was gone.

I didn't say anything at first. Just stared at the door, still swinging slightly from how hard he'd slammed it.

The room seemed to inhale after he left, the momentum of his departure pulling the air in with it.

Lydia sat down slowly. "He'll talk."

"No, he won't," I said. "He's afraid of us—afraid of what we can do. He'll disappear. We'll never hear from him again."

Ellie finally spoke, her voice low. "We keep losing people."

I didn't respond. That wasn't the point.

Winning isn't about who you lose.

It's about who you control.

Terry had always been a choice. He just didn't know it until tonight.

And now he'd made it.

Rey Hughes slapped the Friday *Washington Post* onto the polished table like he was laying down a royal flush.

"Well, now ain't that somethin'?" he drawled. "This little beauty oughta hand you the keys to the White House on a silver platter."

Bold black letters screamed across the front page: **WHITE HOUSE LINKED TO FLORIDA MONEY LAUNDERING SCHEME.**

Ted didn't flinch. He just leaned back in his chair, lips twitching into a grin. "I believe you're right, Rey. This could very well secure us the presidency."

Hughes was the nuclear option. Former right hand to President Hayden, exiled but not powerless, now reborn as Ted's secret weapon. He was all Southern charm and sharpened instincts; a fox dressed for the derby. And now that fox had delivered a carcass to our doorstep. Hayden was bleeding out in the headlines. Our path forward had never looked so clear, and never felt so dangerous.

As we filed into the strategy room in Virginia, the air was thick with that too-bright light and the smell of brewing hostility. The Bright family stood near the window: Ted, Evelyn, and Philip. Edward was nowhere to be seen, likely too ashamed or too furious to face any of us. The tension in the room was stretched so tight that it could snap at a whisper.

Rey gave a little nod to the empty seat beside me. "Looks like y'all are short one man today."

"Terry's moved on," I said flatly. That was all they were getting.

Ted lifted the paper again, admiring it like it belonged in the Smithsonian. "Rey has delivered *me* the Oval Office," he said.

Me.

Not us.

Not the campaign.

Not the country.

Just me.

Lydia, sitting beside me, didn't flinch. Her voice came steady and even. "This is huge, no doubt. But Rey, you do realize this could come back to bite you. If the feds start pulling threads—"

"Ain't nothin' to pull," Hughes interrupted with a lazy wave. "All that's left is loose yarn."

"This could lead to prison," she pressed.

Rey just grinned wider. "Hell, if I gotta do time, I'll take a suite at Club Fed with a view. Course, I imagine a future President Bright might be inclined to *pardon* an old friend."

The wink he shot Ted made my stomach turn.

"You knew the laundering was happening. Played a role," Lydia continued.

"Played a role? Darlin', I *engineered* it. That story claims the campaign stopped using stolen funds after the primaries. Bullshit. We spent that money until Hayden took the oath."

"So if it was you who orchestrated the slush fund, why does the story pin it only on Chuck Albert?" Ellie asked, although she already knew the answer.

"Because Chuck always had Hayden's ear. Thought he knew what was best for the governor," Hughes replied. "I just whispered into it. He was hesitant at first, but once he got a taste of that money? He couldn't stop. It's hard to let go of the tit that feeds ya."

I felt the table tilt beneath me, not literally, but politically. We were dancing in the aftermath of a political kill shot, and Ted was holding the gun.

Ted finally cleared his throat, folding the paper with surgical precision. "Alright. Enough celebration. Let's talk next steps."

It was subtle, but I felt the shift. Ted wasn't asking us. He was directing us.

We moved through messaging strategy, polling reactions, ad pivots, surrogate deployment. Ted listened more than he spoke, but every word he did offer was weighted, deliberate. His voice was cooler than usual. Not arrogant, commanding.

Then came the pivot.

"I've asked Philip to take a closer role overseeing media operations," he said, casually, like it was nothing.

My jaw didn't move, but something twisted in my gut. That had been Lydia's lane. Ours. Philip had always been the least threatening of the Brights, more finance than fire. But now he wasn't just a brother lurking on the sidelines. He was the new watchdog. Ted's eyes and ears inside the machine we worked so hard to invade.

Lydia stiffened. "Excuse me?"

Ted's gaze didn't even flick to her. "We've had inconsistencies in rollout. Philip's going to bring cohesion."

Lydia looked at me, but I didn't speak. I was still registering the power play.

"And Evelyn," Ted continued, nodding toward her like a general acknowledging his best lieutenant, "will oversee briefing prep for debates and interviews."

Evelyn beamed. "I'm putting together a new rapid response structure. Something tighter. More agile. We'll share a plan by end of day."

And there it was. The poison under the handshake.

That had been my domain—after the convention. Once Chicago wrapped and the real war began, Ted brought me in to hone the message. Not to make him presidential, he'd already earned the nomination on his own, but to reinforce it. I handled the briefings, the prep, the shaping of answers under fire. He was the candidate. I just made sure he didn't bleed on camera.

Now I was being handed a muzzle and a folding chair while the Bright children circled the ring.

"Who signed off on this?" Lydia asked coolly.

Ted finally looked at her. "I did."

The room chilled. Ted hadn't even raised his voice.

Control wasn't seized. It was *assumed,* just like that.

"I hope we're all clear moving forward," Ted said, standing. "We can't afford divided lanes anymore. The stakes are too high."

It was a rebuke without theatrics. And a warning shot meant for Lydia and me.

Lydia rose, brushing past Evelyn on her way to the hallway. Evelyn, naturally, couldn't help herself. "Funny how something as basic as a delegate memo turns into an unsolvable mystery under *your* watch."

Lydia froze.

Then, she turned slowly. "Funny how someone with no real job title keeps pretending she has one."

Evelyn smiled, wide and cruel. "Oh, Lydia. You've been gunning for me since day one. And I've finally figured out why."

"Oh, please."

"No, really. It's not just because you hate me. It's because you see yourself when you look at me. We're cut from the same designer cloth. Hiding behind Daddy's name. Daddy's money. Daddy's influence. The only difference? I never pretended I earned it."

Lydia's fists clenched. "We are *nothing* alike."

"We are *exactly* alike. Except by November, I'll be First Daughter. And you? You'll be the VP's footnote. Maybe his mistake."

The temperature dropped ten degrees.

Lydia didn't blink. "At least people remember my name. You're just a socialite in a pantsuit."

Evelyn's smile curdled. "And you're a cautionary tale in stilettos."

They stood nose-to-nose for a beat too long.

I stood. "Enough."

The room fell silent. My voice didn't shake, but the control I thought I had? It was gone.

I turned to Ted. "Apologies. That won't happen again."

Ted gave a tight nod. Nothing more.

Evelyn, of course, added one last barb. "Keep your staff in check, Landon. You're starting to look sloppy."

As the room shifted back to logistics and polling data, I realized something I hadn't wanted to admit until now:

Ted Bright had taken back the wheel.

And we were just along for the ride.

15

The Eye of the Storm

September 2028

The House chamber simmered with heat, not from the chandeliers or the summer sun, but from the rage, calculation, and uncertainty coiling between its rows. Beneath the arches and carved woodwork of one of America's most storied rooms, democracy was not in motion—it was in crisis.

President Norman Hayden was now at the center of the largest financial scandal since Watergate. They called it *Publicgate.* Millions were stolen from state infrastructure funds while he was governor of Florida; the money was funneled into shell corporations, laundered through offshore accounts, and allegedly used to build the very fortune that catapulted him into the White House.

The revelations were damning. And yet, the question before the House wasn't legal. It was constitutional. Political. Existential.

Grace Randolph, Republican of Wisconsin, stepped into that fire with steady resolve.

"Madam Speaker," she said, her voice clear over the hum of side conversations and rustling papers. "This is not about party. This is about the law."

The silence that followed was sharp and temporary.

Randolph stood tall, shoulders back, jaw set, her words slicing through the chamber. "President Hayden orchestrated a criminal scheme that siphoned millions from public works and pocketed the proceeds. It doesn't matter *when* it happened. What matters is what it says about the man in office."

Murmurs turned to groans. A low growl began to build from her side of the aisle. "RINO." "Traitor." "Sellout."

But Randolph didn't flinch. The Speaker gaveled once, more for appearance than enforcement, and let the chaos bubble. Randolph kept speaking.

"The Constitution does not demand that a crime be committed in office for it to warrant impeachment. It demands we consider the nature of the offense, and the danger it poses to the republic."

Congressman Clint Hayes, Republican from Indiana and a loyal Hayden ally, rose next. His movements were practiced, almost theatrical.

"Let's be clear," Hayes said, palms open in a performative calm. "The president stands accused of wrongdoing committed *before* his term as president began. He is not accused of abusing the office; he is accused of misconduct before he held it. We are not a court. We are a Congress. And we do not retroactively punish men for past sins once the people have spoken at the ballot box."

Hayes's voice dropped an octave. "Do we really want to establish a precedent where every election is subject to post-facto judicial review by the House majority?"

Some clapped. Some scoffed. Most just leaned in.

On the Democratic side, Congressman Jake Harrison of New York surged to his feet.

"He didn't just 'sin'," Harrison barked. "He laundered money to fund the very empire that launched his presidency. He bought the illusion of success. He corrupted the foundation of his public life. That's not irrelevant. That's the root of this administration."

The Speaker banged her gavel harder this time, but it only seemed to stroke the fires.

Randolph rose again, now without waiting for permission.

"Every day we delay accountability," she said, "we signal to the American people that there are two sets of laws, one for the powerful, and one for the rest of us. If Hayden were a mayor or a school board member, he'd be under indictment already. But because he's *president?"*

Hayes stood again, already shaking his head.

"We are not prosecutors, Congresswoman. We are not judge and jury. And we are not in the business of punishing political allies or enemies for pre-office misconduct."

A slow, deliberate voice cut through the chaos. It was Junior Williams, Democrat from Arizona. Measured. Legalistic.

"Let me remind the chamber," Williams said, "that *Publicgate* may not be over. Yes, the laundered funds primarily trace to Hayden's time as governor. But are we certain none of that network carried over into his current campaign?"

The chamber quieted. The suggestion landed like a weight.

Williams continued. "The Chief of Staff has resigned. The president's own foundation is under audit. We are only beginning to understand the scope. If any of those illicit funds were used in the 2028 campaign, then we're not just talking about the past. We're talking about an active subversion of our electoral system."

The silence held for a long beat.

Finally, Randolph stepped forward one last time.

"You don't have to like me. You don't have to agree with me. But you do have to answer this question honestly: if the presidency becomes a safe haven from prosecution, if it becomes a reward for criminal success, then what kind of nation are we becoming?"

Her eyes scanned her own caucus. Some couldn't meet her gaze.

"History is watching."

As the debate dragged on, the chamber teetered between fury and paralysis. The lines were no longer clearly partisan. The issue wasn't just *if* Hayden broke the law. It was whether Congress had the courage, or the political will, to do anything about it.

And as the shouting resumed, it was clear: the scandal wasn't the only thing unraveling.

So was the unity of the Republican Party.

And perhaps the presidency itself.

The illusion that Ted Bright was ever in control disappeared the moment I turned onto the spiraling driveway outside Dallas. This wasn't his campaign. It belonged to the man waiting at the top of the hill, and Ted had just sent me to kneel before him.

For three weeks, the Bright family had been watching me like I was some kind of political virus; contained, but not cured. No unsupervised moves. No rogue plays. Ted had started locking the doors I used to walk through freely.

Today, he sent a message: I was to take a meeting in Texas. Alone. No staff, no Lydia. Just me and the man who really bankrolled this campaign.

While Ted was out in Florida, shaking hands, kissing babies, pretending to be the second coming of FDR, he wasn't just campaigning. He was circling the ruins of Hayden's presidency like a vulture, hoping to claim whatever was left of the political flesh *Publicgate* had burned away. Meanwhile, I was being dispatched to the lion's den.

They said it was a donor visit.

But I wasn't born yesterday.

This wasn't about money.

It was about reminding me where the power lived, and where it didn't.

Duane Dyer's estate sat like a fortress on the edge of Oakwood Heights; three gates, private security, and enough square footage to house a battalion. The car dropped me at the front circle, and the doors opened before I even knocked.

A butler with dead eyes led me through marble corridors and gold-plated arrogance until we reached a den lined with leather, oil paintings, and the smell of cigars that cost more than my first car.

Dyer didn't get up when I walked in.

"Landon Wolfe," he said, lounging in an armchair that looked like it had been pulled off a plantation. "So you're the pretty face Ted picked for the number two slot."

I forced a handshake. Dyer's grip was limp. Disinterested. "Mr. Dyer. Appreciate you making the time."

"I didn't make time," he said flatly, waving me to the chair across from him. "Ted sent you. That's the only reason you're here."

He poured two glasses of bourbon and pushed one toward me. I didn't touch it.

"You don't drink with me?" he said, raising a brow.

"I don't drink," I replied. "Especially not with people I don't respect."

His mouth curled into a smirk. "Recovering?"

"Ten years."

He nodded. "Same boat. Hard thing to quit."

He took a sip of his own glass anyway.

For a moment, he just studied me—the faint smile, the lazy swirl of bourbon—the quiet arrogance of a man used to buying obedience.

"Ted's boy has teeth, that's cute," he said, tipping the glass just enough for the amber to catch the light. "Thinking you don't have to respect me."

The words rolled across the room like smoke. I could feel him testing me, measuring what kind of animal he'd been sent.

"I'm not Ted's boy."

"Sure you are," he said, eyes dancing with condescension. He leaned forward, the smirk deepening. "I was shocked, to say the least, when Ted picked you. But when we talked, he had nothing but praise. Said you had potential. Potential to do great things. The type of potential I can work with."

I leaned in, voice steady. "You didn't drag me down here for flattery. So let's stop wasting time."

He chuckled. "I like you. A little fire. That'll burn out eventually, but enjoy it while it lasts."

He paused there, letting the weight of his words linger, watching for cracks. When none came, his tone shifted; slower, heavier.

Then he said it, plain and proud:

"When that Publicgate story broke, I nearly broke out champagne. You have *no idea* how long I've been waiting for that bastard Hayden to hang himself."

I gave a polite nod. A performance. Always a performance. "It was quite the bombshell."

He cocked his head. "That's it? Not celebrating?"

"It'll have consequences, sure. But I don't think it's the golden ticket Ted thinks it is."

His eyebrows lifted, amused. "Enlighten me."

I took a slow breath, buying half a second. He wanted spectacle; I'd give him analysis.

"Scandals don't move the needle like they used to. Voters are numb. They expect corruption. They expect rot. We give them another round of shock and outrage, and by next week, it's gone." I paused. "What worries me isn't Hayden's dirty laundry. It's what he's doing, or not doing, overseas."

Dyer leaned back, bored. "Let me guess. The Solomons."

"Jonas Taneoka has taken power. Chinese warships are off the coast. The SLF is sweeping through the islands with Beijing's blessing. And our president's sitting on his hands, letting it happen."

"Because it's a nothing island," Dyer said, waving it off like he was swatting a gnat. "Let them have it."

I stared at him, trying to decide if he was stupid or just greedy.

"And next time it's Micronesia? Or Taiwan?"

He took another sip. "Pissing off the Chinese isn't smart. It's not good diplomacy. And more importantly, it's not good for business."

There it was. The real sermon. The one he didn't even realize he was preaching.

I sat back in my chair, staring at him. "You mean your business."

He didn't flinch. "Bright's entire economic platform will fix what Hayden broke. He's already promised to remove the tariffs, open the trade routes, get our markets breathing again. And if that means letting China play king in the Pacific, well, that's the price of peace, son."

The word *son* landed like a slap, deliberate and smug.

I clenched my jaw. "That's not peace. It's Appeasement 101. You give a bully one island, they'll want the rest of the archipelago."

"Maybe," he said. "But war tanks the stock market. My companies, hell, *dozens* of American businesses, have poured billions into this campaign. We're not paying for brinkmanship. We're paying for normalcy."

I looked down at my untouched glass. The bourbon caught the light, perfectly still, the way power always looks when it thinks it's untouchable.

Lydia's voice echoed in the back of my mind; her bargain for power, her own reasons for wanting me in the Oval Office. Different industry. Same story. War and business. Two sides of the same coin.

Dyer leaned forward, now fully in command.

"Ted told me you'd want a say in the Solomons. Told me you'd think it's your chance to lead on something. But you're not here to lead. You're here to listen."

Something in my chest tightened. That was the moment I realized I wasn't a guest, I was an employee.

That's why I was in Dallas. Not to negotiate. Not to advise.

But to be *told*.

"Ted's doing what's best for the campaign," Dyer continued. "And what's best for the campaign is doing what I tell him to do. You get that, right?"

I didn't answer. Silence was the only weapon I had left in that room.

"You've got your title. You've got your face on the ticket. Smile, wave, say the right things. That's your lane. Stay in it."

My hands were clenched in my lap. Not in fear, but in fury.

Because I could feel it now, how deeply the rot had gone. How hollow the man at the top truly was.

Ted Bright didn't bring me into the fold. He handed me over. Offered me like tribute to the donor class. The boys who run the world from leather chairs and quiet rooms.

And the worst part?

He thought I'd stay silent.

He thought I'd just smile.

But that's the mistake men like Duane Dyer always make.

They confuse silence with submission.

They forget what happens when you push a man with nothing left to lose.

16

A War of Words

The Presidential Debate

Ted Bright stood in front of the mirror in his Cleveland hotel suite, adjusting the American flap pin on his lapel with the precision of a man who knew the cameras would capture every twitch, every blink, every bead of sweat. His baby-blue tie, the same shade he'd worn for every major speech since his Denver days, was tied tight in a Windsor knot. He smoothed the front of his navy jacket, eyes narrowing as he studied his reflection.

He didn't see a man about to debate the President of the United States.

He saw a kid from Colorado who'd clawed his way from city hall to the Capitol, who'd taken on bigger names with more money and thicker Rolodexes, and beat them all. And now, just two hours away from the first and only presidential debate of the campaign, he was staring down the biggest name of all: Norman Hayden.

The bathroom door creaked open behind him.

"You're going to wear a hole in that lapel," Gwen said, stepping inside with a smile that was soft and familiar. Her presence always calmed the static in his chest. She walked up behind him, looping her arms around his waist and resting her head against his back.

"How do I look?" Ted asked, turning to face her. He was smiling, but there was a flicker of uncertainty in his eyes. "Do I look like the next President of the United States?"

"You look like my husband," Gwen said, smoothing his jacket with the same gentle hands that had held him through victories and scandals, heartbreak and triumph. "Which means you're already everything you need to be."

Ted chuckled under his breath, forehead resting against hers. "You remember that night in Denver? The night we stayed up counting precincts until the sun came up?"

"You mean the night I nearly had a panic attack watching you lose Jefferson County?" she grinned. "Yeah, I remember."

"And now here we are."

Her eyes flickered with pride, and fear. She knew the weight of this moment better than anyone. She had carried it with Ted for thirty-five years.

"You were born for this," she whispered. "No matter what happens tonight, don't forget who you are. You earned this."

A soft knock broke their moment. Then the door opened.

Evelyn entered first, composed as always, dressed in a slate-gray power suit. Philip and Edward trailed behind, both in tailored jackets and serious expressions. Alyssa and Pat, the two in-law children, followed, and then came Rey Hughes, wearing a seersucker blazer and chewing a toothpick as if it were a matter of national security.

The room shifted instantly; private intimacy giving way to political machinery.

"You good, Dad?" Evelyn asked. She gave him a quick once-over, always the strategist.

"I'm good," Ted said, squeezing Gwen's hand one last time before letting go.

Philip was adjusting his cufflinks. "Don't let Hayden bait you. He'll try to come off like the wise old statesman. Just stay on message."

Edward chimed in with more energy. "He's a walking scandal, Dad. That's your opening. Don't let him control the tempo."

Pat crossed his arms. "Speaking of, what's your angle on Publicgate?"

The room went still. Gwen's eyes flicked to Ted's, her expression tightening.

Ted opened his mouth, but Rey spoke first, voice syrupy with his Louisiana drawl.

"Ol' Hayden tried to back outta this whole thing," Rey said, sauntering forward. "Told the network if they, or we, brought up Publicgate, he'd walk."

"He tried to cancel the debate?" Edward blinked. "Over that?"

"He didn't want it mentioned," Rey said, toothpick twitching between his teeth. "Told the moderator. Told the campaign. Tried to make it a condition."

"And you agreed?" Evelyn asked sharply, eyes narrowing.

"We agreed to get him on that stage," Rey said, his grin widening. "Didn't agree to keep our mouths shut once the lights came on."

Ted sighed, rubbing his temples. "I gave my word, Rey."

Rey raised an eyebrow. "You gave your word to get the President on a stage. Not to play the role of his defense attorney."

The room buzzed with rising energy. Philip stepped closer. "If you don't bring it up, he wins. That scandal is our edge. You *have* to go there."

"He'll spin it," Ted said. "Say it's all political. Say we're desperate."

"He can say whatever he wants," Edward shot back. "But the people are watching. And they're waiting for *you* to speak for them."

Ted looked at Gwen. She didn't say a word. Just nodded.

He exhaled slowly, eyes fixed on the table, letting the decision settle before he gave it voice.

"We bring it up," Ted said finally, his voice firm. "But we're surgical. Sharp. Clean. One hit. We don't let it define the night."

Rey clapped his hands once. "That's what I like to hear. Let's make the man sweat."

The tone in the room shifted. What had started as anxiety now bristled with purpose. This wasn't just about a debate anymore. It was about shaping the future of the campaign, maybe even the country.

As they gathered their things, Ted paused once more in front of the mirror.

He straightened his tie and tightened his jaw.

He was no longer the man who'd stood here twenty minutes ago, searching his reflection for confidence.

He was the candidate now. The fighter. The one who would face Norman Hayden with a nation watching.

Rey clapped him on the back, the grin never leaving his face.

"Remember, Teddy boy," he said. "You don't win a war of words by stayin' quiet."

Ted nodded, his voice low and resolved.

"Let's go win the war."

The tension in the Rock and Roll Hall of Fame buzzed beneath the lights, crackling behind the eyes of the audience, sparking in the fingers of those clutching their programs. The stage was sleek and dark, lit only by two podiums set before an American flag that spanned the width of the backdrop. It was a temple of modern democracy, the drums and guitars behind glass replaced for one night by politics, ambition, and the weight of the nation.

David Kessler, the silver-haired anchor of *Democracy Now News,* stood center stage. His voice was smooth, composed, and polished with years of primetime gravitas.

"Good evening, America," Kessler began. "Tonight, live from Cleveland's Rock and Roll Hall of Fame, we witness democracy in action. Two candidates. One stage. One nation deciding its future. Let us begin."

A swell of restrained applause filled the hall.

"President Norman Hayden, you have the floor for your opening remarks."

President Hayden stepped forward, unhurried, his posture straight as an iron beam. The cameras caught the controlled blink of his eye, the subtle nod before he spoke.

"Thank you, David," Hayden began, his baritone voice echoing with practiced cadence. "Four years ago, the American people asked for change. And we delivered. We revived an economy on the brink, rebuilt industries that had been hollowed out by globalization, and put American workers, not bureaucrats, not special interests back at the center of our national agenda."

He paused, letting the words settle.

"Through strategic tariffs and fairer trade deals, we've rebalanced a global system that once punished our middle class. We brought manufacturing jobs home. We made America first—again. And we're just getting started."

Muted applause followed. The supporters in the audience were careful not to violate the debate rules. The rest of the room stayed frozen, studying every breath, every blink.

Kessler turned smoothly. "Senator Bright, your opening statement."

Ted Bright approached the podium like a prosecutor at the start of closing arguments. He didn't smile. He didn't blink. His voice cut clean through the silence.

"Thank you, David. Mr. President," he nodded briefly toward Hayden. "America has heard these talking points before. We've heard about tariffs and 'putting America first.' But let's talk about who paid the price."

He shifted his weight, now leaning into the microphone.

"Those tariffs? They didn't punish China. They punished Ohio farmers. They punished Michigan manufacturers. The cost of everyday goods rose while real wages stagnated. Families are paying more for groceries, appliances, cars, and they're told it's progress."

Hayden didn't react, but his jaw tightened.

Bright pressed on. "And now we face a deeper question. One not about policy, but character. Mr. President, you speak of transparency, of restoring trust. But there's a scandal you won't talk about. One that goes to the very heart of your administration's integrity."

The temperature in the room shifted. It was like someone cracked a window in winter.

"I'm talking about Publicgate."

The words dropped like a hammer.

"You've dodged questions, fired whistleblowers, and hidden behind legal technicalities. The American people deserve to know why public money, *their money,* was funneled into shell nonprofits tied to your campaign efforts. Why your former chief of staff, Mr. Albert, is under federal investigation. And why you've refused to cooperate with a full independent inquiry."

For the first time, Hayden turned toward him. His expression was unreadable, but the steel in his eyes said everything.

Kessler, ever the arbiter, stepped in. "President Hayden, this is the first time you've been directly challenged on Publicgate in a public forum. Would you like to respond?"

Hayden inhaled, slow and deliberate. "David, these allegations are politically motivated. Every administration faces smear campaigns in an election year; mine is no different. My team has followed the law. We've cooperated with the Department of Justice, and there has been *no* indictment. No charges. Just headlines from the same media echo chamber that's been against me since day one."

He shifted, his voice sharpening. "What Senator Bright is doing tonight is deflecting from his own lack of a coherent agenda. He'd rather talk scandal than substance. The people of this country want jobs, security, and leadership, not recycled attacks."

Bright stepped in again, crisp and immediate. "With respect, Mr. President, there's nothing recycled about corruption. When taxpayer dollars are misused to benefit your political machine, that's not noise, it's a betrayal."

The crowd rustled. A few in the press pit leaned forward in their seats. Kessler raised a hand.

"Gentlemen, let's move forward—"

But Hayden cut in, his voice calm, but cold.

"I'll remind my opponent that *his* campaign benefited from one of those so-called nonprofits in 2020 when he ran for Senate. But perhaps his memory only works when the cameras are on."

A flash of reaction swept the audience. Bright gripped the edge of the podium.

"That's a lie," he said flatly. "And you know it."

Kessler quickly interceded. "Thank you, gentlemen. Let's pivot. Senator Bright, you've spoken about economic inequality and the strain on the middle class. Can you elaborate on your economic vision?"

Bright didn't hesitate.

"Absolutely. What we need is an economy built *from the middle out.* We invest in infrastructure, workforce development, and small business innovation, not trickle-down tax cuts and tariff gimmicks. My administration will roll back the tax cuts that disproportionately benefited the top one percent and use that revenue to fund paid family leave, affordable childcare, and education reform."

He glanced toward Hayden.

"We've had enough of economic theater. It's time for economic reality."

Hayden raised a brow. "You talk about reality, Senator, but what you're proposing is a European-style welfare state, paid for by raising taxes on families and job creators. You want to grow government. I want to expand *opportunity.* That's the difference."

The crowd murmured again; supporters on both sides responding to the contrast in vision.

Kessler nodded, already pivoting.

"Let's move to another key issue tonight: immigration. President Hayden, under your administration, immigration policy has become a focal point of both praise and controversy. How would you define your philosophy on immigration, and how would that continue in a second term?"

Hayden clasped his hands on the podium, nodding slightly before speaking. "Absolutely. When I came into office, our southern border was a disaster. Illegal crossings were surging, and American families were paying the price, whether through lost jobs, rising crime, or strained public services. My administration responded. We finished the wall. We empowered

Border Patrol. We reformed asylum abuse and stopped catch-and-release. And we did it without apology."

Applause erupted from pockets of the audience. Hayden's supporters were energized, his tone firm and resolute.

"I believe in legal immigration," he continued. "But let's be honest: a sovereign nation without secure borders is not a nation at all. We've prioritized American workers and national security—and we will keep doing so in a second term."

Kessler turned to Ted. "Your response, Senator?"

Bright was ready.

"Let's get one thing straight: border security is important, but it doesn't have to come at the expense of our humanity. President Hayden talks about walls and raids. I talk about solutions. Reforming our visa system. Modernizing immigration courts. And yes, securing the border, but doing it smartly, not cruelly."

Bright leaned forward slightly. "America is a nation of immigrants. We need laborers, innovators, and entrepreneurs from around the world. My plan invests in high-tech screening and a merit-based system that welcomes contributors, not fearmongers."

Hayden chuckled dryly, speaking before Kessler could interject. "Spoken like a man who's never had to actually enforce a policy."

Bright didn't miss a beat. "Spoken like a man who governs with slogans instead of strategy."

The two men locked eyes across the stage, their ideological divide on full display.

David Kessler shifted the topic.

"Let's talk healthcare."

Ted stepped into his message with ease, as if he had rehearsed a thousand times.

"Healthcare in this country is broken," he said. "Millions of Americans are forced to choose between paying for prescriptions and putting food on the table. That's unacceptable. My administration will lower premiums and expand access to affordable healthcare for everyone. No American should have to decide between their rent and life-saving medicine."

The applause was more vigorous this time, more unified.

But President Hayden, ever the tactician, waited only a moment before launching his counter.

"Ted, those are the kind of words you'd expect from a liberal legislator looking for votes," he said with a smile that didn't reach his eyes. "But what you conveniently forgot to mention is that you don't actually believe in these policies."

The hall quieted again.

"You see, Senator Bright is one of the largest shareholders of RXSure, one of the biggest pharmaceutical companies in the country," Hayden said, his tone sharp. "And I believe it was your own running mate, Congressman Landon Wolfe, who made that information public. Wasn't it, Senator?"

Bright's jaw tensed. Hayden had hit a nerve.

"I'd expect better of you, Ted," Hayden added. "You're talking about lowering prices while profiting from the very system you claim to oppose. That's not reform. That's hypocrisy."

Bright replied quickly, trying to keep the momentum. "President Hayden wants to talk about my financial disclosures. Fine. But let's not forget his record. Publicgate didn't disappear just because he stopped talking about it. Money laundering. Shell accounts. Whistleblowers silenced.

That's not transparency, it's a cover-up. And if we don't hold this administration accountable, who will?"

But the moment had shifted. Hayden had successfully dragged Bright into the mud.

Kessler stepped in. "Let's move to foreign policy. Specifically, the rising tensions in the Pacific and the Solomon Islands."

The president returned to his confident posture. "We've maintained strategic neutrality while strengthening alliances in the region. Ted's running mate, Congressman Wolfe, likes to paint a dire picture of Chinese dominance in the region. Let me be clear about China's ambitions: there is no such dominance, and there won't be under my leadership."

The words rang with force, echoing through the hall; an echo of President Ford's famous line decades earlier.

"A Bright-Wolfe administration?" Hayden added. "Let's be honest, what you're signing up for is a road to war. Battlefield Bright and Warmonger Wolfe."

Laughter scattered across the audience.

Bright, unfazed, replied. "President Hayden is living in a fantasy. While he's taken a hands-off approach, President Xian Wei has expanded China's presence across the Indo-Pacific. From ports to airfields to cyber warfare, they're playing chess while we're still playing checkers."

He turned directly to the audience. "We need a president who stands up to them; not one who lets them expand unchecked," he said, his voice tightening with conviction. "That doesn't mean rushing into war. It means strength. Resolve. It means showing the world that the United States doesn't flinch. Mr. President, with all due respect... under your watch, you've become a puppet for Beijing."

The insult landed hard. Hayden didn't flinch. Instead, he leaned forward, his expression cool, voice cutting.

"You're the puppet, Ted."

A murmur rippled through the crowd. Bright didn't miss a beat. He gave a small, amused laugh, then flashed his trademark smirk, the one that drove both supporters and critics wild.

"There you go again," he said, with a shake of the head; soft, dismissive, deliberate.

David Kessler raised his voice slightly to regain control. "Gentlemen, please. Let's keep the focus on policy."

But the gloves were off.

The moderator shifted in his seat, the weight of the moment building again as he turned his focus back to Ted. "Senator," he said evenly, "what's striking is that, despite all the heated rhetoric tonight, your stated position on the Solomon Islands, and even much of your approach to China, actually aligns with the president's. Neutrality. Strategic restraint. So the question must be asked: if you both agree in principle, why the posturing? And more to the point, how do you respond to reports suggesting your stance may be less about policy and more about personal financial interest in the Chinese markets?"

Bright's face tightened, the muscles in his jaw locking into place. There it was. Not just the question, but the way it had been framed. The language, the timing, the sudden precision of it. Kessler wasn't working off a hunch. He'd been handed this. Fed it. And there was only one man in the campaign with access to that level of detail, one man reckless and arrogant enough to just leak it just to keep Bright in check.

Wolfe.

Ted could feel it, down to the marrow; this was Landon, undermining him again, cutting the legs out from under his running mate, all under the guise of strategic control.

He swallowed hard, then turned his gaze to the moderator. "Yes, I've had business interests in Asia," he said, voice steady, deliberate. "And yes, some of those ventures touched the Pacific. But I've divested. I've disclosed. And I've walked away from any role that might present even the perception of a conflict. My position on the Solomon Islands is based on strategy, not self-interest. I answer to no one but the American people, and the Lord, my Savior."

He steadied his posture, bracing for what came next. Because it was never just the moderator in these moments. Not anymore.

David Kessler looked between the candidates, sensing that the night had taken its toll. "Gentlemen," he said, his voice regaining a formal calm, "thank you for your time and your candor. We'll now move to closing statements. President Hayden, you may go first."

Hayden adjusted his cufflinks, then stepped forward with the ease of a man used to control. "America, under my leadership, we have seen progress: measurable, real, and lasting progress. We've stood strong abroad, rebuilt our economy at home, and restored pride in who we are. I'm asking for four more years to finish the work we've started; to keep America first and secure a future built on strength."

The crowd applauded, though the fault lines in the room were clear.

Kessler turned. "Senator Bright."

Ted nodded slowly, his voice carrying a quieter force. "Tonight you heard two visions: one about protecting power, and one about restoring trust. This campaign isn't about soundbites or slogans. It's about families —your families —and the future we all share. I've never claimed to be perfect, but

I promise to lead with integrity, to fight for fairness, and to never forget who I serve."

He paused for a beat. "The American people deserve better. And I'm ready to deliver it."

Applause followed, but in Bright's mind, the noise faded.

The debate ended with a ceremonial handshake, firm yet forced and cold. Cameras flashed. The crowd stood. Kessler signed off. But even as the stage emptied and the candidates vanished behind their respective curtains, the real war remained.

Ted Bright had walked into the Rock and Roll Hall of Fame to face one opponent. He left knowing there were two. Hayden was his rival on the ballot. Wolfe had always been a rival. But tonight, the betrayal was no longer speculation. It was war, on two fronts. One in the public eye. And one within his own campaign. The path ahead would no longer be just a fight for the presidency; it would be a fight for control of the nation. For truth. For survival.

17

Shadows of the Government

October 2028

The afternoon sun slanted low through the Oval Office windows, casting long, fractured shadows across the room, fitting for a presidency gripped by fatigue and haunted by scandal. President Norman Hayden sat hunched behind the Resolute Desk, his posture wilted, a man worn thin by battles both public and private. Arrayed before him were the Joint Chiefs of Staff and Secretary of Defense Claudia Meyers. The room smelled faintly of coffee, paper, and something colder: disillusion.

General Preston Rhodes was the first to speak, his voice stripped of its usual deference. "Mr. President, we have hard confirmation. Jonas Taneoka has declared the Solomon Islands under a new constitutional order, backed by the Solomon Liberation Front. Every pro-American official still loyal to Prime Minister Talifa has been purged, many executed. They're calling it the People's Cleanse."

Secretary Meyers nodded grimly. "Satellite imagery confirms construction on what looks like a deep-water port underway in Choiseul. PLA naval engineers are on the ground. If China completes that base, they'll have a permanent military footprint less than 1,500 miles from Guam."

Hayden didn't look up. "Every decade gets its own version of Havana. Ours just comes with coral reefs and Chinese concrete."

Rhodes didn't disagree. "The region is slipping fast, Mr. President. We've evacuated embassy personnel. Our assets are blind. We need to act. A limited-scope joint operation can restore Talifa's loyalists to power. Quiet, efficient, just enough to show our resolve."

It was familiar: the outlines too clean, the confidence too rehearsed. The Pentagon called it Operation Iron Key: a deniable strike, involving trained locals, and a regime quietly replaced before Beijing could fully consolidate its influence. But Hayden was unmoved.

He leaned back in his chair, eyes dull. "No more. I won't spill American blood on some distant archipelago for the illusion of strength. Not with thirty days until the election."

General Robert McIntyre frowned. "Sir, this isn't about elections. It's about the balance of power in the Pacific."

Hayden's reply was cold and final. "We're done. I want a full withdrawal plan on my desk by the end of the week. All U.S. personnel, including military advisors and naval support vessels, are to be out of the Solomon Islands by January 1st. No exceptions."

Silence choked the room.

General Glenn Bowers shifted in his seat. The man had never been good at masking his anger. He let out a sharp breath and stood.

"With respect, Mr. President... that is cowardice. The Liberation Front is executing people who believed we had their backs. And you're going to leave them to die because of some poll numbers?"

President Hayden's brow furrowed, but his voice remained level. "Watch your tone, General."

But Bowers wasn't finished, not even close. He stepped closer to the Resolute Desk, his voice sharpening. "I've served under three presidents. Republican, Democrat, it didn't matter. Each of them had a spine. I don't know what happened to yours, sir, but it sure as hell didn't make it to this meeting."

Hayden slowly rose to his feet.

"You're not just running from conflict, Mr. President," Bowers continued, jabbing a finger toward the map on the wall. "You're surrendering. You've got more fire in you when a journalist shouts 'Publicgate' than when the Chinese military moves warships into our backyard. You're more outraged by poll trackers than power vacuums."

Hayden's jaw tightened. "You think this is about optics? About survival?"

Bowers nodded grimly. "That's exactly what I think. You don't want to be the guy who goes into retirement with blood on his hands, so instead you'll walk away while a sovereign nation burns. Tell me, how many more allies have to die before you can finally sleep at night?"

"I've buried more soldiers than you've trained," Hayden snapped.

"But you didn't die with them," Bowers fired back. "You sat in this damn chair and told yourself their sacrifice meant something. And now, when people need that meaning to count, you're throwing it away like it's a bad headline."

Something in Hayden broke.

His voice dropped to a dangerous whisper. "You don't know what it costs to sit behind this desk. Every hour, every briefing, every parent who asks why their son didn't come home. You think it's courage to send more of them to die in another jungle half the country couldn't find on a map? No, General. That's arrogance. And delusion."

Bowers' mouth curled into a sneer. "No, Mr. President. That's duty. And right now, you're failing it."

"You're a coward," he added. "A criminal hiding behind the flag to protect yourself from the consequences of your own lies. You don't belong in this office."

That was it.

Hayden's hands slammed against the edge of the desk. "You arrogant son of a bitch. You want to command this country? You think barking orders in uniform makes you a leader? You think wearing stars gives you the moral high ground?"

The room had gone deadly quiet.

"You are relieved, General," Hayden growled. "Effective immediately."

No one moved.

Hayden's voice rose, final and presidential. "Get out of my office."

Bowers straightened, locked eyes with Hayden for one last second, then turned without a word and stormed out, his departure shaking the very air in the room.

The silence that followed was deafening. Hayden, breathing hard, looked out over the stunned faces of his military leadership.

"The order stands. I want this over. No press leaks. No briefings. You'll coordinate the withdrawal under Secretary Meyers' authority. The United States is out of the Solomons."

No one challenged him.

As the remaining generals gathered their materials and filtered out, Hayden remained alone for a moment longer, staring at the faded world map pinned to the far wall. Red circles marked disputed zones. The Pacific was bleeding.

He knew what historians would write—weakness, retreat, appeasement. He just no longer had the energy to fight it.

Outside the Oval Office, reporters gathered in clusters, buzzing with rumors. Inside, Hayden sat back down, alone with the shadows.

The brightly lit set of *The Political Pulse* buzzed with quiet urgency as cameras rolled and lights bathed the studio in patriotic red, white, and blue. Behind the glass desk, hosts Lisa Harper and Mark Anderson sat poised beneath a digital banner that read: "*Publicgate Reopened: 29 Days to Election Day.*"

Across from them sat Ruben Leon, the journalist who had detonated the Publicgate scandal with his explosive exposé in *The Washington Post.* He was the image of the progressive intellectual; round wire-frame glasses perched above a thoughtful gaze, his curly dark hair slightly tousled, a muted brown tweed suit giving him the air of a professor who'd wandered into prime time. The moment the commercial break ended, all eyes turned to him.

Lisa Harper led with practiced calm. "Welcome back to *The Political Pulse.* With us tonight is Ruben Leon, investigative journalist, Harvard alum, and host of *Leon's Take.* Ruben, Publicgate is back in the headlines after a stunning move by the FBI. What should Americans make of this development?"

Ruben leaned forward, his voice cool but charged with purpose. "Lisa, Mark, when the Bureau reopens an investigation into the sitting President of the United States less than a month before an election, it sends shockwaves through the system. The timing is, frankly, unprecedented... or at least it would have been, had we not lived through 2016."

Mark Anderson nodded gravely. "You're referring to the Clinton email investigation."

"Exactly," Ruben said. "The FBI knows the weight of what it's doing. And yet they did it anyway. That tells me something serious is in play. Whether it leads to prosecution or not is almost secondary because politically, the damage is already done. It casts a shadow over the last days of this presidency. The only question now is how deep it cuts."

Lisa raised an eyebrow. "There's debate now on whether a sitting president can be indicted. Does that factor into how voters might respond?"

"It does," Ruben said, his tone sharpening. "Legally, it's a grey area. Politically? It's damning. Voters don't care about Article II interpretations or DOJ memos. They care about trust. Optics. Character. And Hayden's already failed that test in the court of public opinion. Publicgate wasn't just a scandal; it was a betrayal. The President misused public funds to bankroll his 2024 presidential campaign. And now? He's stonewalling."

Mark interjected. "So let me ask you plainly: does this change the election?"

"It could," Ruben said. "The reopened investigation hands Ted Bright a golden opportunity. He doesn't even need to attack; he just needs to look like the adult in the room. A credible alternative. Hayden's collapsing under the weight of his own secrets. The real impact of the FBI move isn't what they find. It's what the public starts to believe they *will* find."

Lisa glanced down at her tablet and pivoted. "Let's shift to the Bright-Wolfe ticket. There's growing buzz around reports of internal tension. You've written about this. What are you hearing?"

Ruben leaned back in his chair slightly, his expression tightening into a wry smile. "The Bright-Wolfe partnership was never built on chemistry. It was built on calculation. Bright needed someone who could help him solidify national security credentials, appeal to swing voters, and reassure moderates in the wake of Hayden's collapse. Wolfe checked those boxes—but ideologically, they're miles apart. Wolfe is hawkish, sharp-edged. Bright prefers pragmatism and control."

Mark added, "And the debate didn't help."

"Not at all," Ruben replied. "Bright tried to project unity and control, but just hours before he stepped on stage, a damning leak hit newsfeeds. According to sources, someone within his campaign provided David Kessler with documents. These documents claim that one of Bright's top donors has deep financial interests in China. That's the same China currently backing the Liberation Front in the Solomon Islands. The implication? Bright's tough talk on foreign policy may be compromised by the money behind his campaign. And multiple insiders say the source of the leak was none other than Landon Wolfe."

He adjusted his glasses, the weight of the moment settling in. "That's not just a political disagreement. That's Wolfe drawing a red line, undermining Bright in real time. He's playing a long game, staking out ground for a future beyond this campaign."

Lisa folded her hands, her expression thoughtful. "So, is this just friction, or something deeper?"

Ruben didn't blink. "If Bright wins, the administration will start with a cold war inside the West Wing. That's the risk. If Wolfe pushes for a harder line on China, for example, and Bright resists, we're talking about a White House divided on fundamental policy. And that can become chaos. The ticket may have been necessary, but that doesn't mean it was built to last."

Mark leaned in. "Could voters see that as a reason to hesitate?"

"They might," Ruben said. "But here's the irony: next to a scandal-ridden incumbent being re-investigated by the FBI, even a fractured ticket can look like stability. That's how low the bar's fallen. The real question isn't whether voters trust Bright and Wolfe. It's whether they trust them *more* than they trust Hayden."

Lisa offered a tight nod. "As always, Ruben, we appreciate your insight."

The camera pulled back into a wide shot, the panelists' silhouettes bathed in the cool glow of the studio lights. In the control room, producers queued up graphics for the next segment. Across the country, millions of voters watched, brows furrowed, wondering not just who would win the White House, but if anyone could be trusted to hold it together.

The suite at the Riverside Elegance hotel in Harrisburg had been cleared of campaign staff for the morning. Outside, a light drizzle slicked the windows, softening the sound of the city below. Inside, the atmosphere was quiet but dense; an airless sort of silence that often accompanied briefings too dangerous for public record.

Ted Bright sat with his tie slightly loosened, his campaign schedule cleared for the next hour. Across from him sat Nathan Kirk, Deputy Director of National Intelligence. A former Army Ranger turned intelligence hawk, Kirk had served in both Iraq and Afghanistan before climbing the ranks in Washington. He was in his early fifties, tall and straight-backed, with flint-gray hair combed tight and a jaw that looked like it hadn't unclenched since 2003.

He wasn't a relic of the Cold War; he was its spiritual successor. The kind of man who still thought in zones of influence, who saw diplomacy as delay, and who'd once said in a closed-door session, "Soft power doesn't keep Beijing awake at night."

Nathan Kirk removed a leather folder from his briefcase and placed it gently on the table between them.

"Senator Bright," Kirk began, voice crisp, "as part of the national security transition protocol, we're continuing periodic briefings for both major candidates. Today, we're focusing on the Pacific theater, specifically, the Solomon Islands."

Ted nodded silently. He already had a sense of where this was going.

"As of this morning, the situation remains fluid," Kirk continued. "Our embassy and diplomatic personnel are being quietly repositioned. There's been limited contact with pro-U.S. figures in Honiara. The State Department is preparing for full evacuation."

He paused, letting the first shoe drop.

"The president has two main options on the table. One: full withdrawal. Pull out the remaining forces, abandon the provisional government, and let the Solomon Liberation Front consolidate power under Jonas Taneoka. It would be fast, and disastrous. Beijing would have its puppet regime within weeks. Hayden knows it. He knows what the history books might say, that he was the president who handed the Pacific to China. In my opinion, he appears to be tired. Tired of bleeding capital on what he sees as a losing front. Tired of fighting wars no one at home supports. And with his presidency hanging by a thread, he's not looking for a stand. He's looking for an exit."

"And the other option?" Ted asked.

Kirk opened the folder and pushed a document forward. Redacted lines. Satellite maps. CIA insignias.

"Operation Iron Key," he said, lowering his voice. "It's a limited covert action, built on doctrine we've used before. We're arming and training an indigenous paramilitary unit made up of anti-SLF factions: exiles, defectors, loyalist tribes. The teams would move in under cover of night, launched from a carrier group staged just outside contested waters. No U.S. flags, no boots on the ground. But make no mistake, this is about removing Taneoka. Taking the head off the snake."

Bright let the word *removing* hang in the air like smoke from a just-fired gun.

Kirk pressed on, his tone clinical. "The plan calls for simultaneous strikes on SLF infrastructure: airstrips, comms hubs, weapons caches, followed by a fast inland advance. The proxy force would move to seize the capital. With Taneoka gone and the leadership fractured, the assumption is that the rest will collapse. We've run simulations. With surprise, it's possible."

Ted raised an eyebrow. "*With surprise, it's possible.*"

Kirk didn't blink. "That's how these operations succeed: clean, precise, quiet. No American boots, just our influence shaping outcomes."

Ted's voice turned flat. "Or fueling a disaster."

He leaned forward, hands clasped. "You're talking about handing rifles to splintered factions and hoping they can take out a regime we've already conceded is dug in. This is the kind of plan that looks good in slide decks and ends with body bags and blame."

Kirk's jaw tightened, just slightly. "Respectfully, Senator, this isn't some throwback. We've modernized our approach."

"Have we?" Ted asked, his tone sharpening. "Because what I just heard sounds like someone repackaged a Cold War failure and gave it a new name."

He let that sit before continuing. "Tell me, did the President approve this?"

Kirk hesitated just long enough to betray something. "The President has it under consideration. He's weighing both options."

That was a lie. Or, at best, a careful omission. Hayden had already made his decision, and it wasn't the one Kirk was pushing. The Joint Chiefs had their orders: prepare the withdrawal. Hayden wasn't interested in salvaging the Solomons; he was trying to cut his losses. He saw what it was: a quagmire. Not a battleground, but a graveyard. His legacy couldn't afford another open-ended intervention. Not this late in the game.

But Kirk wasn't looking for exits. He was looking for permission.

"You're giving me two options," Ted said, narrowing his eyes. "But only one of them is real. Hayden's already walking away. So why the performance? Why are you pushing Iron Key?"

Kirk's response was smooth, practiced. "I assume you understand the stakes in the Pacific. Your proximity to Duane Dyer. I figured that meant you were paying attention."

There it was. Not a threat. A test.

Ted's jaw clenched, not out of guilt, but calculation. Dyer had made his position clear: stay out of the Islands. China was where the future and the money were. A skirmish over some hard-to-find cluster of islands wasn't worth upsetting the balance. Not when Dyer had factories, assets, and markets on the mainland. If Beijing was irritated, that irritation could ripple, both economically and diplomatically.

Ted didn't need a classified briefing to understand the implications. He was already aligned. Like Hayden, he didn't want a fight. He just couldn't say why.

"This isn't about Dyer," Ted said, though they both knew it was. "It's about not getting dragged into another proxy war we can't win. You want my administration's first move to be a covert invasion? That's not a strategy. That's a suicide pact."

Kirk steepled his fingers, gaze steady. "I want to prevent Chinese naval dominance of the Southern Hemisphere."

"And I want to prevent American fingerprints on another failed regime-change operation." Ted stood now, slow and deliberate, his voice even. "If Hayden *was* considering this, which I don't believe he seriously is, someone should talk him out of it. Because this isn't a plan. It's a provocation."

Kirk stood, mirroring him. Not hostile. Just resolute. Like a man used to being told no, and waiting for someone else to say yes.

"I'm giving him options," he said. "The same I'm giving you."

Ted didn't flinch. "Then here's mine: we don't green light Iron Key. We don't arm militias, we don't outsource coups, and we sure as hell don't start another Cold War because some spook in Langley misses the good old days."

Kirk's mouth twitched, whether from offense or recognition, Ted couldn't tell.

"You may want to reconsider, Senator," he said quietly. "Because if you win, and odds are you will, this mess won't belong to Hayden anymore. It'll belong to you."

Ted stared him down. "Then I'll own it. But I won't inherit your disaster."

A beat passed between them. Then Kirk gathered his folder and snapped it shut with the clean precision of a closing case.

"Very well," he said. "Shall we move on to Russia?"

Ted nodded, his voice cool. "Yes."

But even as Kirk pivoted to Russia's latest threats, the ghost of Iron Key lingered, unspoken but alive, hanging in the space between them like a fuse no one wanted to admit had already been lit.

The evening sky over Landover looked like a bruise, deep purple bleeding into gray as we cut through the beltway traffic. I sat stiff in the back of the SUV, barely hearing Lydia's voice as she flipped through talking points beside me. Ellie was up front with the detail, scrolling through her phone, eyes narrowed. I was supposed to be focused. Energized. Instead, all I felt was a low thrum of exhaustion, until we turned into the convention center's circular drive, and I saw him.

Edward Bright.

He was standing outside the venue, flanked by two junior staffers and a half-assed grin that told me everything before he said a word.

An agent opened my door and I stepped out fast.

"Ed," I said, my tone clipped. "What the hell are you doing here?"

He straightened his tie like he belonged here. "Ted asked me to cover tonight's remarks. He thought you could use the night off."

I stared at him. "You're speaking, *instead of me?"*

"That's the agreement," he said, calm as a fucking priest. "You've been doing a lot lately. Thought it might be good optics to rotate some of the spotlight."

Lydia stepped in, voice sharp. "Is that what this is now? A rotation?"

Edward didn't blink. "It's strategy. You brought me into the spotlight, Landon. Your move, not mine. I'm just doing my part."

I wanted to laugh, or hit something. Edward wasn't smug, not like his brother would've been. That's what made it worse. Edward *believed* this bullshit. Thought he was helping. That he hadn't just cut the ground out from under us and called it strategy.

"You're not playing your part," I said slowly. "You're playing *his.*"

His face flickered, just a second, then the smile came back. "People inside want to hear from the future of the party. We're all on the same team, Landon."

"Sure," I muttered. "Just make sure you remember whose team you were drafted onto."

Ellie was already tugging my arm. Lydia looked like she wanted to slap someone. I gave Ed a long look, turned, and headed back to the car.

Back in the SUV, silence cracked under the weight of it all.

Then I snapped.

"Un-fucking-believable," I spat, slamming my palm against the leather armrest. "I prep a damn speech, come all the way out here, and find out Ted's latest puppet show stars Edward fucking Bright?"

Lydia was seething. "They didn't even warn us. They knew we'd protest if they did."

Ellie's voice was flat. "This wasn't an oversight. It was a message."

"Oh, I got the message," I muttered. "Loud and fucking clear."

I leaned forward in my seat, elbows on my knees, the security detail silent in the front as if they couldn't hear the storm behind them. Ted wasn't just sidelining me, he was dressing it up with a smile and a handshake, sending Edward to do the honors. A clean suit, a polished script, and a podium I was supposed to own. This wasn't about ego. It was about power. Control. Ted had started closing the circle, and I was watching it from outside the rope.

"He's grooming him," Lydia said. "That Senate seat. Ted's finally letting Edward back in."

"And using him to sideline *us.*" I shook my head. "They think I'm just going to roll over. Smile for the cameras. Let Edward wave the goddamn flag while I sit like some leper in the back row."

Lydia didn't speak. She didn't need to. She was staring out the window, jaw tight, same rage brewing just beneath the surface.

"You know what this means, right?" I said, voice lower now. "We thought we had a pawn. Turns out Ted took him back."

Ellie nodded once. "So what do we do?"

I looked out the windows as the venue lights blurred past, glowing like a mirage I'd never reach.

"We change the board."

The McLean house hadn't changed, but everything else had. Same velvet drapes swallowing the daylight, same polished floors and heirloom oil paintings hanging like ghosts on the walls. It was the place where Lydia and I first shook hands, where all of this began in earnest. Back then, it felt like the start of something hopeful. Tonight, it felt like walking into the command post of a quiet war.

The air was heavy with cigar smoke and ego. Crystal glasses clinked softly in the background, dull echoes against the thunder building in the room. One voice rose higher than the rest.

"That coward sold me out," General Glenn Bowers barked, mid-stride, pacing like a bull too long in the pen. "Hayden's a puppet. A goddamn mannequin in a Navy suit." He stopped short, turned on a heel, and hurled his empty glass into the fireplace. It didn't shatter, it thunked dully off the stone and rolled to a stop, a pitiful little anticlimax to his outburst.

I lingered in the doorway with Lydia at my side, Mitch Ferguson just ahead of us. It felt like walking into a sealed chamber; no fresh air, just fumes and fury. Lydia's eyes scanned the room like she was pricing it, and knowing her, she was.

"Evening, gentlemen," Mitch said, tone slick and unbothered. He swung a bottle of French brandy like a trophy. "Apologies for the delay. Thought we could use something top-shelf tonight."

Three heads turned. Bowers stood by the fireplace, face flushed with liquor and betrayal. Preston Rhodes sat on the edge of a leather armchair, his scotch nearly empty, expression tighter than a noose. Robert McIntyre leaned back with a kind of cold detachment, the glint in his eyes more dangerous than the whiskey in his glass.

Mitch motioned to us like we'd just been initiated into some dark cabal. "You all know Congressman Wolfe, and this is Lydia Barnes, the face of Barnes Industries."

No one nodded. No one smiled.

Lydia turned to the decanter on the bar. Poured herself two fingers of something older than the war in Afghanistan. Her nails clicked against the glass like punctuation.

I didn't grab a drink. Not yet.

I gave the room the thinnest version of a grin. "Figured this was a better use of my time than glad-handing a bunch of undecideds at a convention center."

Bowers snorted and grabbed another drink from a nearby tray. "What's eating at you? Ted screw you over?" he asked, voice hoarse.

I didn't answer right away. Just looked around at the faces of these so-called guardians of the republic; men who'd seen too many wars, and

Lydia, who probably knew how to start one if she needed the market to move.

"He sent his son," I finally muttered. "Last minute. Right before I went on. Ted pulled the rug and handed the stage to Edward. Had the cameras already rolling."

Bowers gave a guttural laugh. "Sounds about right."

I took the glass Mitch handed me and stared at it for a moment. Ten years sober, and yet the room already tasted like regret. I took a sip. Just a sip. Brandy lit a fire down my throat and didn't stop until it reached my chest.

Rhodes waved a hand like he was brushing off smoke. "Your campaign drama doesn't matter. Not tonight. What we're dealing with; it's bigger than speeches, sons, and stabbed backs."

I hadn't met Rhodes before, but I knew the type: silver hair clipped to the scalp, a face like it belonged on a Vietnam memorial, and a demeanor carved from years of discipline and unspoken wars. Next to him sat General Robert McIntyre: square-jawed, buzzed haircut, posture so rigid it looked like he'd been carved from concrete. He didn't say a word. Just sat there, eyes narrowed, studying everyone in the room like he was reading a classified file. Cold. Methodical. The kind of man who'd fought proxy wars before breakfast and slept just fine.

McIntyre set his glass down. "Solomon Islands," he said simply.

The name alone tightened something behind my eyes.

Bowers stepped forward, brimming with fury. "Hayden's ordered a withdrawal. Full. Comprehensive. No footprint left. He's handing the South Pacific to Taneoka."

"To China," McIntyre corrected, voice like ice. "Don't bother dressing it up."

I leaned forward, glass in hand, not sure whether I wanted to throw it or drink it dry. "You're saying we're just walking away? After everything?"

Rhodes nodded grimly. "The Liberation Front's already filling the vacuum. Taneoka has total control. There's evidence, including satellite movement and joint exercises off Nendo Island. Taneoka has Chinese arms and Chinese advisors. It's a liberation. It's annexation with a new flag."

"And Hayden knows," I said flatly.

"Oh, he knows," Bowers snapped. "I told him in the Oval Office. We all did. Laid it out with maps, intelligence, timelines. He smiled like I was giving him stock tips and told me I was "too delusional. Two days later, I'm retired."

My stomach knotted. This wasn't policy drift, this was surrender, plain and simple. Taneoka had always been loud, theatrical, a nationalist firebrand with just enough anti-colonial flair to play well on international stages. Two years ago, he was a fringe figure clinging to a ragtag insurgency. Now he was Beijing's man in the South Pacific. A regional pawn dressed up like a liberator.

Mitch poured himself a drink but didn't sip it. He looked at me, voice low. "What they haven't told you is this: Taiwanese SIGINT picked up chatter two weeks ago. Taneoka is coordinating with a Chinese naval detachment off the coast of Manus Island. This isn't just about the Solomons. They're laying the foundation for a corridor, stretching from Nauru to Vanuatu. Beijing wants a strategic vice. And Taneoka's the pressure point."

Lydia leaned forward, calm but sharp. "And what happens to the defense contracts tied to that corridor?"

McIntyre didn't blink. "Gone. Scrubbed from the books. Or worse, handed to Chinese SOEs under regional security partnerships."

It hit me like a punch in the chest. I'd known the Solomon Islands were unstable—hell, I'd pushed for covert support against Taneoka for months. But I hadn't known this. Not the withdrawal. Not the surrender. Not the quiet, bloodless handoff of the Pacific to Beijing.

This wasn't just Hayden being risk-averse. It was deliberate. A doctrine of retreat. An empire collapsing without even bothering to slam the door on its way out.

And Ted Bright? His fingerprints were all over this. A "pivot" to Pacific markets, foreign holdings wrapped in shell companies, green lit defense divestitures in Congress. He didn't just know this was happening; he was profiting from it. Ensuring the Americans didn't bark while China took the leash.

I stared into my glass. The brandy didn't burn anymore. Just tasted like smoke.

Bowers tilted his head toward Lydia. "She sees it. This isn't foreign policy, it's business. There's money in war. But there's just as much in pretending you don't want one."

And there it was.

The room had gone quiet. The pacing had stopped. Even the ice in the glasses was no longer cracking.

Nobody said it, not yet. But it was there, between the hardwood and velvet, the rage and resignation.

This wasn't about strategy.

Not about diplomacy.

Not about a pivot or a withdrawal.

This was about who would fill the vacuum.

And whether we'd let them.

Not a decision.

A reckoning.

Then, the doorbell.

It cut through the silence like a rifle shot. Mitch moved fast to answer the door, and a moment later, two more figures stepped inside.

Nathan Kirk from the Office of the Director of National Intelligence. Neat, unreadable face. Pressed cuffs. The kind of man who never entered a room without already knowing what happened in it.

And Emil Rollins: CIA. Older, grizzled, scar over one cheek like a signature. The kind of scar you didn't earn behind a desk.

Mitch raised his glass toward them. "Kirk, Rollins, you're just in time. We were discussing our friends in the Solomon Islands."

Rollins chuckled, that broken-glass voice of his rasping out over the tension. "Or should I say, soon-to-be *former* friends of America and *newly purchased* friends of Beijing."

A low hum of agreement moved through the room, like wolves scenting blood.

I sat back in my char, watching it all unfold. These weren't politicians or press secretaries. These were men who built empires out of ashes and called it stability. Lydia's gaze lingered on Rollins a second too long, professional history, no doubt, but something colder, too. An understanding.

Rollins took a slow sip of the French brandy before continuing. "Truth is, we've been gaming this out since January. My shop's got a working scenario file for a Bright presidency. If you're wondering whether he'll get tough on China or push back against the Solomon Liberation Front... don't. He won't."

I didn't even flinch. I'd known. I'd *always* known.

Kirk nodded. "We ran parallel assessments. The trend lines are clear: under Bright, the U.S. is out. No hardline stance. No containment doctrine. Just silence, and a market exit."

Rollins leaned forward. "Taneoka has Chinese backing, state-trained paramilitaries, logistics pipelines across Guadalcanal. The SLF has better communications than some NATO units. And we're pretending they're an internal matter?"

He shook his head, amused and disgusted.

I felt my jaw tighten. "So what's the countermeasure?"

Kirk didn't blink. "There *was* one. Operation Iron Key. Black-budget op. Pentagon-CIA joint backchannel. We arm local resistance cells, hit SLF compounds before the Chinese can dig in. Minimal exposure. Maximum disruption. And if it works, Taneoka never sees the end of the year."

I looked at Lydia. Nothing on her face. But her glass had stopped moving.

"And Ted?" I asked.

Kirk's mouth tightened into a grim line. "He killed it. Said, quote, 'We're not getting dragged into another colonial mess.'"

McIntyre, silent until now, rose from his seat like a storm building offshore.

"A colonial mess?" His voice cracked like thunder. "What the hell does that spoiled little coward know about war? About containment? About deterrence?"

No one answered. No one dared.

McIntyre turned to face the room, jaw locked. "If we don't push back now, we hand Beijing the keys to the Pacific. Next it's Kiribati. Then Fiji. Followed by the Philippines. We used to draw red lines. Now we draw up press releases."

The air was thick. Charged.

Bowers stood, pacing. "And don't think the Chinese don't know it. They're baiting us with Taneoka. He's their revolutionary icon. This is the trial balloon for the Pacific Prosperity Sphere. They want to see if we blink."

The room went still, no one moved, no one spoke. Only the low hum of the ice machine from the fridge broke the silence. Bowers's outburst hung in the air like smoke after gunfire.

Then Rhodes cleared his throat, slow and deliberate. He didn't stand; he didn't have to. The authority in his voice was enough to command the room.

"I've served under seven presidents," he said. "Watched some rise to the moment, others crumble beneath it. But I'll tell you this: Washington wouldn't have stood down. Roosevelt would've mobilized the fleet yesterday. Eisenhower would've had boots on the ground before Taneoka learned to hold a rifle. Even Reagan, for all his pageantry, understood power and how to wield it when the world blinked."

He turned his gaze on me. "And now we've got Hayden, grasping at whatever scraps history might give him on the way out the door. More worried about bronze plaques than battle lines. And Bright..." Rhodes paused, shaking his head. "Bright is too far inside China's pocket to find his way back out. He's not a leader. He's an asset."

There was nothing theatrical in the way he said it. Just a cold, precise statement of fact.

"And the office itself?" Rhodes went on. "It used to mean something. Used to be a weight no man could carry without trembling. Now it's just another stepping stone for corporate men and cowards."

The words hit like a sermon delivered at a funeral; the kind where the casket's still open.

I felt the room tilting, shifting. Years of doctrine, diplomacy, backchannel maneuvering; none of it meant a damn now. Not in the face of what was coming. The Pacific was burning. China was moving. And all we had were tired hands waving white flags from the steps of the Capitol.

I looked around at the faces: McIntyre, jaw tight with rage; Kirk, chewing the inside of his cheek like he might break skin; Rollins, leaning forward, waiting for someone to say the unsayable. Lydia sat composed as ever, but even she had that calculating gleam, like a trader who saw the shape of the market before it moved.

The anger in me wasn't hot; it was cold now. Controlled. It pooled in my chest like a current waiting for the dam to break.

I leaned forward, rested my glass on the table with care, and met Rhodes' stare.

"What if Ted isn't the one calling the shots?" I said, voice low. "What if it were me?"

The silence that followed was surgical. No one breathed. No one blinked.

Rhodes didn't flinch.

McIntyre leaned back, the hint of something dark curling at the edge of his mouth; satisfaction, maybe. Or recognition.

Because I'd said it. The thing none of them wanted to say out loud, but all of them had been circling like vultures over a dying republic.

And now the words were out there, daring someone to deny them.

"I know what you're all thinking. You've been circling it. Afraid to say it out loud." I looked each of them in the eye. "You've all served. You've seen the costs. And yet, here we are; being led by men who wouldn't know the stakes if they were tattooed across their chests. Ted Bright is a coward. Hayden is a relic. And we're still pretending this system will right itself?"

Mitch shifted in his seat, trying to lighten the air. "Landon, I think you've had a little too much to drink."

"No, Mitch." I shook my head. "I've never been more clear."

I rose to my feet, picking my glass back up, the brandy sloshing at the rim. "This isn't about the Solomons, not just about Taneoka or Beijing. It's about a turning point in our history. It's about what kind of country we leave behind. And right now, it's one where America retreats, apologizes, and dies quietly."

"And?" Bowers asked flatly, arms crossed.

I met him with a steady gaze. "And I say we don't let that happen. We don't wait for the system to devour itself. We act."

McIntyre's voice was a low warning. "What are you suggesting, Congressman?"

"I'm suggesting we stop pretending the ballot box is going to fix this. If Ted takes the oath, the war is lost before the first shot is fired." I looked to Lydia, then back to the men. "So we take him out of the equation."

The silence that followed was razor-edged.

"You mean... remove him?" Rhodes asked, testing the phrasing, the air.

"Yes," I said plainly. "Remove. Eliminate. Call it what you want. But Ted Bright cannot be allowed to take the oath."

Rhodes exhaled sharply, shaking his head. "You realize what you're proposing?"

"I do."

"It's treason."

"It's survival," I snapped. "And we need to start calling things what they are."

McIntyre stood. "And what? You take over? Is that what you're angling at?"

I didn't answer immediately. I let the silence hang there long enough for them to feel it settle into their bones.

"I'm not angling at anything," I said at last. "I'm just stating the obvious: the wrong men are in charge. And maybe the only way to fix that... is to stop waiting for someone else to do it."

Mitch's voice was low. "And if we do this... what's the plan?"

I leaned forward slowly and deliberately. "We make it clean. Controlled. Ted's death looks like a tragedy, not an execution. We control the succession. We place the right people in the right rooms. And we reclaim the Oval, not with tanks in the streets, but with strategy. Precision. Subtlety."

Bowers nodded slowly, not in agreement yet, but no longer in opposition. "We'd need absolute discipline. A black operation inside our own borders."

Before I could respond, Rollins leaned forward, his fingers steepled like a devil in the confession booth. A sly grin pulled at the corner of his mouth, never wide enough to be honest, always sharp enough to draw blood.

"My agency has experience in these sorts of operations," he said. His voice was smooth, too smooth, like silk over glass.

Lydia's eyes narrowed. "The CIA isn't allowed to operate on U.S. soil. You know that."

Rollins chuckled. Not a laugh. A knowing sound. Low, practiced, and dangerous. "You think that ever stops us?"

The room didn't react, not outwardly. But I felt the shift; subtle, seismic. A tilt toward inevitability.

"We've been running ops inside the U.S. for years," Rollins continued, brushing invisible lint from his cuff like he was clearing conscience from his sleeve. "Surveillance, sabotage, character assassination. Real assassination. If we want this done, we can make it happen. Quietly. Permanently."

The air thickened. We weren't theorizing anymore, we were building. Blueprints of betrayal, scaffolding for sedition.

Like Roman senators on the eve of the Ides of March, we convinced ourselves this was salvation cloaked in treachery; necessary, righteous, inevitable.

The outlines of the coup began to harden. Not just *if,* but *when.* Not just *how,* but *who.*

I took stock of the room.

Mitch Ferguson was methodical: calculated. A man who lived in flowcharts and probabilistic kill ratios, who treated geopolitics like a game of Go, not poker. As Director of War-Games and Intelligence, he'd modeled a hundred theoretical conflicts and counted the cost of each down to the last digit. What he craved wasn't spotlight, it was control. *Secretary of Defense,* I thought. Let him turn theory into doctrine, simulations into policy. Give him the authority to reshape America's next war before it starts. That would keep him locked in, not with loyalty, but with purpose.

Rollins and Kirk? They were bought and sold the minute I mentioned Iron Key. A covert invasion of the Solomon Islands disguised as a stabilization mission. A return to the Pacific theater, a modern echo of Guadalcanal, but this time, the spoils wouldn't be freedom. It would be rare earth minerals, global shipping lanes, and contracts. Billions in contracts. For them, it was legacy wrapped in dollars and draped in the flag.

Bowers? That was easier. A man stripped of his command, humiliated by a White House that saw him as a relic. All I had to do was offer him restoration. Not just of his stars, but of his name. His honor. He'd march into hell if it meant getting his rank back.

The others, including generals, aides, and a few career operatives who had joined the meeting late and stood in the shadows like ghosts, needed something simpler. Faith. A reason to believe that the Republic still had teeth. That we weren't just a nation rotting from the inside while the outside world closed in on us. I promised them that. A rebirth of American strength. A spine of steel where there had been nothing but soft apologies and red lines in the sand.

Then Lydia.

Her silence had its own language. I knew her better than the rest. She wore ethics like jewelry; selectively, stylishly, never too tight. She didn't like this. She didn't *want* this. But she *understood* it. And more importantly, she stood to gain more than anyone else. Her family's defense conglomerate would be first in line to "rebuild" the Solomons after we lit the match. Government contracts. Infrastructure. Weapons. Logistics. She'd be the invisible empress of the Pacific.

And she knew it.

The hours dragged on, but none of us noticed the time. We were mapping treason in real time, shuffling pieces across a blood-soaked chessboard. Voices rose, tempers flared, but no one left. Because deep down, we'd all come to this room hoping someone would say what we were now all planning.

The target: Ted Bright.

The buyers: Us.

The mechanism: American fear, dressed as salvation.

We discussed logistics, leaks, and deniability. Ted's security detail. His movements. The inauguration window. Possibilities narrowed. The plan began to breathe.

And somewhere in those fevered hours, in that gray hour before dawn, it was done.

"When you make me president," I said, not as a boast, but as a warning, "be prepared for the storm that follows."

No one laughed.

I felt it then, the transfer of weight. Like a crown, invisible and burning, lowered onto my skull. No ceremony. No applause. Just consequence.

Their eyes were on me: Lydia, Mitch, Rollins, the generals. Not in awe. In calculation. In allegiance.

We were no longer just patriots.

We were architects of a quiet war.

If we failed, we'd hang.

But if we succeeded...

We'd become the new founding fathers.

The first light of morning cracked through the blinds, cold and pale. We didn't rise. We didn't speak. The silence now was heavier than any oath.

History wouldn't remember this room. But it would remember what we did next.

There was no turning back.

We had built the machine.

Now, we only needed to pull the trigger.

18

Democracy's D-Day

Election Day Morning | November 2028

The special morning edition of *The Political Pulse* opened with a camera shot just above the National Mall: columns, monuments, and American flags caught in the blue-gray dawn of November 7th, 2028. The Capitol stood still beneath clouded skies, but the republic it governed was in motion. Lines had already begun forming outside polling stations from Phoenix to Philadelphia. Democracy, battered and cynical, was showing up anyway.

Inside the polished glass set just across from the White House gates, the mood was subdued, reverent, and electric.

"Good morning," Lisa Harper said, the words crisp, unflinching. "It's Election Day, 2028. America heads to the polls."

Her voice didn't carry the false uplift of campaign season. It had the weight of a reckoning. Behind her, a montage played: Senator Ted Bright waving to packed rallies in Atlanta and Charlotte. President Norman Hayden, caught in grainy footage, stands stone-faced as he exits Air Force One under the night skies of Tampa. Then, footage of a Miami protest shows people shouting, holding signs about Publicgate, indictments, and backroom deals.

Co-anchor Mark Anderson picked up without missing a beat, flipping through notes but barely needing them. "The final seventy-two hours have redefined this race. Ted Bright, charismatic, disciplined, and unrelenting, was always seen as a serious contender. However, what we're witnessing now is something entirely different. A movement. A phenomenon. He's surged in the polls with the kind of momentum we haven't seen since Reagan in 1980 or Obama in 2008. His message, bipartisan, optimistic, relentless, has captivated millions. They're calling it Bright Fever. And this morning, it's burning hot.

Lisa nodded, adjusting her earpiece. "It's the kind of closing momentum you can't script. In the last three days, the Bright campaign has barnstormed the Rust Belt, locked down South Carolina, and, most surprising of all, put Florida into play."

"Florida," Mark repeated. "That's the shocker. President Hayden's home state. A decade of Republican dominance. Now it's truly purple, and slipping."

The camera shifted to a live shot outside a high school in Broward County: young voters, college kids, Cuban grandmothers in folding chairs, all waiting. The line stretched around the block.

Lisa's voice lowered. "Let's not forget what's driving this. Publicgate has decimated the Hayden campaign. What began as whispers in early September has metastasized into a full-blown crisis of legitimacy. Shady PAC money, favors traded in Tallahassee, and that damming exposé from *The Washington Post,* it's left Hayden reeling."

Mark leaned back in his chair, a touch of skepticism on his face. "The President's tried to cast it as a media smear. He's stuck to the 'witch hunt' script. But the damage is done. Independents are turning. Suburban moderates have gone silent. And his firewall in the Sun Belt is cracking."

The screen displayed a heat map of battleground states, glowing like nerve endings. Ohio, Michigan, and Arizona were pulsing red-orange.

Pennsylvania? Toss-up. Georgia? Leaning Bright. Florida? A fifty-fifty deadlock.

Lisa tapped the tablet in front of her. "Let's be clear. If Bright flips Florida, it's not just a swing state. It's a bellwether. A red state gone blue would signal a national rejection of Hayden. A referendum on his entire presidency. And the polls? They've got Bright with a four-point edge, within margin of error, but rising."

A gust of wind rattled the glass behind them. Outside, the White House loomed, marble, fortified, almost indifferent.

Mark's tone darkened. "And it's not just the White House on the line. Control of Congress could swing, too. The Republicans currently hold the House. The Democrats cling to the Senate by a thread. If Bright wins and Republicans retake the Senate? We're staring down a divided government, one that could stall or even sabotage his agenda from day one. But if Democrats hold the Senate and manage to flip the House? That's a mandate. A unified government. A hard reset on domestic and foreign policy."

"Gridlock or green light," Lisa said. "That's what today decides. A Bright presidency with a divided Congress would mean trench warfare on Capitol Hill. But if Democrats hold the Senate and somehow flip the House? We could see something we haven't witnessed since 2008: a newly elected Democratic president with full legislative control. It would be sweeping. Fast. Transformative."

She looked off-camera for a moment, then back. "But if Republicans hold the House and retake the Senate? We enter uncharted territory: a populist Democratic president boxed in by a hostile Congress. Nothing passes. Everything stalls. Chaos becomes governance."

Mark's expression shifted, no longer just reporting, but sensing history.

"Today isn't just about who wins," he said. "It's about what kind of country wakes up tomorrow. Unified or fractured. Functional or paralyzed."

Lisa didn't speak right away. When she did, her voice had softened, the weight of the moment settling between them.

"Whatever happens tonight, it won't just shape a presidency. It'll test the system itself."

The silence that followed was heavier than any commentary.

The broadcast rolled on, state maps, pundit panels, exit poll projections, but the message was already clear.

By midnight, the American experiment would either survive another round or begin to break in ways no one could have predicted.

Claire Hayden muted the television just as the segment came to an end. The screen froze on Mark Anderson's furrowed brow, a chyron running beneath: *"BRIGHT FEVER GRIPS NATION AS VOTERS HEAD TO POLLS."*

The remote clicked softly in her hand. The silence that followed felt cavernous.

She didn't turn around when she heard the door open. The familiar shuffle of polished oxfords on the carpet, the faint scent of cologne that had long since become synonymous with her husband, these were the final quiet details of a life slipping through her fingers.

Norman stood behind her, adjusting his cufflinks in the reflection of the dressing mirror. He looked tired, not just in the way campaign trails exhaust a man, but the deeper kind; exhaustion that comes when the gravity of loss can no longer be outrun.

"You watching the news?" he asked gently.

"I was," Claire replied, setting the remote down. "I turned it off before they said anything worse."

He gave a dry smile, walking over to the window. The city below was stirring. Flags flapped, distant motorcades wove through intersections, and somewhere, voters in wool coats were queuing up outside schools and churches.

"D.C. loves the drama of it all," he said. "Election Day. Crowds. Speeches. Long camera shots of people pretending they're changing the course of history."

"You used to love it too," Claire said.

He didn't respond. Just kept watching the street below.

She stood, brushing down the sleeves of her tailored coat, and walked toward him. "You're already gone in your mind, aren't you?"

Norman looked at her then. He looked older in the morning light. His eyes, once sharp with ambition, had dulled. "I'm not gone," he said. "I'm just... ready. For whatever comes next."

Claire studied him. "That's not you. The man I married, the man who clawed his way through every election in Florida, even when nobody gave him a shot, he never folded."

A beat.

She stepped closer. "Do you remember Clay County? The state senate race?"

He let out a soft, humorless chuckle. "They called me *the ghost candidate.* Said I didn't have a chance in hell. Had a broken-down pickup truck, seven volunteers, and a budget smaller than the school board's bake sale."

"You knocked on every door in the district," she said. "Even the ones with dogs. You campaigned through a hurricane warning."

"And I won," Norman said quietly.

"Damn right you did," Claire said. "Because you didn't float. You dug in."

He exhaled, the memory softening the defeat that clung to him.

"I don't want to leave," she whispered. Her voice cracked like ice on a pond. "I know we're supposed to be gracious and measured, but I love this place. I love the work. The platform. The people. I don't want to be... irrelevant."

He turned toward her. She was more than the First Lady. She was the one who kept the campaign sane in 2024, the one who'd held his hand when the Publicgate headlines rolled out like a funeral procession.

"You're not irrelevant," he said, his voice quiet. "You were never just the First Lady. You're Claire. You'd still matter if I lost every office I ever held."

She pressed her forehead to his chest, drawing the scent of starch and memory. "I'm just not ready for the lights to turn off."

He didn't have an answer to that. Only silence and the ticking of the grandfather clock down the hall.

Publicgate had done its damage. It would stain the history books. His name would come with an asterisk, an entire chapter in some future textbook about American decline. But here, in this room, he wasn't the embattled incumbent. He was just Norman; tired, aging, unsure of what came after.

"I don't know if I have another fight in me," he admitted.

Claire looked up. "Then borrow some of mine."

He smiled at that; genuine, the first in a while.

A knock came at the door. Secret Service, right on schedule.

Norman kissed her forehead. "Let's go vote for a president."

Claire straightened her coat. "And let's pretend it's still you."

They left the residence hand in hand, the echo of their footsteps swallowed by the halls of a house they might never walk again.

But for now, they were still here. Still standing.

The skyline of Denver rose like a jagged crown against the slate-gray sky, its high-rises framed by the snowy silhouette of the Rockies in the distance. The motorcade coursed west on I-70, cutting through the early morning haze with a lawman's urgency; empty lanes cleared by flashing lights and police escorts, the city's pulse slowed to make way for the would-be president.

Inside the lead black Suburban, Ted Bright sat in silence, his face turned toward the passing buildings, eyes narrowed in quiet reflection. Denver had always felt like home, and it was home. He had walked these streets as a young city councilman, governed them as mayor, rallied them as Colorado's governor, and now, as their senator, he had carried their hopes to Washington. Today, the city stood not just as a backdrop, but as a stage, ceremonial, and symbolic. The place where his journey from the city hall to the White House would come full circle.

This morning, Denver was no longer just his hometown. It was the heartbeat of the campaign's closing chapter, the place where the three tiers of American government converged in a single man's rise. City. State. Federal. All roads, for Ted Bright, led here.

Across from him, Rey Hughes tapped his fingers against a tablet, a thick accent curling around his words like molasses. "Well, I'll be damned. Look at this here," he muttered, tilting the screen toward Ted. "Landon's on a goddamn tear. Been bouncin' through Arizona, Pennsylvania, Wisconsin, Michigan. The man's movin' like he's runnin' for president *himself.*"

Ted didn't look up. He simply gave a faint, dry exhale through his nose. "About time he earned his keep."

Rey chuckled, that slow, rasping bayou laugh. "Hell, boy's been quieter than a possum playin' dead since we benched him last month. But now? He's workin' the trail like he just saw Jesus at a diner in Des Moines."

Ted finally turned. "Because he's not working for *me,* Rey. He's working for *himself.* Every handshake, every rally, every clipped little interview, it's Landon Wolfe laying bricks for his own goddamn future. He wants to look indispensable."

Rey leaned back in his seat, tapping a cigarette against the side of the tablet, though he didn't light it. "Ain't the worst idea to let him think he still matters. Let the man puff up like a blowfish, and then we drain the tank. Send him somewhere far, far away."

Ted's brow lifted. "Like?"

Rey grinned. "Solomon Islands. Place he's so fired up about. Sure, we're pullin' out, but we still gotta make it *look* like we care. Send him on a little post-withdrawal goodwill tour. Shake hands, take photos, and tell the world it ain't a total loss. JFK used to send ol' Lyndon all the way to Vietnam just to keep him outta the West Wing. Could do the same with Wolfe. That boy's itchin' for an island vacation? Fine. Give him one."

Ted considered this. "Let him strut around on the other side of the world while we start setting the real agenda back home."

"Yessir," Rey said, pleased with himself. "And when the time's right... resignation. We feed the press some horse-shit about 'personal reasons' or a 'health scare.' Get him out clean. No scandal. Just fade him out like an old bumper sticker on a car you're about to trade in."

Ted's voice was low, even. "He thinks we're partners."

Rey grunted. "That boy ain't your partner. He's a spare tire. Only good when you've got a flat, and even then, it's temporary."

Ted turned his gaze back to the window, the glass now reflecting the tops of Denver's federal buildings and the gold dome of the state capitol. The city was waking up around them, commuters rerouted, shops opening, bundled pedestrians watching from the sidewalks as the Bright motorcade sped past.

"I'll let him have the inauguration," Ted said. "Let him stand behind me and wave like he belongs there. Then we gut him, quietly. One cut at a time."

Rey gave a low whistle. "Cold. I like it."

"No mess," Ted replied. "No headlines. Just... irrelevance."

Outside, the convoy turned off the interstate and into the heart of the city. Ted watched as the morning fog began to burn off the glass towers, and somewhere in the distance, a massive digital billboard flashed: THE FUTURE IS BRIGHT!

But inside the car, the future was being plotted, calculated, brutal, and methodical. And Landon Wolfe, for all his ambition and fire, was already being written out of it.

Philadelphia never changes: brick and blood, cobblestone and ambition. It wears its history with pride, but today it felt like camouflage. A city voting like the republic depended on it, while I moved among them like a ghost.

I wore black. Not for the sake of symbolism, but because it felt fitting. Funerals deserve dignity, and this would be no exception. Ted Bright would die tonight. America would hear a lie so vast, so meticulously rehearsed, that by morning it would be gospel. That's the thing about lies, they don't need to be small to be believable. In fact, the bigger the better. People don't question what feels like destiny. They just applaud it.

Since that night in Virginia, when the generals came to the estate like Roman senators in civilian suits, this has been inevitable. The coup didn't begin with tanks or troops; it started with nods across quiet tables, with brandy and bitterness and oaths muttered like prayers. We were patriots, after all. Disillusioned, yes. But not defeated. The system had failed us long before we ever considered returning the favor.

They call what we're doing treason. But what do you call a nation whose leaders sell off power like cheap property? What do you call a president who let the Pacific fall into Chinese hands while insisting on "diplomatic restraint"? What do you call a candidate like Ted Bright, propped up by the media, insulated by wealth, preaching unity while preparing for tyranny?

I call it rot. And rot must be cut away.

The plan is already in motion. Denver will be the stage, ironically fitting, the city where Ted rose from mayor to governor to senator, now to president. He'll stand under that triumphant skyline, believing he's reached the mountaintop. He'll smile for the cameras. And then, as the nation watches, the curtain falls.

It will be quick. Efficient. Surgical.

A gunman. Live television. Blood on the marble steps of a Denver government building. The moment will be burned into the collective American psyche before the echo of the shot even fades. Children will cry.

Anchors will stammer. Secret Service agents will descend like vultures. And in the confusion, in the blinding, deafening chaos of it all, the lie will begin.

They'll say it was a lone actor, some disgruntled extremist, maybe foreign, maybe domestic. It won't matter. We'll make him what the nation needs him to be. A symbol. A scapegoat. A villain they can hate while we tighten the bolts of the machine.

And while the country mourns, shocked, broken, terrified, we'll move. Martial authority. Emergency powers. The kind of sweeping control that's only possible when the rulebook is too soaked in blood to be read.

Technically, I won't have a claim. Not right away. Ted will have been president-elect, not sworn in. The Constitution doesn't speak clearly in moments like this; it assumes the dead man would still be alive. And into that void, the old vultures will descend. Kennedy Hickman, Ivan Chang, Patrick Callahan: all of them will see their chance. They'll cry for a convention. They'll whisper about legitimacy. They'll try to scramble the order.

But while they argue over fine print and nomination rules, I'll already be in front of the cameras. Calm. Measured. Presidential without the title.

The people won't want another politician clawing their way into the spotlight. They'll want someone strong. Someone who stood beside Ted on the ticket. Someone the military trusts. Someone who doesn't blink when the world burns.

They'll want me.

Because while the party tears itself apart trying to interpret constitutional nuance, I'll be the only one offering certainty. Offering order. Offering strength. And in the end, that's what they'll choose, not legality, not precedent, but survival.

And I won't take the reins outright. Not at first. The optics have to be perfect, me stepping forward reluctantly, humbly, as the one steady voice in the storm. The grieving nation won't want a senator, a governor, or a progressive darling. They'll want a protector. And I'll become one, even if I have to build the throne out of the wreckage Ted leaves behind.

So let the others shout. Let them file motions, call for votes, wave copies of the Constitution in front of cameras. By the time the Electoral College meets, there won't be any debate left to have. The path will already be paved. The public will demand it.

And I will oblige them.

Because history isn't written by the victors.

It's written by the ones who survive the storm... and convince everyone they were the eye of it.

The police escort curved down Speer Boulevard, cutting through the heart of downtown Denver like a scalpel through flesh. Skyscrapers loomed overhead, casting sharp shadows onto the concrete sprawl of the Metropolitan State University campus. From above, it looked like any other Election Day: orderly and ceremonial. But on the ground, it pulsed with urgency. Students gathered like storm clouds, huddled behind barricades, waving campaign signs and phones in equal measure.

Ted's SUV came to a halt near the campus library. When the doors opened, the noise surged; cheers, chants, the sharp crack of a reporter's camera flash.

Ted stepped out into the Colorado morning with the confidence of a man returning to consecrated ground. His navy coat flared slightly in the wind as he adjusted the sleeves, flanked by Secret Service agents Jackie Bell and Allen Jordan. He nodded politely as they moved him forward, their eyes scanning windows, rooftops, every twitch in the crowd.

The path to the polling station had been cleared, but still, a hundred voices broke against the barricades.

"Senator Bright! Do you think you'll take Pennsylvania?"

"What would you say to undecided voters still on the fence today?"

"Senator Bright, what's your plan for student loan reform if you win?"

Ted slowed. Jackie Bell gave a firm glance as if to say, keep moving, but Ted ignored him.

He turned toward the crowd and raised a hand. "One at a time," he said, his voice warm but commanding, the kind that made people listen. "Pennsylvania? It's going to be close. But I've always believed in the power of a good ground game, and I believe in the voters there."

"Student loans? The plan is to stop treating students like an ATM. No interest on federal loans. And real forgiveness, not empty promises."

Another voice called out, "What would you say to voters who think this country needs more than politics-as-usual?"

Ted smiled without showing his teeth. "I'd tell them this: politics-as-usual didn't build the America we love. It was vision, discipline, and service. That's what I've offered every day I've been in public life, and what I'll offer as president."

There was a pause, a shift in the crowd's energy. Then a college student near the front, flushed with excitement, barely older than twenty, shouted the question that landed with a hush:

"Senator Bright, how does it feel to vote for yourself... to be president?"

Ted's expression flickered for the briefest moment, as if the weight of the question tapped something personal. He stepped closer to the barricade, hands in his coat pockets, and answered with the grin of a man who knew how to wear legacy.

"Not all that different from when I ran for mayor. Or governor. Or senator," he said. "But just to make it special, I'll circle my name in blue ink today instead of black."

The crowd laughed; a kind of laughter that carried relief, hope, and pride. Denver loved its favorite son.

Bell leaned in again, murmured something about optics and time, but Ted waved him off with a slight nod. He stood there just a moment longer, soaking it in: the cheers, the cold air, the cathedral of glass and steel rising around him like witnesses.

Today, he would vote for himself to become President of the United States.

Not many men got to do that. Fewer still had done it from the city that had shaped them. Denver wasn't just the backdrop; it was the proving ground. And now, it stood with him one final time.

He offered one last wave to the crowd before turning toward the polling station, set up inside the campus library, flanked by his detail. The chants of "Bright for America!" echoed behind him like an anthem.

He didn't look back.

Whatever came next —victory, legacy, or destiny —it was already in motion.

And by midnight, the whole world would be watching.

19

The Ides of Victory

Election Night | Denver, Colorado

The Wellington E. Webb Municipal Building pulsed with electricity. A thousand moving pieces, advisors with tablets, interns on headsets, the campaign's legal team tucked into corners, each part played like a note in a rising political symphony. The last votes were being cast. Across the country, the sun had set and the verdict of a nation had begun to take shape.

Ted stood apart from the chaos, alone in a private war room just off the main operations floor. The space was sleek, polished, and almost sterile; three wide televisions bathed the room in the cold light of competing news anchors, while a long buffet table offered untouched food he had no appetite for. A few unopened bottles of wine and bourbon stood behind glass, like museum artifacts, symbolic and unreachable. He poured himself a glass of water instead.

He paced slowly, hands behind his back, eyes flicking occasionally to the electoral map as it shifted and pulsed in real-time. His mind wasn't on the numbers. Not yet. He was thinking of the shape of power, of legacy, of how many decades had come and gone to reach this precise, fragile moment.

A knock pulled him from his thoughts.

Jackie Bell stepped in with his usual strength, the line of his Secret Service suit crisp and unyielding. His voice was low and measured.

"Senator. Civic Center's locked. Barricades are up on Bannock, fencing wrapped around the amphitheater. We're secure. It's... electric out there. Feels like a coronation."

Ted allowed himself a faint, skeptical smile. "Let's not say that word just yet."

Jackie nodded once. "Crowd's pushing a hundred thousand. One of the biggest Denvers ever seen."

Ted gave a gentle nod and looked back toward the window, where the distant lights of Civic Center Park shimmered through the glass. "Thank you, Jackie."

With a polite exit, the door clicked shut again, and silence returned.

And then, another knock.

This one was softer. Slower. Almost reluctant.

Ted turned. Edward stood in the doorway.

He was dressed for the night, the campaign pin on his lapel gleaming under the fluorescent light, but the confidence was a façade. His posture carried the stiffness of a man bracing for impact. Behind his eyes was something unspoken, raw.

"Dad..." he began, closing the door gently behind him. "Can we talk?"

Ted studied him, really looked at him, for a long second. Then, with a simple gesture, motioned toward the couch.

Edward crossed the room and sat carefully, like the furniture might break beneath him. He didn't speak at first. His fingers played with the edge of the campaign button, turning it over and over in silence.

"I've been carrying something," he finally said, barely above a whisper. "Since the convention. Since Wolfe."

Ted sat across from him, elbows on his knees, calm. Waiting.

"I screwed up," Edward said. "I let them in. I let Lydia in. I let Wolfe take the reins. I gave them power, *your* power. And I knew better. But I just... I wanted to matter."

He paused, swallowed hard, and stared down at the carpet.

"I got drunk. I got careless. I got manipulated. And I gave away the one thing you've worked your whole life for."

Ted didn't flinch. He didn't interrupt. He watched his son unravel.

"I should've been stronger," Edward said. "You could've picked anyone. McCoy. Karen Ortiz. You ended up with a snake. And I—" he choked on the word, "I handed him the damn keys."

The silence that followed felt thick enough to cut.

Ted leaned back slightly, drawing a long, controlled breath.

"You're right," he said at last.

Edward tensed.

"You made mistakes. And I won't pretend they didn't cost us. I was furious with you. For a while."

Edward's jaw clenched. He nodded once, as if ready to accept whatever punishment came next.

"But," Ted continued, his voice quieter now, gentler, "you're not the first Bright to be reckless. And you won't be the last to come back from it."

Edward looked up, startled. "You mean—?"

"I forgive you, son," Ted said. "I mean it."

The words hit Edward harder than any rebuke ever could. His posture crumbled. The breath he'd been holding escaped in a ragged sigh, and he buried his face in his hands for a moment before letting his shoulders drop.

"I didn't think you'd ever say that," he said softly.

Ted gave a faint smile. "Took me a while. Took *you* longer."

Edward let out a short, weak laugh. "That's fair."

The quiet between them was no longer heavy; it had turned warm. The air had shifted. A long, bitter winter between father and son had finally broken.

After a pause, Edward sat up straighter. His voice steadied.

"I've been thinking," he said. "About what comes next."

Ted raised an eyebrow. "Next?"

"I want to run for your Senate seat. Colorado. When you resign."

Ted studied him, his expression unreadable.

"I figured that would be Philip's path," he said.

"Philip's the golden child," Edward replied, a slight smirk forming. "But I've seen this campaign up close. I've seen what real power looks like. What it costs. I want to earn something of my own. I want to serve."

Ted didn't respond right away. He looked at his son, not the boy he'd tried to shape, but the man finally beginning to stand upright.

"You know the Senate's a war," Ted said. "A brutal one."

"I'm not afraid of it," Edward said.

Something in Ted's gaze flickered then, an idea, a distant horizon suddenly visible.

"You know," he said slowly, "only two father-son pairs have ever reached the White House. The Adamses. The Bushes."

Edward blinked. "You think I could—?"

Ted's tone shifted, quiet and measured, yet full of intent.

"I think," he said, "if you don't waste the second chance you've been given, you might just make us the third."

The words stopped Edward cold.

He had spent years chasing fragments of this, his father's pride, his approval, his faith. Now, here it was. In full. Offered freely, like grace.

"I won't let you down," Edward said, his voice thick with sincerity.

Ted reached across the table and placed a hand firmly over his son's.

"I know."

And for a moment, rare and fragile, there was peace.

No handlers. No staff. No crisis.

Just father and son.

Edward wiped at his eyes. "When I run," he said, smiling through the emotion, "remind me to make 'No Landon Wolfe' part of the platform."

Ted chuckled. "Make it your first executive order."

Laughter lingered between them as the glow of television screens reflected the early red and blue tide of results. Outside, the city braced for a celebration. In here, history paused.

It was a quiet triumph.

One, no network would capture.

And in that moment, just that one, Edward Bright had everything he had wanted.

Everything, except time.

I stepped into the war room just as the buzz reached a fever pitch. The air was heavy with stress, caffeine, and the sharp tang of nerves; a battlefield thick with anticipation, if not smoke. I'd flown in from Pennsylvania, with a stop in Columbus before that, the ground still practically shaking from the helicopters and rally music. Now here I was, in Denver, surrounded by glowing maps, murmuring strategists, and a candidate who looked like he hadn't slept since the primaries.

The room itself felt like a pressure cooker. Multiple TVs bathed us in bluish light: NBC, CNN, *The Political Pulse,* all spewing numbers, counties, margins. Steve Kornacki's voice filtered through everything like a metronome: steady, clinical, detached from the emotional carnage his numbers inflicted. The electoral map was beginning to fill in, with some red and some blue, just as always.

Ted stood in front of the central screen, arms crossed, face unreadable. His tie was slightly loosened, his collar damp. He wasn't saying much, but the tension in his jaw said everything. This wasn't the Ted Bright of the campaign trail, shaking hands and quoting scripture. This was something colder. Focused. Worn.

"NBC can now project that President Norman Hayden will win North Carolina and the state's sixteen electoral votes," Kornacki announced.

Ted didn't flinch. Not great news, but not unexpected either.

"And Senator Bright will win South Carolina, the home state of his running mate, Congressman Landon Wolfe," Kornacki continued.

The room popped like a champagne cork. People clapped my back, whooped, grinned at me like I was Atlas holding up the damn map. But I didn't grin back. One state didn't mean anything. Not tonight.

Ted hadn't moved. He was staring at the screen like a general surveying a battlefield from a hilltop. The Carolinas were split. A small win, but not momentum.

Then Virginia turned blue.

"Senator Ted Bright will win the state of Virginia, capturing sixty-five percent of the vote," Mark Anderson declared from *The Political Pulse,* his voice animated, maybe even surprised.

The room *erupted.* Virginia was no coin toss; this was dominance. Ted let out a breath, almost a sigh. Still, his arms stayed crossed. Still watching.

I moved closer to him. "Everything's going to plan. Just 192 more to go."

He turned his head slowly toward me and didn't bother hiding the fire in his eyes. "Wolfe, shut the fuck up. It's way too early for that kind of talk."

I raised my hands slightly, a casual shrug. "Just trying to keep it light. Virginia's a big deal. We should take the win."

"We'll celebrate when we win the damn thing," he muttered. His voice was low, tight. Presidential, in the way a man has to be when he's watching history balance on a fault line.

The next update hit like a hammer.

OHIO: PRESIDENT HAYDEN PROJECTED WINNER.

The red bar ticked forward on the screen. The room fell quiet, just a murmur or two, and the static hum of a losing heartbeat.

Ted stared, unmoving.

Someone whispered, "Ohio's gone." It felt like shouting.

Ted didn't explode. Didn't throw a chair. He just dragged a hand through his hair and whispered, "Dammit."

Not loud. Not theatrical. Just the sound of something cracking deep beneath the surface.

He took two steps back and looked toward the floor, then back up at the screen; his mind playing chess against fate.

Michigan was next: *Too close to call.*

Then Georgia: *Dead heat.*

The silence in the room turned brittle.

Ted looked at the map, then slowly shook his head. "What the hell is going on here?"

From the corner of the room, Rey Hughes stirred. He'd been half-lounging, a glass in hand, eyes half-lidded like he was watching a minor-league baseball game instead of the future of the country.

"Looks like we're tryin' to skin a cat with no blade," Rey drawled.

I blinked at him. "What does that even mean?"

Ted cut in before Rey could answer. "I knew I should've gone with McCoy," he said, almost to himself, but then he turned to me. "He's from Georgia. He would've locked it down."

My spine straightened. "Georgia was always going to be close, Ted. McCoy or not. You picked me for a reason."

Ted's eyes snapped toward Georgia's electoral count, then back to me. His jaw twitched. "I *picked* you," he said, spitting the word out like it tasted rotten. Then came the scoff, dry and bitter. "*Right.*"

I didn't flinch. "Yeah," I said calmly. "You did. And like it or not, I've been carrying the weight ever since."

He didn't respond. Just stared at me for a moment longer, eyes hard. Then turned back to the screen, as if the map might offer a better conversation.

Rey lifted his glass slightly. "If Georgia breaks blue, Florida might follow. And if Florida goes..." He trailed off with a smirk. "Well, let's just say I'll be buyin' myself a Cuban cigar."

Ted's jaw clenched, eyes locked on Georgia. "Yeah, and if it calls the other way, we're screwed."

I stepped in, my voice steady. "Ted, a few minutes ago you told me it was too early to celebrate. Well, it's too early to be throwing in the damn towel either."

He didn't look at me, but I could see his shoulders rise and fall; controlled, but tense.

"We still have three paths," I continued. "Michigan's in play. Pennsylvania's still counting. And Georgia's not gone yet. You know that."

He stayed quiet for a beat too long, eyes flicking between the numbers on the screen and the weight of everything he had riding on them. Then he spoke, softer but still sharp. "If we lose Georgia and Florida... I'm holding you responsible."

I gave a tight nod. "Fair enough. But if we win them, I expect a cigar too."

A flicker of something passed across his face, annoyance, maybe, or just fatigue. Then, finally, a smirk. "Don't get cocky."

"I'm not. Just... focused."

The screen flickered again. Another projection was coming.

The room leaned in, every breath held.

Election night wasn't over. But the real fight had only just begun.

I'd been back in the private room for a while now, long enough for the tension from my earlier fight with Ted over Georgia to fade into background noise, replaced by the relentless churn of numbers, projections, and half-formed hopes. The room had settled into an exhausted rhythm when Lisa Harper's voice suddenly cut through the television chatter, sharp and surgical.

"*The Political Pulse* is first to project that Senator Ted Bright will carry the state of Florida, President Norman Hayden's home state."

The room went dead. Just... silence. A kind of stunned, unnatural stillness. Then—chaos.

People jumped to their feet, gasping, shouting. I could feel the shift like a jolt of electricity running through the floorboards. Florida flipped. Thirty electoral votes. All ours.

Mark Anderson's voice followed on the broadcast, muffled now by the noise. "This is a stunning development. Almost no one saw this coming. A devastating blow to the president's reelection chances."

Ted was frozen. Hands on the back of a chair, staring at the screen like he didn't trust his own eyes. Honestly, I didn't either.

I pushed through the crowd toward the glass side room where Lydia and Ellie had set up their command station. "Lydia!" I called as I entered. "Can you confirm? Pulse just called Florida."

She didn't look up. Her fingers danced across the keys. "Already on it. Checking precinct data."

Ellie had a phone to her ear, talking in a low, fast voice. I waited. My heart was hammering, not just from adrenaline, but from the implications. If this were to hold, the map would tilt. The math would change.

Lydia leaned back, finally. "It's real," she said. "Miami-Dade turnout crushed expectations. Hispanic independents swung hard against Hayden. Our data's confirming it across multiple counties. Florida's gone."

I grinned and let out a sharp breath. "Holy hell."

Out in the war room, the buzz reached a new pitch. CNN, NBC, and even FOX are all confirming it. Florida was blue. And with it, our count leapt. Ted's total ticked up to 168.

Then came the second blow.

"Breaking now," came the anchor from ABC. "Senator Bright will also win the state of Georgia. Atlanta's urban turnout, combined with late-breaking rural swings, appears to have given Bright a clear lead."

The map lit up again. Red state turned blue.

It was a clean, devastating one-two punch.

I stepped back into the private room, as applause broke out like cannon fire. Aides were embracing. Journalists in the back scrambled for updates. Ted's family gathered around him, clapping, hugging. For the first time all night, he looked like a man who believed it was happening.

I drifted toward him. "You still worried about Georgia?" I asked, keeping my voice light.

Ted gave me a sideways glance, tired but buzzing. "I'm not worried about a damn thing right now."

I let the corner of my mouth twitch into a grin. "Glad I could pull my weight."

He didn't respond. Just nodded slightly, barely.

From the corner, Rey Hughes raised his glass with the calm of a man who'd already played this scene out in his mind months ago. "There it is," he said, to no one in particular. "That's the flip."

I didn't stick around. I slipped back to the side room, where Lydia and Ellie were still at it, feeding off the energy, focused as ever. The map was unfolding in our favor, all according to plan.

"What's the story with the congressional races?" I asked, sliding in beside them.

Ellie looked up, her eyes sharp, her voice already half-excited, half-lethal. "Democrats are flipping the House. Senate's holding. Even with Ted's seat open."

That gave me pause. "A Democratic Congress? That's real?"

Lydia nodded, scrolling through her data feed. "It's a wave. The exit polls are brutal for the GOP. Voters turned on them in the suburbs, especially after Publicgate. They didn't punish Hayden; they protected him. That's the backlash."

Ellie added, "Some of those Republican incumbents? They're not just losing; they're getting wiped out. The voters are calling bullshit on the cover-up."

I caught a name on the screen and felt my heart skip a beat. Iowa's 3rd Congressional District. Morgan McClain. Red bar shrinking. Blue wave swallowing it whole.

She was losing.

The woman who'd taken my seat back in 2016. The one who smiled through every televised betrayal of what I'd built. The one who lit the match on the long road that led me here.

Gone.

Poetic, I thought, but even revenge has its limits. I leaned back, watching the numbers settle. Ted wasn't handing himself a Democratic Congress. He was giving one to me. That was always the plan, buried beneath the noise and theater. And now, it was coming into focus, one flipped district at a time.

But something twisted in my gut. The calculus wasn't as clean as I'd hoped.

"If we've got a Democratic House," I said, my voice low, calculated, eyes fixed on the screen, "how the hell do I sell them on the Solomon Islands?"

Lydia didn't answer right away. Her jaw tightened. "That's a different kind of battlefield."

"No Republican war hawks to lean on," Ellie added, scanning her tablet. "No easy path to a use-of-force resolution. This new Congress? They'll choke on the word 'intervention.'"

"They'll want panels, envoys, humanitarian drops," Lydia muttered. "Not boots and ships."

I nodded slowly, watching district after district flash blue. We had won, but not cleanly, not without complications. For a brief moment, I felt it, a miscalculation. A gap in the line. Then the thought was gone.

"They won't march for war," I said, almost to myself. "So we won't ask them to."

Ellie looked up.

"We'll give them something else. Fear." I let the word hang. "The kind that creeps in under the skin. The kind that doesn't ask for permission, only reaction. A sunken patrol boat. A missing team. Grainy satellite footage and a leak to *The Post.*"

Lydia met my eyes, her voice quiet. "False flag?"

I gave a slight smile. "Doesn't have to be a flag. Just fear. Manufactured or not, it makes policy move."

Ellie shook her head, impressed and unsettled all at once. "You don't need hawks, do you?"

"No," I said. "I just need an excuse. One that the doves can't say no to."

Mark Anderson's voice boomed from the television, crisp and final.

"*The Political Pulse* can now project that Senator Ted Bright of Colorado has won the 2028 Presidential Election and will become the 48th President of the United States."

There was a moment, just a sliver of stillness, before the room detonated in sound. Applause. Shouts. Someone let out a scream. Champagne hissed open, and Philip Bright hurled a cork across the room like a grenade. Edward followed with a spray of Moët that hit the ceiling tiles. All around me, the room turned into a roaring theater of triumph.

But I didn't move. Not at first.

I stood near the back wall, half in shadow, watching them all celebrate. Watching *him* celebrate. Ted, the man they just crowned, was hugging his wife, his daughter clinging to his side. He looked like a president. The networks would talk about that. The look. The smile. The effortless grace.

But I knew better. That title America just handed him? It had an expiration date.

The on-screen commentary continued. Lisa Harper's voice cut through the chaos like a needle. "Ted Bright didn't just win an election tonight; he launched a movement. A new American frontier, one rooted in unity, in optimism, and in justice. His 'Future is Bright' movement will define a generation. And in doing so, Bright has cemented himself as the face of 21st-century liberalism."

A not-so-subtle invocation of Kennedy. I almost laughed.

"And yet," Mark Anderson added, "this victory is inseparable from Publicgate. From the backlash. From the consequences. Florida flipped tonight—Florida. The state Hayden governed. Georgia followed. Voters rejected the GOP's silence. Their refusal to act. They wanted someone to challenge the rot. And Bright gave them that."

He was right. But they didn't see the real irony. Ted didn't challenge the rot, he repackaged it. Sold it as hope. And I made sure it sold.

As *The Political Pulse's* commentary droned on, I felt a buzz in my pocket. One name on the screen: Mitch Ferguson.

His message was brief.

"He won. Time to prepare the next phase."

That was all. No names. No emojis. Just the calm, clinical confirmation of something long in motion.

I locked the screen and slid the phone back into my pocket, heart steady. Ted was president-elect. But he wasn't the future.

I was.

Behind me, the war room pulsed with euphoria. Staffers hugged, cried, laughed like survivors. But the screen told the true story.

27 states. 336 electoral votes. Hayden limped away with 202.

A historic victory. A mandate.

And the perfect cover for what comes next.

Seated at the Resolute Desk for one of the last times, President Norman Hayden stared into the warm shadows of the Oval Office, its soft lamplight catching the gold trim of the drapes and the edges of a world slowly moving on without him. The air was still, reverent. This was a room built for myth and memory, an echo chamber for power. And tonight, it felt like a tomb.

The portraits watched in silence. Washington, austere and stoic. Lincoln, weary-eyed. FDR, mid-turn in his wheelchair. Hayden let out a slow breath. His presidency was over.

He dialed the number without hesitation. Not out of obligation, but principle. His hand didn't shake. His voice, when it came, was firm. This wasn't surrender. It was duty.

Ted answered quickly. "Mr. President."

"Senator," Hayden replied, the edge of fatigue tracing the words.

"Congressman Wolfe is here with me," Ted added, brisk but respectful. "What can we do for you, Norman?"

Hayden leaned back, the leather of his chair creaking faintly beneath him. "Ted, there's no script for a call like this. Only tradition. You ran a strong race. You and Wolfe pulled off what many thought couldn't be done. I'm calling to concede, and to congratulate you. I know you'll make a fine president."

There was a pause. A quiet breath on the other end. Then Ted's voice, more human than Hayden expected: "Thank you, Mr. President. That means a great deal. I know this wasn't an easy campaign."

"No," Hayden said. "It wasn't." His eyes wandered to the corner of the room, where the flag stood motionless. "I'm sitting at the Resolute right now. Looking out over the Rose Garden. It hits you differently at the end. You'll see soon enough. This office, it's not just power. It's isolation. Every crisis ends here. Every failure lands here."

Ted was silent. Listening. Maybe realizing.

Hayden continued. "There's a loneliness to this job, even with a cabinet and advisors. In the end, it's your face in the Situation Room when the missiles fly. Your voice calling the next of kin after a drone strike goes wrong. History won't remember the sleepless nights, but it'll remember the decisions."

"I understand," Ted said. "I don't take any of it lightly."

"I know you don't," Hayden said, more gently now. "That's why I'm calling. Some men cling to power until it kills them. I'd rather pass it with dignity."

A flicker of something passed through Hayden's chest, sadness, perhaps. But not regret.

"There'll be briefings waiting. National security, economic transitions. The outgoing staff will cooperate fully. I've made that clear."

"Thank you," Ted said. "We'll make the most of it."

"Just remember something," Hayden said, voice firming again. "The office is never really yours. You borrow it. Steward it. And if you're lucky, you leave it a little better than you found it."

Ted's voice steadied. "That's the plan."

"Good," Hayden said, allowing a pause to settle between them. "Then I'll leave you to it."

There was no ceremony. No need for more. Just the quiet understanding between two men, divided by power but bound by duty.

On the other end of the line, Ted turned to those gathered in the private campaign suite: the Brights, the strategists, the hangers-on, and gave a slight nod. "Clear the room," he said quietly. "Give me a moment."

Now alone, the two presidents, outgoing and incoming, spoke not as rivals but as caretakers of a nation. The conversation shifted to the machinery of the republic: daily intelligence briefings, the weight of the nuclear codes, foreign adversaries cloaked in diplomacy. Hayden's voice grew heavier as he detailed the invisible wars already underway; cyber probes from Beijing, naval standoffs in the Pacific, the quiet dance with Moscow.

After a while, the line went quiet. No more platitudes. No passing of the torch with cameras flashing. Just a phone call. Just the burden changing hands.

Hayden gently returned the receiver to its cradle. The room seemed to exhale with him, its stillness settling into something sacred.

Outside the Oval, staffers moved like shadows, packing boxes, transitioning power, preparing for what came next.

Hayden remained at the Resolute Desk a moment longer, running a hand along its edge. Soon, the Oval would belong to another.

But for tonight, it was still his.

As I stepped out of the private room, the noise of the war room hit me like static; chatter, celebration, the mechanical churn of a machine that didn't yet know it was being dismantled from within.

Ellie stood near the edge of the chaos, sharp as ever in a lavender dress that cut through the crowd like a violet flame. Always poised. Always deliberate. Her eyes met mine before her feet did, and she broke through the tangle of staffers and aides with the grace of someone who knew precisely where history was about to tilt.

"Mr. Vice President-elect Wolfe," she said, her voice smooth, rehearsed, yet laced with that private electricity we both carried now. She handed me a bound speech, with clean lines and an official seal, printed on thick paper that smelled of ambition.

"It hits all the necessary notes," she continued. "Unity, continuity, a shared vision with Ted. Restoring virtue, rebuilding strength, all the right applause lines."

I gave the document a quick glance. The language was noble, statesmanlike, yet utterly fictional. I didn't need to read it to know that. "Let's hope this one never sees daylight," I said under my breath.

Ellie's smile was subtle, but it curled at the edges like a secret. "It won't. But we had to make it look good."

She handed me a second, unlabeled, unassuming envelope. Thinner. Deadlier. The real speech. The one history would remember. A eulogy dressed as a call to order. A public reckoning for a nation that, in less than an hour, would watch its president-elect fall on live television.

I slid the decoy into the outer pocket of my jacket and pressed the real one to my chest, tucking it inside like a confession. The weight of it against my ribs felt colder than paper should. Colder, even, than steel.

"You've done your part brilliantly, Ellie," I said, voice low, careful. "Whatever comes next, history will remember it."

She didn't respond immediately. Just looked at me, the flicker of conscience in her eyes warred with calculation, and calculation won. She'd started with poetry in her blood, back when speeches were meant to inspire, not manipulate. But now? Now she was a co-conspirator, her words drafted like blueprints for power.

Footsteps behind us; heavier, purposeful. Secret Service. The shift was happening. You could feel it. The invisible clock ticking down to zero.

"We're moving soon," one of the agents said to no one in particular. "Civic Center Park is staged. Lights are hot, cameras rolling."

Ellie nodded and gave me a last, almost imperceptible touch on the sleeve. Two speeches. Two outcomes. One podium. Only one version would be spoken aloud tonight.

20

The Whole World is Watching

Civic Center Park | Denver, Colorado

The elevator opened with a quiet chime, and suddenly we were below it all; beneath the war room, beneath the cheers, beneath the weight of history itself. The underground garage of the Webb Building was cavernous and cold, lit in long fluorescent stripes that gave everything a pale, ghostly hue. Victory had been declared, but in this basement bunker, it felt like something darker was being loaded into the back of black cars.

The Secret Service moved with precision; Jackie Bell barked into a radio as agents swept corners and gestured hurriedly. Ted and Gwen were ushered into the first vehicle, a reinforced limo codenamed Apollo. Their family followed close behind into a second one. Smiles, hugs, flashbulbs. All of it felt like a well-rehearsed play barreling toward the final act.

I was directed into the third vehicle. Lydia slid in beside me, Ellie just behind her, clutching her satchel with a grip that could have cracked stone. Then came Rey Hughes, ever the contrarian, ever the barnacle clinging to whatever hull was cutting through the water fastest.

The door shut behind him with a heavy click, and we were sealed in. The interior was sleek and shadowed, thick with tension. Outside, the low hum of engines echoed against concrete as the motorcade aligned for departure.

Rey broke the silence with a smirk and that oily Louisiana drawl. "Well, I'll be damned. You actually helped win this thing."

I didn't look at him. I stared forward, into the black-tinted window, watching reflections flicker across the glass like ghosts.

He leaned forward slightly, smugness dripping off every syllable. "Tell me, Landon... when you tried to sabotage the campaign from within, did you think you'd be sittin' here tonight? Watching it all go the opposite way?"

I turned my head, slowly. "And here I thought you were done with amateur psychology."

Rey chuckled. "Come on. We both know what you wanted. You figured you'd poison the well, tank the ticket, and ride the chaos into the Oval. Problem is, you underestimated him. Ted's not just a politician. He's the whole goddamn movement now."

I gave him a half-smile, one of those dry, exhausted ones meant to hold back something deeper. "Let's not rewrite your part in this. You broke federal law running money for Hayden. Publicgate wasn't a leak, it was your golden parachute. You jumped from one sinking ship to the next, and here you are again. Ever the patriot."

Rey shrugged, undeterred. "Hey, I've always said, I back winners. I'm just lucky my winner turned out to be the real deal. And you?" He grinned wider. "I hope you packed light, Mr. Vice President-Elect. You won't be spending much time in the West Wing. Ted'll have you shaking hands in hot zones and kissing ass in Asia. Soldier-diplomat. The workhorse behind the show horse."

I didn't bite. I just met Rey's gaze and said, flatly, "I look forward to that."

He leaned back, smugness intact, satisfied to get the last word.

Outside, Denver came into view. The limo climbed out of the underground and into a city alive with triumph. The streets were lined with people, shoulder to shoulder, waving flags and holding homemade signs.

Some had tears in their eyes. Others danced in the cold, as if the November wind was no match for the warmth of hope.

The Future is BRIGHT.

Bright-Wolfe 2028.

Colorado's Son. America's President.

The energy was infectious, but I couldn't catch it. Not tonight. Not knowing what was coming.

Civic Center Park loomed ahead, a sea of light and sound. A hundred thousand voices pressed against the barricades, chanting Ted's name like it was both a blessing and a battle cry. The city had turned itself inside out for its favorite son.

Ted was about to have his moment under the stars.

And I knew, as our limo rolled into place behind his, that it would be his last.

The agents moved quickly again, opening doors, sweeping the plaza, radios crackling in their sleeves. Lydia adjusted her scarf. Ellie didn't say a word; she just watched the crowd of people, her expression unreadable. Rey shifted beside me, humming something tuneless, probably convinced he'd won whatever private game he thought we were playing.

I stared out at the Civic Center Park stage, lit like a monument. The sky above was starless. Denver roared as if it were witnessing the birth of a new age.

And maybe it was.

Not the one they thought. Not the one they'd cheer for.

Just beyond the lights, something irreversible waited. A fulcrum in the shadows. Once crossed, there'd be no going back.

History was about to begin its next chapter; loud, brilliant, and soaked in blood.

We moved through a narrow path behind the stage; cordoned off, guarded, soundtracked by the distant roar of a hundred thousand lungs. Floodlights swept across Civic Center Park in rhythmic pulses. The air was electric with celebration, a city ablaze with pride. A Colorado Native had won the presidency, and the capital of the Mountain West was throwing the biggest party in the republic.

The tent behind the stage was half war-room, half sanctuary, lined with gas heaters and stocked with water bottles, folded chairs, and Secret Service agents who looked ten seconds from pulling their sidearms if anyone made the wrong move.

Ted stood near a stack of flag-draped trunks, fixing his tie in the reflection of a turned-off monitor. Gwen was adjusting their grandson's collar. The atmosphere was light, warm, and touched by history.

Then the staff photographer appeared, a mid-twenties man, nervous, chewing on a pen cap.

"Can we get a shot of the President-elect and Vice President-elect?" he asked.

Ted slung an arm around me. His grin had the brightness of someone convinced he had just climbed Olympus. The camera snapped. He turned to the lens and said, "That one's museum-worthy."

Then the moment died. Ted's arm dropped. The smile evaporated.

"You know what you are, Landon?" Ted said under his breath, just loud enough for me to hear. "You're the fog that rolls in after the battle, covering the dead. You wait, you hide, then you scavenge what's left."

His voice was even, detached. He didn't need volume. He had certainty.

"I've watched you slither through every campaign room, every donor dinner, every backroom handshake, hoping no one would see the fangs."

He paused, eyes scanning mine.

"But despite everything... despite *you*... I want this to work. I want a real partnership. Like Eisenhower and Nixon, before it all went south. Like Clinton and Gore, when it still mattered."

He glanced at his family, then back at me.

"You and I—this country—we don't get a second shot at this. So here it is, plain as I can offer it. We start fresh. Clean slate. You give me loyalty, I'll give you respect."

He extended his hand.

I took it.

His grip was firm, like a man shaking on a treaty he knew would be broken before the ink could dry.

"You have my word," I said.

We both knew it meant nothing.

Ted turned to Gwen, then to Evelyn, Philip, and Edward. His family gathered near the tent opening, wrapping themselves around him like a fortress. It was his moment, the culmination of everything he had built, sacrificed, endured.

I stepped away, drifting toward Lydia and Ellie. They were seated at a folding table beneath a small portable TV. The feed showed the empty stage, lit like a cathedral. Flags fluttered in the thin mountain air, their shadows flickering against the backdrop of Civic Center.

None of us spoke.

Then the voice rang out, heavy, official, amplified across downtown Denver:

"Ladies and gentlemen, please welcome the next President of the United States... Theodore Bright!"

The speakers thundered to life, and with it came the unmistakable opening riff of *Don't Stop* by Fleetwood Mac; a song that had become more than just a campaign anthem. It was a promise, a prophecy. *"Don't stop thinking about tomorrow..."* The lyrics rang out like scripture across the night sky, carried on waves of cheers from the crowd. This wasn't just music, it was the overture of a new American chapter. A brighter day was coming, the song insisted, and Ted Bright was the herald. He stepped into the spotlight with his family behind him, basking in the roar of a hundred thousand voices. *"Yesterday's gone... yesterday's gone..."*

I watched the stage, not the man, not the music, but the space he walked into.

The roar of the crowd, the chorus of *"Don't stop thinking about tomorrow,"* still echoing through the air.

The past had been buried in ballots. The future, they believed, had just taken the stage.

The whole world is watching.

Mako Elias Tanu passed through the Civic Center Park checkpoint at 8:32 P.M. with nothing more than hand warmers, a phone, and a folded pamphlet wedged in his back pocket. He wore a dark Patagonia puffer over a thrifted CSU hoodie, the kind worn by students and dropouts; and a pair of faded jeans. Nothing about him looked out of place. That was the point.

The air smelled of popcorn carts and city concrete. Crowds pressed in on every side, their chatter bubbling with anticipation for the president-elect. Flags waved from every railing. Searchlights swept the sky like it was the Fourth of July.

No one gave Tanu a second glance. No one saw a threat.

He walked with a quiet, deliberate rhythm, half-listening to the technician sound checking the stage, half-scanning for movement in the shadows. Beneath the puffer coat, his fingers closed around a small, heat-sealed envelope taped inside the lining. A message. A confession. A manifesto. Maybe it would be read. Perhaps it wouldn't. But he needed the world to *see something,* even if no one ever knew his name.

Not far from the perimeter, seated on a park bench near a vendor cart, a man in a navy coat watched through mirrored sunglasses. His hand didn't move much, just a slight lift of his wrist to glance at a watch, then a soft tap on an earpiece tucked under his collar.

"Asset is in play," he murmured to no one, the words absorbed into a low-frequency mic.

He didn't look again. He didn't need to. The machine was already turning.

As Mako approached the inner barricades, a man brushed past him. The contact was seamless, invisible to the eye. Just another shoulder in a crowd of thousands. But in that instant, the mission changed.

Emil Rollins; older, grizzled, the scar on his cheek catching light like a signature, moved with the calm precision of a man who'd done this before. He blended just enough to be ignored in a crowd, but anyone who looked twice would remember the face. His gloved hand had left something behind. A Glock 19 slipped expertly into Tanu's palm beneath the folds of his coat.

No words were exchanged. No confirmation. Just the cold weight of steel and history merging in one man's hand.

Tanu didn't flinch. He adjusted his jacket, folding the weapon deeper into the warmth of the fabric, and continued walking. Not fast. Not slow. Just another man finding his place near the stage.

No one knew where he came from. Few knew his name. He had been seen on the Metropolitan State campus, alone, days before, drifting through lectures, ordering coffee with cash, reading dense books on imperialism and power structures. He barely spoke. He barely smiled.

There were whispers, always whispers, that he had once been recruited. That someone in Langley had seen value in him. That maybe he'd been trained, or tested, or simply used.

But what mattered now was this: he was here.

Whether he believed he was carrying out justice or playing a part in someone else's grand design, Mako Elias Tanu moved forward, and the world, unknowingly, inched toward chaos.

Soon, the lights would rise. Ted Bright would step onto that stage. One shot would start the fire. The rest, just smoke and ash.

Ted Bright stood tall at the podium, the sea of faces before him electric with anticipation. Civic Center Park pulsed with life; over a hundred thousand strong, packed shoulder to shoulder, their breath rising like fog into the icy Colorado night. A low hum filled the air; excitement, nerves, the weight of history pressing in. Before them, the Capitol dome shimmered, lit in patriotic blue. And from every screen in America, millions watched the man they'd just elected to lead them into a new era.

The music faded. Fleetwood Mac's *"Don't Stop"* gave way to silence. A silence think enough to feel.

Ted's voice broke the stillness; confident, steady, presidential.

"My fellow Americans," he began, "tonight isn't just a celebration of victory, it's a mandate. A call to something higher than party, higher than politics. It's a call to unity."

A roar thundered from the crowd, rising with the sound of flags snapping in the cold wind. Families cried. Young people chanted. The promise of something new was in the air.

"We've spent too long being divided," Ted continued. "Too long talking past each other. But tonight, we turn the page. This country does not belong to red states or blue states. It belongs to all of us."

The stage lights flared as he spoke, casting long shadows. The teleprompter glowed faintly. Secret Service agents stood still along the periphery, their eyes scanning the crowd with clockwork precision.

"I am not the president-elect of a single party. I am the president-elect of the United States of America."

More cheers. Deafening this time. A storm of applause. Ted's words carried echoes of Reagan's optimism, Obama's hope, JFK's call to courage. The crowd believed in him. And tonight, belief felt like a weapon.

But belief cuts both ways.

Just beyond the stage, in a crush of bodies near the silver barricades, another kind of belief stirred. A colder, quieter kind.

Mako Elias Tanu stood motionless near the front of the crowd, surrounded by celebration but utterly detached from it. The people around him cheered, cried, clutched each other in joy; but he remained still, his eyes fixed forward. His right hand rested calmly inside his coat, fingers coiled around the grip of what waited beneath. His breath was steady. Measured.

He had been waiting.

Waiting through the sound checks. Waiting through the music. Waiting through the flags and the fireworks. And now, as Ted Bright spoke of unity and healing, the Asset was in play.

They wouldn't know his name. Not yet. That part would come later, replayed in grainy footage and chyrons. For now, he was just a face in the crowd.

On stage, Ted pressed forward, swept up in his own rising conviction.

"We will not be defined by our fears. We will not let foreign powers shape our destiny. We will not be pawns to another nation's game. We will lead. We will rebuild trust in our democracy. And we will do it together."

A breeze rolled through the park, carrying confetti and the faint smell of gunpowder from the fireworks that had come before. No one noticed.

Mako's fingers curled tighter around the grip of the Glock 19; cold, precise, American-made. Its weight anchored him, focused him.

A whisper crackled through a Secret Service earpiece. The agents moved, but they were too far, too slow.

Ted's voice hit its crescendo.

"Tonight, we take the first step into a future where every American can dream again. Where justice is real. Where hope is more than a slogan. We will not go backwards, we will move forward. The future—"

He didn't finish.

A single breath hung in the cold.

Tanu raised the gun.

Six rapid flashes of light split the air.

Bang. Bang. Bang. Pop. Pop. Pop.

The sound ripped through the night like the sky itself splitting open.

Ted's body jerked once, twice, before he collapsed behind the podium. Screams replaced applause. The flags stopped waving. Chaos descended.

Secret Service lunged forward, too late. Spectators dove for cover. The great American celebration unraveled in an instant. Lights strobed. Helicopters veered. Somewhere, someone shouted into a radio. Somewhere, a soldier stepped onto foreign soil—and a nation changed forever.

But up front, among the shattered euphoria, Mako Elias Tanu stood still.

For a moment, the world seemed to hold its breath.

Then the gun dropped to the pavement. A metallic thud.

And everything began to burn.

Acknowledgements

They say that the most challenging part about writing a novel is beginning. Everyone can come up with a great idea or concept, but what separates an author from others is that the author has sat down and written it.

The earliest idea for *The Campaign* emerged in 2019, as I was completing my undergraduate studies at the University of Colorado, Colorado Springs. I imagined a different version of Landon Wolfe then; still hungry for power, still cunning, but already sitting in the Oval Office. That version of the story revolved around a terrorist attack, quietly engineered by a desperate president to cling to relevance. But something was missing. The concept lacked soul, lacked stakes. I shelved it.

Then the world changed. When COVID hit in 2020, I picked up the idea again, this time scribbling the opening scene on yellow legal pad paper. It didn't go far. But the desire was still there. The world I was imagining —the America of 2028, fractured by ambition and ideology —kept tugging at me. I wouldn't finish a complete draft until three years later, but I had begun to understand the story's shape.

The "oh shit" moment, as one of my college writing professors called it, came in October 2022. The headlines were filled with naval tension in the South China Sea, and it finally clicked. Landon Wolfe wouldn't just run for president, he'd run because he wanted control over how war itself would be waged. A soldier-turned-candidate. A man who thought he could navigate America through the storm. That was the underlying plot.

Taiwan and China felt too immediate, too close to home. So the Solomon Islands Crisis was born. And with it, a new kind of American power struggle.

The structure came next. I always envisioned the novel opening with the end, a choice that helped shape Wolfe's voice. A voice that's cold, composed, and always two steps ahead. My earliest drafts had him from Philadelphia, not Iowa. He even won the presidency outright in those versions. But it didn't ring true. I realized the story worked better if he wasn't on top, but close to it. Tempted. Clawing his way back into relevance as someone else took center stage.

That someone was Ted Bright. A character I've carried with me since 2019, but who didn't come into focus until I recognized the tragedy at the heart of his rise. Ted is the idealist, the reformer, the symbol of everything that seems pure in politics. His arc is modeled on history, full of echoes of Kennedy, Reagan, and Obama. His dynamic with Wolfe, a shadowy, almost Shakespearean rivalry, owes something to the tension between LBJ and JFK, and this dynamic shapes the book's emotional core.

I finished my first 125,000-word draft in May 2023. It wasn't perfect. But it was written. On a road trip, my wife, Victory, read it aloud while I drove. I could hear what wasn't working. Lydia Barnes lacked dimension. Terry Park and Ellie Poole were flat. The coup storyline felt too tangled. Victory told me what I needed to hear: "You don't quite have that female voice yet." And she was right.

So I cut. I rewrote. I carved the story down to 90,000 words. A cleaner structure. A more ruthless Wolfe. A stronger Lydia.

By December 2023, the second draft was done. Victory read that one too, and this time, she said something I'll never forget: "I'm reading this and forgetting that you wrote it."

That version was close. But not quite there. I wrote a third draft in the fall of 2024 and set it aside for months, as Stephen King recommends. I let it breathe. And then I returned for the fourth and final time, clarifying the Cold War echoes, deepening the Solomon Islands crisis, and reshaping Lydia's arc into something sharper and more calculated.

This final draft, the one you've just read, is the result of years of thought, work, failure, and rewriting. I poured everything I had into it.

Thank you.

To my wife, Victory, this book is dedicated to you. You saw its potential before anyone else. You told me when it didn't work, and gave me the tools to fix it. From long walks unpacking Landon's rage, to giving me the idea of Kelly replacing him with Governor Mathis, to reading every painful draft, I couldn't have written this without you.

To my sisters, Allie Schaal, you nailed the cover design. Your work brought the visual world of *The Campaign* to life. Reagan Lange, thank you for capturing my author photo.

To my parents. My mom, who gave me a love for presidential history. My dad, who was writing his own book as I finished my first draft. That father-son competition helped drive me forward.

To the readers, thank you for giving this dark, morally complex story a chance. It's not an easy read. It's a story about ambition, betrayal, and the fragility of democracy. A story that feels uncomfortably close to home in 2025.

And finally, to Landon Wolfe. The master manipulator. The villain we're drawn to. Part Nixon, part Emperor Palpatine, part something else entirely. His story is not finished, not by a long shot. Now that he has the power, I'm just as curious as you are to see what he does with it.

With gratitude,
Hunter Schaal
July 2025

About the Author

Hunter Schaal holds a Master's in Library Science from the University of Missouri and a Bachelor's in History from the University of Colorado. He lives in Colorado with his wife and dog. *The Campaign* is his first novel.

www.ingramcontent.com/pod-product-compliance
Lightning Source LLC
Chambersburg PA
CBHW030826310726
48980CB00006B/659/J

* 9 7 9 8 9 9 9 6 4 6 0 0 2 *